You and
EVERYTHING
After

~ book 2 in the falling series ~

a novel

by Ginger Scott

For you, sweet and wonderful and amazing readers.

Prologue

Ty

Here's the thing about a really good dream: no matter how hard you try to stay in it—eyes closed, hands gripping the sheets, face pressed deep into the coolness of your pillow—you always wake up.

Always.

My dreams are always the same. I can feel the pull of the bat in my hands, swinging it around my entire body, the pressure on my thighs as I push my weight back on my right leg, my hips twisting, the bat cracking against the ball. Then I'm running. *I'm really running.*

I can feel it all.

Sometimes, when I can hold on long enough, Kelly is there after I round the bases. I feel her weight in my arms, her hands along my ribs, reaching around my back as she curls her legs around my body, and I lift her. It's all so effortless. I kiss her, carry her, touch her—breathe her in.

And then it all just stops.

The buzzing of the alarm is harsh; everything about my *now* a painful contrast against the dream I was forcefully removed from. I spend the next few minutes grieving. I have to get it all out of the way here and now, because I can't make my goddamned useless legs anyone else's burden. And I have to get up. I have to pack and get my ass on a plane back to Louisiana to make sure my brother follows through with college. I know if I go where he goes, we'll both make it through—through life.

He doesn't know this, but I need him, probably more than he needs me. But I'm the strong one, and Nate's the gifted one with the big heart. Those are our roles in life; I was crowned at birth by being born first. I take care of Nate, no matter what. Even if I'm fucked up and broken.

"Hey, you're awake." I barely register the half-naked brunette exiting my bathroom. It's all a bit of a fog. There was a party, and there were a lot of underclassmen there, and I remember the flirting. *Huh*—I must have been charming last night.

I force my typical smile to my face, and push my body up so I'm sitting on the edge of the bed, still wrapped in my sheets. Reaching for the T-shirt half hanging from my dresser's top drawer, I indulge in a quick glance at the back of her naked body while she's facing the other way. She's hot. Super hot. But she's not my type. Nobody is.

"Hey, sweetheart." I hate calling chicks that, but I have no idea what her name is. "Thanks for last night, and I hate to be a dick, but...I gotta go," I say as I pull myself to the chair, and bend forward to grab my jeans.

"I know; you told me. *You don't do girlfriends,*" she says, making air quotes with her fingers. Good...glad I was with it enough to have that conversation with her before anything else. "You planning on coming back to Florida next semester though?"

And there it is. She knows my deal, we had the conversation—but they always want more. "Sweetheart," I say, her name's still a total blank, "I'm probably never coming back to Florida again. And if I do, it will be in my private jet as CEO. Now, I have a flight to catch in just a few hours...and that towel you're in? I need to pack that. So—"

She looks like she wants to punch me, and I don't blame her. But I never make any promises I can't keep. I'm on the hook for too many promises as it is. Promises to my parents to "be strong for my brother" and to "do something *big* despite my disability." I'm good at playing strong—sometimes I even believe it myself. But other times...hell, I'm just fuckin' tired.

"In case you change your mind," she says, handing me the corner of some paper she just ripped from one of my magazines. *What the hell?* I turn it over and see her number and, *ah*...that's right—Beth.

"Yeah, thanks," I say, tossing it in the trash right in front of her. That pretty much seals the deal; she's gone seconds later, giving me the finger on her way out. I deserve that. I probably deserve a lot worse. But Beth is better off without me, and as selfish as it sounds, I need to keep all of my energy in reserve to get through the things I want in *my* life. I don't have the capacity to share with anyone else. I lost that the moment I dove off that cliff.

Finally alone, I stop everything for a few minutes, pushing myself to the window so I can watch everyone going about their lives outside. Pressing my forehead to the windowpane, I watch a couple say goodbye; the guy picks the chick up and swings her around, and then they kiss like they're in love. You can tell the difference. My kisses are all about using and avoiding. They're great in the moment, but I don't taste anything, except maybe vodka or Tequila—or, sometimes, smoke. I don't feel anything, other than my need to get off. But that kiss—the one happening two stories down from my window—is so foreign. It's about love and happiness and the future.

My phone buzzes on the bed, so I snap myself out of my torture and put on my mask. It's Nate. "What's up, man?"

"Hey, I'm picking you up from the airport. Parents are staying put," he says. "Anything special you want since you're getting in late?"

"Yeah, to hit the strip club on our way home," I say, half kidding.

"Right, so a bunch of singles then. Got it," he says, without even as much as a laugh. We're playing this straight, like we always do. I love my brother. He's my best friend. But Nate's not strong enough to bear the weight of everything that happened to me. So I finish making plans with him on the phone, and when I hang up, I spend the next two hours packing the rest of my things—a job that would take anyone else fifteen minutes.

Before I leave, I push myself back to the window to watch my life that *should have been* happen outside, but only for few more seconds. With the heaviest bag on my lap, and the roller behind me, I make my way to the hallway and ask another student to help me wheel the roller to the taxi out front. Once the door is shut and we're on our way to the airport, I forget it all—the dream, the scene out my window, the last four years at Florida State; it's all meaningless. And so is everything that's to come. I'm just going through the motions. You know...being strong.

Whatever.

Chapter 1

Ty

"Come on, princess. Get your ass up! It's time for workouts. Early bird gets the worm, and all that shit," I practically sing to my brother, whose head is buried under two pillows. He's still nursing himself a little after our late night. Nate's not used to my schedule. I've never needed much sleep, a side effect of constantly waking up in pain—however real, or not, it may be. I pretty much filled my undergrad years with party after party, and I still finished with a 3.8 grade point average.

"Gahhhhhhhhh," Nate bellows, his voice muffled by his mattress as he throws the top pillow at me, hitting me in the chest. "What are you, part robot? How are you not tired?"

"I'm just that awesome. Awesome people don't need to sleep as much as you mere mortals," I say, tugging the blanket from his body to really piss him off.

"All right! I'm up. I'm up," he says, pushing his fists into his eyes and rubbing like he did when he was a kid. He's still that kid to me—probably always will be. "The team doesn't even start workouts until nine anyway, asshole!"

He's complaining, but he's still getting dressed. I push Nate. I push him because he takes it, which means he secretly likes being pushed. And I push him because the kid is seriously talented. I was good...before I got hurt. I *maybe* could have played college ball, probably for some junior college back home. But Nate, he could go all the way, as in big leagues, and stay there—for years.

"Hey, that's *awesome asshole*, thank you very much. Now get your shoes on so we can get our miles in," I say, pushing into the hallway to wait for him.

We go five miles every morning—Nate takes the treadmill at the gym, and I work the hand cycle. My body, at least what's left of it, is something I can control; so weightlifting and fitness have kind of become an obsession. School has always been easy, which is probably why the partying never seems to get in my way. But throwing myself in the pool, and making my arms pound the water for a mile or two is a challenge—I need those challenges to remind me that I'm still alive.

"You're like this happy little morning elf, and I hate you," Nate says, throwing his workout towel at me before turning to lock up our room.

"Dude, it's not like I'm the one putting the hard stuff in your hands. You know, you can get drunk on just beer, bro. You don't have to do shots and shit like that. That's why you're always so tired in the morning," I tell him.

Nate was a goody two-shoes in high school, always hanging with the same group of guys and his girlfriend. The switch flipped when he found out she cheated on him. Thank God I was home when that happened. He left the party, came home to me, and we shared our first bottle of Jack. Damn, maybe it is my fault—I should've started him out on something weaker.

"About that, man...I think I'm out," he says, pausing right before the doorway exiting our dorm.

"Out of what?" He's lost me on this one.

"Out...of this partying and trolling-for-random-chicks thing we're doing every night. It's...it's just not me," he says, and I can't help but laugh, but Nate's not in the mood. "Fuck off, I knew you'd make fun of me."

"Sorry, sorry dude. That was just—"I have to pause again, trying to keep a straight face. Tucking my big-ass grin into the side of my arm to hide it, I force myself to take a deep breath—and to take my brother seriously. "I'm sorry. I guess I just don't see the downside."

"You wouldn't," Nate says, walking ahead. My smile's gone at that—he's right, I wouldn't. And that stings a little.

Workouts go the same, and when Nate heads off to join the team, I put in some extra time. There's a posting for personal trainers that I've been looking at, I just haven't had the balls to ask about it yet. But today's the day. There's a cute girl working the main counter, so I hit her up first.

"Hey, Nike!" I call her *Nike* because that's what her shirt says. She looks down, smirks, and then looks back into my eyes.

My grin makes her smile and bite her lip, and I know I've got her. "Sorry, didn't know your name."

"I'm Sage," she says, leaning over the counter just enough to give me a nice view of the frilly white-lace trim on her bra.

"Sage, nice name," I smile, falling right into my routine. "I was checking out the posting for the personal trainer. That filled yet?"

"Nope," she says, her smile bigger now. "You interested?"

"Yep," I say, playing off of her flippant answer. She's oblivious though.

"Hang on, I'll get the manager," she says, pushing back with a skip from the counter and heading into a back office. I allow myself a glance at her tiny shorts and perfect ass while she bounces away.

The manager wasn't as charmed by my dimples and good looks, so I had to win over all six foot four of him with my skills. After six years of physical rehab, I know my stuff; he was happy to hire me to work with freshman students who were just looking to stay in shape.

I type Nate a text on my way back to the dorm, making our now-regular lunch plan for burgers at Sally's. It's probably our dad's fault. Preeter boys like their routine. I think maybe only two or three days have passed that we haven't eaten at least one of our three meals at our new favorite hole-in-the-wall.

I have a good hour to kill before Nate's practice is done. Alone time. At least during school, I can sink my mind into something for one of my classes; I usually end up working ahead—just because I can't stand being idle. But there's not much to distract me now. Even *Sports Center* is lame in August. McConnell is not known for its football team, so like hell am I going to get into *that.*

It's a bad idea—it always is—but my phone is in my hand, and my fingers are typing and hitting send before I can stop myself. It's been three weeks since I've talked to Kelly. She had her baby two months ago. That was a slap in my face, a reality dose I probably needed. That's why I broke up with her in the first place—so she could have these things. I did it because I loved her; I wanted her to have it all. But damn did it hurt seeing her live her life and move on from me so effortlessly.

Kelly stayed with me after the accident, through our junior year of high school. We were going to go to the same college, too—that was always the plan. But I could tell by the look on her face, the look she wore more and more every day, that she was forcing herself to go through with it all. She wanted out. But she loved me too much to hurt me. So I pushed her away instead. I broke it off and went on a dating binge at the end of my senior year. Somehow, through it all, she stayed my friend.

My phone buzzes back with a response, and I hover over the screen for a few seconds, afraid to open it. I just asked her how things were going at home with Jack, the baby. We've managed to remain friends for four years. *Friends*—even though every conversation with her is like driving a stake through my heart. Last year, she got married. A few months later, she told me she was pregnant, and I died a little more.

Swiping the screen, the first thing I see is a picture of tiny feet nestled inside Kelly's hands—the diamond ring on her left finger like a banner waving in my face. Her husband, Jared, tolerates me, but I don't think he'd mind at all if Kelly and I just stopped communicating...completely. I have a feeling he'll get his wish one day; distance and time, they do funny things to the heart—they make you...forget. Or at least, want to forget.

He's beautiful. That's all I can say.

Thanks. Her message back is just as simple. I know we're near the end, and I feel sick. I'm getting drunk tonight—with or without Nate as my wingman. Hell, I might just pull up a stool at Sally's and join the regulars who plant themselves there all day.

Cass

"Oh my god. You literally brought your entire life from Burbank to Oklahoma, didn't you?" I huff, dragging two extra bags, as well as my own trunk, along the walkway toward our dorm.

"That was the deal. I would come *here*, but I still get to be me—and I like to have my things," my sister Paige says, prancing ahead of me with the lighter bags. She's a full minute older, but you'd think years separated us with the authority she holds over my head.

When it came time to decide on a college, Paige's choices narrowed down to Berkley and McConnell, and Berkley was definitely her preference. But for me, it was always McConnell, and only McConnell. They had the best sports and rehab-medicine program in the country, and that's what I wanted to do—what I was destined to do. But my parents wouldn't support me moving thousands of miles away without someone around to keep an eye on me. Supervision—the word made my skin crawl, I had heard it so often. *Supervision* and *monitoring* were words bandied about so often—in conversations about me, but never in conversations with me. God, how I wished just once someone threw in the word *normal.*

So, as much of a pain-in-the-ass as my sister is, she's also a saint, because she picked McConnell...and I'm the only reason for that. I owe her—I owe her my life.

"Okay, so here's the deal," Paige starts as soon as we get our bags, mostly hers, loaded into our dorm room. "I want this bed. And I'm still going to rush a sorority. Mom and Dad don't need to know that I won't technically be living *with* you."

"Works for me," I say, already unzipping my bag and flipping open the lid on my trunk. I feel Paige's purse abruptly slam into my back. "Ouch! What the hell?" I say, rubbing the spot where the leather strap smacked my bare skin.

"The least you could do is pretend to miss living with me," she says, her eyes squinting, her frown showing she's a little hurt.

"Oh, Paigey, I'll miss you. I just hate that you have to be my babysitter—*still!*" And I do hate it. I think that's the worst part about being a teenager with multiple sclerosis—everyone's always waiting for something to go wrong.

It started in the middle of my freshman year. I would get this pain in my eye. It would come and go, weeks between each occurrence. When I couldn't ignore it any longer, I told my parents, and we went to the eye doctor. My vision was fine. He told them it was probably stress from school, or the running in soccer leaving me dehydrated. What a simple and succinct diagnosis. It was also complete crap.

The fatigue hit next. Again, easily summed up with too much soccer practice, which, of course, led to truly uncomfortable fights between my parents—my mom wanting me to quit completely, my father saying I just "need more conditioning." It was because of these fights that I hid the tingling from them. That went on for months, until it was summer. Then one day, I couldn't walk.

I could stand from my bed, get to my feet, but that was it. The second I attempted to move toward my door or drag my feet toward my closet to get dressed I wobbled and fell. I felt like the town drunk without the benefit of the booze in a paper bag. I screamed for Paige and my parents, and I knew by the look on their faces that my life as I knew it was done.

After my first steroid IV treatment, I was able to walk again—all of my symptoms gone, like the round ball the magician waves in front of your eyes until it isn't there. Only, just like that magician who secretly tucks the ball behind his hand, my MS isn't really gone either. It's...hiding.

The fights continued, and my parents separated for a while. After the MS diagnosis, my mom insisted I quit soccer. I got depressed. My dad supported my wishes to play again—of course, under strict circumstances, and with limited workouts. Everything pretty much sucked for the next year.

It was a series of med trials, seeing how certain drugs affected me, then finding out what side effects I could handle. I also got really good at giving myself a shot—three times a week, for three years, until they came out with the pill version last year. I didn't mind the shots, though. What I minded were the constant questions and lectures from my parents: "How are you feeling? Are you fatigued? You should rest; stop working so hard."

Paige never lectured. Through it all, she just stayed the same. True, she's terribly self-absorbed—there were moments that she resented the attention I got because of my disease—but it was more about the *attention* and the fact that it wasn't on her. And I liked that.

We made a deal with my parents, coming here as a package. We fought for it for months—my mom really wanted to keep me at home. But that's the thing about MS. It never goes away; it's always with me. The shots, drug trials, therapies—they can't cure the disease; they can only slow it down. Like the front line of the Pittsburgh Steelers—except nowhere near as effective. Maybe more like the front line of the Miami Dolphins. So in the end, I got my way. Now that I'm here, I'm not going to let MS be a part of any conversation. I'm just Cass Owens, and my story ends there.

"Hungry. Now," Paige says, snapping her fingers at me. I smile out the window, not offended in the least. I'm free.

"Let's go eat greasy fried crap," I say, grabbing my purse. Blowing right past her, I ignore her eye-roll protest and impending whine about needing a salad with low-cal dressing. Freedom!

Ty

I'm two beers ahead of Nate by the time he walks into Sally's, and I can already see the lecture building with every step, the closer he comes. He's doing that thing, where he cracks his neck on one side and looks down, shaking his head at me in shame.

"Save it, bro," I say, picking up my glass and finishing off the last of my second beer while he sits down and admires both empty mugs.

"You called Kelly, didn't you?" It's not really a question, so I don't answer. "I don't know why you torture yourself. It's not like you can't meet other women. Damn, Ty—that's like your best skill. You meet women every five minutes, and they're in love with you after ten minutes."

"Yeah, but I don't love them. No one is Kelly," I say, feeling every bit of my self-loathing settle over my body.

"No, but maybe...just maybe, someone could be better, you know, like *different* better. If you'd just give it a damned chance," Nate says, stretching his legs out from the booth, and pulling a menu out from the rack on the wall. I can't help but watch his muscles stretch, and I hate him—just for the smallest second—for being whole. I don't really hate him, but sometimes it's hard to be so damned positive all of the time. "Order me a cheeseburger and chili fries. I'm hitting the head," he says, pushing out from the booth, and walking to the restrooms in the back.

Our mom always says that Nate's the romantic one. Me, I'm all numbers and practicality and logic. But I don't know, I think my romantic-side is alive and breathing—it's just tortured. It's this sliver of my soul that feels certain that there's only one girl out there who could ever love me, and her love wasn't meant to last forever.

"*Hahahaha*! You are sooooo not the sexy one," a chick's voice squeals from behind me so loudly that I'm compelled to turn around. That, and she said the word *sex*, pretty much an automatic for me. I glance over my shoulder, and at first all I can see are two blondes. I can't quite make out their features, but if pushed, I'd say they were both probably pretty damned sexy. When they pass me, I breathe in and the air smells like the ocean. One of them is taller than the other—lean, but built, clearly a runner. The other one is curvy; she's wearing a sundress that, if I had to guess, was hiding no bra, and probably a pretty sexy pair of panties.

"You're, like, *predictable* sexy," the tall one says, and I hear a bubble snap from her gum. "I'm like *ninja* sexy."

I can't help but smirk at what she says. This chick's funny. And I'd have to say, that might just give her the edge on sexy. I keep my gaze forward, pretending to look at something on my phone screen on the table, but I notice the pair of them slide into a booth across the room.

"What'll you have today, Ty?" Cal says, pulling the pencil from behind his ear to write down our order. I don't know why he bothers asking. Four weeks we've been coming here, and I'm pretty sure we've ordered the same thing every time.

"Cheeseburgers," I say, nodding to Nate, who's now standing behind Cal and waiting to slide back to his seat.

"Oh, hey Nate," Cal says, writing down our order, and putting the pen back in its spot somewhere within his disheveled of hair and the mesh Budweiser hat he wears every single day.

"I'm starved, man. Today's practice was brutal. It's just...so damned hot," Nate says, pulling his own phone out and looking at the screen. I'm glad he's only half paying attention to me, because my focus is dedicated to the booth about twenty feet away.

"Do you have any low-fat dressings? Like, at all?" the curvy blonde says, a strand of her hair wrapped around her finger when she asks.

"We have Italian," says the older woman taking their order.

"Yeah, but is it just oil? That doesn't mean low-fat. Is it fat-free or low-fat?" This chick is high-maintenance.

"It's...Italian," the waitress says. A small chuckle escapes my lips, and the other girl, the *ninja*, looks my way briefly. I don't know why, but my heart kicks a little at getting caught.

"She'll have the Italian. Just put it on the side," the ninja princess says, and the waitress walks away.

"Good thinking. It's low-fat if you put it on the side," the diva says. My ninja princess just stares at her, watching her pull out a mirror and check her lipstick; then she flips her gaze to me. This time, I don't panic; instead, I just lift the right side of my lip in a tiny grin to let her know I'm with her—hell, I'm *so with her.* She shakes her head at me in disbelief, and then returns her gaze back to her friend.

"Putting the dressing in a different bowl doesn't change its chemistry, Paige," she says, and I smirk again.

"What's so funny, dude?" Nate interrupts, but I shake my head and hold my hand up against the table.

"Hang on, I have to hear this out," I whisper; he bunches his brow before turning to look at the two girls behind him who have me completely rapt.

"Then why the hell did you make me get it on the side, Cass?" she asks, and I commit that name to memory the second it leaves her lips.

"So you could use less," Cass huffs back.

"That's stupid," Paige says.

12

"Yes, I see that now," Cass says, stepping out from their booth to head to the restroom area. She gives me one last smile before she leaves, and I hold up my empty beer glass to toast her—the sexy ninja princess, with the patience of gold, and the next girl I want to get to know in Oklahoma.

Chapter 2

Cass

"Is it bad that I'm excited? I shouldn't be so excited. I should play it cool. Right, cool...*phew*...deep breath, and ready. Okay, I'm being cool. How's this?" Paige only rolls her eyes and picks up her stride. "What? Not cool? It's the shoes, isn't it? Or my shorts? I should have worn a dress, or something cuter. I'm so bad at this."

"Jesus Christ, Cass! You look fine. You're cute. Boys are going to think you're cute. Just like they did back home. If you're going to get like this every time we go to a party, I'm going to start going without you," Paige fires back her short fuse with me, and my nerves kick in quickly.

"You're right," I say, blowing out a huge breath into the few strands of my hair that have found their way in front of my face. "I wish Rowe would have come with us." Rowe's our roommate. We have one of the big rooms at the end of the hall, which means there are three of us in a room, and Rowe seemed pretty cool. I liked her music, and she seemed like she was hungry for friends outside of her tiny circle—just like me.

"Ugh. I don't. I don't know about that chick. She's...*quiet*," my sister says, punctuating that last word like there's something wrong with being quiet. I'm quiet. Or at least, I was. But I left that all behind in high school. Here, no one knew my history. No one knew about my bad choices for boyfriends—and the reputation that only took months to create and a thousand miles to run away from. Here, I was going to be loud, and confident, and important, and someone's girlfriend. And I would settle for nothing less.

"You're just being a bitch. She's nice," I say, feeling defensive of my barely eight-hour-old friend.

"Probably. But I still don't like her," Paige says, making those annoying last touches on her hair she always makes before she knows we're about to enter a room full of strangers. I should probably do the same thing, tuck hair behind an ear, or make sure my lips are pink or shiny or kissable or, I don't know. Paige did my makeup. That's her thing—hair, fashion...exteriors. Me, I'm more of the crack-open-the-beer, chug-faster-than-the-guys, and then kick-their-asses-in-something kinda girl. I brush my fingers through my hair anyway though, because change is good.

The second we open the door, we're weaving through a crowd of people. We're at some old apartment complex, right off campus. One of the fraternities took it over for housing. The living room is filled with smoke, which makes everyone look just a little dirtier.

College parties aren't like they seem in the movies. They're not even close. There isn't some band playing in a corner, or some DJ spinning records. It's just an iPod plugged into a nice set of speakers, playing the same rap album over and over again. The girls here aren't all wearing major label designer clothes. Most of the guys are wearing hats, and they sport newly minted beards that haven't been groomed properly—and *way too much* cologne. It's just an apartment overcrowded with people, most of whom are gathered around a Goodwill sofa in the living room or the giant table pushed against a wall in the dining area.

"I'll get us beer," I say to Paige, doing my best to push through the group of girls who are gathered around the kitchen island. My experience has me waiting for them to say something to me—or spill their drinks on me on purpose—but instead, I slip through unnoticed, their conversation continuing without pause as I move through them.

I grab two cups and a marker, writing *PAIGE* on one. I'm about to write my name on the other when my hand suddenly writes out the name *ADRIANNA*. I put the pen cap back on and can't help but smile at the idea of being a mystery woman, just for the night. Once I've filled each cup from the keg, I slip back through the crowd to find my sister.

"Adrianna?" she asks, taking a sip from her cup and pointing to my persona scribed on mine.

"Yep, tonight I'm Adrianna," I say, taking a big gulp, and challenging her stare with my mouth pressed in a hard line—just like Adrianna would.

"You're weird," she says with a slight eye-roll, turning her focus to the rowdy crowd of guys piled on the couch in the living room. Nudging me to follow, she leads us closer.

"Oh shit!" one of them yells, leaning to the side with his controller in hand, as if his body movement actually had an effect on what his character was doing on the screen. They're playing *Battle Wound*. I recognize it immediately.

"Dude, you suck at this, Cash! Give your turn to Preeter; he'll save your ass," one of the other guys playing yells.

"Fuck no, man! I can save this shit. Just move out of my way..." Cash starts, and then we all watch as his guy on the screen flies through space and gets absolutely ass-hammered with alien bullets.

"Shit," his friend says, tossing his controller on the table. "I'm out. Cash, you suck!"

"I don't suck. I just need the right partner," he fires back at his friend, who just flips him off while he leaves to get another beer.

I don't even hesitate, grabbing the open controller off the coffee table and flopping myself onto the old couch cushions between two very large guys. "You're right, Cash," I say, giving him a wink. "Your partner bailed on your ass. Let's go again. I got your back. Who wants a piece?" I ask, instantly realizing the sexual innuendo I just threw out there. A few of the guys seem to have picked up on it, and they chuckle. Back home, that would have mortified me. But I let it roll off of me now, especially tonight, because I'm *Adrianna*!

"You're on, princess," one of the bigger guys next to me says, pulling his body forward and leaning his elbows on his knees. Paige has found a spot near me along the sofa arm, and she's already surveying the room for some guy to hit on. There are a few here that are typical Paige targets—I'm pretty sure the two I'm stuffed between are football players.

"Okay, watch my tail," Cash says, biting his lip and leaning, just like he did last time; we run our guys through the dark corridor of the space ship. He has no idea what he's doing, and I would venture to guess he hasn't played this game before. That's okay, though, because I'm about to make him look like a bona fide video-game nerd. I've played every version of *Battle Wound* at least a hundred times, and I know all of the surprises. I'm shooting milliseconds before the bad guys attack, leaving in our wake a digital hallway full of carnage as our soldiers run through the various scenes on the screen.

"Cover me!" I yell, surprising Cash, who almost fumbles his controller out of his hands.

"Oh, uh...okay," he says, looking from me to the screen, not really sure what to do. It doesn't matter. I know where the explosives are hidden in this level. It's one of those secret weapons only people who read *Gamer* magazine know about— one of those tiny tips printed in the margins of a recent issue. My fingers work the controller, pushing my guy into a roll with his weapons drawn. I barely miss the bullets flying at me—Cash is clearly no use as a backup—and fire away at the barrels stashed along one of the walls.

"You're so dead, peaches," big guy on my right says. *Peaches*, I like peaches. Not sure I like the nickname, and I'm pretty sure I'm going to love kicking this guy's ass. But I don't really have anything against the fruit. Just three more seconds. *Two. One.*

The explosion is the best part. They really upped the graphics on version eight, and the way it melts everyone when the pod explodes is cool as hell. I know Cash is going to be pissed, because he thinks we're dead, too. But he'll know soon enough.

"Shit, Cash! She's worse than you," my peaches friend says.

"You are so taking that back in about ten seconds, Marcus," says a voice from the other side of the room. It's the guy I saw at Sally's yesterday—the one who laughed at my conversation with Paige. He's still in a wheelchair, and I'm not sure what that means. I didn't mention him to Paige yesterday, because I'm not sure how she'll react. She isn't what I would call...well...nice. He's really cute, and I can tell he must work out like crazy, because his shoulders actually have that cool dent that runs along the entire length. He smirks at me now, just like he did at the restaurant, and I can feel my blood pump just a little faster from his stare.

"I don't think so, Ty. Chick just nuked us all," Marcus *peaches* says, and while he's talking, I watch the screen, where Cash's character, and mine, are rescued by a cloaked starship that suddenly appears and saves our bodies before they melt. Since tonight I'm Adrianna, I stand up with both of my hands in the air, turning to face my opponents, pumping one fist a little higher than the other in victory.

"You're so dead...*pumpkin*," I grin, tossing my control back over to Cash, and backing away, serenaded by a few whistles and the sound of Marcus's ego being absolutely torn to shreds by every other guy in the room.

"Uhm, do I need to teach you how to flirt?" Paige asks, hooking her arm through mine, while we head out the back door to the large patio where everyone else seems to be gathered.

"What? You think that's going to turn guys off?" I shrug at her, lifting myself up to straddle the block wall around the patio.

"Cass, how do I put this? *That*? It doesn't really make a guy think about taking your clothes off. You pretty much made that entire room of men feel inferior," she says, her attention split between me and some tall jock who just sat on the other end of the wall.

"Maybe," I say, swirling the last remnants of beer in my cup before chugging the last sip. "But there was one I don't think minded all that much."

Ty

Sexy ninja. It took her less than five minutes to have every videogame-playing asshole at this party by the balls.

"Dude, that was hot," I say, punching Nate on the shoulder while everyone else in the living room scrambles to recover— Marcus and his brother, mostly. Once Cass defeated the game, they shut the Xbox off, clearly not wanting a repeat ass whooping.

"You have a strange set of standards for what's hot, man," Nate says, handing me an extra beer and heading to the back patio. The second we pass through the door, I see her sitting on the wall on the other side.

"Maybe I do, bro. Maybe I do," I say, not able to take my eyes off her. Her legs are tan and long, and I love that she's wearing shorts and a T-shirt. The high-maintenance chick that's obsessed with salad dressing is with her, and she looks like she's dressed for a goddamned prom. "What do you think...freshman?"

"I don't know. Yeah, probably, I guess," Nate says, half paying attention and pulling himself up to sit along the block wall. "If you hit that, you're keeping that shit in her room, though. I need my sleep, and I'm not hanging around the hallway waiting on you to get some."

"Oh, Nathan. You and your beauty sleep," I tease, doing my best to eavesdrop on their conversation a few feet away from us. Cass keeps flitting her eyes my direction, trying not to smile. It's cute, the way she's afraid of getting caught.

"Come on, bro. You owe me one," I say, untying one of Nate's shoelaces and pushing forward to approach the two blondes.

"Goddamn it, Ty. I don't owe you shit, and you know I hate it when you fuck with my shoes," Nate says somewhere behind me. I'm already zeroed in on everything in front of me though, and the adorable smile playing out on Cass's face as she bites the side of her bottom lip, trying not to blush.

"You read *Gamer*," I say, knowing full well she does—based on the ass whooping she displayed a few minutes ago. I don't sleep well, and when I can't sleep, I play video games—*all* of them.

"Maybe," she says, sipping at the beer in her cup. She's being coy; it's cute. "You...read *Gamer*?" she asks, one eyebrow cocked upward.

I grin in response, wink, and then tip my cup back finishing off my beer. Her cup's empty too, so I take this opportunity. "Get you another?" I ask, brushing my hand into hers just to see how she reacts. She looks down when I do, rapping fingers against the cup where I touched skin—almost like she's not used to being touched that way.

"Yeah, I'll have another," she says, handing me her cup. I notice the salad dressing blonde scoot in closer, nudging her in disapproval.

"Relax, I'm not an asshole. I won't drug her," I say, and her friend just stares at me, hard, her brow low and her facial expression clearly not trusting me at all. She grills me with that gaze for a few seconds before turning her attention to Nate, suddenly forgetting all about me.

"Be right back," I say, holding both cups in one hand and pushing myself back inside.

The crowd around the keg is thick; I move toward the kitchen and pick up a few smaller cups, filling them with the tequila I brought. I pour eight shots, putting them on a plate in my lap, knowing I can probably talk Nate into doing a few with me. I know he said he was *done* with this...but I think he'll play along just long enough for me to get in with Cass.

By the time I get outside, the other blonde—*Paige* was her name, I think—has made herself at home on Nate's lap; I catch his glance and wiggle my brows at him. He shakes his head and rolls his eyes a little. I know if he truly *hated* having this girl crawl all over him like she's doing—he'd put an end to it. My brother might think he's done with his partying ways, but he also has a hard time saying no to certain things.

"Shots?" Cass says, wrinkling her nose.

"Beer line was long," I say, glancing over my shoulder. When I turn back to her, I hand her the still-empty red cup from my lap, but not before noticing the name she's scribbled on it. "Adrianna, huh?" I ask, glaring at her and wondering why she's pretending to have a different name. I know her name's *Cass*—I heard it loud and clear the other day, and there's no fucking way I was going to forget it.

"That's me," she says, pulling it from my hand and kicking off from the wall, "and I'll just get my own beer then."

Her friend is still working on Nate, but I can tell my brother's not taking the bait this time. He keeps checking messages on his phone, asking about scores when other people walk by—scores for games that I know there's no way he's interested in. Cass, or *Adrianna,* is standing on the tips of her toes looking over the crowded living room for the keg. The party is starting to really get going now, and I know she's not getting to that keg for at least fifteen minutes. And when she does, there's a good chance it'll be dry anyway. She turns back to me; I hold up my makeshift platter of tequila and raise an eyebrow.

"Yeah, tequila it is, I guess," she sighs, coming back to lean against the wall next to me. I hand her one of the tiny paper cups, and when our fingers touch, we both react, almost dropping the liquid.

"Damn, sorry. I thought you had that," I say, catching it just before it spills, minus the few drops that splash over the side onto her. I'm nervous in front of her, and it's really fucking weird. She licks the tequila from the top of her hand, then reaches to take a new cup from my lap, my pulse racing the closer she comes to touching me. *What the hell?*

"Paige?" she says, elbowing her friend and handing her a drink. They have an odd exchange at first—her friend looking at the drink for several seconds and then at Cass—almost like she's scolding her. "Just take the stupid drink, Paige."

Before the quiet grows any more uncomfortable, I pick up a cup and hand it to Nate, raising my brows high, urging him to do one shot—*just one, man. Come on.* After an eye-roll and a heavy sigh, he takes the drink from me, tilts it back, and lets it slide down fast, which thankfully, has Paige mimicking his actions and doing the same. Without pause, Cass downs hers quickly. Before I can blink, she reaches for another, and it goes just as fast.

I'm pretty sure she's drunk *way* before she realizes it. I've had two, maybe three shots, but she's gone and refilled the cups twice, which would put her at about...six, I think. "So...wanna play a game?" she slurs, as she sloppily pulls up one of the patio chairs, pushing it right in front of me, and sitting down—our knees touch. I can't feel it, but I swear just seeing her bare legs grazing mine is the hottest sensation ever. Or maybe I'm drunker than I think I am, too.

"Sure, I'm in," I say, moving the plate of empty cups from my lap to the table at the side of us. I lean forward and crack my knuckles, watching as she tries to crack hers. It's cute, the way she acts tough. She holds her hands out flat and nods at me to do the same. When I hold them in the air in front of her, she studies them for a few seconds and then pulls them a little closer before resting her hand flat in mine, her knuckles on top.

"You hit the top of my hands, I take a drink. I hit the top of yours, you drink," she says, and her friend coughs loudly behind me. "You're not playing, Paige. Butt out!"

"I know I'm not *playing*, Ca—" her friend starts, but Cass interrupts.

"Adrianna!" she inserts, then pulls the corners of her mouth into a proud grin. She'd be the worst spy ever, but I'll play along.

"Yeah, Paige. Wait your turn. Adrianna and I are playing now," I say, keeping my eyes on Cass's the entire time. When I stick up for her and use her fake name, she smiles and her cheeks flush red.

"Fine, *Adrianna*," Paige says. "Just don't go crazy with tequila. I'm not taking care of you."

"Okay...*Mom!*" Cass says, breaking our stare, and raising her eyebrows a hint at her friend. "You go first," she says, her gaze on me again.

I know this game. Nate and I used to play when we were kids during long car rides. I don't think I've ever played it as a drinking game, though, so this should be interesting. I stare into her eyes and feel her hands hovering against mine; I twitch two or three times just to see her jump.

"When am I gonna do it? Is it...now?" I shout and jerk, but don't really move my hands. On instinct, she quickly pulls her hands into her chest; I have to admit, I'm impressed that she's still so nimble—given how lit she is on tequila. Slowly, she slides her hands back over mine, her eyes intensely watching for any muscle twitch or movements. Then, in a flash, she looks into my eyes again.

"Pussy," she teases, a tiny smirk tugging at her lips, and holy fuck is it hot when she talks like that. I can't help the grin that crawls up the side of my mouth as I keep my eyes locked on hers.

"Princess, I'm no pussy," I say, slowly enunciating each word, and pushing my hands so they're firmly against hers. Her breath hitches when I do, and her palms heat up from the friction of touching me. Her eyelids grow heavier, and I can tell the alcohol is really hitting her system now, so I don't waste my time. With a swift movement, I swing my right hand out from under hers, reaching for the top of her left hand—catching her unexpected. Only somehow...what the hell? My hands are flat together, and I've missed her completely.

"I'm no *princess*," she says, her hands untouched against her chest and the mischievous grin lingering somewhere between sexy and pissed as hell. "My turn."

Yes, I do believe it's her turn. Because *I* have no fucking clue what to do now, but goddamn do I want to figure it out.

Chapter 3

Cass

"How, in the name of all that is holy, are you awake...and moving!" Paige's voice is muffled by her pillow, which she has secured over her mouth and eyes to block out the closet light I just turned on.

"It's just easier if you push through the pain. Want me to open the window?" I ask, laughing when she pulls both hands away from her pillow to flip me off. I love teasing Paige when she's hung over.

"Touch that curtain, and I will end you," she seethes, which only makes me laugh harder. Paige has flair for drama.

We drank a lot last night, but I've drunk more before. It's been a while, but my tolerance still seems to be okay. And we came home early—mostly because the guy Paige had her eye on left early, and she got bored. I could have played the flirting game all night though. We never talked about anything personal me and...*huh*, mystery man. No names—at least, not my *real* name. I think he knew I was faking it, but he played along, which was...nice.

I slapped hands with him for about thirty minutes, maybe longer, and our conversation stayed on the surface. Double-meaning comments, laced with flirtation, but nothing deeper. As soon as I could tell it was going somewhere, I left. He went to the bathroom, promising he'd be right back, and I told Paige I was ready to go home. I'm a little embarrassed by it now that I'm sober, but as far as he knows, I'm Adrianna—might as well be Cinderella.

"I've got a noon with the personal trainer. I'll be back in a couple of hours," I whisper, knowing Paige has already drifted back to sleep.

When I found out they had someone on campus that worked with people...like me...I jumped on the appointment. Not that I really need anyone to push me through workouts, or to teach me things. I'm pretty self-driven when it comes to exercise, which my mom is always quick to point out I should do *less* of. The doctors disagree—or rather, they don't *all* agree. So I do what makes me feel good. And since I left soccer behind in high school, I'll stick with pushing my body in the gym.

Rowe is standing by the elevator, and I can tell she's talking to someone, but I can't see the other half of the conversation until I'm right behind her. And suddenly, he's here. Our eyes are like magnets. My heart starts to literally throb, my chest pounding with a quick rhythm I'm pretty sure I can't hide. My palms are sweaty, my mind racing with fear that he's going to call me Adrianna—or that Rowe is going to call me Cass. Either way, I'm going to look like a lunatic to both of them. And I can tell by the way his mouth is curling into a knowing smirk that he's ready to pick up where we left off—the flirting game. Thing is, I'm *way* better at that after I've had a few shots of tequila.

"You missed a hell of a party last night. You're coming to the mixer with me tonight, no excuses," I say to Rowe, looping my arm with hers, basically using her as a human shield for my embarrassment.

"Hey…" he starts to speak, and my body instantly flushes from the piercing stare of his eyes. "I think I met you last night."

"Yeah, we hung for a bit I think. I got pretty shit-faced," I say through a nervous laugh. I feel like such a loser, and I have no idea why I'm pretending I don't remember every second of my time with him last night. *He* was the first vision in my mind when my alarm went off this morning…and I've been daydreaming about his stupid dimples and crystal-blue eyes ever since I first saw them at that burger joint I went to with Paige.

"What was your name?" He's calling me on my bullshit.

"Cass." I give in quickly, my secret identity of *Adrianna* now dead here in a freshman-dorm hallway.

"Cass," he says, his damned dimples punctuating my one-syllable name as it glides from his smirking lips. "That's right. I'm Ty."

I can't help but admire his arms as he stretches his hand toward me in introduction. They're strong and toned in a way that screams of discipline, and as much as the girl part of me wants to admire them for the sex symbols they are, the physiology nerd in me wants to study his arms and learn how to make more just like them. I catch Rowe staring, too, and I realize we've both been gawking at him like a piece of meat for several seconds now.

"Rowe and I were just heading out to the gym. We were going to stop by a few of the buildings on the way. You know, scout out our classes? Wanna come? You look like you're heading that way," Ty says.

I have no idea how he knows Rowe, and I also have no idea where the jealous pang deep in my chest is coming from. All I'm sure of is that I hate the way it's making me feel, and I'll be damned if I act out on it and add to my checklist of crazy. "Sure, sounds great," I say, plastering on a fake smile to hide the twisting feeling in my gut over the thought that maybe Rowe took my place in line for Ty's attention.

The elevator ride is...awkward. Rowe's hands are fidgeting together like she's nervous, and Ty...he's still grinning. I catch his glance at me, and I keep trying to speak, but every time I open my mouth, my brain shuts down. I'm utterly void of anything clever, funny, or interesting. God, why did I even get up this morning?

By the time we get outside, Rowe's grip on my arm is so tight, it's turning into a tourniquet. "Hey, are you...okay?" I whisper in her ear.

"Sorry," she says, letting go of my arm, realizing exactly how hard she was squeezing me. "Not good with strangers."

"You don't really know him?" I ask, my nerves inching up another tick. Ty is a few feet ahead of us on the main walkway, but I swear he's trying to listen to our whispering. His head is tilted just enough—it's the same tell I have when I'm dropping in on someone's business.

"Just met him this morning," Rowe says, her arms stretched out on either side, her face panicked. Now I'm really curious why he was talking to her in the first place, and I can't help but wonder if he knew she was my roommate—*goddamned stupid hope and heart*. I grab her arm again and tug her forward with me so we can catch up.

"So, ladies, where are you from?" Ty asks, and I catch his eyes start at my legs and work their way up to my face. The attention is intense, but I like it. This is *way* better than that jealous feeling I had a few minutes ago.

"My sister and I are from Burbank," I say, and immediately I can tell he's trying to see the relationship between Rowe and me. Rowe clears it up quickly though, explaining we aren't sisters. Then, they're both looking at me a bit puzzled.

"My sister's our other roommate. You met her last night, too. Paige?" It hits me suddenly that Paige and I never really mentioned this to Rowe, and her reaction is priceless. She stops short of calling my sister a bitch—not that it wouldn't be accurate, or at least partially accurate—so I make her feel a little better by calling Paige's bitchiness out for her.

"I'm from Louisiana originally," Ty says, and suddenly the honey-glaze accent that smolders from his mouth comes together like a gorgeous puzzle. "I'm in grad school, but my brother's a freshman. We thought it'd be cool to live together, so we both settled on the same school. They have a great business program here, and a hell of a baseball team, so it worked out."

"Nate's your brother," Rowe says, and now I'm wondering who the hell Nate is. God, do I hope he's not the guy Paige was all over last night...for Rowe's sake.

"I think I saw him last night, too..." I say with a questioning face, just feeling him out on this. "My sister was *all over* him," I say, and Ty quickly confirms it.

"I remember her. She's cute," he says, and I don't know why it feels like such a massive punch to my ego that he thinks my sister's attractive, but it does. "Not my brother's type, though."

Great. So does this mean she's yours? I keep that conversation in my head, and do my best to look unaffected, letting my eyes take in the various buildings on either side of us, the trees, the other students—anything to keep me from frowning a big, fat-ass frumpy face.

When we get to the gym, Ty offers to find Nate for Rowe. I turn my focus to my friend and her bright pink face. I'm not sure when she met the man Paige called *Mr. Dreamy Muscles* half of the night, but it's clear she's into him. Her face grows even redder when he walks over, and when they talk she starts to stare at her feet. It sounds like they had plans this morning, and while she originally thought he stood her up, it turns out it was just miscommunication. When Rowe's not paying attention, I let myself get a good look at Nate's face—I can tell by the way he's looking back at her that whatever is sparking between them goes both ways. Paige is going to be pissed. But she'll get over it, and she'll find herself a different poster boy to chase down. She always does.

And me...well, I had a nice round of flirting, but it looks like that's as far as this train goes for Mr. Dreamy's brother and me, since he's fully engrossed in something on his phone, barely paying attention to me or his brother anymore.

"Rowe, I've got to go. I have an appointment with a personal trainer in ten," I say, glad to have an excuse to leave Ty without looking desperate or uncomfortable. "I'll see ya back at the dorm."

I slip my watch from my wrist and tuck it into my workout bag, willing myself not to look at Ty, not to see if he noticed I was leaving. I give a small wave to Rowe and grant Nate a smile, then spin on my feet and head to the main doors to meet with my trainer. But I'm weak, and I turn at the last second, pushing through the door with my hip and looking up—and damn if he isn't staring right back at me—smile, dimples and all.

Shit. I like this one. And he is going to play me.

Ty

I'm not sure what I did to deserve this fortunate run of luck, but I'm going to enjoy the ride. Cass just left for her personal-trainer appointment, and my first appointment is in exactly ten minutes. I'm pretty confident that isn't a coincidence.

I pass through the men's locker room so I can see if she's the one waiting for me, and I actually bite my knuckles when I see her sitting there at my appointment table. With a quick "thank you" to the heavens, I push through the locker room doors and almost make it to where she's sitting before she notices me.

"So, you must be...Cassidy Owens," I say, flipping through the forms tucked on my clipboard, pulling the cap from my pen with my teeth. I'm doing my best to keep my grin in check. Her entire body flushes the second she sees me—the light shade of pink taking over her skin, even brighter next to the yellow blonde of her hair.

"Tyson Preeter," she says, her eyes closing just a little while she puts it all together.

"Well, this is going to be easy; you've already heard about me," I wink and hand her the check sheet to go through her goals and objectives for our first session.

"It was in the email. And now I feel...well...pretty stupid that I didn't put that together. Ty...Tyson," she says with a slight wince. Her eyes stay on me for a few seconds as she taps the pen to the top of the clipboard. "This...is weird now, isn't it?"

"It's only weird if you make it weird...*Adrianna*," I tease, wanting her to know that yes, I in fact remember every little detail from our first encounter last night. Hell, I remember every detail from the first time I saw her—even the smell of the gum she popped when she walked by my booth at Sally's. And, not just remembering all of this shit, but obsessing over it? Yeah, for me, that's a little weird.

"Right...Adrianna," she laughs, whipping through a few items on the check sheet, pausing at the goals section, and looking up at me through a few wavy strands of hair that she quickly pushes back behind her ear. "That...uh...that was an experiment. You know, just to try out being someone else. Just for an hour or two."

We stare at each other for a heartbeat longer than normal, and I can feel this tiny shift in the air between us. "Yeah, I get that," I say. No joke or jab, just me getting it. And I do. She has no idea how much I *get* that.

"I don't really have any goals," she says, pushing the barely-filled-out checklist back at me.

"That's fine. We'll come up with those together after today," I say, giving a quick glance at her history. My clients are all supposed to be working through something—injuries, disabilities—but she didn't write anything down. "You rehabbing something?" I ask, my pen hovering over the line to fill it in for her.

"No, I've got nothing. I mean...my joints pop from years of soccer, but that's about it," she answers fast, and now I'm worried that she's not supposed to be working with me.

"You...sure you're supposed to be *my* client?" I ask, hoping like hell that even if she's not, she'll stay.

"Oh, I'm yours; I requested you," she says, her eyes flashing wide quickly with embarrassment. I pounce on this.

"Ohhhh, I get it," I say, turning around and filing her paperwork in the lock drawer.

"Get what?" she asks, her eyes squinting with hesitation.

"You're a stalker," I smile, just in case she doesn't realize I'm bullshitting her. "I mean, it's understandable. This happens all of the time."

"What does?" she asks.

"Me. Stalkers," I say through a feigned sigh. "I've had...many."

"Oh, I'm sure you have," she says, folding her arms up in a challenge. I like this. I like this a lot.

"Oh yes, there's an entire cellblock at campus police for the women who have tried to get to me in the past and failed," I say, grabbing my gloves and urging her to follow me to the bench for some basic weightlifting. "You're the first one to completely make up a name and sign up for my...ahem...*services*, though."

"I did NOT sign up for your services!" she chokes, half playing and half real. I can tell she's a little offended.

"Uh..." I start, looking at her—taking in her entire body, which is wrapped perfectly in those tight-ass workout pants and a matching tank top. Then I turn to the side and gesture to the sets of weights on either side of us. "You sort of did."

"Well, yes, I signed up for your personal training. But I'd hardly call that *services*," she says, straddling one leg over a workout bench and positioning herself in a way that has me feeling a lot less like working out. I'm staring; I'm staring and I'm thinking and I'm...not hearing a single thing she's saying right now.

"Sorry?" I say, suddenly aware of how fucking creepy I must look.

"I *said* I actually thought I could learn a thing or two from you. I want to get into rehab work," she says, and for some reason, her purpose for being here, for choosing me, makes me...sad. She wants to learn from me. And I know it's not because I'm some rehab workout king. It's because I'm disabled myself, and that makes me unique. A novelty. I'm fascinating to her, but not the same way she's fascinating to me.

"Oh," I say, not really in the mood to *play* anymore. "Well, let's start with a good upper-body combo, something that is good for leveling. We'll see where you're at, and then work up from there."

I guide her through a few exercises, and every time I'm in a position to touch her, I don't. It just feels weird now, and I don't know why. She's gotten serious, too, and a few times, I catch her looking at my eyes while I'm going through a motion. I'm used to people watching me lift myself from my chair, and they usually say something about how strong I am and how amazing it is that I can *do things like this with only my arms.* But that's not the way Cass is looking at me. Her gaze is...different. And I'm frustrated by it.

"We should go out," I say, overcome with this urge to get back to me, and everything I know. "Tonight. We should go out. Hang, you know?"

She stares at me, still finishing up her bench press, her lips barely moving with a silent count of each number until I barely hear her utter, "...fifteen."

"No," she says, standing quickly and dragging her long leg back over the bench; I swear she's teasing me with it.

"No?" I question. I'm not used to *no.*

"No," she says, picking up her small pink towel and wiping the sweat from her forehead and the back of her neck. I'm actually left speechless by her rejection.

"Well, all right then," I say, blinking and looking out at the other students lifting around us. No. She said no.

"I just...I have a feeling about you," she says.

"Right. A feeling," I say, pulling myself back to my chair. "And what kind of feeling is that?"

She sighs heavily at first, then leans against the rack of weights before finally looking at me. "You're...nice."

I'm sure the laugh that bursts out of my mouth is jarring, but I can't help my reaction. "I have been called a lot of things, but *nice* has never been one of them. Even my brother doesn't call me *nice*," I say, still laughing when I realize she's doing that staring thing again, the kind that makes me feel uncomfortable. I quiet then, pausing while I nod, just trying to figure her out.

"Look, you're...good company," I say, letting my eyes settle into hers. It's strange how natural it feels. "I was thinking it might be nice...to be friends."

"Friends," she repeats, her tone oozing with skepticism and her eyes studying me like she's waiting for me to jump at her and yell, "*Boo!*"

"Yeah, friends," I say again. "Your roommate seems to be into my brother, so I'm thinking you and me, we'll be hanging out a lot, and you're funny. I like that," I say, not really paying attention to a damn word coming out of my mouth, but suddenly feeling desperate to make this girl my friend. What the fuck is happening to me?

"I'm...*funny?*" she asks, moving closer to me and sitting back on the workout bench, her knees doing that thing where they graze against mine.

"For a girl," I joke. Without pause, Cass pushes her hands against my chest, I'm sure her intent to chide me, but I take advantage of it and trap her fingers against my body, forcing her to stay close, in my space. Her laugh comes out nervously, and for some reason, I'm overcome with this urge to make her feel...okay. Reaching up with one hand, I tip her chin so our eyes meet. "I'd really like to be your friend," I say, and strangely, I mean it.

For a few seconds, we are completely alone. I don't notice the athletes starting to clank weights around us, or the people firing up the nearby treadmills. All I notice is how cold her hands are, how fucking amazing her fingers feel, and how much I want

32

to kiss her. And I would totally fight the urge, but goddamn it, I want to kiss her.

So I do.

One second I'm teasing her and begging her to be my friend, and the next my hands have slid up her completely perfect arms to the side of her face, and my lips are begging hers to relax. I—and my damned impulsivity—am going to blow my shot to hell in a split-second decision. At first, she's taken off guard, and I feel her threaten to pull away. I'm pissed at myself, and my grand romantic fantasies. I should know better. I'm not the romantic one.

But then, her hands wrap around my wrists, and she's kissing me back. Everything about her—her tongue, her soft bottom lip, the sharp edges of her teeth—is tempting me and begging me to go on. But the loud thud of the fifty-pound dumbbell dropping on the floor next to us snaps us out of *whatever the hell that was.* Cass's fingers release their hold on my arms, and she pushes away from me.

"I'm sorry," I say, just wanting the redness to leave her face, and for her to look at me again like she was before I got all impulsive and shit. "I didn't mean to do that."

"Yeah...you did," she says, standing and moving away from me even more. Distance—so I can't do *that* again.

"Yeah...I did," I admit, giving in to the smirk threatening to take over my lips. Her chest is heaving in-and-out like she just finished running a mile, and her eyes have this frightened vibe, like they're torn between wanting me to kiss her again and wanting to run.

"I'll be your friend, Tyson," she says, swinging her towel around her neck and picking up her small set of keys from the corner of the weight room. "*Friends.*"

"Absolutely. Friends. Totally got it," I say, chewing at the inside of my lip. When she's just far enough away, I call out to her again. "Hey, but Cass?"

"Yeah?" She turns and nods, her face still flush from everything that just happened.

"I'm totally going to kiss you again sometime. You know...like friends," I say, pushing back from the floor mats without waiting to see her reaction. I don't have to, because I know she wants me to kiss her again. Nate is going to give me hell for this, but I think I might just really like a girl.

Chapter 4

Cass

I told Rowe about the kiss, but not really. I just dropped it on her and pretended it was no big deal. I did that because Paige was in the room, and as far as Paige knows, things like me randomly hooking up with boys for flirting and making out is no big deal. It's just a continuation of my senior year of high school.

But Paige never really knew the full story. And I think I'd rather keep up the façade that *being flirty* is just part of my personality, rather than open that shit can up again.

I knew she'd have a reaction over Ty. He's...different. Yes, he's in a wheelchair. And Paige...that's all she sees. But it's kind of the last thing I see. There's something about him. He lifts about three times as much as I do, and his body is cut to perfection. And his eyes—oh, that's why I let him kiss me. That's why I kissed back! It was like hypnosis. But there's something else when I'm near him, and I can't quite put my finger on it. It's like we're playing this intense game of chess, studying one another to find strengths and weaknesses. Only, I don't want to exploit his. I only want to understand them.

He's going to the mixer with us tonight, and I know I'm going to see him in about five minutes. It's been six hours since our friendship pact—sealed with a kiss, I suppose. I can't be easy with him, though. I like him this much and I barely know him. If I give in to what my body wants, and then he ends up moving on to the next girl, it will suck. No, it will more than suck—it will completely derail my promise to myself to make this year all about me and what *I* want. Instead, it will be all about Ty and how sucky it is to live down the hall from him.

"Ladies?" Ty says with a rhythmic knock on our half-open door. "Hope you're decent. We're coming in."

He has his hands over his face, but his fingers are spread so he can see everything. It's stupid, but it makes me giggle. Paige just rolls her eyes, but she straightens up fast as soon as Nate trails in behind Ty. I look over to catch Rowe's reaction and notice her frame growing smaller. If the race to win Nate's heart comes down to confidence, I'm afraid Rowe doesn't stand a chance in the shadow of Paige Owens, who has decided to wear her silk dress tonight, lest someone on campus not have the chance to know exactly what her nipples look like.

Paige seems to be ten steps ahead of us, all the way to the gym; I know this too is strategic. She's always looking for the angle, the way to make sure the guy she wants has no choice but to notice her ass. My sister is a beautiful girl, and she'd be beautiful without all of the tricks. But I tried to tell her that once, and she just told me I was jealous. So, if she wants to wrap herself in see-through fabric and parade in front of me like a stripper for attention, I let her.

As soon as we enter the gym, Paige turns it on heavily, pulling out every stop she can think of to make sure Nate's eyes are on her, and only her. Of course, the way she pops her chest out seems to have Ty's entire focus too, and something in me...just...snaps.

"They're tits, boys. Get over them," I say, walking ahead to the registration table. I can feel Ty move closer to me, but I don't give him the satisfaction of eye contact. He can take this opportunity to get in a few more good looks at Paige's breasts. My sister is oblivious, still preening in front of Nate, competing even harder now that he's moved his hand to the small of Rowe's back.

As soon as we enter the gym, an announcer starts giving directions to break people up based on middle names and birthdays. I always hated these types of mixer games. We did this a lot at soccer camp on the first day. I always got stuck in the worst groups—with girls from rich schools, who weren't really good at soccer—so our group ended up losing whatever drill they made us do.

It's the same now. There aren't many *J* middle names for females, and the guys starting to form the *J* group in the middle of the room all look like the kind who yell out their car windows and whistle at women they think are *hot*! Before anyone can ask me my middle name, I backtrack to a seat against the wall in the corner and pull out my phone to pretend I have something important to do.

"Me, I'm more of an ass man," Ty says, settling into the space next to me.

"Wha—?" I ask, probably still a little pissed that he blatantly ogled my sister's tits.

"I mean, don't get me wrong, your sister makes a good case for boobs, but I'm just more into asses," he says, stretching his hands behind his neck, cracking it to one side before pulling up the corner of his lip into this cocky half smile and winking at me.

"I take it back. We can't be friends," I say, turning my attention back to my phone.

"Good," he says, which gets my attention, and I snap my eyes up to look at him again. "I was thinking about it, and this whole friends thing is going to make it awkward when I kiss you again."

"I'm not kissing you..." I say, but I sort of run out of words, because as irritated as I am with him right now, he's so damned handsome that it stuns me.

"Again?" Ty speaks the word for me, his eyebrows raised. "You mean again, because baby, you already kissed me. Please say you haven't forgotten it."

"Oh...my god. You did not just call me *baby*," I'm starting to wonder if I imagined all earlier versions of Ty, because *this* one is not impressing me.

I sink my focus back into my phone, playing one of those stupid games that I'm sure I'll obsess over and sit awake at night trying to master. Several seconds pass before Ty finally leans over into me with a nudge. "Baby hater," he says. I fight it at first, but a small snort laugh squeaks out through my smirk. "There she is."

My first instinct is to roll my eyes, but as soon as my vision locks onto his face, I'm reminded of the fact that there's something about him I also find irresistible. "Your smile...is breathtaking," he says—all traces of his crass jokes from before, gone. We stare into each other for several more seconds, and he's the first to break. "So, no circle-mingling for you? What, bad Girl Scout camp experience?"

"Ha," I snicker. "You're half right. Soccer camp. And yes, it was the worst. I hate forced icebreakers. You?"

"Well, I'm not exactly built for square dancing," he says with a slight shrug, gesturing to the circles of people grouped out on the gym floor, all linking arms, walking in circles, and giving each other these uncomfortable-looking back massages. "You should be out there, though. You might meet someone."

"I'm good here," I say, letting my smile linger in a way I hope like hell looks sexy from his perspective. His pause signals that it might.

"So, Cass Owens is a soccer player, huh? You mentioned that during our workout. You still play?" he asks.

"Gave it up," I shrug. "It was a high-school thing for me." I stay away from the details, but he watches me closely as I speak, and I get the sense he's trying to tell if I'm bluffing with my words. I'm not—not entirely, at least. I did give it up, and it *was* a high-school thing. But I miss it. My stupid body doesn't like that kind of exertion, though, and even if it could handle it, my parents' marriage couldn't take me rebelling against what makes my mother comfortable. So the deal was I get to study exercise in college, but my shin guards and soccer cleats get hung up for good.

I look out at the circles of people and catch Rowe's attention. I'm pleased to see she's right next to Nate. Paige is on the other side of the gym. It's not that I'm rooting against my sister, but I just feel compelled to root for Rowe in this. Nate seems like a good guy, and Rowe reminds me of me. And I guess I want to know one of us can get the prince in the end.

"It'll happen again. Just so you know," Ty says, his voice bringing me back from my trance.

"What, me? Soccer? I doubt it," I say, not doing a very good job at masking the sadness in my response. Ty's eyes stay on mine as I try to work my lips back into a natural-looking smile. His mouth pushes into a tight line as he draws in a deep breath and slowly starts to nod his head.

"I was talking about me trying to kiss you. But now, I sort of feel like a dick, so..." he says raising his brow and clapping his hands together in his lap. "Yeah, uh...hey, I know. How about I just help you get back into soccer-shape instead, and we'll see about walk-on tryouts in a few months?"

I'm not sure what I'm struck by more—the fact that he's so hell-bent on kissing me again, or the fact that he thinks he can get me back out on the field. I start to smile and open my mouth to respond when I hear a few people scream in front of us and turn to see Nate lifting Rowe in his arms, then laying her flat on the floor.

"Shit! I think she just passed out!" Ty says, pushing forward, but stopping before the thick crowd of onlookers. I work my way in and urge people to give her space. Her eyes are already blinking, but she seems disoriented.

"She's totally faking," Paige says behind me.

"I don't think so," I say in return, watching my new friend have a full-blown panic attack on the gym floor. It takes several seconds for Rowe to realize she's safe, and after she comes to, we lift her to stand. Nate is glued to her side the entire walk back to our dorm.

"Drinks in our room?" Ty asks everyone, but his eyes are on me. I shouldn't go. I've had one night of partying already, and a second—in a row—is probably a bad idea. Paige is already squealing, though, and Rowe is walking a little slower behind us with Nate, so it all seems to come down to me. I nod a small *yes*, and Ty responds with a grin that stretches his entire face. Somehow, all I notice is the way his beard has grown into this really sexy stubble that only makes the dimples stand out more.

When we make it upstairs, Rowe pauses, and I can see Nate hesitating. She's not feeling well, and I think he's considering staying with her. But he eventually gives in and joins Paige, Ty, and me back in their room.

Ty is twenty-two, so their mini fridge is well stocked with beer and their shelves with hard liquor. Just one look at the tequila makes my stomach turn, so I make a face at him and cover my mouth. "Overdo the tequila last night did you?" he teases, and I immediately nod *yes* in return.

One thing I learned from my mistakes in high school is not to be embarrassed to admit I'm drunk—or that I don't want to drink. Paige, however, seems more than willing to have a repeat performance, and she downs a few shots within the first five minutes we're in Nate and Ty's room.

It's comfortable in here. Everything is darker than our room, probably because they have a blanket looped over their curtain rod to keep the room extra dark. Their space also feels more masculine. It's void of extra stuff, only necessities and the random magazine or two.

Ty is quick to pull himself from the chair into his bed. He pulls his shoes from his feet and lets them fall to the floor before unbuckling what looks like a very expensive watch and tossing it on the dresser right next to his bed. He looks up at me when he's done, scoots his body closer to the wall, and then pats the space next to him.

"Uh uh," I say, surveying the small stretch of open floor, not really ready to *get horizontal* with Ty.

"Come on, it's just a bed," he says, that perfect smirk luring me. Do I want to lie next to him? Of course I do. It's just that I've learned through painful experience that the easy ones never stay long—they leave scars and change the course of your life without sticking around to see the fallout. I don't want Ty to be easy. I want him to be a challenge—slow and thoughtful. A boyfriend. Easy ones aren't boyfriends either.

There isn't much room on the floor, though, and I will look ridiculous if I pull over Nate's desk chair. My stomach sinks with that dropping sensation, because I hate that I'm giving in. But I do it anyway, and I slide onto my side to face Ty, careful to keep myself at least an arm's length away.

"Oh my god, I can't believe you bought that line. Now that I have you in my bed, I'm totally going to take advantage of you and turn you into my sex slave," he says, only able to hold the serious look on his face for a fraction of a second before rolling his eyes.

"You're an ass!" I say, smacking lightly against his chest, pulling my hand back quickly this time, so he can't catch it.

"Yeah, I know," he says, the corner of his lip curled up in that perfect way. "But I *am* going to kiss you again. Sometime...soonish. Just FYI."

40

"We'll see about that," I say, taking note of the pleasant flutter in my belly. I love that flutter. I haven't felt it since before the diagnosis—since before I turned myself into a doormat for heartbreakers. "And FYI? Chicks don't dig it when you woo them about kissing with an FYI like some five-minute business deal."

"Oh, I don't know," he says, his eyes boring into me. "I get the feeling you mean business."

"Oh, I'm *all* business," I tease, pursing my lips and crossing my arms in front of my chest in defiance. I'm enjoying this game.

"Pity," he says, rolling to his back and folding his arms behind his head. "Me? I'm all pleasure."

FYI, you can go ahead and kiss me now.

Ty

Cassidy Owens is a goddamned goddess. I have no idea what she's still doing in my bed, but she's still here—I must have a shitload of karma I'm cashing in. We've spent the last hour talking about everything. I mean *everything*!

Cass likes cheeseburgers, and she dips her fries in mayonnaise. But she runs an extra two miles when she knows she's going to eat like crap. She cares about her body, but not for vain reasons. She says she just likes to feel healthy. Usually, I'd call bullshit when a chick says something like that. Chicks always play off wanting to look hot, and they do it so you'll tell them they look hot anyway. It's stupid. But I really don't think Cass gives a shit about the physical side effects of her workouts. She wants to be strong—like a killer.

She didn't get too deep with me about soccer, but I get the sense she misses it. I'm not sure why she gave it up. From what I gathered, she would have made the team at McConnell, easily. She's a competitor. I understand—so am I. And there isn't a day that goes by that I don't miss running the bases. If my body would let me round third just one more time, I would in a heartbeat. But when I brought up the idea of her training for tryouts, Cass just shrugged.

Paige passed out a few minutes ago, and I catch Nate over Cass's shoulder, pulling the extra blanket from the box Mom sent, and tucking it under his arm.

"Dude, what are you doing?" I ask, but I already know. Nate looks at the pile of blonde hair and wrinkled silk on his bed, then at the neatly folded quilt in his arms before answering.

"Some shit just ain't worth it, bro," he says, grabbing my watch off the side table, which makes my stomach tense. "Gonna need the Tag tonight; have to set the alarm so I don't miss workouts. I'll drop it off before I leave."

"Whatever," I say, pretending it isn't a big deal. I'm full of shit, though, and Nate knows it. Kelly gave me that watch, and I never go a day without it on my body.

"Yeah, I'll still bring it back though," he smirks, then fastens it to his wrist and quietly tiptoes out the door.

I let my eyes settle back on Cass, and she's looking at me with what I can only describe as wonder, and it's making me really fucking uncomfortable. Lying on my back, I flop one arm over my eyes. "Dude, you can't look at me like that. It's like...an invasion of privacy or something," I say, sliding my arm down enough to see that she's still there. Still staring.

"Stop it!" I tease, pulling the pillow from the corner of my bed and shoving it at her. When I open my eyes the second time, she's hugging the pillow close to her body, and her stare has only grown more intense, and full of...fuck...I don't know...*fondness*? "What already?"

"You love your brother," she says. Not a question; just a statement of fact. All I do is nod *yes* in return, and I'm no longer embarrassed by her attention. She's right, and I'm glad it shows. When she scoots a little closer to me, I feel my muscles tighten on instinct, and everything in me freezes. It feels like minutes pass, but I know it's only seconds ticking by before I feel the tickle of her hair along my arm and the warm touch of her hand sliding flat over my chest until she's completely cradled against me. I need to know what I did to deserve this moment. I need to know so that way as soon as the sun comes up, I can go do it again.

"I know it doesn't seem like it on the outside, but Paige loves me like that too," Cass says, her voice a whisper. I'm sure she doesn't want to wake her sister up, but I saw the amount of shots she put down. I'm fairly confident we could invite a mariachi in to perform, and Paige would sleep straight through.

"You and Paige...are you close?" I ask, my arms still flat against the bed, though I slowly start to let my fingers relax into a curl. At this rate, I may finally get to put my arm around her by sunrise.

"We are. Sort of," she says, stifling a chuckle. "We're different. I know, I know—that's pretty obvious. But we still always have each other's backs. When Paige wanted to win homecoming queen, I campaigned for her. And when I wanted to come to McConnell, Paige stood up to my parents for me and told them they needed to loosen their grip. That's really the only reason she's here, you know. She came to McConnell so they'd have to let me come with her."

"That's kind of crappy," I say, defensive against Cass's parents, whom I've never met, and realize mid-sentence could honestly be lovely people. "I mean...why would they let Paige go away, but not you?"

Cass pauses at my question. She doesn't even open her mouth to answer for a long time, instead reaching over to touch a loose string on my blanket—her eyes intensely staring at the string while she thinks. When she finally does speak, I can tell part of what she says is a lie. "Paige was always planning on staying in California, and my parents wanted us to both be near home. Empty-nest syndrome or something like that, I guess. But she's better at standing up to them. She fought them so I could go," she says, keeping her gaze locked on my chest and that damn thread. I play a lot of poker, and I know that if what she just said were really no big deal, I'd be looking into her eyes.

Lying is usually a deal-breaker for me. That's one thing I don't do. Do I omit the truth? Yeah, I do that all the time. But I don't lie. But for some reason, I'm compelled to give her this one. I'm breaking the rules, my rules...*for her.*

"So honestly, when do I get to kiss you again?" She laughs at my harsh left turn in our conversation. I love the way she laughs.

There's this rasping sound that comes from deep inside her, showing it's genuine, and her smile creases deeply into her cheeks.

She flops to her back, and I instantly kick myself for causing her to move away. "You're really trying to wear me down, aren't you?" she asks, her hand running along the side of her face until she covers her eyes, peering at me through her barely-spread fingers.

"Wow, well...I've never really had to wear anyone down before..." I say, shielding my slightly dented ego.

"And that's precisely why we need to be friends, and why I can't kiss you..." she starts, and I interrupt.

"Again," I say.

"Right, again," she whispers, and moves her hand back to cover her eyes. I take this opportunity to roll onto my side and really look at her, the way her lips barely part when she breathes, the small twitches they make when she fights against her body's urge to smile, the tiny movement of her tongue as it wets her lips. I *have* to kiss her again.

"But...and hear me out," I say, startling her with how close I am. She uncovers her eyes and turns to face me, scooting back a few more inches just to maintain this new self-imposed *safety* distance. "Maybe the fact that I am willing to work so hard just to get you to say *yes* makes you different."

She stares into my eyes for several long seconds, her lips slightly parted as she considers this. "Am I? Different?" she asks.

"Now see, there's the catch," I say, running my thumb softly over the wrinkles in the sheet between us. "I can't know for certain unless I kiss you again."

"Oh *really*," she says, smirking.

"Cross my heart," I say, motioning my hand across my chest. "It's in the handbook."

"There's a handbook," she says.

"Uh, duh. There's *always* a handbook," I challenge back.

"And your handbook says you can't tell if I'm worth your time without jamming your tongue down my throat?" she fires back.

"Wow. Again with the word slap," I say, secretly loving this back-and-forth we've got going now.

"Word slap?" she questions.

"Yeah, like, you just bitch-slapped me in the face with your words. Word slap," I say with a shrug. She holds my gaze after this and bites at the corner of her lip, her eyes squinting as she decides her next move.

"Okay, how's this," she says, leaning in a little closer, closing the gap in the invisible barrier she seems to have instituted when I started talking about kissing. "You can kiss me again..." I move toward her on instinct, but she's quick to put her hand against my chest to stop me. I grip it, tightly, and meet the dare in her eyes. "But not until you mean it."

There's a fire in her eyes when she says this—one that I don't disrespect, and don't dare cross. It's not threatening, but it's serious, and I have this feeling churning in my stomach that Cass Owens is what Nate and I like to call a *game changer*. Her words have my heart racing, my mind worried that I can't mean it enough, at least not yet. All of our playfulness from seconds before has ceased with this line she's drawn, and I will obey it.

Holding her gaze, I lift to my mouth her hand I've trapped against my body, pressing my lips to her open palm. I don't speak, and I don't break our line of sight. But I don't kiss her, either.

Chapter 5

Ty

My mom's voice is consuming my ear as Cass slips out of my room with the shyest smile. *Damn.* I wanted to give her a proper goodbye. But that's the Preeter parents for you. It's like they have a special alarm that goes off and alerts them when to interrupt the best parts.

When I was a seventh grader, Mom had this way of driving up to pick me up at school right when I was about to get handed the porno mag from the cool kid whose dad kept a boxful under his bed. And in high school, there was no sneaking the Cinemax late-night shows on the big TV. Somehow, Mom would suddenly need to sit in the living room for reading, her back "bothering her in bed." And Dad's no better. Though his timing always seems more aloof, he was the king of flipping on the porch light right when your hand was about to find the right place underneath a girl's shirt.

That's what happened when my phone chirped at ten this morning. It kept chirping. And I knew it would keep chirping until I picked up. Persistent—that's Cathy Preeter.

"No, Ma. It's not too early. I was awake," I lie. I lie through my teeth. I hate lying, and I'm a total hypocrite now, but Mom doesn't count. Not when it's for Cass. Not that my mom would lecture me over having a girl in my bed. 'Cause hell, this ain't the first time she's interrupted *that*! She'd lecture me for wasting my day away, not getting an early start on such a "wonderful morning." I'd trade in a thousand sunrises to spend another night like that.

"Good, that's my boy," she says. I grin at her verbal pat on my head, because I love it when my mother's proud of me—even if I made up the reason for it today. "Your dad and I are coming in for the game in two weeks. We've got the box. Thought it'd be nice to take you boys to dinner. You know, do that parent-spoiling thing a little."

"Spoiling's good," I say, lifting a T-shirt from the floor and sniffing it to make sure it's *clean enough*. It isn't. I toss it back into the closet and try the next one, which smells a little less ripe, so I pull it over my head.

"All right. Well, we have extra tickets, so if you—or your brother—you know...have anyone *special* you'd like to invite? We'd love to host them. And have them join us for dinner, of course," she says, her voice in that super syrupy tone that she started to have the first time I went to a junior high dance. My mom loves the idea of her boys meeting the right girls. She's a romantic. And it's always driven me nuts, which is why I never take the bait and *always* show up alone. Every time...except this time. Maybe. *I think?*

"All right, we'll see," I shrug her suggestive questioning off because I haven't asked Cass yet. And I still might not. I feel like I need to *mean it*—like Cass would say—if I were going to toss her into the equation with my parents. And I'm going to need to think that through a little more before I plant the seed in Cathy Preeter's fairytale imagination.

"Nate, too," she says, adding that last part because she knows how burned Nate was after his breakup with his high school girlfriend, Sadie. She was a bitch, and she proved me right about her when she cheated on my brother with his best friend.

"Yeah, yeah," I say. Sometimes, I think my mom forgets that her offspring are men, and we have a low tolerance for the gushy, mushy shit. "Hey, I gotta go, okay? Send cookies. And by cookies, I mean money. Love you!"

"Love you too, Tyson," she says, and I hold out hope. "Oh, and bake your own cookies...*sweetheart*."

Damn. Worth a try.

Cass

I have that hopeful grin on my face. I wore it all the way back to our room, and as much as I want to straighten out my lips and come across indifferent when I open our dorm-room door, I can't. I'm just too...happy.

"Looks like *someone* had a good night," Paige teases, still primping herself at the mirror. I saw her slip out of Nate and Ty's room a little before me. I almost left then with her, but it felt too good to be there, warmly tucked under his heavy blanket with my back pressed against his chest. He did that thing where a guy strokes a girl's hair; at least, I think that's a thing? I read about it, and I've seen it on TV and movies. But I've never had a guy do that to me. All of my intimate scenarios have been...*less* personal.

I don't answer Paige, but I don't lose the grin either. Tossing my shoes to the corner, I pull my backpack from the seat of my desk chair, setting it down on my bed with me so I can start sorting through things and getting ready for class this week. I'm keeping my hands busy, and my mind occupied, because I don't want Paige to ruin this.

"What are you doing, Cass?"

She's going to ruin this.

I huff. I literally huff, because the pressure boils in me so fast that it has to come out just as quickly. *Whooosh*, the air blasts through my nose as I shake my head. My sister, the protector—she will never understand. "I like him, Paige," I say, challenging her with my stare, and waiting for her to tell me about all of his flaws.

"Seriously?" That's all she can say in return, and the way she's looking at me makes my stomach sick.

"Paige, unlike you, I don't rule people out of my life based on superficial physical shit," I say sternly. I've ramped up to pissed off now.

"Oh, fuck you," she says, surprising me a little that she's really going to spar with me over this. Raising my eyebrows, I ready myself for one hell of a one-sided debate, but she moves to sit next to me and grabs my ankle, which is folded over my leg in my lap, disarming me.

"I'm *not* talking about the fact that he's in a wheelchair, Cass. My god, give me a little credit," she says. I purse my lips tightly, trying to force myself from launching into all of the reasons I shouldn't give her credit when it comes to how she sees other people. "I'm talking about his rep—everything I've heard about Tyson Preeter...the stories *you* have heard. What other girls said at that party. What the sororities said when we took the tour our first day."

"I don't know what you're talking about," I lie.

"Don't bullshit me, Cass. You like him, but that doesn't give you a good enough excuse to go blind to everything about him that screams *douchebag*. He's charming, and then he's a dick. That's Tyson Preeter in a nutshell—and I'm sorry, but I'm not going to let him use you like that. You've been used enough!"

Her last comment bites. She winces a little when she realizes what she said, and I feel the apology coming.

"I didn't mean it that way, Cass," she starts, but I unwrap my headphones and put them in my ears to drown her out. I get it. I was the slut in high school. I've got notches on a bedpost, and was voted *most likely to sleep her way to the top* in the unofficial yearbook. But I've taken my lumps. Believe me, I've felt the wrath of what I did, and Paige has *no idea* how bad things got. My guard is up, and I'm willing to wait for Ty to wear it down— to *earn* it. And I believe he will.

"Cass," Paige says, tugging one of the ear buds from my head, forcing me to look at her. "I just don't think he deserves you. That's all. And I mean it."

I push my earpiece back in place and quickly return my focus to the class list in my lap, pretending to read. Paige walks back to the mirror and returns her focus to making everything on her perfect. And in my head, I twist the words she said to how I really feel.

"And I don't think *you* deserve *him.*"

An hour ago, I walked out of Ty's room feeling like the princess in a Disney movie—cartoon birds and butterflies whistling around my head as I tiptoed barefooted along rose petals. Now, I feel dark and sick and ugly. I feel just like the girl I was my senior year of high school—like the girl who let any guy make her feel better, feel special for the *then and now.* It's the same way with drugs. The high lasts in the moment, and then the lows crash over you after, and the shame becomes so unbearable, you lower your standards to find the high again even faster. I lowered my standards to almost non-existent.

I was popular, and I had such a great story—the star soccer girl who was overcoming the limitations of MS. I was on the shots my senior year, and while they were supposedly helping me to keep the number of MS flare-ups down, they often left me feeling wiped out and tired. But worse than that were the red welts left behind on my stomach, thighs, and arms from the needles. I didn't mind at first, and was only happy to be rid of the constant worry of a flare-up, when actual cell damage was occurring in my spine and brain. But the summer before our senior year, I joined Paige on a lake trip to Palm Springs. She wore her typical bikini—her body smooth and perfect, and the only thing every guy we came in contact with could look at. I wore board shorts and a long T-shirt, because despite being thin and toned, I knew when guys looked at me, the welts would be the first things they saw.

After that, upon my urging, my parents switched me to the oral meds. And when the popular and hot Jeff Collins started to flirt with me at the end-of-the-summer bonfire down at the beach, I let him take my virginity the same night. I did it because it felt good to be wanted and looked at the way Paige was. When he didn't call the week after, and started dating someone else as soon as school started, I turned my attention to his best friend Noah, thinking I would make Jeff jealous. I waited a week before I slept with him. And then I waited—waited for word to get back to Jeff, for Jeff to get jealous, for the both of them to fight over me and want me to be *theirs.* That fight never happened—they both moved on, leaving me behind. The pattern of making myself feel loved and wanted by being easy became an addiction, until it almost ruined my life.

Maybe Paige is right. Maybe I'm falling into old habits. Being in Ty's arms, being the object of his desire—it feels good. But maybe that's not enough.

I'm absorbed in my own doubt and thoughts when I hand my student ID over to the woman at the front desk at the rec center. The beeping sound, when she passes it under the scanner, finally wakes me from my trance.

"Back so soon?" Ty's voice comes from behind me, like the finger of the devil scratching at my soul and beckoning me to come to him.

"What can I say? I'm dedicated to my workouts," I say, not turning fully to look at him, not wanting to get locked under his spell.

"Well, I don't have any clients for the rest of the day. How about we workout together? Maybe get started on your conditioning?" he asks. He's actually serious about training me, and the hungry competitor deep inside is even more attracted to him because of this.

"You were serious?" I ask, allowing myself to turn to face him. He's wearing a black ball cap turned backward and a gray T-shirt that's tight enough to curve with every peck and ab muscle on his torso. He's also wearing black sweats with a white stripe down the side of each leg, and I realize I've never actually seen his bare legs. He even wore his sweatpants to sleep last night.

"I know my body's hot, baby, but if you wanna touch it all you have to do is ask," he smirks, and I flush red now that I realize exactly how long I've been staring at him.

"Didn't we have a conversation about this whole you calling me *baby* thing?" I change the subject.

"That's right. You hate babies," he says, and I laugh on instinct. I hate that he makes me laugh so easily. And I love it.

"I'm just going to get in a quick workout. Really, I won't be here long," I say, caught somewhere between wanting him to take my hint and let me go—and wanting him to challenge it, to challenge me.

"Chicken," he says, and my tummy fires up with giddiness that he's chosen door number two.

"I'm so *not* chicken. And oh my god, could you be more of a third-grader?" I ask. He's followed me to the cubbies by the weight room. I push my small gym bag into one of the shelves, not even bothering to get out my iPod, because I'm totally transparent; I want Ty to stay and talk to me.

"I'm an awesome third-grader. That was my favorite grade. First kiss, class clown, record number of detentions. Yeah, I was *king* in third grade. So, are we conditioning or what?" he says, getting right back to his point without pause. He stares into me, his eyes taking a brief second or two to roam down to my waist before coming back to my face. I can feel my lips tug at the corner wanting to mimic the smirk he's giving me. We're flirting, and it feels good. But Ty's also messing with my biggest weakness by dangling the soccer carrot out there in front of me like that. And I may not be strong enough to refuse his challenge—no matter the shit storm it will cause with my parents.

"What did you have in mind?" I relent, and his smirk grows into a full-blown smile.

Ty pulls a folded paper from his pocket and flattens it against his chest before handing it to me. I can't help but gawk at his chest muscles for a split second before bringing my attention back to the paper. It's a workout plan, a good one, completely customized to me. My heart melts that he's serious about turning me back into a competitor—so serious he spent time and energy devising a plan. My muscles actually jolt with a tiny charge, the familiar desire of wanting to push myself settling deep inside me. But there's also a faint stabbing sensation in my side, the one that comes from responsibility.

"I want to do this," I say, sucking in my bottom lip, and holding my breath, trying to stave off the sting of tears in my eyes because I miss soccer so goddamned badly. "But I just can't."

I fold the paper along the same creases and toss it back to him, but he only stares at it in his lap, snickering once.

"Seriously, Ty. That time...*my time.* That part of my life is over. I can't work at that level any more," I say. I don't even realize I've started to chew on my thumbnail until Ty reaches up and pulls my hand away from my face, tucking the workout plan back inside my fist.

"Yes, you can," he says, squeezing my hand closed around the paper and looking at me, determined to get me on his side. My heart started kicking the instant he touched me, and the longer he holds my hand in his palm, the faster my pulse races. I haven't begun my workout yet, but I feel a single drip of sweat form at my neck and race down my spine. My conscience is screaming at me: *you can't do this*! I can't do this because I'll be breaking a promise I made to my mother, and because I told the doctors I would quit pushing myself so hard, and because Paige promised my parents she wouldn't let me go overboard.

"Yes you can," Ty repeats, squeezing my hand a little tighter, almost as if he can hear my inner battle. But he doesn't understand. I have limits. I have responsibilities. And my body...it can't handle any more pushing. It gets tired.

"I have MS."

I say it so fast, I don't hear the words leave my lips. But my breath is stripped away—it's panic, the kind you get when you're terrified, or when someone rips a painful bandage away.

"I have MS."

I say it again, just to be sure I hear it this time. I won't look at him because I don't want to see the sympathy on his face. I don't want to see that moment he gives up on me. I don't want to see it, because I like the way he looked at me before—the flirting, the wanting, the desire, the kiss. Goddamn it, why did I tell him?

"Pussy," he says, squeezing my hand even harder, and shaking it to get my attention. My eyes go to his on instinct, and there isn't a single trace of pity on his face. His lips don't twitch, and I can tell this isn't a front. He isn't trying to put on a strong face for me. He isn't *pretending* that he doesn't care what I just said. He honestly and truly doesn't. He's just calling me a *pussy*.

"Ty, did you hear me?" I ask.

"Yeah, I heard you. You have MS. I can't feel my legs. *La di fuckin' da*. Are we training or what?" His expression hasn't changed once, and the armor I just started to build up around my heart is already cracking.

I pull my hand from his and unfold the paper again to really take it in. Everything on here—every exercise and the time associated with it—is familiar. I know I can do it. I've done it before. I also know I may experience setbacks. And I know my body will be tired. But I want this. Maybe it's because Ty's the one believing in me, and maybe that's making me want it even more. It's probably the *wrong* decision based on a medical plus-and-minus chart, but it's the right one in my heart.

"Where do I start?"

The way his mouth slides into a prideful smile melts any remaining doubt away, and I take a slow, deep breath, my chest almost puffing at feeling strong *and* wanted all at once.

"We need to get your miles back up," he says, grabbing my bag from the small shelf and tossing it to me. "No weights today. Today is all about the treadmill."

I follow him to the aerobic machines, and everything feels lighter, yet nothing between us has changed. And I think I like that most of all. "Oh, by the way," he says, glancing at me over his shoulder, "my parents have a suite for the first home game. They're taking Nate and me, and we have extra seats. I'd like you to meet them. Wanna go?"

It may not be the right move, and I may be blowing any *future strategy*, as Paige would say, but I smile and let my eyes light up anyway, because Ty is actually doing it—he's earning me, like I'm something to be earned. "I'd like that," I say.

He nods in response, like it's no big deal, but I also hear him exhale heavily, and I can tell asking me made him nervous. *I* make him nervous. And I like that, too.

Chapter 6

Ty

I have never done a load of laundry in my entire life. Not once. Ever. Nate calls it my gift, my *one* super power.

Mom always takes care of it when we're home. It's her thing. She always says she loves the smell—the way the fabrics feel when she pulls them from the dryer—and the warmth. I get it. When I was a kid, I used to love tagging along with her while she did the weekend chores, and we'd always end up in the laundry room. I would sit in the corner, in the basket filled with freshly dried towels, and eat a bowl of grapes. Something about the dryer sheets lulled me to sleep. To this day, when I'm at home, Mom practically bakes my blanket and pillowcases in the dryer, and I swear to god I sleep like a damned baby.

You think my addiction to the smell of warmed lavender would be enough to learn how the whole process works. But as much as I love the end result, I absolutely loathe the manual-labor part of laundry. It's just so...tedious! It's not like dishes or vacuuming, not that I do any of that often either, but at least when you do the dishes, it's done...in like...fifteen minutes. Or you put them in a machine and just come back later and pull the dishes out when you need them. Laundry, though—laundry requires waiting. And carrying. And folding. And sorting.

While I was in Florida, I was usually able to get someone to do my laundry for me. Nate's taken care of it for the last month, throwing my laundry in with his. He says I'm so good that I even have him trained. I know he'd do it again. I know he'd do it every week, for the rest of the semester. But I just saw Cass go into the laundry room, and suddenly here I am, halfway down the hall with a full basket of laundry in my lap.

"Hey, fancy meeting you here!" I shut my eyes and release a breathy laugh when I hear myself speak. I'm so fucking lame.

"Oh, hey," Cass says, jumping at my voice. She's sorting her laundry, so I pause and watch.

She's wearing tiny running shorts and this thin T-shirt that makes me want to toss water on it just to watch it stick to her skin. We haven't really talked much since our training session a couple days ago. I have a feeling she thinks I'm freaked out because she told me about her MS. But I'm not. I haven't gone to see her because every time I do, I want to kiss her. But then I think about her one stipulation, and I wonder if me—and all of my *crap*—won't find a reason to hurt her once I'm done. That would be the end of it, too. No more training sessions, no more not-so-random laundry room run-ins. I don't think I want to be done with that.

I'm starting to realize there's a difference between *wanting* her and *needing* her. Problem is, I'm victim to both. I want her, God do I *want* her. But lately, I need her too. I *like* needing her. It feels...I don't know. It just feels. But if I blow one side of the deal, I'll lose the other. It's a delicate balance, and kissing her—that would tip the scales for good.

"Right, so I just shove all the clothes in this one and then pour in...what? Like, two cups of this stuff?" I'm not even close. Even I know this much. But I thought it would be better to play full dumbass rather than have her see me flounder and look foolish for real.

"Uh, yeah, if you want to repeat that episode of the *Brady Bunch* where Bobby floods the laundry room with bubbles," she says, giggling and taking the full cup of soap from my hand, pouring almost half of it back in the bottle.

"That's a classic," I say, making my move, pushing back and waiting for her to take over.

"Oh, I don't think so. Get over here. You are going to learn by doing, not by watching," she says, reaching her hand to mine. I come willingly, hungry to touch her, but my fire is put out quickly when she pushes the detergent back into my hand.

"What, no hands-on instruction?" I tease. She smirks, but she also rolls her eyes, so I give up on the overt flirting—for now. "Okay, okay, fine. I put in this much, but where?"

Cass points at a small drawer on the side of the machine, and I pull it open and pour in the soap. "Now what?" I ask, honestly clueless. She's laughing at me genuinely now.

"WOW," she mouths, big and slowly.

"Hey, don't make fun of me for not knowing how to do domestic shit. That's not nice. I'd like to see you swap out an air filter and put in a quart of synthetic," I say, practically growling when I'm done with my testosterone-filled comeback.

Cass is staring at me with her hand on her hip. "That make you feel better?" she asks, her mouth pursed, and her eyes doing that slow blinking thing that my mom's do when she's about to tell me to knock it off.

"Yes," I actually growl and beat my chest once for added effect. "Yes, it did."

Without pause, Cass proceeds to talk me through every single step involved in swapping out a goddamned air filter and putting in a quart of oil on a sixty-seven Dodge Charger. A sixty-seven Dodge Charger that "yes, you can switch to synthetic from ten W forty...if you know what you're doing!" And somewhere in the middle of it all, I admit to myself that there's a really good chance that I'm falling for her. It was at about the point that her lips slowed down to delicately toss out the words *valve covers* and *oil filter cap*.

Scales. Are. Tipping.

"Right, so, I sort the whites from the darks then, and put them in here," I say, swallowing my pride—with an actual swallow—and replaying the hottest damned dressing-down I've ever had.

"You're getting it," she says, pulling herself up to sit on the counter, her legs swaying back and forth like wind chimes while she watches me do my first solo load of laundry in my entire life. I'm actually kind of proud.

I look at her over my shoulder, and her bottom lip is caught between her teeth while she tries to hide her smile. I like the way she's looking at me.

Time to test the scales.

I press the start button and the machine begins to whirl and buzz quietly. It also says *forty minutes*. "Forty minutes?" I protest, but Cass just laughs, and then pats the counter next to her. I see her eyes flash when she realizes what she's done, but I won't let her feel bad.

"I'm good down here," I say, making a joke out of it and positioning myself right in front of her, moving my hands to grab the meaty calves of her legs. "Damn. Those feel like weapons."

I let my grip loosen, but I don't move my hands away, and she doesn't ask me to.

Cass

He's touching me. And it's not like the way he touched me in the gym, when he pressed my muscles to make them work harder. That touch was purposeful. This is a thoughtful touch, a strategic touch—an opening that he is taking.

"So, how do you know how to change the oil on a sixty-seven Charger?" he asks.

"I drive one. Back home. That's my car," I say, and his top lip curls just enough to make his left cheek dimple.

"That's hot," he says, and I laugh at his bluntness. It's probably my favorite quality about him, the way he just says things—whatever he's thinking. There's no filter, no *wall.* That's how I operate, or at least how I *try* to.

"I know," I say back, matching him. I match him. *We. Are. A. Perfect. Match.* These thoughts have flooded me ever since I told him I had MS, and he acted as if I said I liked pepperoni on my pizza.

His gaze lingers, and his smile grows a little bigger. I can see him chewing on the sides of his tongue, small twitches working in his jaw as if he's deciding whether or not to say something. He looks at me like this for a while, and his hands stay locked to the underside of the bottom of my legs. Eventually, he starts to tap at them teasingly with his fingertips, causing them to sway toward him as if he were toying with a balloon.

"How are the weapons feeling this morning?" he asks, giving each leg one more rub and squeeze before letting his hands fall back into his lap. My skin grows cold and tingles, wondering where he went.

"Good. I was tired yesterday though. But I think I can go again today." I'm exhausted, but my stomach is doing that urgent fluttering thing that is making me say irrational things and convince myself that I'm fully recovered from our first killer workout—all because I simply want to spend more time with him.

"Liar," he smirks. He knows I'm bullshitting, and I feel the burn of embarrassment starting to move up my neck. "I won't judge you, just so you know. Humans, we get...tired."

I twist my mouth and squint at him, not sure what he means.

"You're tired, because I probably worked you harder than you've ever been worked. And it's okay. You're allowed to be. I won't think it's because of the MS, which I know is what you're afraid of," he says, his brow lowered and his eyes zeroed in on mine. "I won't think you're weak. Ever."

My head nods in agreement and my lips form a relieved smile. I don't tell him that he's off-base, because as much as my *real* reason for pretending I'm not fatigued is to be near him, I do also worry that he'll think I'm weak. I worry because everyone else in my life thinks I now have limits. Ty is the first person who, so far, doesn't set them for me.

Ty catches a glimpse of my opened notepad and anthropology book next to me on the table. I had planned on getting a little of my homework done from the first day of classes, but that was when I thought I'd be in here alone for the next hour. My plans changed the second he said "Hello."

Before I can reach for the book, Ty takes it in his hand, and begins flipping through a few pages.

"Ah, undergrad classes," he says, sighing dramatically. I know he didn't mean anything by his statement, but suddenly I feel embarrassed, and maybe a little inferior, by the fact that I'm not yet nineteen and he's twenty-two, by the fact that I'm taking one-hundred-level courses and he's getting an MBA.

"I was just getting ahead, but...I can put it away," I say, taking the book from him quickly, and zipping it up in my backpack along with my notes and pen. I like the heaviness of the pack in my lap, like a shield—so I leave it there, hugging it to my body while my legs dangle.

I wonder if I look as uncomfortable as I suddenly feel. He's smiling at me, sort of. He looks uncomfortable too, and now I'm beginning to wonder if he's starting to calculate all of the negatives that come along with our age gap. He keeps looking at his watch, nervously twisting it around his wrist, like he wants to leave.

He wants to leave.

"I could just come and get you. You know...when your laundry's done?" I practically blurt out my question. He's blinking at me, like he's trying to decipher whatever language just spilled out of my lips. I'm pretty sure the dialect is young, naïve, and stupid.

"Are you...getting rid of me?" he asks, his head cocked slightly to one side as his eyes shift between my backpack and me, growing wider with each pass. Suddenly, he smirks as if he's discovered something. "Wait a second...were you looking at a porno mag? Is that why you put your book away?" He grabs my backpack from my lap so fast that my reflexes fail their mission to grip it back.

"No, I swear. I was just studying," I say through nervous laughter, sliding from my perch on the counter in an effort to get it back. I know Ty is just teasing, and at first we're in a cute game of tug-of-war. But when he unzips the side and reaches inside—his fingers threatening to pull out the pamphlets and self-help books I just picked up from the library—my fight to regain possession grows more manic. Ty, however, still thinks we're playing; his hands grip one end of the bag and mine the other. He yanks hard, his strong muscles really only knowing how to do one thing, and it forces the zipper open completely.

I thought I felt foolish about being younger. But that was *before* I made a floor display of every cliché low-self-esteem brochure printed in the state of Oklahoma. Naturally, the most embarrassing one is in Ty's hands right now.

"*How to Love Yourself So Others Will Too,*" Ty reads, flipping the book in his hands and skimming his eyes over the description on the back. I take this opportunity to scoop everything else up in my arms and sit on the floor with my legs crossed, quickly stuffing things back in my bag. "Oh, this is good. Wait, listen to this one..."

60

He starts to quote a few of the passages, mocking the stereotypical affirmations and examples in the book. I know they're stupid—and hearing them now, I'm not sure why I picked the book up. But reading it made me feel good an hour or two ago. "Wow, what class is making you read this shit?" he asks, finally putting the book down. His laughter cuts short when he sees me, my eyes buried in my lap.

"It's not for a class," I say, looking up long enough to get the book from him. "My stuff's in the dryer. Just...just knock on my door when it buzzes done." I leave quickly, clutching my things close to my chest and feeling ridiculous.

I don't bother to zip my bag up again, instead carrying it all into my room and letting everything spill out into a pile on my bed. I don't know what made me check all of these things out. It all started with the book Ty was reading, actually. My hands gravitated to it while I was looking through some of the health and wellness books. At first, my attraction was the same as Ty's—I found the book amusing. But some of those cheesy sayings actually rang true, especially the ones about feeling inferior to siblings and how we use self-deprecating humor as a crutch. Next thing I knew...I had two books, four magazines, and a dozen brochures.

Ty's knock on my door is soft. I hadn't shut it all the way when I walked in, so he takes advantage and comes all the way into my room with little warning.

"Dry already?" I ask, doing my best to pretend none of *that* happened. I pick the pillow up from my lap, laying it over the embarrassing evidence.

"No," Ty responds, moving closer until he's at the foot of my bed. Without pause, he slides from his chair to the bed until he's sitting next to me. He picks up the pillow, and my stomach sinks. His smile is soft as he scoops everything into my bag, and slides it all to the floor, closing the distance between us even more until his hand is suddenly cradling my cheek.

"Just so we're clear here, *I mean this*," he says, pressing his lips softly against mine as his other hand moves to my chin, tilting my mouth toward him. I've been kissed by some pretty convincing boys in my life, each one wanting to make me believe something by the way their mouth worked against mine, the way their tongues coaxed their way inside. This one kiss from Ty was like removing a blindfold.

No kiss has ever felt like this. His thumbs are soft against my cheek, and his fingertips are gentle in my hair. His lips pause over mine, stroking softly before crashing into me with more force. I'm used to guys using this move to disarm me, to get me on my back so they can see how far I'll let them go. But Ty is only pulling me closer to him, his hands sliding from my face to my shoulders and arms until I feel his strength lift me completely so I'm on his lap.

When his hands find my face again, he stops long enough to breathe, our foreheads pressed together and the tips of our noses touching. Even this simple touch is perfection. My heart is beating wildly, and I can feel my body trembling as Ty slides his hands deeper into my hair, bringing my lips to his again, this time sucking on my top lip until I give in and open up for him completely as he tastes me with his tongue.

The longer the kiss lasts, the stronger his grip on my body is, and when he finally pulls away from my mouth, he continues to hold me close, cradling my entire body to his. I feel every heavy breath escape his chest, and I start to wonder who is feeling this more—me or him? My knuckles are white from the tense grip I have on the back of his shirt, and when I finally let go, I notice how sweaty my palms feel. I don't know what Ty has done to me, but I know I will never be the same.

Not after that kiss.

Chapter 7

Ty

The first time I kissed Cass was just my damn impulse. But this last one, yesterday…that was…

The moment she looked up at me from the floor, I was done weighing my options. Watching her hands quickly trying to cover up the brochures and pamphlets with promises to make you feel happy, pretty, popular and whole—whatever bullshit promises brochures like that make—that was enough.

I have a box full of those brochures and books, buried under an equally old tub of trophies and CDs tucked somewhere in the depths of my closet at my parents' house. I'd get a new brochure with every new group I went to—or with every therapist I spoke to. I got them from the school, and from my mom's whacko circle of friends who believe in holistic powers and positive thinking. And every time I got one, I'd thank the person, bring it home, and throw it in the collection.

When her backpack opened, I saw all of her insecurities spill right onto the floor, and I just knew. This one. *This girl*— she's that other half my mom always talks about. I didn't kiss her because I felt bad for her. I kissed her because I *felt* her. Cass is me—in every possible way. We're both broken and pissed, fragile yet strong, careful with our hearts, but free with our words. And seeing the look on her face when I caught her in a moment of feeling *less*, in a moment that she felt unworthy…

"You are so much *more* than your sister," I whisper to myself, amused that somehow she thinks she has something to prove. Fuck that. I have something to earn.

"Mail call!" Nate yells, tossing a hefty envelope at me as he busts through our door. It lands on my chest, so I sit up in my bed and look it over. It's from Baker, Louisiana. *Kelly* lives in Baker. I toss it to the side and give Nate my full attention.

"Not gonna open it?" he asks, one eyebrow raised, tempting me.

"Nope," I say, moving to my chair and pushing to the desk. I flip open my laptop to check my training schedule for the rest of the week.

"Wow," Nate says. I can feel him staring at me, and I know there's a grin on his face. "You're smitten."

"Shut up," I say, following it up by tossing a pen at him from my desk. I'm more than smitten, but I'm also the one that does the dishing of crap around here. The crap doesn't flow both ways. "You ask Rowe about the game and dinner with the parents yet?" I know he hasn't, but this should get the focus off me and...*feelings.*

"Yeah...no..." he says, falling flat on his back and pulling his pillow over his eyes. "I don't know what it is, dude, but this girl—she intimidates me."

"Are you still tiptoeing around the boyfriend thing?" My brother saw Rowe hanging up a picture of her with another guy, and he's too pussy to come right out and ask her about it—so instead, he's taken to permanently moping. It's annoying.

"I brought it up. She doesn't want to talk about it. That's about as far as it goes." He blows out a heavy sigh.

"Well, if you don't ask her, Cass won't go. And if Cass doesn't go, I'm going to kick your ass. So quit being a douchebag," I say, grabbing his shoe and throwing it out in the hall like I always do when he irritates me. I've been doing this to him since he was a kid and used to want to hang out in my bedroom while I was talking on the phone to a girl.

"Fucker. I hate it when you do that," he says, standing with a heavy slouch as he drags his feet toward his sneaker. He keeps walking down the hall when he picks it up, though, so I know he's just as smitten as I am.

I push the door closed and turn to look at the simple brown package lying on my bed. It's one of those over-sized envelopes, and it's super puffy. It looks like a shirt. I bet it's a shirt. That was Kelly's thing—she loved those shirts with really silly sayings, and I thought they were a tremendous waste of resources, human labor, and money. She would buy me one for every birthday, holiday, anniversary, or whim just to tick me off. I loved it. I loved her for doing it.

Suddenly, I'm back on my bed, holding the package in my hand. For some reason, I smell it, wanting to know if it carried any sign of her along with it during its postal route. It just smells like cardboard and ink.

When I tear the corner open, I see the white fabric and confirm my suspicion immediately. I can't help that it still makes me smile, and I rip the rest of the envelope away to hold the shirt up and reveal the punch line. It's a stick man, humping the word *it*. Fuck it. Ha! Okay, that's funny.

I toss the envelope in the trash and fold the shirt up and slide it in my top drawer. There really might be a time and place to wear that one—it's a keeper. She finally found the one joke shirt I think is worth the twenty bucks she probably spent on it.

There's a Facebook message waiting for me when I open my laptop, and I see Kelly's picture looking back at me.

Well?

She must have followed the tracking code to see if I got it yet.

It took you something like 15 shirts to finally find one I think is funny, but I have to admit it—that shirt kicks ass. Thanks!

I hit send and start to close my laptop, but a message from her pops up right away. She must be online.

I KNEW IT! Glad you like it.

Happy Anniversary, Ty.

There's this feeling that accompanies stress and anxiety, it's like a spoon pushing into the side of your gut. It's similar to that sensation I get when I go on a really charged roller coaster—only sicker. Yeah, I have that feeling...*right now!* I don't respond. In fact, I exit out of Facebook completely, and turn my laptop off, worried that somehow some internal camera is switching to *on* allowing Kelly to see my forehead broken out in a cold sweat.

It's our anniversary. She's right, and the thought floated through my mind once this morning, but I quickly dismissed it. I think of it every year at the start of September, and I wonder if she's remembering our first date at the fall-festival dance, too. The first year she just sent me an email, acknowledging it. The last two years, she's blown it off completely. This is the first time she's gone as far as to send me something though.

Maybe it's just a funny shirt. And maybe she was just trying to be thoughtful.

Maybe I won't wear it now, though.

My afternoon appointments rescue me from overanalyzing shit. I grab my workout bag and lock up our door. I can hear Nate and Cass talking down the hall, so I follow the sound of their voices. I have to give Nate a key anyhow, so I use it as an excuse to invite myself in.

I enter the room and catch Cass at the door.

"You love me and you know it!" I hear Nate say around the corner. Cass bends down quickly, kissing me lightly on the lips before rolling her eyes and whispering, "Your brother's a pain in the ass." She winks and picks up her step toward the elevator, clearly making her way to the gym.

"You better not!" I say, not really liking Nate using the word *love* with Cass. Stupid and petty? Yes. Do I give a shit if he thinks so? No.

Nate's elbows-deep in Rowe's drawers, flipping them over so they dump out all of her clothes when she comes back. It's funny, and really, I'll take any excuse to rifle through Cass's drawers. I join in and flip her drawers over, too, paying special attention to the lacey things in her top drawer. I am looking forward to seeing those things in action.

My brother's in love; I can tell. It's not so much the way he talks about Rowe all of the time, but rather the way he *doesn't* talk about her...it isn't transient. And as much fun as I had playing big-brother-little-brother party time with him this summer, this feels more like the way things are supposed to be. And it's not just him—it's me, too.

He pauses on one of the drawers, and he's holding a picture. I can see over his shoulder it's one of Rowe and the other guy; I wince before he turns around. "This is like the one I was talking about. Do you think she has a boyfriend?" he asks. I have no clue, so I tell him he should ask, but I also make a mental note to ask Cass about Rowe and that picture, and then it hits me—I have someone to *ask*. Cass is *someone*—*my* someone. Holy shit, how the fuck did that happen?

We get the drawers back in place and lock up behind us, heading to the elevator. I'm running late for my first training session, but I hear Paige's voice as the elevator doors open. I shift my eyes to Nate and urge him to pick up his step. I follow him back to our room.

"Dude, I can't stand that chick! How is it that I'm crazy about her sister?" Nate's shit-eating grin clues me in on my big slip, but I don't really care that he knows how I feel. I like a girl, a girl that isn't Kelly. Kelly, who just wished me a happy anniversary from her home in Baker, where she lives with her husband and brand new baby boy. *What the fu—*

"She has great tits!" Nate says, bringing me right back to *my* Cass and her annoying-ass twin.

"Ah, that's a good point. Way to focus on the positive. She does indeed have great tits," I respond, waiting just long enough for her elevator trip to be complete, and her to be gone, before I head back down the hall to race to my training appointment. I pull out my phone to send a text that I'm running late to Sage, the girl who works the front desk, but I pause when I see one from an unknown number.

I miss you...baby ;-)

Cass, you just took another little piece of me.

Miss U 2, reformed baby-hater.

Chapter 8

Cass

I can tell something's wrong as soon as I walk into our room. Rowe's clothes are in a pile on the floor, her dresser drawers all empty and stacked on her bed. It looks like a break-in, only a really lame break-in. I can't figure out why someone would just go through Rowe's drawers and nothing else.

"Hello?" I say, my heavy backpack now clutched to the front of my body, like *that's* going to protect me. I kick the closet door open, and it ricochets off the back wall, shutting closed again. It's empty, as is the room.

I toss my bag on my bed and sit down looking at the strange mess of Rowe's things across from me. Curious. I stand and tug on the top drawer of my dresser, and the second I do, I feel the tickle of my socks and underwear slide down into a mound around my feet.

"Son of a bitch!" I pull the next drawer, and the heavy thud of jeans and sweatpants follows where undergarments went. I'm about to pull open my third drawer when I hear Rowe come into the room behind me.

"Damn it, Rowe! I didn't want to be a part of this war, but looks like I'm in it now!" I pull the third drawer out carefully, my hands doing their best to hold my clothing in place, but it's useless, and shorts and workout clothes land in the heap too.

"Who's messing with you?" Paige asks, hooking her book bag over her desk chair and sliding her shoes from her feet.

"Ty! And Nate! They flipped our drawers," I say, stuffing—not folding—clothes back into my drawers so I can slide them in. Paige brushes by me; at first I think she's going to help, but instead she starts pulling on her drawers to see if she's been pranked too. When nothing happens, and her clothes all stay in place, I feel a little bad. I can see the hurt on my sister's face over the fact that Rowe and I are part of something she isn't. But that's how this was supposed to go, wasn't it? Paige finally gets her life, and I get mine? Yes, that's how it's supposed to go. But I still don't like seeing my sister slighted.

"Okay, tell me what you girls need me to do. Let's get those assholes back," Paige says, and I know this is just her way of joining—of finding a way *in* on the attention. My gut instinct is to tell her not to worry about it, but then I look at Rowe, and I can see my new friend is happy to finally have my sister's approval, in some small way, so I let it slide. I'll let Paige be a part of this, even if she has nothing to do with it.

"I have an idea, but we're going to need to go to a hardware store," Rowe says. I can tell this has Paige losing interest right away.

"Yeah, I'm not doing that," she says, sitting back down on her bed, and pulling her phone from her purse.

"Hey, you wanted in. Either you're in or you're out," I say, taking the phone from her hands and tossing it a few feet away. I stare Paige in the eyes, challenging her to just drop her damn *better-than-everyone* complex for now. My sister is being a bitch because she doesn't want to like Rowe, she doesn't like taking orders from Rowe, and I know it's just because Rowe has the attention of Nate. But my sister needs to get over herself, because Rowe is nice. I need Rowe. And that should be enough.

"Fine," she says, blowing the bangs from her face with a dramatic huff of air. "Let's go to the hardware store. But I'm borrowing a car. It's too hot to walk anywhere," she says, grabbing her purse and leading us out the door. Out of habit, we follow.

Pain in the ass or not, my sister is good at getting things. Within minutes, she had a car borrowed from some frat guy, and she also managed to get us two gallons of free paint from the guy working the counter at the hardware store in town. We hid the paint and supplies in our closet overnight, and I woke up extra early this morning to set our plan in motion. Now, I just need to catch Ty before he is really ready to leave.

Rowe's long brown hair is all I can see hanging out from our doorframe down the hall. One more step, and she's out of sight. I know she's still listening, though. Somehow, I was nominated for this job—the *inside* job, as Rowe called it. I feel like a criminal, and I'm really bad at things like this. But Rowe got really excited when we picked up the supplies, and she was the first one awake this morning. For some reason, I feel like I need to pull this off for her. I take one more deep breath and knock softly on their door. Ty has a business class early this morning, so I know he's up. I can hear him making his way to the door. When it opens, I lunge at him before he has a chance to make conversation. I sit on his lap, kissing him until he lets the door fall closed behind us.

Phase one: complete—*I've made it inside.*

His kiss is intoxicating, even at seven in the morning, and I almost forget the real reason behind my mission. I hate that my next *real* kiss with him isn't really real at all. Ty pulls away begrudgingly and lets his eyes wash over my body before he speaks—his attention tuned in to my workout pants and bare stomach, a tactic I have to give Paige full credit for. My sister knows men. I may have slept with more of them, but she's had more of them chase her.

"I'm sorry, did I...order a wake up call?" he says, his tongue barely licking his bottom lip as his perfect smirk slides into place. My body suddenly feels a million degrees hotter, and my pulse is beating like a drum, firing away in my head, arms, and chest.

"No, I was just getting back from an early workout, and I remembered you would be up," I say, hating that I'm lying to him, but knowing it's not for a *bad* reason. He studies me, and for a few seconds, I think he might be seeing right through our little plan, but then his smile is back. He's pulling my head in close to kiss me again. *Oh god, his kiss.*

"Baby," he practically growls. "Wait, I can call you that now, right?" he asks, one eyebrow slightly cocked while he looks at me from only a few inches away. His face is shadowed with the perfect layer of unshaven stubble, and I allow my hands the pleasure of feeling it.

"I don't know; I'm still on the fence about the whole *baby* thing. Let's just say I'm *trying it on,*" I say, secretly loving that he calls me anything at all.

"Okay, well then...*baby*...while I would love to stay right here and kiss the honey flavor from your lips all morning, I have to get to class," he says, losing me somewhere around the word *honey*. That word—which would sound like the hokiest line in the world coming from anyone other than Ty—slides from his tongue, his southern accent caressing it, and making it my new favorite flavor. I had no idea my lips tasted like anything.

"Cass? You with me?" He's waving a hand in front of my face. *Shit!* I was off daydreaming about him.

"Oh, yeah...uh, yeah. Sorry, it's just...I don't have my key. Paige and Rowe are both out." *Lie, lie, lie*—holy damn my hands are suddenly sweaty. Don't look panicked—hold it together!

"That's fine. Just hang out here. Nate won't be back until late. Just lock it from the inside when you're done," he says, pulling his backpack over one shoulder and turning his chair swiftly with his other arm.

"Oh my gosh, that'd be great. Thanks, and yeah...I'll lock it up," I say, a little too quickly, bubbly, and about a million other ways that are no doubt shouting at him not to trust a damn thing I'm doing. Shit, I'm talking too much! Just smile, Cass. Smile and act natural.

I make myself comfortable on his bed, tucking my hands under my legs because I fear if I don't, they'll just start waving in protest against me, as if to tell him I'm a big fat liar who is tricking him so my girlfriends and I can exact our revenge.

"All right then. I'll come by later?" he says, winking. Gah! Even that wink is so good it's practically scripted.

"Sounds good," I say, going for simple. Two words and done. Once the door shuts behind him, I flop onto my back and let the rush of blood take over. Holy fuck that was the hardest thing I've ever had to do—and I had to confess some pretty ugly things to my parents my senior year of high school. Maybe it was just my state-of-mind at the time, but this little performance for Ty—just so I could get access to his room for a prank—has damn near exhausted me.

"Excellent work, Smithers," Rowe says, quickly sliding into the room with Paige behind her.

"Nice, a *Simpsons* reference," I say, giving her a high five while I still lie flat on my back. Paige has no idea what we're talking about, so she interrupts and takes over the conversation.

"So what now?" Paige sits down on Nate's bed, and I can tell she's trying to stake a claim over it. My sister still thinks Nate's up for grabs, but I'm starting to think Rowe just might have this match won.

"We paint," Rowe says, handing each of us a roller and a pan.

Rowe cracks open one of the cans and fills both my pan and hers with a thin layer of a color called *Pretty Princess Pink*. Paige is slow to join in, but eventually she gets to her feet, fills her own pan, and begins rolling the color on the wall over Nate's bed.

For three hours, we work tirelessly—covering every inch of wall in their dorm room, as well as the ceiling, with the most obnoxious sweet-sixteenish color known to man. There's still a good hour's worth of work to do, cutting in on the corners and near the floor, but I'm already late for open tutoring in physics. I bombed my first week's quiz, and I know that if I don't get help early, it's only going to get worse. I'm not a natural learner—my grades take work.

"Rowe, I am so sorry, and I know this is totally sucky, but I have to go," I say, setting my brush down on a paper plate on the floor.

"You're bailing? And leaving me here with *her?*" Paige asks, and I can't help but chuckle lightly because I'm sure Rowe is thinking the same damn thing.

"It's okay. We're almost done anyway," Rowe says, jutting her hip out with a little extra flair to show my sister how little she cares about her comment. I kinda think she cares a lot, though.

"Thanks," I say, wiping my hands off on a paper towel and tiptoeing my way around our paint supplies until I can safely exit the room.

I'm a bit of a mess, but I don't really have the time to shower, so I just quickly run a brush through my hair while back in our room and pull it up into a ponytail. I peel a few spots of paint from my hand and arm during the elevator ride, and by the time I hit the sidewalk that leads to the science building I look a little less like a contractor.

The lab room is quiet; only one other student is in there. I wonder if this is the normal turnout, or if it's only the two of us struggling so far. I take a seat near the front of the room and pull out my book and my last quiz. The instructor is still busy reading whatever is amusing on his iPad. I don't even know if he saw me come in.

"Ehemm," I clear my throat, trying to make it sound natural, but it doesn't come out natural at all. And the way he quirks his eyebrow up at me over the top of his iPad is a good indicator that it probably sounded a bit snobby.

"Yes?" he asks, his eyebrows raised and expecting some great response.

"I'm here to go over my last quiz." My voice comes out small. I feel intimidated, but I can't quite put my finger on the reason. I suppose it was his *oh-so-warm* greeting. The metal of his chair digs into the floor and makes the most abrasive sound as he slides it out from his desk and drags it along with him to sit next to me at the table.

"Let's take a look," he says, his arm reaching across me and slowly dragging the quiz into his view. His arm skims against mine lightly—an accident—but it sends a sharp sensation through my nerves that feels all kinds of wrong, so I pull my hands into my lap, making myself somehow smaller.

"Cassidy...what was your last name?" he arches one brow at me.

"Owens. Cass Owens," I say, my voice hoarse again.

"Right. You're missing the final step. Here, let me see your pencil," he says, reaching in front of me again. He slides his chair a few inches closer so we can both look over my paper. I can feel his breath. It's not like Ty's breath. It smells of stale coffee and old cigarettes. "You need to divide by that number to get the total sum, like this."

My brain is working overtime to make sure I remember every step he's jotting down, and I'm grateful he's writing it on paper so I can use it as a guide later rather than having to ask him again. I don't want to go through *this* more than once. He slides the page squarely in front of me and holds the pencil out for me to take.

"You try the next one," he says. When I grab the pencil, I swear his grip stays on it for a second too long, almost like we're playing a mini-game of tug of war, and I think his lips might curl into a small grin. He's young—probably a grad student like Ty. He's also very attractive with light brown hair, closely shaved to his head, and forearms that look like they could throw something heavy with very little effort. As good looking as he is, his effect on me is opposite.

I force myself to stay focused on my work, and I manage to correct six of the problems in front of him. He relaxes while I work, leaning back in the chair, which also gives me some very welcome distance. The hairs on my arm are no longer standing. But for some reason, I can still hear him breathe. It's a steady sound, masculine—unsettling.

"I think I get it now. I can't believe I blew it on the quiz. It seems so easy," I say, staring at my redone work with a little disappointment that it won't matter to my grade. Suddenly, he reaches for the paper, folding it in half as he stands.

"I'm not done entering grades yet. Maybe this is the one I look at instead," he says, winking as he heads to his desk and his iPad. I'm so uncomfortable by his suggestive tone, but I'm also pretty sure I'm overreacting. He's flirtatious—that part I'm not mistaking. But I keep looking over at the other girl, sitting in the opposite corner—she hasn't looked up from her work once. Surely, if something were really off, she'd be staring at us.

"Thank you...really," I say, gathering my things and pushing the chair under the study table. "I will do so much better on the next quiz. This totally makes sense now."

"Sure thing," he says, putting my reworked quiz in a small folder on his desk and propping his feet up on it while leaning back in his chair. "Here every Friday."

"Right, got it," I say. Got it—you're here every Friday. As in, I should come more often, and you'd like to see me here? Or as in, this is a courtesy to students, don't blow your studies dumbass, and get tutoring *before* the quiz. I'm actually laughing

74

to myself as I exit the class, and when I turn to look at him over my shoulder, he's already returned to reading whatever is on his iPad.

When I return to our room, Rowe is listening to music and looking through a few art books on her bed, and Paige is squealing on her phone about some party.

"Oh my god, of course I'm going. I don't know what I'll wear though, hang on...let me ask..." Paige says, snapping her fingers at me while she riffles through things in her section of the closet.

"I'm sorry, are you *summoning* me?" I ask, my eyes zeroed in on her long lavender nails.

"Yeah, party tonight. Pete's. That place we went the first week of school. You wanna go?" She's barely registering me while she talks, inserting *yeahs* and *uh huhs* to the other person on the line while inviting me to a party I really don't think she wants me to go to.

"I don't know, Paige. I think I'm just going to hang with Ty," I say, and she's already shrugged and moved on. Well, that was easy.

"So, how'd it turn out?" I ask, sitting down next to Rowe on her bed. She startles when I do, and I realize she was listening to her music still. "Sorry," I cringe.

"It's okay. Had it up kind of loud," she says, rolling the ear buds up in the cord and setting them to the side. "The room looks fantastic. They are going to flip their lids. Seriously, I took pictures."

Rowe pulls out her phone, and we scroll through half a dozen shots of a room that looks like it has been hosed down with Pepto-Bismol. I'm kind of proud, actually. "Wow, this is the coolest thing I've ever done," I say, handing her back her phone. She studies the image left on the screen for another second, and then looks back at me.

"Yeah, me too," she laughs.

Rowe is still going through the books on her bed. I move back to mine and open my backpack, digging to the section where I've tucked away my physics syllabus. I've been trying to remember the instructor's full name ever since the tutoring session. I remembered his first name, Paul, but that's all that was coming to mind when he was hovering over me with his hot-ass breath and...I don't know...lurkiness? I browse to the top of the syllabus to find it—*Cotterman.* That's right, Paul Cotterman. His cell phone number and email is underneath his name, and it catches my attention. I don't know why. I have no reason to call him now that I understand the lesson, but something about seeing it there listed out draws my attention, and it makes my stomach twist.

The knock on our door stops us all instantly. Even Paige whispers into her phone, telling the person on the other end that she'll have to call them back.

"Shit! Shit! Shit! Shit! Shit!" I whisper, my stomach suddenly overcome with the thumping of my heart. "Rowe, what do we do? It's them. It's totally them."

"Maybe not," Rowe shrugs, and I just push her off balance, because *like hell* it isn't them.

Paige is standing on her bed now, biting her thumbnail and pacing in place, like she's hiding from a mouse. I hold my finger to my lips, like somehow if we're all quiet we'll be able to get away with this. I get closer to the door, now able to see the shadow of someone standing on the other side.

"It's Molly. I'm out of printer ink, and I need to get this paper done. Can I borrow yours? It will only take a few seconds," says a soft voice, clearly the shy girl that lives next door. I relax, and wave off Rowe and Paige as I put my hand on the door.

"One second," I respond. But the instant I turn the knob I feel the pressure of the door push in on me, and before I know it, Nate has slid past me, and Ty is staring at me—his arms folded over his chest, his face scowling.

"Run, Rowe! Run!" I try to save her, but Nate is swift, and he quickly carries her over his shoulder out our door. She giggles the entire way.

"You are in soooooo much trouble, ladies!" Ty's voice fills our room as our door closes behind him.

"Oh please, like you didn't have it coming," I say back, standing my ground. I'm still not sure if he's truly angry or amused.

76

"Pink. I fucking hate the color pink," he says, his arms relaxing finally until he locks them behind his neck, and then it's there—that tiny hint of a smirk that wrinkles the corners of his eyes and clues me in, lets me know that Ty is playing with me.

We're locked in this staring contest for a few long seconds when Paige interrupts. "Right, well I think I'm done here. Cass, I'll be out late. You sure you don't want to come to the party?" Paige asks. She glances between Ty and me, and she already knows my answer. No, I don't want to go, because standing in front of this man beats the hell out of a dumb party.

"I'm good," I say, not once taking my eyes off of his. Paige leaves without saying goodbye.

"So, tell me, Cassidy Owens..." he starts, and I wince at hearing my full name.

"Ooooooh, that's the *I'm in trouble* tone. I know that one," I say as I walk backward until I feel the backs of my legs hit the bed, forcing me to sit.

"Oh, you're in trouble all right," he says, constantly coming closer until he can reach forward and put his hands on my knees. His touch is a faint tickle at first, but soon his hands have a firm grip on the tops of my legs.

"You started it," I say, tilting my chin up, keeping the volley going. On instinct, Ty turns and looks at my dresser, remembering his small prank. He curls the side of his mouth into the sexiest smile, the dimple in his cheek shaded by the dark stubble.

"Yeah," he says, bringing his eyes back to mine. "I sure did."

I push myself back on the bed, and Ty slides his hands so they're resting on either side of my body, and then begins to lift himself so he's hovering over me. I succumb and lie on my back while he pulls himself completely from the chair—holding his chest above mine with his massive arms. They're perfect, and his biceps are working so hard that his T-shirt looks as if it's about to rip from his arms, the white fabric hugging it so tightly.

Unable to stop myself, I run my hands up his forearms, onto his biceps, and under the sleeves of his shirt until I can grip his shoulders. Every curve of his body is warm and smooth, the muscle underneath so powerful. "You have the most unbelievable arms. Like, seriously—when I have to write a thesis paper, can I use you as my subject?" I say, letting my gaze wander over his biceps while my hands slowly stroke his skin, admiring every dip and ripple. I know I sound gushy and corny, but seriously, I love his body. It's a masterpiece.

"Well, fuck," he says, dropping his forehead to mine and shutting his eyes. He chuckles lightly and shakes his head softly from side to side, our foreheads rolling together. "How am I supposed to be mad about a little pink room when you say shit like that?"

I drag my hands back up his arms until they're around his neck, and then I let my fingers glide over his jawline, my thumbs in heaven against the rough texture of his chin. God, I swear this man is a lumberjack. "I'm sorry I tricked you," I say, my lips twitching with nervous energy, just begging him to kiss them again. I have to tuck the bottom one under my teeth just to mask my quivering nerves.

"Yeah, that wasn't very nice," he says, licking his lips lightly, his breath hot against my mouth. "I thought that kiss this morning was real."

"It was," I say quickly, tilting my face just enough so he's forced to look into my eyes. I know we're playing a game right now, but it's important to me that Ty doesn't think I'm the kind of girl to give kisses out freely and dishonestly. I'm not that girl anymore, and I'll never be that girl again. "The only part of this morning that I made up was the part about being locked out of my room. The *kissing you* part, that was just a perk."

"Yeah? So I'm, like, on your list of benefits?" he smirks.

"Yeah. It goes: medical, dental, PTO, and Ty Preeter," I say.

"PTO? What the hell is PTO and how is it before *me* on the list?" he asks, pushing me flat on the mattress, slowly letting the weight of his body cover mine.

"Uh, paid time off? Like vacation? Sorry, but I need my vacation. I have plans...BIG PLANS! Like Tahoe, the Hamptons, Venice, and London," I say with a false shrug. Truth be told, Ty's number one on my list—and he might be the only thing on it at this very moment.

78

"Well, I'm sorry, but I'm afraid you don't get vacation. You've been a very bad employee," he says, and his eyes flash this devilish look that warms my entire body.

"What, are you going to write me up or something?" I ask, trying not to break character despite the desire to giggle.

"Something like that. Let's just say this is all going in your file," he says, his hands combing through my hair while his lips graze mine, his touch faint, but leaving behind a trail of fire.

"I've been written up before," I say, every muscle in my body weakening, beckoning, and begging for him to take over.

"I think we're going to need to schedule you some more on-the-job training then," he says, his laugh slipping through the serious face he's trying to hold. His smile is perfection, and it melts me completely. "I'm sorry, this whole bad-boss act isn't working for me. I'm just going to stick with what I know."

His kiss comes hard and fast after that, his hands strong on either side of my face while his tongue tangles with mine. His body is so warm, and all I want to do is touch every inch of it, my hands instinctively moving to his back and lifting his shirt until he rolls to the side and lets me remove it from him completely. He takes advantage of this move, pulling me on top of him now—kissing me with even more force while he works his fingers slowly around the arch of my back, his thumbs grazing the bare skin just above the waistband of my shorts.

"I fucking love the Beach Boys," he says, and I can't help but laugh, falling with all of my weight into his chest while he wraps his arms tightly around me, then works his fingers through my hair until he can see my face.

"That was...pretty much the strangest mood killer I've ever heard," I say, unable to hide my giggle and the smile that is permanently tattooed under my nose. It's bliss.
This...everything...this moment—it's bliss.

"You know, that song? The one about California girls, and how perfect your skin and hair and shit is. They're just dead on, that's all," he says, nuzzling his nose against my neck and taking small bites out of my ear.

"You should write them, tell them to change up their lyrics. That song would be so much better your way—California girls have perfect skin and shit." I can't even fully finish the sentence without laughing, and Ty can no longer hold his in either.

"Was I even close? God, how does that song go?" he pulls me against his side and tugs one of my pillows over so he can tuck it under his head. He's humming the tune to *California Girls*, and his chest is vibrating with every note. He's actually not a horrible singer. I wonder if he'd ever sing me to sleep?

"You have a nice voice," I say. When he looks down at me with a pinched brow, I reach up and cross my heart. "I swear, I'm not feeding your ego. You have a nice voice."

"Lots of choir. Nate's actually better. He stole the solo from me in the community Christmas play one year when we were kids. Little thief," he says, still wearing that same smile he does every time he talks about his brother. I love it.

His stare at me is intense. His smile is soft, but there's something working behind his eyes. "Penny for your thoughts?" I ask.

He smiles at my question at first, then watches his hand as he slides his fingers deeper through my hair, fanning the strands out along my bare shoulder. "My mom always says that," he says. "She's going to like you."

God I hope so.

Ty

I have been lying here with Cass, her and me alone, on her bed, for more than an hour. And I still haven't taken her clothes off.

What the hell is wrong with me?

Normally, I would start to think that I must not be into a chick. No, screw that...normally I wouldn't even *be* here by this point. I wouldn't even worry about making up a good excuse. I'd just leave. But leaving is kind of the very last thing that I want to do. Rowe just came back, and she made a face at Cass, one that I could tell meant, "He's leaving soon, right?" She left with her things to shower. She does that, showers late at night—I only know her habits because my brother stalks her in the hall. Ever since he ran into her that first night, he leaves our door open in the evening and listens for any sign of her.

I should probably go. But I don't want to. And I don't think Cass wants me to go. It's weird how I can lie in one spot—not even a hint of sex on the horizon—and still be this content to be with a girl. It's more than content. I feel whole. I haven't felt that since...since Kelly.

"I should go," I finally get myself to speak.

"What if I just hide you? I'll keep you under my covers. Rowe won't even notice," she says, and I flip her cover over my six-foot frame, my feet dangling out.

"I think she might notice," I say, pulling the cover back and stroking her hair from her face so I can kiss her forehead.

"How'd it happen?" I think this question has been on her mind for hours, days maybe. I wish I could get inside other people's heads, because I wonder if it's the first question people have when they meet me. Was I born this way, or did something happen along the way? I don't mind answering. I never do. But I don't think Cass has really ever cared to know, until now.

"Accident," I say, simple at first.

"Like, a car accident?"

I smile softly and shake my head. "No, not a car accident," I say, pushing myself to a sitting position, my weight held by my arms for balance. Cass moves her head to my lap, and it strikes me that this is something nobody has ever done to me. It feels strangely intimate, the kind of intimacy that goes along with trust. "It was at this lake that Nate and I always went to over the summer near our grandparents' house. There was this one area, lots of cliffs and a deep, pooled area. The summer before, Nate watched a bunch of teenagers jump from the cliffs into the water. He was too afraid to try, and he regretted it for an entire year. It was all he'd talk about."

"How old were you two?" she asks, and on instinct I thread my fingers through her hair without even looking. It feels so natural having her lie here in my lap.

"I was sixteen. Nate was twelve. At least, when it happened. He wanted to jump because he chickened out the year before, but when the time came, he got really scared. I know I pick on him, but that's my brother, and I don't know…. He was this little boy, not really even a teenager yet, and he was just so afraid to try something. I've tried to rationalize it in my brain for years now, but at the time I just felt like I needed to help him through this. I didn't want my brother going through life afraid to try things. I wanted him to be something. So I told him I'd go first."

"And you jumped."

"And I jumped."

"And that's when…" she says, her voice a soft whisper now.

"And that's when I didn't come up," I say, a shrug of my shoulders really the only punctuation I've got.

"Are you ever angry?" she asks, and her question actually surprises me. Over all of these years, no one has ever actually asked me this. I talked to Kelly and Mom about it, but only because I needed to before I crumbled.

"Yeah. Sometimes I'm *really* angry," I say, and I'm so surprised by my honesty that it forces me to take in a deep breath, like a reflex.

"I'm sorry, we don't have to talk about it," Cass says, noticing my sigh.

"No, no. I just…wow, I've never had anyone ask," I say, almost laughing with my words. I smile when I look down at her, and she looks concerned. "I'm not angry now. Sometimes, yes…I get angry. But I don't dwell on it. I don't want to slip into a bad place. I need to stay positive, for Nate."

"Just for Nate? Nothing for yourself?" she asks, and once again, her words give me pause. I pause because she's right. It used to be for Nate. But the self-challenging, the drive, the focus I give to everything I *can* do—that's all for me.

"You are awfully insightful. Are you sure you're not a psych major?" I ask, kissing the back of her hand as I squeeze it. I lift her head from my lap gently and move myself to my chair. "Your roommate has been hovering in the hallway, and I like her. If it were Nate out there, I'd make him wait. But Rowe, she's good people. So…I'm gonna go."

"Okay," Cass says, her eyes sleepy as she kicks her feet under her blanket and fluffs her pillow under her head. "Sweet dreams."

"Oh, I'm going to have dreams all right. Feeling your head in my lap, that did *things*." I wink, joking, not joking. "I'll see you tomorrow for the game."

I press my lips to my fingertips, and my hand to her cheek; she smiles this perfect goddamned smile. I have never wanted anything as much as I've wanted to be able to run again—until now. I want her, and I hope like hell I don't fuck this up.

Chapter 9

Cass

The tingling is familiar. It was there when I woke up this morning. Faint, but there. A sensation in my legs—my nerve endings firing a reminder that something is not right in my body. It went away, but I've spent the rest of the day waiting for it to come back, terrified of a flare-up.

MS relapses are like traffic pileups that happen in my nervous system; my body gets hit with one or more of the symptoms for a long period of time. The flare-ups usually don't go away without a few days of an IV steroid treatment, and sometimes that doesn't even do the trick. I know my current symptoms are because of how hard I've been pushing myself. I'm more than fatigued. But Ty has me believing that I can do this— not just try out for, but actually *make* the McConnell women's soccer team. At first, I just liked having him believe in me. But somewhere along the way, I started to want this for myself—to believe I could do it.

I still haven't told my parents about the soccer tryouts. I'm not officially signed up. I haven't even spoken to Paige about it. I'm not ready to hear all of the reasons it's a bad idea—all valid points, but I don't want to penetrate my daydream just yet. There are a few weeks left before I have to face the facts, before I have to fight those who won't want me to do this. So for now, I'm just going to enjoy the possibility. That is, unless the damned MS decides otherwise.

I've been flare-up-free for several months—since the oral meds, really. But I'm playing with fire—all of this running and lifting that I've been doing. Exercise is good. In fact, it's something my doctors *want* me to do more of. But *this* kind of exercise—it sort of crosses the boundaries. The tingling this morning—that was hard to ignore. But it went away, and I try to focus on that.

It went away.

"This is your fault that I'm in this situation," Rowe says, spinning in front of me in another outfit option from her closet. Nate finally asked her to join us at the game tonight. I'm glad, because I didn't want to meet Ty's parents alone. I'm glad to have an ally.

"Stop giving me shit, and get in there and try another dress on," I say, spinning her around and pointing her back to the closet. Rowe and I are so much alike. As much as I have confidence on the surface, I'm still a tangled mess of self-doubt on the inside. I think maybe I've just gotten farther along in the process of knowing my worth than she has.

"This one looks ridiculous," she says, coming out in another dress—this one short, falling above the knee. There's nothing wrong with the dress, but Rowe...she just looks uncomfortable in her own skin, and I am the last person on earth who knows how to fix that. I can barely keep my own fire lit, let alone light someone else's.

"Something's not right. Why don't you just wear jeans and a shirt, like you always do?" Rowe shoots me a pained look, and I know immediately that was the wrong thing to say. Honestly, I just meant that she looks great every day, but I get the sense that tonight—going to the game with the boys and meeting parents—is as important to her as it is to me. And it's one of those occasions that call for something better than a T-shirt and jeans, something better than looking *nice*.

"I'm not good at this," she says, her entire posture simply defeated. Shit...I think I did that.

"What do you mean? Paige would *kill* to be the one to get Nate's attention," I say, trying to boost her confidence with a last-ditch effort. My shoulders cringe the second I hear my sister walk in. I know she picked up on her name. She'd never miss a mention.

Cue the Paige Owens show...

"Paige would kill for what? For you two chickadees to get your asses off my bed?" And there it is, the subtle shift that is about to make Rowe's discomfort all about Paige.

Rowe is looking at me with a face full of panic. I've got this one handled though. I lie back and spread my arms on Paige's bed, wrinkling her bedspread *just enough* that I know it's going to irritate her. "Your bed is always so much more comfortable than mine," I say, rolling to the side and smelling her blankets. They actually are nicer than mine. "And your sheets are softer. What the hell?"

"Mom and Dad like me better," Paige says, pushing me out of her way so she can straighten the wrinkles I made. Rowe doesn't know this, but I took a bullet for her there. It's all about the art of distraction with Paige.

My sister is stationed at the small vanity mirror and counter in our closet, working on her makeup. She's good at makeup. And clothes. And confidence. Oh god, we need her.

"What?" she asks, catching me staring at her in the reflection.

"Rowe, I'm afraid we're going to need her help," I say, looking at my friend whose eyes are so wide, I think they may actually fall out of her head.

"Help with what?" Paige asks, only semi interested. What I'm about to tell her will get all of her attention though. I'm sorry Rowe; I'll make this up to you.

"First, you have to promise me you're not going to get pissed," I say, taking my time to watch my sister consider my offer. Her movements are sharp and calculated. She has the ability to make the simplest act—even putting the lid back on a tube of gloss—look threatening.

"Pretty sure I can't promise that. Just a hunch," she says, her eyes squarely on mine now. She probably thinks I'm about to get her into some pile of trouble, because historically, that's been the case. But no, I'm actually just going to break her heart. And I kinda hate that more.

"Nate invited Rowe to come to the game with me and Ty tonight...to meet their parents. She doesn't have anything nice to wear, and I'm not good at makeovers, so we've pretty much just been failing in our attempts for the last two hours—and we have to leave in like thirty minutes," I say, all in one breath, because I feel like the more I can pack in, the less likely my words are to sting. I know they do anyhow—I can tell by the crushed face my sister makes at me, for just a fraction of a second. She looks at

Rowe, not with jealousy, but with envy. There's a difference between the two—however small it may be—and the fact that my sister's face is full of envy means a part of her actually likes Rowe. And there's also a part of her that sees what Nate sees in her. She just wishes he saw whatever it was in her, too.

"Stand up," Paige says, jolting Rowe and me both to attention. She studies our roommate's face, and then moves the garments left hanging in our closet. She holds a few things up, but nothing is the perfect fit. I can see the options dwindling, and there really is only one dress that works; I know it's Paige's favorite. It's a simple, deep-blue cotton dress, and Rowe would look like a knockout in it.

"Come here," Paige says, twirling Rowe around, and with a little force, pulling down the zipper of her dress. She's still hostile, and I hate that. I'm about to call her on it, when Rowe's dress suddenly falls to the floor. Our roommate stands in front of Paige and me with what I know—in an instant—is her worst nightmare bared to us.

Rowe's body is riddled with scars. They are deep and pink, and a few are a dark red. They appear surgical, for the most part, but others...I don't know. Something bad happened to her. In that moment, I find Paige's eyes, and I make a silent plea to her. *Paige, come on...you cannot mention this. Don't say anything. Give her this—give her the safety of us.*

I'm wishing so hard, I swear my lips are moving. But I see it in my sister's eyes right away. Rowe and I—we are so similar. Her scars stayed, while mine disappeared. My welts from the MS shots faded in time—with massaging, and oil, and work. And I get to become *just Cass.* I have a choice, and I can choose not to tell anyone. When my sister looks at me again, I can see the recognition in her eyes. I know she's also urging me to share. Rowe can be trusted; she wouldn't sum me up as *just the girl with MS.*

But I'm not sharing tonight. This break—this moment that happened between the three of us—this is Rowe's. It's for Rowe and Paige. As I watch my sister drape her favorite dress over our roommate, squeezing her hand to give her courage to feel beautiful, I know that Rowe has also earned herself a new warrior. Once Paige Owens is on your side, heaven help the person who tries to do you harm.

My story can wait. Tonight—right now—this is for Rowe.

Chapter 10

Ty

I've played the voicemail over at least a dozen times. I feel like a child, hiding in the hallway while I listen, like I'm doing something wrong. Maybe I am. But I don't know. I just can't figure out what this means.

It's Kelly. She left the message late last night, probably while I was in Cass's room—*in Cass's room, with Cass, where I want to be right now.* Instead, I am here at the end of the hall, bent forward in my chair by the fire exit and laundry room, holding a finger to one ear and my phone to the other. I play it again—hoping to get one more clue into what's going on.

"Hi, Ty. I know, it's...it's late. I'm so sorry. I wasn't going to call, but...gosh."
Kelly laughs nervously.
"Wow, your voice. I haven't heard it in so long. It's just always been text messages, emails, Facebook. You sound...good. You sound good."

It's the pause—this pause—in her message that worries me. She is crying. I've held that girl through tears before, and I recognize the hiccup in her breath. She's hiding it, but I know it's there. She has to know I'd know, that I'd recognize it. And then her mask goes up.

"You know what, it's okay. I'm just probably being stupid. It's late, and the baby's been up a lot. So, you know what? How about maybe I see you over Thanksgiving? Yeah. Let's plan on it. You can meet Jackson."
She lets out a single, breathy laugh.
"I bet you'll get a baseball in his hand. Okay, so...I'll just talk to you then. Really, don't worry."

Thing is, I'm worried. I've been worried since I checked my messages at midnight. I woke up at three in the morning and listened to it again, and if I'm being honest, I never went back to sleep. Every time I listen, I worry.

"Shit wagon, where the hell are you?" Nate yells down the hallway. I told him I was looking for a shirt that I thought I left in the dryer. I've been gone longer than it takes to look for a shirt.

"I'm coming, I'm coming. Quit the damn fussy fuss," I say, pushing my phone back into my pocket before our door comes into view.

"I found your stupid shirt. It was under your bed," Nate says, throwing the gray McConnell T-shirt at my face.

"Of course it was," I say, pulling the green shirt over my head and exchanging it, just to keep up my act. I check the watch and pause, re-clasping it to make sure it's on tightly and running my finger along the sharp edges of the band. Kelly's watch.

"Dude, what time is it?" Nate asks. Right, my watch...I was checking the time.

"We should go. You know Mom—if we're not there when we say we're going to be there, she calls for the flare guns," I say.

"No kidding. And I don't want them seeing this crap," Nate says, throwing a pink Barbie pillow into the corner, on his bed.

"I don't know...it's all kinda growing on me," I smirk. We went in town today—originally, to get ideas for ways to get the girls back for their painting stunt. But I've got to give them props; it was good, too good to top. So we decided to embrace the pink, go full sparkle and shit. Our room is now accented with Barbie blankets, ponies, fluffy pillows and rainbows. Mom will love that we blew the hundred bucks she sent in the card on teenage-girl shit at the Target. Well worth it, if you ask me.

Nate locks up the room and I push ahead. I can already see the girls walking toward us. Rowe is beautiful. She's always wearing jeans or shorts and T-shirts, but she went full out for this, and her legs...damn. My brother is in trouble.

"Pick up your chin, bro. Your girl is *smokin'*," I say, slapping him once on the back. He's grinning like a fool.

At the elevator, I reach for Cass's hand. As good as Rowe looks in her blue sundress, Cass is all I'm going to see for the rest of the night. She looks like sunshine—like real, actual sunshine—caught in a bottle for me, and me alone, to enjoy. She's walking warmth; the gold of her hair is twisted in a braid on top of her head, small pieces tickling the nape of her neck. And god that skin, so golden, so soft...I can see tiny bumps rise on her flesh; I swear it's because I'm staring at her like this.

When the elevator opens, I pull her onto my lap and wrap my arms around her tightly. "I had to see if you smelled as good as you look," I say, my nose running along the inside of her neck. I let my lips suck in the bottom of her ear away from Rowe and Nate, and she takes in a sharp breath when I do. "You are lovely."

"Lovely?" she giggles. "When did you drop into a Cary Grant movie?"

"The second you walked out of your door looking like sunshine," I say, and she blushes.

"I like that. *Sunshine*," she says, her lip finding its way in between her teeth as she tucks her head into the space near my shoulder and chin. My sunshine. Careful, Cass, or I'll trap you in a bottle and keep you forever.

It doesn't take us long to get to the stadium. That's one of the best things about McConnell's campus—everything is close. When you depend on your forearms to get you places on time, proximity is important.

Somehow, Cathy Preeter always finds a way to stand out. We're more than two hundred yards away, but I can spot my parents' tailgating setup within the sea of McConnell red and gold.

"Why do they do that?" Nate asks, shaking his head at the overboard display of school pride my parents have set up.

"You know Mom. Doing something halfway is like getting an *F*. She's an *A* student, bro. Besides, don't worry. I'm bringing a girl, that should pretty much take up all of her focus for the rest of the night—and blow her freakin' mind," I say as we get close enough for my parents to finally recognize our approach.

As I suspected, Mom's eyes laser in on Cass. I put my hand on her back, and she turns to look at me, swallowing her nerves. "They are going to love you," I reassure her, and she nods once with big eyes. I love that she's not sure they will. I've never been surer about anything though.

"What is all this?" Nate asks, breaking the ice right away. He gestures to all of the McConnell things my parents have set up—chairs, a tent, cups, plates. What's funny is we have the same stuff in our room, only it's ponies, and Barbies, and princess crap. The thought makes me chuckle.

"You know your mother. She just likes a reason to shop," Dad says, shaking Nate's hand, and then mine. He's already curious about the two girls standing behind us, and when he raises an eyebrow at me, I shrug. *I know, this is a big deal...but let's not make it one, Pops.*

"Mom, Dad, this is Rowe and Cass," Nate says, taking care of the introductions. That's probably a good thing, because I would probably screw this part up. Without even realizing it, I've brought my hand to my mouth and I'm actually biting my knuckle. What the hell? I'm nervous!

"Cass," Dad starts. Thank the heavenly lord Dad's the first one to talk to her. "We have heard absolutely *nothing* about you," he says, and I want to punch him. Yes, it's true. I'm not a sharing kind of person, but fuck, Dad? Seriously? Way to make me sound like an insensitive dick.

"That must mean you're pretty special. We only hear the breakup stories, and we used to get one of those a week," Dad continues. Okay, so that's a little better.

Cass smirks at me quickly, like she just got some secret that she plans to use against me. "It was touch and go there for a while," she says to my dad, giving me a wink. Ninja princess. "I painted his room pink."

That's right. She painted my room pink. And I may never change it back, because it reminds me of her. I look right into her eyes, my smile big, and shake my head while my dad laughs and looks to my mom, who's also pretty impressed.

"It was Rowe's idea," Cass says, wanting to give her friend credit. This girl, she owns me, and I pull her into my lap without even thinking. And when my mother's eyebrows shoot up to her hairline in shock, I hug Cass tightly, just to punctuate my point. *That's right mom—she owns me. And you're going to love her.*

92

My parents can be cool when they try. Nate and I sat near the front of the suite, the row making it easy for me to push between two of the sections. Our parents stayed near the back, at the food tables, giving us some space. There are a few people here from my dad's office. He's in accounting, which on the surface sounds about as sexy as working in cardboard. But my dad's kind of high up with a big firm, and his accounting works in numbers with lots of zeroes, and that...*that* gets exciting. I get my business sense from him. So does Nate, though Nate's more public relations.

The girls are sitting in front of us, their feet propped up on the bar at the front of the box, and their skirts tucked tightly around their legs. If I were a cameraman on the other side of the stadium, I know where I'd be focusing.

"Dude, there's a lot of whispering going on up there," I say to Nate, nudging him to look at Cass and Rowe, their heads close together. Every few seconds, Cass cups Rowe's ear, then she pulls away again, crossing her arms. Rowe looks like she's getting upset. Fuck me. Are they seriously fighting?

"Hey, mind if I get some time with my date?" I ask as I push in closer to their row. Cass climbs over to sit on the other side of me, and Rowe doesn't flinch or bother to look our way. I cast a look to Nate, who takes a deep breath, then climbs over the seat to sit next to her.

"I made Rowe mad," Cass admits. Shit. I hate girl fights. I have a brother, and I love that I have a brother. I'm also glad we don't have a sister, because I wouldn't know what the hell to do with all of her damn girl fights.

"Okay," is all I say. I suck.

Cass turns to look at me swiftly, studying me for a few minutes with her brow pinched, trying to tell if I'm serious, so I shrug.

"You are such a boy," she laughs, laying her head on my shoulder and cupping my bicep with her hand. It feels like she was meant to do this always.

"Yeah, but I prefer the term *man,* if it's all the same to you. Just sayin'," I joke, and her light laugh shakes my arm. I lift it up to put it around her and squeeze her to me. Looking over my shoulder, I notice my mom watching me the entire time. Her grin could not be any more obvious.

"Paige is spending the night at the sorority house tonight," Cass says, bringing my attention back to her. "She's joining one. She'll be moving out." I feel her breath stop. Mine stops too. It froze the moment I realized what this means: Paige will be gone, and if Rowe is with Nate, we would be *alone*. Not gonna lie, my pants just got a little bit tighter, and I'm pretty sure Cass can tell. There are some things that are difficult to hide.

"So...you're saying..." I start, not wanting to presume anything—I usually do, but this one, this time? This is different. I need to be careful here.

"I'm saying...that..." she starts, then stops, biting her lip. Her cheeks turn red, and I can hardly stand it.

"Come on, Cass," I say, shaking her lightly to my side. "You can do it."

She buries her face into my bicep, and it's so cute that I can't torture her any longer.

"Do you want to have a sleepover?" I ask, *sleep* the very last activity on my agenda. Cass nods her head *yes* against my arm, then pulls her face out just enough to look up at me. I kiss her forehead the second she does.

"Done," I say.

"But I'm worried about Rowe. She's kind of...nervous. I don't know, I feel bad kicking her out of our room. That's...that's what we were fighting about," she says, and I can tell she honestly does feel bad. And now I feel like a royal prick—because, as much as I should care about Rowe's feelings being hurt, the only thing I can think about is getting back to Cass's room, getting her alone, and getting her out of that damn yellow dress.

"She's with Nate. Trust me, we would be doing those two a massive favor. My brother is pretty whipped by that girl," I say. A smile cricks up in the corner of her mouth, so I kiss it. "I promise. Think of this as our good deed. Rowe will thank you. I know it."

Shit, I hope she doesn't punch her. Either way, I'm getting this girl into her room, alone, tonight. I don't care if it fucking

94

kills me. Well, yeah, I care if it kills me. Let me sleep with her first, *then* kill me, universe.

Here is why baseball is better than football. No matter how many runs your team is down by, you always have a sense of hope. One inning—one inning can change it all. You can score, and I've seen it, a dozen runs in an inning—especially at the college level. There's no time limit. The game could go on all night, as long as it takes.

With football, there is a clock, and everything is measured against it. For example, McConnell is down by four touchdowns, and in a few minutes, it will be five. Given McConnell's average time taken to score, there is not enough time left on the clock for the Bulls to make a comeback. It's a mathematical improbability.

But here is why football is better than baseball—just for tonight. If this were a baseball game, I would have to stick it out. My competitive nature and the promise of hope—of a comeback—would keep me here. I hate missing a good comeback. But there is no hope. Not even an ounce. So I am free to leave, with Cass, to go to her room and do a shitload of dirty things to her that I have been thinking about pretty much non-stop for the last hour. So for tonight—and just tonight—I thank football.

Thank you, football. You are king.

Cass has just walked back over to sit next to me. I think she wanted to try to ease Rowe's worry one last time, but from the looks of things, I don't think it worked. Rowe has completely shrunk down in her seat, and Nate is staring at her, his hand over his mouth like he doesn't know what to do. He knows...he's just afraid.

I hope Cass isn't backing out. When she sits down next to me again, I pull her close, reminding her, like a damn dog humping her leg. "I think this game is pretty much a lock. You?" I ask her, my lips close to her ear, close enough that I give the bottom of her ear a tiny tug with my teeth. Her lips quiver when I do.

Yeah, she's still in.

"Let's go," she says, sliding her hand sensually across my chest as she stands and steps around me. I almost lose it right then and there.

"Mom, Dad—see you guys tomorrow at dinner," I say, not wanting to linger. Our timing could not have been better as my parents were in the middle of a discussion with another couple. They pause just long enough to say *goodbye* and shake Cass's hand, then we're out the door.

The trip back to our dorm feels three times as far as the way here. Cass is making small talk. It's cute. I can tell she's nervous about this whole thing.

"Do you have a dog at home?" she asks when we get to the front door to our dorm. This is her fifth random question, and I've indulged every single one.

"...Yes, I can drive a stick shift. It just has to have a hand clutch...No, I've never had a Mohawk. But if you think it's cute, you can shave my head. I don't care.... I pierced my right ear in high school. But I don't like wearing an earring. I'm a lazy shit, so the hole closed up.... My favorite color is green. *No, blue!* No, green. Monty Python joke, lame. Sorry."

Finally, we get to the elevator. "We don't have a dog. My dad's allergic. Breaks my mom's heart, because she loves animals. She visits the neighbor's dog all the time," I say, pulling her back on my lap as the elevator doors close. "Now, why are you so chatty?" I ask, tugging her hair loose from the tie that's kept it in place on top of her head. Her braid unravels into these blond waves, and I swear to god she looks like a mermaid.

"I need to put you in water," I say out loud, my fingers finding their way to the base of her neck and then digging deeply into her soft, sunshine hair.

"You...you have a thing for *water?*" Her eyebrow quirks up at me, and I laugh.

"No, sorry. You just look like a mermaid. I like this," I say, pulling a few strands of her hair in front of us and holding the waves out for her to see.

"Oh," she smiles, her face showing her shyness. "Thanks. It's how I hide being a ninja."

"Right, good secret identity. No one would suspect a mermaid," I say, my teeth grazing her neck as I let my smile form against her skin. "You even smell like sunshine. How is that possible?"

When the doors open, she tries to stand, but I keep her firmly in place on my lap and push us forward. This is why I workout so much. Here is the payoff, right here. I can do these two things at once.

We hit the wall a few times on our way to her room, mostly because I can't seem to get my mouth off of her damn neck. I finally relent and let her get to her feet when we're at her door, and she drops her keys trying to unlock too quickly.

"Sorry, I'm a bit of a jumble," she giggles. She really is nervous.

"Relax. I'm not in a race," I say, reminding my lower region to behave—*for now.*

She smiles and takes a deep breath before turning her attention back to the door, this time slipping the key in easily and letting us both inside. She drops her purse on her desk and heads to her closet, drawing the door closed almost the entire way, but leaving a small sliver of space where I catch her dress slip from her body and see the curve of her breast. Yep, that's not helping me keep downstairs in check. My dick is pretty much at full attention now, ready to war with my conscience, which is not in great shape—it doesn't get a workout much.

Shit.

She comes out in a small white tank top and black cotton shorts. She's barely wearing anything, and the fabric is so thin, it practically glides over her features.

"I wanted to be comfortable. I hope that's okay," she says, sitting down on her bed and folding her legs over one another, like we're about to play UNO.

"I'm good with comfortable," I smile, suddenly unsure of my next move. Fuck, maybe we really *should* play UNO. Looking around, I'm not sure where I fit. Do I sit next to her? Do I just start kissing her and pulling her clothes off? Do I take my shirt off? Or does she just want to talk? I usually don't care—and, normally, I've been at a party...I've already had the talk with the girl about how *I don't do girlfriends* and shit, and she usually says she's fine with that, and there's whiskey, and bad tastes, because sometimes the chick smokes. I hate smoke. And there are hints that I'll regret sleeping with the girl. But none of that applies here. I am a fish out of water.

"So, are you my girlfriend?" I'm a goddamned fourth grader.

My heart is pounding like I'm a sixty-year-old man on heart medication, and I'm actually sweating. Cass looks right into my eyes; I think she thinks I'm joking at first. But I'm not. I'm actually having a panic attack; it's getting harder to breathe. Slowly, realization hits her, and her smile follows.

My lungs fill up.

"I'd love to be your girlfriend," she says, doing that cute thing where she bites her lip and looks at her lap.

I should be over there.

I'm going over there.

I pull myself up and sit next to her on the edge of her bed, then reach down and pull my shoes from my feet. "I wanted to be comfortable, do you mind?" I mimic her from earlier, and it makes her laugh nervously. Her lip goes right back in her teeth, so I scoot closer and touch her mouth softly with my finger, pulling her lip loose.

"I'm going to kiss that, if that's okay?" I ask, and she nods slowly, her eyes wide and on mine.

I move in, watching her eyes track the movement of my lips toward her. I've never paid attention to these little things before, but god do I want to watch everything now. I need one of those out-of-body experiences. When I'm so near I can feel her breath, her eyes close. I finally shut mine too, letting my lips fall into hers.

She was waiting for me. The second my mouth hits hers—all nerves are gone.

I have a girlfriend. This is my girlfriend. This is Cass Owens, and she is my undoing, and I go willingly. Her lips grow hungry. I thread my fingers through her hair until a few of the strands wrap around them, and I tug her head gently backward so I can taste her neck.

"Tyson," she breathes out my name, my full name. Fuck, I have never loved my name more than I do right now.

I lay her back gently and lean over her to the side, my lips still on hers and my hand cradling the side of her face. She is like a furnace, the heat radiating from her neck and chest. I know her body is as much in control of her decisions as mine is.

I slow our kiss and let my hand glide down her cheek until I'm only touching her with the tips of my fingers. Like a feather, I trace the profile of her body through the thin cotton of her tank top. I slow as I come to the crest of her breast so I can admire how hard her nipple is underneath. I love this shirt. I don't know who makes it, but I want to invest in their company, and then fill Cass's closet with nothing but this simple, thin, white tank top.

My hand slows around the curve of her breast, and I allow myself one squeeze, pulling the peak in between my thumb and finger until I can finally see the pink color show through her shirt. *I want to bite that. I should bite that.*

Lowering my head, I glance at her face first; her eyes are closed, the lip back at home between her teeth, and it makes me smirk. This is one of her tells. If this were a poker game, I would know she's all in. Her eyes flutter open when she feels me move. I smile softly, and touch my finger to her hardened nipple.

"I'm going to kiss this now, if that's okay," I say, studying her every move, every breath. She nods slowly. I let the coarseness of the fabric glide across my tongue as I take her breast into my mouth, until I can no longer stand the barrier. I pull her shirt up and over her breasts roughly.

Goddamn, she is built like a goddess. Her body is so muscular, but not in that gross, posing, I-want-a-protein-shake-sponsorship kind of way. It's still soft, and supple and...*oh yes.* It tastes so good. As my lips finally make contact with her bare skin, she arches into me. I reach around her body, caging her in my arms, and lifting her to my mouth so I can suck harder, until she's almost raw.

I let her fall back to the mattress and look down at her. She's breathing even harder now, and her body is covered in a light sheen of sweat. I don't think I have ever been so turned on in my entire life. This is it. I'm no longer in control.

"You are so goddamned beautiful," I say, her eyes opening when I speak, her smile curling at the corners of her lips again. "And I want to consume you. My eyes, they don't know what to take in first, and my mouth wants to taste every inch."

I attack her lips again, but this time she rolls me onto my back, her warm hands finding their way to the bottom of the T-shirt, pulling it up just enough so I feel her hot skin press against mine. For the briefest moment, I'm afraid I am being too aggressive, that I'll scare her. But she seems to be craving this, craving me *like* this.

Cass moves to her knees, straddling me at the waist, and slowly works my shirt over my head, kissing a trail down my neck, chest and stomach—she is about to see how hot she makes me. Something clicks inside me. I reach down and touch her face, stroking the hair away that's fallen into her eyes. I don't want to push her, make her feel like she isn't something special. Because she is. She's the most special person I've ever met.

"Baby, you don't have to—" I start, and she puts her fingers to my lips to stop me cold.

"Shhhhh," she says. "Don't call me *baby*." Her smile is wicked, and I know she feels me react beneath her, my hardness pressed against her bare breasts, dying to be set free from the damn jeans I'm wearing.

I pull her head to me again, holding her mouth just a few inches from mine, looking back and forth from her lips to her eyes—just so I can savor this moment before I roughly crash my mouth into hers, my tongue exploring every inch of her, and my teeth tugging at her lips each time she tries to free herself. I feel her hands working at my jeans, struggling, so I let go of her face long enough to help her. Soon, she's pulling them down my legs to the floor.

She's standing before me—nothing but a small pair of cotton shorts on, and I swear I've found religion. Everything about her is like a gift, and as much as I want to hurry up, to push inside her and feel everything that I'm seeing...I also want to take my time. We have the entire night, and I want to use it all up.

"I think I might just be addicted to you," I say, holding myself up on my elbows and reaching forward to tug at the waistband of her shorts. She catches my hand when I do and holds it in place—not because she's scared, but because she wants to seduce me more. She wants to take control of everything, and that...that's scary to me. But I let her have it. I give it over and hold my breath.

The movement of her hips is hypnotic, like a clock pendulum swinging slowly. I watch as she traces the thin waistband of her night shorts across her hips until she gently works her thumbs underneath and begins to peel the silky material away. She isn't wearing anything underneath, and the lower the shorts go, the less I breathe. My heart could stop right now, and I wouldn't even be aware.

She is standing in front of me, completely naked. I. Am. Mesmerized. With a delicate push, she has me once again flat on my back. She runs her hands up the sides of my legs until she reaches the top of my boxers, and she pulls them down until I'm free.

"Do you...have anything?" she asks. I nod *yes* toward my jeans on the floor. I have kind of been hoping for this moment to present itself for a few days. I actually almost left the condom at home tonight—given that we were going to be out with my parents. I'm happy as hell I talked myself out of that idea now.

Cass pulls the packet from my jeans and tears it open, holding it in her hand while she crawls back up to me, her knees on either side of mine. She slides the condom on slowly, and I let a small groan escape my throat.

"Hang on...*baby*," she teases me.

"Cass, I don't have much left. I mean, there's a thread, and then there's me, and I am hanging with the tips of my fingers," I say.

"Well then..." she says as she slides her fingers up my chest until her palms are flat against my muscles, and she's sitting exactly where I need her to be.

I'm not good at being dominated. Not that I need to be a dominant—it's just, I'm usually the one making the decisions, telling the girl how to be with me. But for some reason, I'm willing to give this to Cass. I take my hands and run them up the length of her arms and then slide them down her hips, and as they fall lower, so does she. And then everything. Feels. So much more.

"Oh my god," I can't help the rush of words from my lips, but I also lose my breath all at once. "Cass. You…" I'm incapable of finishing a sentence, of completing a thought.

Her hair falls forward as she leans toward me and kisses my mouth, her teeth taking in my top lip with a gentle tug. Once her mouth hits mine, she rocks forward, and I'm no longer able to hold back. I let my hands take control of her completely, running them up her sides, over her breasts and into her hair, pulling her to me—hard.

I hold her against my body, my right hand running over her back until I feel along that sexy dimple that she has just above her ass—a byproduct of how hard she trains. "Fuck me, you are so unbelievable. This…feels…unbelievable," I speak as she continues to move around me, stopping our kiss and pressing her forehead to mine.

I don't have much longer, and I can tell she's close, so I touch her lightly with my fingers as I penetrate her again and again, my thumb circling her swollen sex until she arches her head back, gasping—her orgasm entirely taking her away. "Tyson, oh my god. That, like that. Ohhhhhh," her voice quivers, her hips shake, and I lose myself, unable to handle hearing her making those sounds without falling apart.

"Holy fuck, Cass," I say, one final pull of her hips down onto me. She collapses on my chest, her hair sticking to my sweat-covered skin. I think minutes pass before I even breathe, Cass's body just rising and falling on top of me as we both catch our breath.

"Are you okay? I mean…was *this* okay?" I ask, again not sure who has taken over my brain, mouth, and body.

"I'm fine," she says, opening her eyes to look at me, her mouth curving into that smile that had me dead to rights the first time I saw it. This girl is mine. And I am hers whether she wants me or not. This is my girlfriend. I have a girlfriend!

"Oh, good. Glad. I'm just okay. I mean, that was...like, all right, I guess," I tease, and she pushes herself up hard against my chest, slightly knocking the wind from me.

"Just okay? You guess?" she says, her face suspicious, and maybe a little pissed.

"Well, you said *fine*! I mean, all of this and you're...fine?" Now she's embarrassed, and she buries her head in my chest again.

"Oh my god, I did say *fine*. I'm so sorry," she says, lifting her head just enough to look into my eyes. I'm smiling, so I hope she knows I'm not serious. Her lip quickly finds its way back to her teeth, and she shrugs one more apology.

"I was teasing you. Cross my heart," I say, thinking how strange those words sound right now.

My heart. Huh. She kind of owns that too.

Cass is quiet for several more minutes, but lets her hand stroke along my chest, and I can tell she's thinking. I wonder if she's uncomfortable? Does she want to get dressed, or is she going to sleep like that? God, I hope she sleeps like that. I'll keep her covered if Paige comes home. I'm about to offer to let her sleep in my shirt when she speaks.

"Please don't leave," she says, her voice soft—a far cry from the confident goddess who was taking control of my body minutes ago.

"Uh...where would I go?" I chuckle, but I stop quickly. I kind of want to be funny, but I also feel a sharp sting in my chest because I think Cass is being serious. And the way she asks—the way she won't look at me right now—damn it, she actually thought I would leave.

"Look at me," I say, my hand gentle, but strong along her face, lifting her enough so she can see my eyes, my mouth, my expression. "Where would I go?" I ask again, this time my tone a little different—softer, and heartbroken for her.

"I thought—" she starts to speak, but stops, letting her eyes fall to my chest. I pick her chin up with my finger and run my thumb softly over her lip.

"Guys that do that are dicks," I say, without a hint of humor.

"But isn't that...kind of...your reputation?" She's embarrassed to ask, and I know it's because she doesn't want to hurt my feelings. But my rep is my fault, and the fact that she is worried about offending me with my own actions makes her maybe the sweetest girl on the planet.

"Yeah, well, I was a dick. Now I'm not," I say, testing out a small smile. When she mirrors me, I let out a sigh and cradle her head, pulling her forehead to mine and pressing my lips to it softly. "Sometimes, we meet people that set our shit right. And you were like a bullet. You pierced straight...right about here." I hold her hand over my chest, and I panic that she can feel how hard my heart's beating.

She's quiet at first, but slowly she comes back to me. "That...is the cheesiest line I have ever heard," she says, unable to stop the grin from spreading into a full smile and soon a laugh.

"You love it," I say.

"I do," she responds quickly, pausing to look into my eyes for several long seconds, her lips making those tiny twitches that look like she wants to say something more. But she doesn't, and instead leaves a kiss on my lips as she steps away from the bed and heads to her closet.

"You can wear my shirt." I don't know why, but I want to see her in something of mine. When she picks it up and pulls it over her head, as she disappears behind her closet door, I feel instantly satisfied.

My mouth is dry from saying the word *love*, and my heart is running about a million times faster than it was just seconds before. I know I didn't really *say* that I love her. But my god it sounded like I maybe meant that. I don't love her. I don't love her—because that's something you spend years looking for. And I have known this girl for a few weeks. I've only loved one girl...and she left me a fucked up cryptic voicemail that I haven't thought about until right this second. I haven't thought about it because Cass...she stops all time for me. When I'm with her, it's only her—she's all I see, and all I want. She consumes me.

But I don't love her. *I can't*. Not that fast. And what would Kelly think, if I fell for someone else after telling her I wanted to spare her from having to live a life with me.

What would Kelly think...if I fell in love? With someone else?

If I fell in love with Cass?

Chapter 11

Cass

I woke up for the first time around six in the morning. The sunlight was barely peeking into my room through the thin curtains, so I knew it was still early. I fell back asleep, but not until after watching Ty for almost an entire hour—every breath, every rise and fall of his chest, the way his arm twitched slightly from the weight of my head—I was building a mental scrapbook of all of these tiny little things. This is what a boyfriend is supposed to feel like.

My eyelids finally conceded again, and for several more hours, I fell into the comfort of safe arms and nonsensical dreams. But now that I feel the tiny tickle of fingertips up and down my back and arms, I'm fairly confident Ty has been watching me—locking away memories of his own. The thought makes me smile.

"There's my ninja," he whispers in my ear, nuzzling at my cheek and leaving soft kisses down my neck and shoulder.

"I sleep with one eye open. Ninja stuff. You wouldn't understand," I say.

"Or would I?" he says, one brow arched.

"You look like one of those cartoon superheroes when you make that face," I tease.

"I know. Captain Gorgeous," he winks, and I can't help but laugh. He gives me the stink eye when I do, pretending to have hurt feelings. "You think I'm kidding, but you can't detect my superhero-ness, because I haven't unleashed my super powers on *you* yet. You weren't ready—ready to withstand the blast of my full gorgeousness."

"Oh my god, you are literally full of crap this morning, aren't you?" I say through heavier laughter.

"Mere mortal. You may be ninja, but you could never compete with my secret weapon," he says, lifting himself with his massive forearms until he's above me, forcing my head and body to fall deep into the mattress and pillow.

"And what weapon is that?" I ask, suddenly feeling a little out of breath.

"This," he says, closing the small gap left between us and kissing my lips with a rawness that he didn't show last night. His mouth possesses mine wildly—as I lie, practically helpless and caged between both of his arms—his forehead finally comes to rest against mine when he pulls away from our kiss to breathe.

"Totally unaffected," I whisper, wanting to tease, but unable to execute my joke because holy hell...*that* quite honestly might really be a super power.

"Liar," he says, the corner of his lip pulling up at the side just enough to produce that perfect dimple—going in for the final kill.

When he pushes away from me completely, to sit along the end of the bed, I feel cold, and there's a part of me that wants to pull him back down to lie next to me. But that would be *needy*. I know that needy isn't good. Needy doesn't get you a boyfriend. Needy doesn't keep a boyfriend. So I just look at him and smile as I watch him pull his jeans up his legs and bend forward to reach his shoes.

"What's on your agenda today?" I ask, immediately worried that even *that* sounds needy.

"I have some things to take care of, and I think I have one client at two. But then..." he leans forward one final time to reach me for a soft kiss, "then I'm all yours. Don't forget—dinner with my parents tonight."

"I'll be ready," I smile, trying to keep the covers over my body, which is now full of nervous energy, knowing I won't have the distraction of a football game to keep conversation—the one-on-one kind—to a minimum with Ty's parents.

Ty moves to his chair and he pauses, looking at me with a strange expression, and then I realize why. I'm still in his shirt.

"Oh! You probably need this, huh?" I say, sitting up and pulling one arm through the shirt before Ty stops me.

"You keep it. I've got a whole closetful down the hall. I think I can make it safely a few feet to the east," he says, his eyes moving down to the exposed skin on my stomach and my black underwear. He's practically undressing me, and I let him. I

107

actually move the blanket a few extra inches away for a better view. My move makes him smile. "Damn."

"Damn what?" I ask, knowing, but wanting to hear it anyway. I'm insecure, and I admit it. I like hearing him talk about me like I'm sexy.

"Damn...I should have waited until you got the shirt off completely before I stopped you," he smirks. I want him to stay, but he's backing away. So I let him go, and simply blow him a kiss as he disappears out my door.

Play it cool, Cass.

I bury my head in my pillow when I hear the door shut, then I replay everything I did and said over the last twenty-four hours—hoping it was enough, but never too much.

After a fast shower, I head back to our room and slip into my cotton shorts and T-shirt. My body is tired today. It's been tired all week. The few hours I have before my dinner—the one where I have to sit down and talk with Ty's parents—are necessary, unless I want to spend the entire night worrying about tingling legs or strange eye pain. I haven't had any symptoms since the leg tingles a day or two ago, but I'm on this constant look out, questioning everything I feel.

Rowe walks in only minutes after me. She's smiling—like *big time* smiling. And that makes me smile too.

I don't like that we fought. I know it wasn't a *real* fight, but still...I was pushy. I was pushy because I really wanted my way, just this once. I wanted the night, last night, with Ty. But before I fell asleep, I did think of Rowe, worried that she wasn't as okay as I was. The smile is still there, though, even as she slides a small, opened cereal box onto her desk shelf.

"Saving up to win the prize?" I ask, kind of wanting to test the waters, seeing if she's still angry with me.

"Something like that," she says, and the smile remains, maybe even grows bigger.

"So...how was *your* night?" Please let it have been as good as that smile on your face is making me believe it was. Please, oh please, oh please. "Does that smile on your face mean what I think it means?"

108

"Nooooooo," she says, but her cheeks are darn near fire-engine red. She looks like a thermometer in the ER during flu season. "We just...*slept*. But it was really, really, *really* nice."

She's still smiling. This is good. I think this might be *very* good, and I didn't blow this friend thing with my selfishness. And Rowe looks happy.

"Hmmmmmmmm, sounds really, really, *really* boring," I tease her, feeling good that I can. "Wanna hear about my night?" I am dying to tell someone about my night! And it can't be Paige.

"Oh god, no!" she says, her face immediately shifting back to a bright shade of red. I'm about to force her to listen anyhow, because *oh my god I have to tell someone,* but suddenly, Rowe is changing her clothes in front of me, and she freezes.

I freeze too.

I saw them earlier. The scars. But she's not hiding them now, not even attempting. Her eyes are locked on mine, and she's waiting to see how I'm going to react. I can see her terror. I've been that terrified. I've lived that terror. *Oh, Rowe, your scars, they're your story.*

But the second that thought passes through my mind, I realize that the moment the welts, from years of shots, finally disappeared from my body, so did my story—by choice. The proof of MS was gone, and I was going to leave it erased.

Rowe doesn't have that option.

"They've gotten better," she says, turning slowly. She's letting me see everything, and I can also see her body shivering with nerves as she does. This is scary to her.

"What happened?" I'm looking at her, because I think that's what she wants. I am in awe of her bravery.

"Two years ago, there was a shooting at my school. You ever hear of Hallman High?" she asks. *Hallman?* I don't even know if the name truly sounds familiar, and my mind has already raced ahead and filled in the blanks. Rowe has been through hell—actual living hell. And sadly, I can't tell her hell apart from the dozens of other *hells* I've seen on the news lately.

"This sounds awful, but there are just so many school shootings—" I'm embarrassed saying this aloud, but Rowe is shaking her head in understanding. I watch her walk to her dresser and pull out a small stack of photos. I saw her hide those the other day, and my stomach is sinking even lower into the depths of grief for my friend.

She shows me a photo of Josh, her boyfriend, and I immediately think about Nate. A few days ago, Ty asked me about Rowe having a boyfriend, and he mentioned that she seemed strange about the topic. We haven't talked about it in a while. But I have a feeling the picture is about to become crystal clear.

"Josh...he saved my life," she says. "He was hit. It wasn't fatal. But..."

She can't finish her words, and I can tell her eyes are starting to overflow with tears, so I just nod and offer a silent smile. Josh was hurt—and he'll never be the same.

She shows me photos of her best friend who died. Betsy. I love that name. I bet I would have loved her friend too. I flip through the pictures she hands me, and I soak each one in, my heart breaking for my friend with every face I see in those pictures. What gets me most, though, is Rowe's face in those photos. She was so happy, so free. I look at her now, and I realize she's a ghost.

She's waiting for my reaction. And I bet she's rehearsed this—the telling of her tale. And I know what it's like to get the fake hugs and *I'm so sorry* utterances. I hate when people apologize because I have MS—like they bumped into me accidentally, and because of that I got MS. It's ridiculous. I have a mental collection of all of the pep talks after my diagnosis:

"You can beat this, Cass."

No, actually, I can't. I can live with it, but I can't *beat* it.

"It's just a little adjustment."

Right...to my *life!*

Oh, and my all-time favorite—*"You have MS, but MS doesn't have you!"*

What the fuck does that even mean?

I'm looking at Rowe, and I want to tell her that I understand. I want to tell her why I understand. But Jesus...a school shooting? My problems are not even in the same ballpark. I understand, but I feel like I'd be comparing her bowling ball to my marble, and it would just be insulting. So instead, I give her a break from the pep talks and the pats on the hand and the *understanding* bullshit that no doubt she's heard a dozen times.

"Wow," I say. "That's...sucky. That's just sucky."

It is sucky. My MS is sucky. The crap deck life deals out randomly is motherfucking sucky!

"Oooooooh my god, it is soooooooo sucky!" Rowe says, her lips cracking a smile, and a hard laugh follows. She's breaking a little, trying to hold on—taking my life raft, my free pass to go ahead and laugh at her situation, and how fucked up it is. And I want to laugh, too. Not at Rowe's experience, but at my own. I want to laugh at it because it takes away its power, and it feels good. And I've never done this.

"Riiiiight?" I say back to her, mimicking her Valley-Girl tone. I start to giggle when I do. It's that crazy, emotional track-wreck kind of laugh that could veer off into a cry at any moment for both of us. But I won't let it. I'm driving this train, and tonight, we mock our shitty circumstances.

We give them the finger!

We laugh. We laugh hard. And when my sister walks in, we keep it going. We tell Paige everything, about Rowe's boyfriend—who is practically in a coma—about her friend who died, and about how shitty it all is. Then, for a small second, my sister catches my gaze, and she looks at me hard. "Tell her," she's saying. I nod *no.* I don't want to; I may never want to. And tonight, I'm going to give her laughter instead of sympathy. Paige can play the role of *serious.*

After a few minutes, our laughing starts to fade, and I can tell Rowe feels the sadness of it all sitting on her shoulders again. I feel it too.

She sits next to my sister and shares the same story with Paige that she shared with me, and as Paige always does, she listens—she listens well. And she sympathizes. And she says those positive little things that I know are probably making Rowe cringe.

She means well. But I'm fairly certain Rowe would rather go back to laughing—as insane as it was. It feels better. And I want to go back to laughing too.

Paige's sympathy is earnest, but it's also short-lived. Before long, she finds a way to bring the spotlight back where it belongs—on her. She's moving out; I knew this was coming, and as predicted, I'm excited at the prospect of living *without* my sister. Surprisingly, though, there's a small pang deep inside. I love my sister, but I never really thought I'd miss her—until now.

"I'm going to need some help moving," she says, always slipping right into her natural supervisory role, doling out orders.

"I'm sure Nate will help—" Rowe offers, cutting her speech short when she realizes what she said. There's a brief awkward silence, but it passes quickly, and Paige thanks her for asking him. Rowe smiles and busies herself in her book bag, I think partly trying to end her conversation with my sister on this high note.

"Cass, perhaps you can help me with my clothes and things?" my sister asks. I'm half-listening, still a little lost in the realization that I will be without Paige soon, so I nod in her direction. "And we're going to need to shave your head."

"Yeah, sure. Whatever you need," I say.

"Seriously, what's with you? Did you even hear me?" Paige asks. I feel her weight suddenly next to me on my bed and finally allow myself to bring her face into focus. Rowe is reading her textbook, her ear buds deep in her ears. She listens to her music loudly; I know she's missing all of this.

"I'm trying out for the soccer team." *Where the fuck did that come from?* My urge to suddenly bring my sister into my scheme was instant and overwhelming. Maybe I'm scared to be without her. Maybe I'm scared of trying out. Maybe I'm afraid of failing. I think, maybe, all of those statements hit the mark. And I think the fact that I have a *boyfriend* is making me act out, too. But I'd rather talk to Paige about soccer than talk to her about Ty. So, that's what came vomiting out of my mouth.

"You can't," she says, just like I knew she would. Her arms are folded in that I'm-older-than-you (*by one freaking minute!*) way. Her smugness pisses me off. I stand and move into the closet flipping through my clothes, picking out something for dinner tonight. The closet also puts us a few steps farther away from Rowe, and I don't want her hearing my sister scold me.

"Yes, Paige. I can. I've been training..."

"You've been...*training?*" I hate this tone she has. She gets it from our mother. It's almost self-righteous. I am definitely my father—easy, willing, and competitive. Paige is Mom—creative, but stubborn and always right. Problem is, Paige and Mom both tend to gang up on me. By God's grace, my parents kept Paige out of the worst of my issues my senior year of high school. Otherwise, she'd probably serve me with nightly lectures—and she sure as hell would have more questions about, and snarky remarks for, Ty.

I take a deep breath, pausing on the dress I think I want to wear tonight. Pulling it into my hands, I shut my eyes and run my thumbs along the soft fabric, breathing in once more through my nose before I dive into my defense.

"Yes. I've been training. And it feels good. No..." I pause, letting the dress slide through my fingers and dangle back on its hanger. "It feels amazing. My body feels amazing. I look forward to exercising—it's more than just part of my treatment. I have a purpose, a goal! Ty has been training me, and he pushes me, but never too far. I can take it. I am *thriving* off of it! But it's not just my muscles, and me being competitive, Paige. I'm running hard. I forgot what working for something like this felt like—and I think I need this...my *soul* needs this!"

"Your...*soul*...needs this?" she scoffs at me, a rude laugh breaking through as she speaks. "Cass, Mom is going to worry herself sick. She's going to nag Dad until he makes you stop, or worse—she'll make you come home!"

"Then don't tell them!"

And there it is. I'm asking Paige to keep a secret. This is where things between us have always been raw. Paige was the one who told the school about my diagnosis. She didn't do it to be mean—she just wanted something to talk about with her friends. She wanted to talk about how hard life was for *her*, because everyone was doting over me. Then, when I slept with Jeff and Noah, and neither of them looked my way again once they took what they wanted, I turned to Paige, devastated and confused. To her credit, I honestly believe all she wanted to do was defend me, but she confronted them...in a crowd.

And then it was out there. Cass Owens was the girl who slept with two best friends, only weeks apart. When the boys practically formed a line—I obliged. My reputation spread fast, and for the most part, I kept up—all the way until the end.

I never said it aloud, but it always hung out there between Paige and me. This lack of trust—it runs deep. So deep, that once I ask Paige to keep this secret, this new secret, the one that is bringing me more joy than anything has in months, she doesn't know how to answer. I can see the redness fighting to take over the whites of her eyes. I've hit a nerve, but Paige Owens doesn't cry. She never shows weakness. And she doesn't make promises she can't keep.

Without a word, she grabs her purse and keys and walks away, careful not to slam the door in her wake—always under control, even when she wants to stab me.

It takes Rowe almost an hour to realize that Paige is gone. She finally turns her iPod off and looks around as she wraps the cord up neatly. "Paige left?" she asks.

"Yeah, she had some party or something. I think she's dating a football player now," I respond, quickly returning my focus to the dress in the closet and the perfect shoes to go with it. It's not a total lie—I think Paige really is into a football player. But who the hell knows about the party. I just know she's not coming back tonight.

That's the weird thing with twins. You fight enough—you start to really understand the idiosyncrasies of your match. And I know Paige won't step foot in front of me again until she can look me in the eye and tell me *I'm* the one who's being unreasonable. And when she does, her face will almost convince me she's right.

Chapter 12

Ty

When Kelly looks at her phone, she's going to think I'm a crazy man. Scratch that—a *crazier* man. I've called, heard the start of a ring, and hung up a dozen times. I know it records every missed call, and I know there's a chance Jared is probably going to see my name lighting up her phone screen about a million times. And it's going to piss him off. But he won't say anything. Not directly, at least. So I dial again, my finger hovering over the END CALL button while I force myself to hear two rings this time.

Once I make it to two, I power through, like I've passed some stupid barrier. Once the third ring finishes, I almost press to end the call, but Kelly's voicemail picks up.

Hey, it's Kelly. I can't talk now, but I'll be sad I missed you, so please leave a message.

And then there's the beep.

Fuck! I've already let two or three dead seconds pass before I stutter into talking.

"Kel, hey," I start. This is weird—this whole thing is weird. She had to know this would be weird. And she had to know that there was no fucking way I would be able to wait until Thanksgiving—almost two months away—to find out what's wrong.

"I'm returning your call. You kind of, well...left me hanging there with that message. I was just worried about you. So, uhm...yeah. Give me a call when you can. I'd love to talk."

Beeeeeep.

My heart sounds like a goddamned drum line. I'm waiting for a prompt, something that tells me I can erase and rerecord, add to my message, get more time. But nothing happens. Soon, there's a dial tone. That's it—I called her back. I don't even remember what I said, and I hope like hell I didn't sound like an asshole. I don't think I sounded like an asshole. Returning call...worried...call me—no, I was okay. That message was okay.

The banging on the door saves me from my own head. It's almost time for dinner with our parents, so I bet it's Nate, and I bet he forgot his key.

"You're running *wayyyyy* late, fucknut," I say, pulling the door open and feeling it release from my hand as it swings fully into the opposite wall. Paige marches in, sliding past me with finesse and speed. She turns, her arms folded over her chest, her fancy purse pulled up high on her shoulder and stuffed under one arm.

"Mind shutting that?" she says, nodding to the door. She sounds pissed. What the fuck? I'm pretty sure when I left Cass, she was good—things were good. No, things were...*great!*

I shut the door and move closer to her, my eyebrows low and my eyes unable to move away from the shiny long fingernails she is tapping against her own arm. How is she making that noise on her skin? Those things sound like they're rapping on a tabletop.

"You and me need to have a chat," she says, popping one leg out a step so this balled-up energy she's holding onto can seep out slowly through her tapping toe.

"Okay," I say, literally biting my tongue to avoid saying something that will only make whatever the fuck is happening right now worse. "Can't say I know what about, so...enlighten me?" Yeah, that probably wasn't the right choice of words, but it's better than the first few things that popped into my head.

"My sister," she says, the nail tapping picking up speed against her arm.

"I'm pretty sure Cass is a big girl, and wouldn't like whatever *this* is you think you're doing," I say, ready to kick her out of my damn room.

"Oh, I *know* she wouldn't like it. And I know you'll probably tell her I was here—even though you shouldn't. But I don't care," she says.

"Allllll right," I say, dragging the words out while I look at her for some clue where this is going.

"I don't like you," she says. Wo—wow! Paige has balls.

"I'm good with that. See ya later," I say, my hand actually on the door handle now.

116

"Let me say my piece, and then I'll leave. Just give me the respect of listening," she says, so I drop my hand and turn to face her again.

"Kinda hard to respect someone whose opening line is 'I don't like you,'" I say, somehow finding myself with my arms folded just like hers. It irritates me, so I grab Nate's ball glove that's sitting out on his desk just to have something to hold onto.

Paige relaxes, though very little. She takes a seat on my desk chair, setting her purse on the floor and folding her hands in her lap. I suddenly feel like I'm in an interview—the part near the end, and it didn't go well, and the interviewer is about to tell me I didn't get the job.

"I don't have to like you, Ty. My sister does. And she does. She likes you...a *whole* bunch," she says, and I smile on instinct. She holds up a hand fast, though. *Don't get too comfortable, Ty.* "My sister has a big heart. She loves easily. She's also been through...she's been through a lot. Soccer was everything to her, and she tells me you've been training her. You have to stop."

"No way," I say. Not a chance. I know Cass wants this. And I know what it's like to feel that drive, to accomplish something you aren't supposed to. I won't back out on her on this.

"I figured you'd say that," Paige says, her voice getting softer, but still with an edge to it. She reaches down and pulls her purse in her lap, preparing to stand. "This is a bad idea. If she fails...she won't recover. She'll be devastated."

"She won't fail," I say, my words sure and fast.

Paige pauses to take them in, waiting for me to hedge my statement. I keep my lips pursed and hold her stare, and finally she sighs.

"Maybe not. But there's a chance. Whether you believe there is or not, there's always a chance things won't work out. And if she fails—" she says, and I interrupt.

"Which she won't," I say, and this only brings back Paige's fire. Fuck it—she already doesn't like me.

"You better hope not," she says, standing and smoothing out her shorts and shirt before she leaves. She stops abruptly, right in front of me, and leans forward, one hand on the side of my chair, her eyes piercing mine with a surprisingly heavy effect.

"If she gets hurt, and it's your fault—in *any way whatsoever*—I will ruin your existence."

"Get in line, sister," I say, going toe-to-toe with her, but also a little surprised at her strength.

She walks to the door and pushes it open with her hand, stopping me from closing it behind her. "It's not that I think you're a bad guy," she says, forcing a gut-busting laugh out of me, and fast. "I just don't think you're good enough for my sister."

Well, damn. She kind of has me there. I watch her walk away, no longer ready to slam the door in her face—caught somewhere between being impressed and feeling bad about myself.

I catch the buzzing sound on my phone and move to my desk to pick it up. One missed call.

From Kelly.

Motherfucking son of a bitch!

"Sorry I'm late. We should get dressed. Mom hates it when we make her wait for dinner," Nate says, barreling into our room and forcing me to put my big fat pile of shit on hold.

Shaking my head, half shell-shocked from the last thirty seconds of my life, I renew focus on the dress shirt hanging from the closet doorknob, and I think of Cass. And I smile—in an instant.

She won't fail. Kelly is okay. And Paige can go fuck herself.

Yep, I'm good.

Chapter 13

Ty

Cass flew through dinner with my parents like a champ. When my dad asked her what she was studying, and she answered, "Physical therapy, to help people with special physical needs,"—I saw my mom swallow hard. It's a weak spot in my mother's heart, and it's because I am...well, how I am.

My mom isn't just one of those parents who starts to take up a cause because her child is affected by something, though—she's always been an advocate for people who have something to overcome. She never uses the word *disabled*, and she's not too keen on the *handicapable* thing either. She just plain doesn't like a label—period. She says we all have differences, and we all encounter differences throughout our life, and that's what they are—differences. Some make some things hard, and some make some things easy.

It took me a while to see things her way. Nate, however, thinks I just bounced right back—and that's because I wanted him to think that. I don't want guilt to ever plague him, make him give up on something, or sacrifice his wants. I love him too much for that. But in the beginning, when I wasn't putting on my brave face for him or my Dad, I was downright angry. And I let it show, but only to my mom. And Kelly.

I knew that my mom would hug Cass by the time dinner was over, and she did. And it is all Cass has talked about since. I'm glad she wants my parents to like her. I want them to like her. I like her.

My parents offered to drive us back, but Cass wanted to walk. I can tell she's cold, the way she keeps hugging herself. But she won't admit it. She's stubborn too. And I also like that.

"You want my sweatshirt, and you know you do," I say, pulling it over my head. She nods *no*.

"No, no...I'm fffffine," she actually shivers the word. I look at her and dare her with my eyes to say it again, but her lips are literally chattering. "Okay, I'm not. Thank you," she finally concedes, taking it from my hands and pulling it fast over her body. I like seeing her in my things.

"My mom loved you," I say, sparking a renewed grin on her face, her lip tucked between her top and bottom teeth while they seesaw as she recalls our evening together. Her hair falls in front of her face when she finally turns to look at me, and she reaches around to tuck it behind her ear. I like watching her do that.

"She really did, huh?" she says, and I can tell she feels proud.

"I told you she would," I say, and her smile only gets bigger. I have to mess with her. "I mean, I paid them forty bucks. I do feel a little ripped off though, I was promised three compliments for you, but I only heard my mom say two."

"Oh, that's because I caught her in the bathroom and told her that if she gave me twenty-five percent of her earnings, she could skip one," she smirks.

"Smart," I say, winking and finally letting my laugh break through.

The air is cold, and it's making her face the sweetest shade of pink, like bubblegum. When we left the restaurant, she pulled the pins from her hair, and the curls have danced in the breeze during our entire trip home. If I could just reach a little higher, I would try to catch one. She's like a firefly, so beautiful—flashes of light that I have to hold. "Can I draw you?" I ask, slightly surprised to hear myself ask that aloud.

"What are you, Jack from *Titanic?*" she responds.

"Are you mocking DiCaprio?" I spar back.

"Wouldn't dare," she says, shaking her head slowly. I hold her stare for a few minutes, admiring the curve of her lips—the way the pink almost matches the color of her cheeks.

"Good. I like Leo. He's a man's man. If you made fun of him, we'd have to rethink things." She laughs at my diatribe. "I'm being serious. There are two things you don't fuck with— baseball, and Leo."

She crosses her heart dramatically as we get to the front of our building. "Wouldn't *dare* mock Leo then," she says, unable to hold her snicker in.

"You laugh now, but were you laughing when he went all rogue in *The Departed*? I think not. He was badass. And what about *Gangs of New York*?"

"Never saw it," she says, and I grab her wrist, spinning her around to face me at the elevator bank.

"Seriously?"

"Never saw *The Departed*, either. Just *Titanic*," she admits.

The elevator opens, and we move inside. "That's just...well...shameful. That's what that is. No wonder you don't understand the full power of the Leo," I say, shaking my head. "That's it. When I go home for break, I'm bringing back my DVDs. We're fixing this."

"Whatever," she says, skipping ahead of me when the elevator opens.

"You know what, I don't want to draw you any more. Not if you're going to have that attitude," I joke, and she turns to face me, her face the most fucking adorable pout ever.

"Nope, not going to work on me. No drawing for you," I say, and she comes closer, sliding one leg over my lap and wrapping her arms around my neck, seducing me. It's totally working. I was only kidding to begin with.

"Nope, you're seduction powers are useless," I say, a breath or two before her lips dust over mine.

She whispers, "Please..."

"I don't know, it's going to take some convincing," I say, taking her top lip between my teeth.

Just then, she reaches down lower in my lap, rubbing along my hard-on and completely jarring me from this little fantasy we've created. I am fully present in the now, and suddenly, the last thing I want to do is draw.

"Please? Draw me, Ty. Please?" she's running kisses down my neck when we hear the elevator *ding* down the hall, and Nate and Rowe's laughter fills the silence. Instead of getting up from my lap, Cass remains seated—her hand staying in place while she moves her other finger over my mouth, keeping me quiet while we listen if Nate and Rowe go to my room. When we hear the other door shut, I nip at the tip of her finger, and she leaves it in my mouth. So fucking sexy.

"Get inside. I'll draw you. But then, I'm undressing you and living out all kinds of fantasies," I say, and she hops up from my lap, opens her door and practically pulls me inside with her.

I didn't expect her to strip. But she did. She's actually playing out that scene from *Titanic*, lying topless on her bed, rings of her hair teasing at her nipple. I so don't want to be drawing right now. Why is this pencil in my hand?

"If I find out you can't really draw, and this was all some ploy, I'm going to be pissed," she says, only half kidding.

"One, I never asked you to get naked," I say, pausing and gawking, mouth wide open. "Sorry. Little distracted. And two, I *can* draw. So hush and don't move so I can get this over with," I say, pulling her spiral notebook to my lap so I can begin sketching and shading.

I'm doing my best to block my view of most of her body with the notebook so that maybe, just maybe, I'll be able to get a decent portrait of her face done before I completely lose my mind. "How long have you drawn?" she asks after a few minutes of silence.

"Shhhhh," I say, and she whispers an apology. "I'm teasing. You can talk. I already have your lips and face. I started drawing for fun in high school. Superheroes and stuff like that. My mom is really good at this stuff. She's an artist. I guess I picked up a few things."

"Do you paint or do other stuff?" she asks, something tickling her nose and forcing her to crinkle it so she doesn't move. I lean forward and run the back of my knuckle down her nose for her. "Thank you," she says, the redness creeping up again at my nearness. I can't believe she's just lying there for me to take—and I'm *drawing*. What the hell?

"I paint. Not as much as I used to. But after...you know...after the accident? I painted a lot. It was sort of therapeutic," I say.

"Why don't you study art?" she asks.

"Oh no. That would ruin it. It's a hobby. I never want it to be a job. And it's really hard to make money at it. My mom, she's one of the lucky few able to make it a career. And I like money, so...hence the business degree," I say, caressing my thumb over

122

the lead lines that shade Cass's breasts. I'm touching the paper with the same reverence I use on her.

"Can I see it?" she asks, pushing herself up a little, trying to sneak a view.

I tilt the notebook quickly and throw my pencil at her. She throws it back. "No peeking. Patience, young grasshopper."

"Grasshopper?" Nose crinkle and sour face follows.

"Do you, like, have any pop culture references? Like...at all?" I continue shading her legs, and then begin filling in her hair.

"Not from the seventies, old man," she fires back.

"Oh, ha ha. I'm four years older than you; I'm not a senior citizen. I watched a lot of Nick at Nite, and I appreciate the classics. Plus seriously, that's like saying you don't know Elvis."

"Grasshopper is nothing like Elvis," she says with a little sigh.

"Valid point. Nevertheless, now you're watching Kung Fu DVDs too," I say, putting the final touches on her sketch.

"Oh...goody," her tone completely lacks excitement.

"Just wait, you'll like them," I say as I move closer to her, the notebook held to my chest.

"You're done? Lemme see!" she reaches for it, but I hold it tight, for some reason nervous to show this to her.

"Hold on. Before you look at it, remember, I did it fast, on notebook paper, and I haven't done this in a while," I say, but she interrupts with a *tsk* sound and yanks the pages from my hand. When her eyes hit the paper, and soften, and her bottom lip gets sucked up under her teeth, I finally breathe.

Cass

I wish I really looked like this girl in the drawing. What Ty has done on a spiral notebook in ten minutes is one of the most beautiful and heart-melting creations I have ever seen.

"Well?" he asks. His face looks nervous. It's cute that he's nervous, wants to please me.

"Ty...it's beautiful. I mean, I don't look anything like this, but what you drew...it's beautiful," I say, letting my eyes wash over the softness in pencil sketched in front of me.

"Yes, you do," he says, pulling himself closer to me. "I really need paints to do you justice. But yes, this is what you look like—how *I* see you."

I think I love him. I know it sounds ludicrous, and yeah, maybe I'm easy, because he just said a full string of magic words that pretty much just flushed the air from my lungs, and wrapped all of him around my heart. But I don't care. I would risk it all to have him say something like that about me, just one more time.

"Ty," I say...the rest of what I want to say hung on my tongue, my nerves keeping my feelings on hold, but my will fighting, wanting to push them out. Maybe it's reason working against me. I know most of what I'm feeling right now is complete and utter swoon from the fact that this older, sexy man has just made me feel beautiful—truly beautiful. But screw reason. I want to jump in with both feet, arms in the air.

He runs the back of his hand along my cheek, grazing my arm and breast until he hits my hand, and he brings it to his lips to kiss softly. I love you, Tyson Preeter. I practice the phrase over and over in my head while he looks at me, touches me softly, and seduces me until I'm ready for anything. Then—there is a chime on my phone, and one on his.

Ignore it, Ty. Ignore it. We're both frozen, having a silent conversation about how whatever *that* is, can wait—it isn't important. And then our phones chime again.

Ty breaks first. And it burns a little that he does.

"It's Nate. He said he and Rowe—" He doesn't finish, because I'm reading my phone now. It's a text from Rowe. She needs to come home, to our room. She and Nate had a fight.

"We could pretend we didn't hear—" Ty starts, his mouth twisted into a half smile full of equal parts hope and disappointment.

"We could. But we're not assholes," I say.

"Well, *I'm* an asshole. But...no...you're not an asshole," he says, taking a deep breath. "All right, you better get dressed. I'm going to go try and console my needy brother and knock some sense into him."

"Maybe we can pick this up again...tomorrow?" I ask.

"Baby, you can count on it," he says.

"Don't call me *baby*," I smirk, and he kisses me one last time, hard, whispering "*Baby*," against my lips with his perfect, self-righteous, I-own-you smile.

When he leaves, I pull my clothes on and flip through channels on the TV. Rowe comes in soon after, and we spend the rest of the night watching bad music videos on MTV and not saying a word. That's probably for the best, because she looks sad. And all I feel is happy. I wouldn't be a very good friend if I had to speak tonight.

Happy. Happy. Happy.

Chapter 14

Ty

Her call comes when I least expect it—on my way to the gym, to run Cass through her workouts. It's a special day. I lined up a visit with the McConnell women's coach—nothing formal, just a quick meet-and-greet. I still feel like Cass is on the fence about trying out, so I thought this might be just the nudge she needs.

Of course, now my focus is shot to shit.

The last time Kelly called, I sent her a text a few hours later. I didn't hear back from her again...until now. My phone is vibrating in my hand, and I'm tempted to pretend I don't feel it—to tuck it back in my pocket until I can lock it away in the gym—and continue to put off whatever is waiting on the other line. But I'm also desperate to know.

So I answer.

"Hey," I say. We've been playing phone tag for weeks; formalities seem forced at this point.

"Hey," she says back. She sounds tired, and not at all like the person she was pretending to be when she left me those messages.

"Hey," I say again, finding a shaded area a few yards away from the gym entrance, away from the busy path of students. That old, familiar smile falling into place.

"You said that already," she laughs. It comes out soft, her voice a little raspy, almost like she's fighting a cold.

"I know. It's just weird...talking to you," I admit. My heart feels heavy. This is why I never called before. I knew it would make me feel bad, would make me...miss her.

"I know whatcha mean," she says back, so much about the way she speaks is familiar. I miss her. *I really fucking miss her.*

"How's Jackson?" I ask, hoping her son is okay, hoping *that's* not her big secret. I breathe in relief when she giggles lightly at my question.

"He's so good," she says, her pride shining through. I always knew she would be a good mother. She's made for this.

"Good. I...I can't wait to meet him," I say, trying to find a way to broach the topic about Thanksgiving—me visiting, and why she *wants* me to visit.

"Me, too," she says, the sudden distance in her voice spurring me to react.

"What's going on, Kel?" I finally ask, unprepared for the tears that I hear my question trigger. She's hundreds of miles away and crying, and I can't help. It hurts that I can't. She's trying to muffle the sound, to hold it in. But she just can't. "Oh, Kel bear...what's wrong?"

Kelly was my whole entire heart for so long—it's almost like muscle memory. The need to care for her when she's hurting—I don't think that will ever go away.

"It's Jared," she says, and I feel my muscles flex, ready to go to war over whatever she says next. "Ty, he used to—"

"Did that son of a bitch hurt you, Kel?" my other hand fisted at my mouth, my teeth biting my knuckles, trying to keep my temper in check.

"No, no...nothing like that. I promise, Ty," she says.

"Then what is it?" I ask, still suspicious, my mind traveling a million miles per second to all of the worst possibilities—each one ending with my fist in Jared's face.

"I think he might be using again," she says, and everything about this conversation takes a U-turn. *Using? What the fuck?*

"What do you mean?" I ask. I don't know Jared well. Kelly met him in college. I wasn't around to get to know him. And maybe that makes it unfair for me to judge him quickly. But I have a feeling my hunch—the one that *Jared is an asshole*—is about to be confirmed.

"He's been clean for a long time, since *way* before I met him. He did drugs when he was in high school. But lately...I don't know. He seems weird. He doesn't come home on time, by...like...hours. And there are so many things that seem...I don't know. Not right? Weird phone calls, strange amounts of money missing from our checking account from cash withdrawals..." she sounds frantic, and I can hear Jackson starting to cry in the background.

"Does he act...like...high or anything?" I ask.

"No. Maybe? I don't know. He's jumpy, and just weird. And he gets a temper—it just comes out of nowhere," she says, stopping to hum something to Jackson, to calm him. Even her humming sounds stressed and sad.

"What was he on...before?" I know so very little about drugs. I've never liked them—not even the prescription kind. My mother begged me to take something for my depression, but I refused. I don't like the idea of chemically changing my mind. It just seems dangerous.

"He took a lot of things. Pills, mostly. But at his worst, he tried meth," she says, and I react poorly.

"Fuck, Kel? Meth? Jesus...and you married him?" I feel bad the second I finish talking, because I can hear her tears picking up again. "I'm sorry. I didn't mean that. I just don't like that he's making you feel this way—for whatever reason."

"I know," she sniffles.

"Can I talk to him?" I ask, seriously considering buying a ticket to fly home tonight so I can choke the fucker.

"No! No...he, he would just get angry that I'm talking to you about any of this," she says. "Ty, I never said anything, but Jared...he doesn't care for you. It's not personal, it's just our history."

"Yeah, well, that goes both ways." I'm hot now, and I don't care to spare Jared's feelings. "Sorry," I throw in at the end, but only for Kelly.

"No you're not," she says, her voice evening out a little.

"You're right," I smirk. "I'm not."

Silence starts to fill our time, and I can hear the sounds of her house in the background—the water running in the sink, her working a bottle together, getting it in her son's mouth, and the soft sounds of a music box starting up behind her.

"I think I just needed to talk to someone, honestly. Maybe...maybe if I feel like there's more to this—or if he starts acting weird again, more often...I don't know. Is it okay if I call? I don't want my parents to get involved. Not yet," I can't believe she's even asking.

"Kel, it's *always* okay for you to call," I say, wishing I could just hug her and make this okay.

"Thanks," she says after a few more seconds. "Listen, I have to get Jack down for his nap. But Ty? Thank you so much...for listening. I think—" she pauses to laugh lightly. "I think I might just sleep tonight."

"Anytime, Kel. Anytime," I say, and I wait for her to hang up.

I'm fifteen minutes late for my appointment with Cass. I didn't want to bring the anger and sinking feeling from my phone call into anything with her. But I'm not sure that's possible, because she's started her workouts, and all I can seem to do is sit here in the corner and bark orders at her—hoping I can pull my shit together by the time the coach shows up to surprise her.

Cass

"Faster. You can go faster!"

Ty's been...he's been a little tough today. I like tough in a trainer. I can take tough. I *thrive* off of tough. It's what made me good in the first place. But there's an extra edge to everything, too. And I *don't* like that edge in a boyfriend.

I push the speed up on the treadmill and go faster anyway, because I also like to win. And if he thinks I can go faster, I'm going to go twice as fast just to prove to him that I'm better than he thinks. *Run, legs! I promise, we'll rest later.*

I barely notice the next two minutes of sprints that pass— mostly because I keep stealing glances to the side where Ty is talking to Coach Pennington. I recognize him from the pictures I've indulged in of the soccer team's website.

McConnell was never one of the schools I dreamt about when I had fantasies of playing soccer in college. I always thought I'd go Pac-12. But that was all before I gave up on myself and spiraled into self-pity and degrading behavior—before my mom cried that I was pushing myself too hard and going to ruin my parents' marriage.

I'm dreaming of playing for McConnell now—dreaming stronger and harder than I have for anything in months. I tick the treadmill up one more level for the final sprint, just to show off how badly I want this.

When I'm done, I spend five minutes walking a lap or two on the indoor track. My body feels alive, my veins pumping blood faster than my muscles can burn it off. It's adrenaline—I'm sure from knowing the coach is here...waiting for me.

"Listen, legs—we're almost done. And tomorrow, I promise—rest. I won't push you as hard," I say to myself, chugging the last bits of my water and walking over to Ty, who's waiting with arms crossed, a cocky sense of pride worn on his face. I definitely like *that* in my boyfriend.

"Those are some fast sprints you were doing there," coach says, reaching out his hand to shake mine. "I'm Matt Pennington. My son works out with Tyson here, and he said you were thinking of coming out for our squad."

Of course Ty has a connection. I glance his way, and he smiles quickly and winks.

"Cassidy Owens, nice to meet you," I say, still a little out of breath. "And yes, I have been thinking about it."

"I remember you," coach says, looking at me sideways. "Your team took state in California, am I right?"

"Yes, sir."

"Striker. You had a mean penalty kick," he says, pointing a finger out to punctuate the fact that he's sold on me. I'm actually a little surprised. While the rest of my team put out recruitment feelers, I disappeared. I figured nobody would remember my name—let alone my stats.

"Thank you," I say, not sure what else to add.

"Well, I'd sure like to see what you can do, see if you can do any of *that...*" he says, nodding toward the treadmill I just lit up, "out on the field. We have some friendlies, non-mandatory, this weekend. Maybe you'd be up for coming out for a workout tomorrow and sticking around Saturday for a game? Inter-squad."

"I'd like that," I answer, and the speed at which I do surprises me. Yeah, I want this. I REALLY want this.

"All right, well, I'll get Ty the info, he can pass it along. We'll see ya there," he says, giving me one more shake, sealing the deal.

When the weight-room doors close behind him, I feel Ty's hands at my waist, and soon I'm trapped on his lap.

"You were amazing today," he says, his lips close enough to my ear that his breath sends shivers down my neck and spine, my skin finally cooling off from my sprints.

"Yeah, well, my trainer was a little pushy today," I squint at him.

"I was," he says, his eyes caught on mine, his mouth in a firm line. "I'm sorry. I sort of brought some baggage from earlier in here with you. That's not fair, and I shouldn't have done that."

He nuzzles his nose against my arm and kisses my skin lightly before looking back up at me. "Wanna talk about it?" I ask, sensing that whatever it is that's resting behind his eyes is weighing on him even more than he's letting on. He takes a long deep breath and our eyes remain locked for several seconds before his lip finally curls into that familiar Preeter smile.

"Nah, it's okay. Just some stuff with Nate, personal—ya know," he says with a shrug, and I almost believe him.

Almost.

Ty

I lied to her. I don't even know why I did it. I don't lie. I'm a truth-teller—even when the truth is fucking brutal and will hurt someone's feelings. I. Don't. Lie.

But I just did.

I sat there, looking into her eyes, my mind conjuring up a thousand images of Cass, everything about her that makes me smile, and then crisscrossing it with the absolute heartbreak I heard in Kelly's voice just an hour before. I couldn't get the two to parallel—Cass making me happy, and Kelly making me sad.

But instead of just telling Cass about Kelly, instead of sharing a little bit of my past—I wrapped it up quickly, cloaked it in a lie, and buried it under a fake smile.

I don't know why I did it, and I'm not proud. I want to fix it, take it back, have a redo...but I replay the scenario over and over in my mind—and it always comes out the same. And I don't know what that means.

Chapter 15

Cass

Rowe and Nate seem to still be fighting. When I ask her about him, she just shrugs, says he's been busy. But I kinda think it's bigger than that. She's been going to dinner in the cafeteria with Ty and me, and I can tell she feels awkward. *We* feel awkward. Rowe just seems sad, like she had this brightness that was really coming alive, and then it suddenly started slipping away after their fight.

I asked her about the fight the other night. One of my moments of absolute eloquence...I just blurted out, "What's wrong with you two?" She couldn't really put it into words, saying something about how her old boyfriend—the one barely alive back home—made it impossible to move forward, and how it was probably for the best. She was giving up. Quitting. And I suck, because I didn't know what to say to get her back into battle. But Ty did. And I love that he feels compelled to take her in. I can tell he's trying to fix whatever went wrong between her and Nate.

Last night was the first one in a few that I went over to his room alone, without Rowe. Nate was at workouts, like he usually is at that time, and their relationship was *literally* all we talked about. And that's when I started to get the strange feeling that Ty might be focusing so much on his brother's problems to avoid something else—something like *me*...and *us*.

This is how one negative thought burns a hole in my chest. It plants a seed, settling in and festering like a wound, an ulcer trying to interrupt my heart's rhythm. There's a cloud over me today. It's black. And I blame the seed. My cloud started to form when I woke up with a little bit of numbness in my toes. It faded, but instead of victory, I waited for the next sign of something *wrong*. My waiting was rewarded when the numbness was replaced by panic after I realized I completely failed to study for my physics test. Now, I'll have to spend the morning before I compete with the women's squad retaking a failed exam in the tutoring lab. And all of it is weighing me down mentally now, making me slow at workouts...where I'm supposed to impress Coach Pennington, and convince him to add me to his roster in the spring.

My cloud—born from that tiny seed—gains power every time Ty doesn't look at me. And it might all just be crazy shit I've cooked up in my head; in fact, the rational side of my brain *knows* this to be true. But it's also so damned real, so tangible, that I feel sick running my heart out on this field while he sits on the sidelines watching. My black cloud tells me it's just a matter of time before he cuts me loose, moves on from his project.

Stupid seed of doubt and black cloud.

I take my break on the opposite side of the field, and Coach Pennington jogs over, slapping my shoulder with approval and a smile. "Looking good, Owens. Keep this up, I think there's more in your tank," he says, reenergizing my tired body and wiping my slate clean of clouds for a few brief seconds. The storm comes again, though, when I feel the scowls of the three girls standing by the cooler next to me.

"Owens. You played for Tech," the girl closest to me says. Her hair is jet black, long, and pulled into a ponytail. She looks strong—fast, too. And she's the only one of the three who doesn't look like she resents me being here.

"I did," I say, my guard still up, albeit a little less.

"Right. My cousin's Tab Snyder. I thought I recognized you," she says. Tabitha Snyder was our goalie in high school—she ended up playing for UCLA, where I would have played if I stayed on the path I was on before my diagnosis.

"How is Tab?" I ask, excited to be starting a conversation with one of the girls. There's almost a sense of relief, but it's quickly extinguished when she doesn't answer my question, and instead pretends not to have heard me at all. She tosses her paper cup into the trash and eyes me one last time over her shoulder while she slithers back up with her friends.

The whistle could not have come at a more perfect moment.

I was done.

Life is a series of choices. My mom is always talking about free will, and how we are like marbles, rolling around through life, our paths constantly shifting based on whatever choices we make. Funny, though—no matter how many times I choose to leave my old life behind, it still manages to find me.

I shouldn't be listening. I should just walk out of the locker room, slamming the door behind me to let them know how close they were to getting caught. But my weaker side forces me to hold my breath, not to zip my bag closed completely, and to lift my feet from the bench and make myself small so I can capture every single cruel word coming from their lips.

"I heard she slept with her coach," one of the girls says, her whisper not really much of a whisper at all.

"No, it wasn't her coach," another girl says. It sounds like the girl I spoke to, Tabitha's cousin. "It was a teacher. She's a total homewrecker. The guy was married."

"Oh my god, do you think that's why she's out here now? Would coach really put her on the team just because she slept with him?" the first girl says.

"Probably. I mean, Coach P. is lonely," Tabitha's cousin says, and the sound of her locker shutting follows, blended with arrogance and laughter.

My vision is clouding, but it isn't from the MS—it's from the sting of tears I'm fighting desperately to keep from falling. It's been months since I've heard the whispers. My father made sure that the whispering back home stopped. It's amazing what a well-written letter from one of California's top law firms can do to gossip. But that letter seems only to have power back home— there are new rules here.

"What a bitch! I mean who does that, sleeps with someone's husband? That's low. She must have no self-respect," the voice says.

Of everything said, this is the one statement that hits the hardest. Yes, there are times when I have had no self-respect. But I have a shitload now. And if you're going to shame me, sum me up with a few rumored whispers swapped in a steamy locker room, then you might as well get the chance to say it to my face.

I zip my bag and stand on the bench on the other side of the lockers, making enough noise to make the other girls nervous. They can see the top of my head as I walk along the bench. I jump from the seat with enough force to cause my shoes to slap the concrete hard, the sound echoing. By the time I round the corner to face them, my chest is full of swagger.

"Oh, *hi*, ladies. I didn't know you were still here," I say, my smile caught somewhere between the words *fuck off* and *bitches*. "Since you are, I thought I'd take this time to maybe clear a few things up."

Their eyes are wide and their hands are limp at their sides—even the beautiful, confident one who started all this in the first place. This vision is priceless, and it makes the pulsating sick feeling in my stomach completely worth it.

"Yes," I say, my lips falling into a comfortable smile, my mouth closed tightly while I wait for one of them to take my bait. The skinny blonde on the end does me the favor.

"Yes, what?" she says, flipping her hair over her shoulder while her eyes roam up and down my body as if she can size me up—everything about me—with this one look.

"Yes, I slept with my coach in high school. And *yes*, I slept with my teacher. Slept with the principal at our school, too. I get around—collect other girls' husbands and boyfriends. I don't know why they always fall for me..." I keep up the false, flippant voice as I talk. "Maybe their women just can't keep them satisfied. I'm so good that after a man sleeps with me, he gives me anything I want. You like being first team?"

When I say this, I turn my head to the girl with jet-black hair, because she's the one I want to hurt the most.

"What? No response for me? Are you afraid I'll spread my legs and fuck my way into your position? I mean, why wouldn't I, right? It's what I do. I don't earn anything myself. Those sprint times that are better than yours, my California scoring records, the goddamned trophy I hoisted up on my shoulders when our team won state—all lies. It's really about the blowjobs I give behind closed doors—to recruiters, to whomever I need to, so I can get ahead. Because, yeah...that makes *way* more sense than the idea that maybe I'm just really fucking good, and maybe I could help your team win nationals, and maybe...just maybe...my skills are threatening to you," I snap my head to the third girl, sitting in the back, her breath held this entire time. "Or you." I revel a little inside when she makes a chirping noise, scooting back in fear. She's afraid of me. Good.

"I underestimated you girls. You're too smart for me. Guess I'll just have to earn my way into the captain's job by showing your asses up out on the field instead of fucking some fifty-year-old married man off campus. Damn, this way is going to be so much harder. Why'd you have to ruin my plan?"

I have left them speechless, each of their mouths opened, but unable to breathe. A year ago, I would have waited for them to leave, would have run home and cried in my closet, my whimpers muffled by my giant teddy bear, and then I would have fixed it all by putting out to some boy who didn't love me, but who I could pretend did—at least for the night.

That was the old Cass. This Cass? She loves herself, or at least she's working on it. She is more than her MS. And she has a boyfriend—who isn't married, and isn't her teacher, or just using her for a few hours and bragging rights.

And these bitches have just lost their starting positions on the team, because tomorrow I am going to humiliate them on that field. I don't care if it kills me.

I slide away from them in my socks and sandals, my gear slung in my bag over my shoulder. I pop my gum once because my hands are both too full to give them the finger.

"See you ladies tomorrow. Hope you're ready for me." I bite down once and force a final smile before I turn and let the door slam behind me.

My chest is thumping wildly with adrenaline. This is the first time...perhaps ever...that I have stood my ground, stuck up for myself, squashed rumors before they got out of control. I feel like I could run a hundred more sprints, or climb a mountain. By the time I get to Ty, who is still waiting for me at the front of the field gate, I leap onto his lap and kiss him—completely forgetting all of the doubt that's been keeping me awake the last two nights.

I'm amazing, and Ty is lucky to have me. And for a few moments, I honestly believe that's true.

Chapter 16

Ty

"You're pushing things kinda close, don't you think?" I ask, watching her shove everything into one bag—her physics notes, her book for the exam, her cleats. I'm fighting every OCD bone in my body not to grab the bag from her and at least fold some of the crap she's stuffed in there. "Awe, woman! You're wrinkling your shorts." I lose the fight and take the bag into my lap, doing my best to organize it.

"I know it's going to be close, but I don't really have a choice," she says, tapping her foot while I do my best to organize this mess she's thrown together. "I failed my test. I mean, like...blew it! This is my only chance to get a retake...just give it to me."

She zips the bag shut, and hooks the straps over one shoulder.

"Okay, but just make sure you leave in time to get to the field for warm-ups," I remind her. Why am I always the nag? Nagging Nate, nagging Cass—huh...I'm Mom.

"Yes, coach," she teases, kissing my cheek as she walks by. "Oh, hey...can I borrow your watch so I can keep track of the time during my test?"

"Oh, uh...can't you borrow Rowe's or something? Mine's so big and heavy," I lie. That makes two, though this isn't really a lie, it's more of an omission. My watch is heavy, but that has nothing to do with my diversion tactic.

"Rowe went home for the weekend. Which means *I'm alone,*" she says, eyebrows waggling. I'm won over by her adorableness, and suddenly I slide the watch from my wrist and hand it to her, somehow keeping myself from clinging to the other end of the band. I watch her slip it over her hand, watch her clasp it shut, and when she looks back at me, I force myself to only look at her face—not at the black and silver time piece that has my soul locked inside.

"I'll see you at the field, right? Nate coming?" she asks as she walks out the door, my eyes still splitting time between her lips and my watch.

"No, he has a tournament," I say, and she freezes at the door, her lip curling on one side.

"You're missing his game," she says. And she's right. I told my brother I had to help Cass with something important, and he understands. There will be thousands of games in his future. But she only has this one shot. He didn't ask what it was, but he smiled and just told me he'd be fine without me harassing him for one game. I shrug and smile at her, pretending it's no big deal. But it is—I don't miss Nate's games—even showed up with pneumonia once. But it seems something finally trumped my brother in the hierarchy of my attention.

She holds her hand over her heart and blows me a kiss when she leaves, and I can't help myself...I stare at the watch when she does. That stupid watch—I hate how attached I am to it. But it's like the glowing pod that lives in the center of Iron Man's chest, and now that it's gone, I feel a little weaker.

I shut her door for her, locking it from the inside when I leave. I make my way to my room to finish some reading before heading to her match.

I'm early. I know I'm early, but she should still be here by now. I told her she was cutting it close with the physics test. Who makes the only retakes available on a Saturday?

Most of the team is here, and coach motions to me across the field, pointing to his watch and shrugging. I wave him off, mouthing, "She's on her way."

Shit, she better be on her way!

I pull the phone from my pocket to my lap because I don't want him thinking I'm searching for her. But fuck, Cass! Where are you?

Are you almost here?

Long seconds tick by slowly, or at least, I think they do...I wouldn't know because Cass has my fucking watch! The more

140

time that passes, the more my chest constricts, like I can't breathe. I hate being late, and even though *I'm* here, Cass being late feels like an extension of me.

I'm watching the phone screen, waiting for any sign that's she's typing, sending me a message. Then I hear a whistle, one of those two-fingered kinds used to call a dog. I look up and see the coach waving his hand in the opposite direction, and Cass is sprinting to the field.

And the breath I've been holding exhales all at once. I'm actually sweating. And she hasn't even entered the game yet.

My eyes zero in on her for the first part of warm-ups. I keep trying to offer her a signal, something to let her know that I'm here, I'm with her—watching. She's got this. You've got this, Cass.

But she won't look up. She's locked in to her own zone, and that's okay. She looks great in warm-ups, not that I know a whole hell of a lot about soccer. But she looks just as good as the other girls out there—girls who have been training with the team, not just some two-bit college trainer in a wheelchair. In a way, it gives me a thrill that I've made her stronger. But I don't think I really did much; I think maybe she was just stronger than everybody else all along.

She looks incredible in her soccer shorts. I sketch a mental picture of the high socks pulled up over her knee. That's a look I'm going to have to beg her to replicate.

Coach subs her in pretty quickly. I can tell it pisses off the girl he subbed out. Good. She should be pissed. Cass is better, and that chick is going to lose her spot. Cass is faster than everyone out there. Her legs work the ball better. She anticipates, and then she capitalizes on her opponent's errors. By the time the first half is done, she has one goal to her name, and plenty of attempts.

I try to get her attention again when they jog by, but she's not looking my way. It's okay—I don't want to be a distraction. I do manage to catch coach, and I nod as he walks by, hoping he says something to give me an indication, something I can pass on to Cass.

"Looking good, Preeter. That girl? She might just save our season," he says.

"Well, what can I say, I know how to scout," I say back, making him laugh as he turns away. I can raise my hand to take the credit until I'm blue in the face. But all of *that*? The forty-five minutes of feet pounding turf that I just witnessed? That's one hundred percent Cass and her drive. I can see she wants this, not just for me. And that feels damn good. I'll take credit for waving the dream back in front of her, but she earns the right to have always wanted it in the first place.

Cass

Nothing is wrong. I'm fine. Everything is fine. Nothing hurts; my body feels good. I'm hydrating, and there's nothing wrong. I lie here on the bench, an ice pack on the back of my neck, my eyes closed to gather my thoughts, the sounds of the other girls and lockers and chatter all melding together into one obnoxious cacophony around me. I've been playing the words over and over in my head, because if I don't, if I let up the mantra for just one second, I know I'm going to cry.

And once I start, I'm not sure I'll stop.

For once, it's not my body that is caging me. My limitations, the ones I'm battling through today, are in my head. The ugly inside me right now is new. And I don't deserve to have to have it there. I didn't ask for it. I didn't want it. I didn't go looking for it. But it found me anyway. I can't deny that the last few hours have scarred me...again.

I shouldn't have stayed. I should have just taken the *F*. But I can't let my grades slip. That's a deal-breaker for my parents. And just one *F*—risks it all.

Maybe I should have risked it? No...don't let those thoughts in. Don't think about it. Just think about the goal, your game—your mission. Your body is fine. Everything is fine. Your legs feel strong. You are winning.

Win. Win. Win!

I was the only one in the room. I knew that was wrong; it's always wrong. But I slid into the small desk. I let him hand me the stapled packet for the retest. I wrote my answers, scribbling quickly, my mind too busy searching for answers and reeling from the excitement of finding them and knowing they were right. I didn't notice how close he'd gotten. I didn't see it coming.

And then his hand was on my thigh.

No. My body is strong—just forty-five more minutes of running. I want this. I can do this.

I jerked my leg quickly, startled, almost as I would be if a spider landed on me. A spider—*this was so incredibly far from a spider.* I would have gladly accepted venom instead. I can still hear it all in my head, his voice battling for dominance with my own. Every second, I fight to keep myself on top, to remain in control.

"Oh, I'm sorry Cassidy. I just wanted to check your work, make sure you were *getting* it this time," he said. So condescending. His breath hot, the stench of stale coffee nauseatingly pungent.

I pretended it was nothing. I played along with the misunderstanding. I told him I felt pretty good this time, that I was sure my answers were right.

And then his hand slid back in place, his chair behind me pushed up against my own. His legs on either side of me, his fingers roaming up...slowly—he wasn't going to stop. He. Was. Not. Going. To. Stop.

A single tear falls down my cheek. I catch it quickly, feeling it fast, and rubbing it away with the back of my hand. I open my eyes and am relieved that I am in a corner...alone. Coach has come in. I missed his entrance. I was lost for a few minutes, but I'm here now.

He's drawing things on the whiteboard, and I nod when he speaks my name. But I'm not hearing any of it. It doesn't matter—I will know what I'm doing on the field, whether I hear his plays or not. It's a friendly—a match up with an OSU club team. Nothing counts here. Except *everything* counts for me, if I want to erase it all—get back on my map. I need to perform here. Forty-five more minutes. I can do this. My body feels strong.

I can shut this out just long enough. I can do it, because I deserve it. And he doesn't get to take that away from me. When it's all over, I'll call my dad, and figure out what I'm going to do about breaking a faculty member's nose.

The game stays on course. My mind stays sharp. The walls stay in place. And his voice—Mr. Cotterman's, *Paul Cotterman's*—it disappears long enough for me to do what I need to do.

I've learned *her* name—the girl with the jet-black hair. It's Chandra. She's good, as good as I assumed she would be. We've been playing opposite most of the game, and we work well together. The only flaw being that I'm pretty sure we share a mutual hatred for each other.

She hates me, because I'm better than her—a disruption to her comfort. I hate her...because she's a bitch.

She knocked my water over when I set it on the table to adjust my shin guards. And she pushed her sharp cleats into the top of my foot a few times, just convenient enough to make it look accidental. But it's not. I can tell. I can tell, because I would have played it the same way if I were strong enough to follow through with such a move. I'm getting there—strong enough? I was well on my way before this morning. But I've had a setback. Today, I'm only strong enough to get through a short soccer match.

I want my shower. I don't want to stay and bond with the girls. I just want to go home and bury myself, hide. And I want to call my father. But coach has other plans. And Ty is waiting for me. And I want to go back to the space in my head when I was flirting with ways to tell him I loved him. But now I just want to be alone. I'm afraid if he touches me, I'll recoil—for entirely wrong reasons. And I don't want to explain them.

I don't want him to look at me and see anything other than the beautiful girl in his drawing.

"You looked at home out there," Coach P. says. "I would never guess that you have MS."

Shit. He knows. Of course, he knows. I bet that's why he gave me this chance in the first place. I bet that's how Ty sold me trying out. Everything feels cheap now, like a gift I didn't earn.

"Yeah, well, you can't really *see* MS," I say, and I know I sound snarky. I can tell because Ty is here now, and he's making wide eyes at me from behind coach. *Tone it down,* he's saying with that face. Oh Ty, you have no idea how close Bruce Banner is to turning into the Hulk right before your eyes.

"I know. I didn't mean...I...sorry, that was insensitive," Coach says. "I just meant you look like you're in top condition, like you haven't taken any time off at all."

"Yeah, well...that's not what you *said*," I say back, and hearing myself, I wake up a little from my trance. I might be overreacting. I need to breathe and remember where I am, what I want. And then take it. "Sorry," I apologize quickly, but he shakes his head *no* and just pats me once on the shoulder, his touch heavy and sharp and as hot as fire. I shudder uncontrollably, but I cover it up fast.

"Bruise. I took a mean collision," I lie. He buys it, nodding and crossing his arms while he looks down at his feet.

"There's some paperwork involved. We'll need to get some additional records. And real workouts don't start until December. But I'd like to have you on the squad, Owens. Honestly...you'd be doing *me* a favor," he says, and I let myself enjoy every word. He's being genuine. And I was good. No...I was *great!*

"I'd like that," I say, allowing myself this little break. I shake his hand and catch Ty's smile behind him.

"Good. Well, we'll see you next week. We work out on Wednesdays and weekends," he says, patting me once more, but this time lightly, as he passes. The light touch—it's actually worse. But I hold my breath and leave my smile in place, my teeth meanwhile grinding against one another at the memory of Cotterman's hand, and how far up my leg it traveled before I stopped it. *One hand* had erased months of progress.

I'm still that girl—the dirty one. Just like the girls in the locker room said. And that's all anyone's ever going to see.

Chapter 17

Ty

"You were awesome. Seriously. I had no idea." I've been gushing for the last hour. I praised her during the entire walk home. I waited in her room, waited while she showered, waited while she changed outfits several times—even though every time it was just a different long-sleeved shirt with jeans. I was the only one talking, just my mouth running off words about how goddamned good she was. It's kind of starting to piss me off.

She smiles. Says *thanks*. But her reactions are that of a beaten puppy. I can't tell what the hell is wrong. I haven't talked to Kelly for a week, since our phone call. And I know I've been a little absent with Cass. I'm there, but I can't help but let my head drift to Kel and Jackson, alone, while Jared is off somewhere...getting high. That pisses me off, to the point of punching things.

Everything in my path lately...pissing me off!

Today, I've been all Cass's. I've been with her every moment. When I asked her if something was wrong—or if someone made her upset—she just said her body was tired. And maybe that's it—but I kind of don't think that's it.

"You almost ready? We should get to Sally's before it gets busy," I say, knowing that we're already going to have to wait an hour just to find a seat. I'm hungry. And *that* pisses me off, too.

"I'll pack you a snack," she says, almost a joke. I think that was a joke. Was that a joke? It wasn't funny. And she's not looking at me, smiling, laughing. I don't think that was a joke.

"Okay," I say, challenging her. She tosses me a granola bar, and I catch it and stare at her while she busies herself with her purse, her hair, her shoes. She won't make eye contact, and it's killing me. PISSING ME OFF!

I follow her to the door, and just before she opens it, I reach for her back pocket and tug, trying to get her close to me. Maybe also trying to add a little of her calming serum to my boiling blood.

146

"Ty, don't," she says, shrugging me off.

"Right. Got it. Wouldn't *dream* of touching you, princess," I say under my breath, moving by her to the elevator so I can be alone with her in an even more confined space. Yeah, tonight should be fun.

I'm careful to keep the conversation on her game, on her training, and her plans now that she's been offered the spot. She seems willing to talk about this stuff. But her answers are still clipped.

We get to Sally's, and the wait is an hour. Surprise.

"Why are you so cranky?" she asks. Seriously? She initiates a conversation for the first time all night...and *this*? She asks me why *I'm* cranky? Pokes the fucking starved-ass bear?

"I was hungry...an hour ago," I say, every acid-laced word that comes out of my mouth making me feel bad. Why are we fighting? Why can't I stop? Why won't she stop?

"I gave you a snack," she says, standing from the wooden bench she's been sitting on for the last ten minutes while we wait. "I have to go to the bathroom."

I don't say a word when she leaves. I do my best to smile, my inner voice coaching me not to make things worse. Maybe this can be a reset button—when Cass comes back, we'll just start over. Begin at *normal*.

She's gone for almost ten minutes, at least, that's how long I'm guessing she's been gone, because I realize that she still has my watch. Which, of course, pisses me off. I make sure it's the first thing I ask when she returns.

"Hey, where's my watch?" I probably could have said that better. I'd feel guilty, but she's suddenly frozen, as in not breathing. Her eyes widen—it's the slightest difference, but I see it. I'm a great poker player, and I look for these things when I'm reading someone. Cass just showed her cards, and she doesn't even know it.

"My...watch?" I ask again, eyebrow cocked. Her eyes fade now, her mouth dropping into an even line. She looks sick.

"Ty, I..." she starts, looking into her lap where her hands are tugging at the edges of her sleeves, pulling the fabric over her wrists, her wrists where *normally* my *watch* should be.

147

"You have my watch, don't you? Cass, this isn't funny. Tell me you have my watch," I demand. She doesn't' have it. I know she doesn't. I knew it the moment her breath stopped.

"Are you *fucking* kidding me?" It's a rhetorical question, so I don't bother to hold her eye contact to wait for her answer. My hands are in my hair, my hat tossed on my lap while I try to imagine how I'm going to be whole again.

Somewhere...somewhere *deep* inside...there is still a faint voice that is telling me it's just a watch. That voice is trying to be heard, trying to tell me that this isn't Cass's fault, accidents happen, it's okay...and I might love this girl. Don't fuck it up over a watch.

I step on that voice. Then I kick it in the groin, and shove it in an alley.

"Did you lose it? I mean...do you at least know where the fuck it is?" I ask. I'm lost to the asshole now. There's no coming back out of this gracefully.

"Ty... please. Don't talk to me like that," she says, and for a small second or two, my voice, the *good* voice, pipes in telling me she's right. I kick it again.

"Cass," I take a deep breath, bringing my voice down to a calm tone because that's really the least I could do. I don't need to make this a show for everyone else. I lean forward to her, my hands folded together while my elbows rest on my knees, my wrist bare. "When you give someone something...let them *borrow* something...say something that might have a certain sentimental value to it—you kind of make this verbal contract. Do you follow me?"

"Ty, I'm sorry. I left it in the classroom. I'm sure it's there. I'll get it," she's talking, but I'm not hearing. All of my senses are closed off. The asshole has moved in, and he ain't budging.

"Go on. Go get it," I say, like there's any chance that could really happen. Fuck, why can't I stop this?

"Ty, you know I can't right now. I'll go, first thing Monday morning. I'll get up early," she looks flustered. Shit. I did this.

"Fine," I say, sulking back into my chair. I watch her open her mouth to talk at least six times, each time lying back in her seat, unable to let the words out. I've stunned her, and I'm such an asshole that I'm proud of it. And then it comes crashing down all at once. I'm blinded by cold hands with manicured nails and a voice behind me hell-bent on ruining any hope I might be clinging to.

"Guess who?" she asks, her voice raspy, drunk. Why do girls do that, ambush you from behind and play this game, knowing the high probability that you're going to guess wrong, and leave everyone feeling stupid?

"No idea," I huff, and as her hands slide away from my face, I get a good look at Cass. She. Is. Livid. A girl with long brown hair slides into my lap. She's dressed like one of the waitresses, and I recognize her. But fuck if I can remember her name.

"Hey, you," she says. "I just got off. You wanna take me home?"

Oh wow. This is really happening.

"Hi, yeah. So...I'm on a date. With my girlfriend," I say, doing my best to encourage her to get off of me. She slides awkwardly down my leg, her stupor causing her to slip and fall on her ass, her skirt sliding up enough to show off her thong, and everything around it.

Cass looks disgusted. She should be. I'm disgusted. I'm disgusted at myself. But I still want my watch. And I can't bring myself to forgive her for leaving it behind...carelessly.

"You know what? It's fine. He *can* take you home. Because it turns out I'm *not* his girlfriend," she says, standing and dropping a ten dollar bill on the small table in front of me to pay for her drink. I blink again, and she's gone.

"Excuse me," I say, pushing through this mystery girl's gaggle of drunken groupies.

I find Cass quickly. She's not even trying to run. She's walking fast, but more angry than running away.

"Hey! What the hell?" I yell, and she halts fast, spinning on her heels and closing the gap between us, her arms crossed in front of her body to fight off the night chill.

"Go on," she says, waving her hand to direct me back inside. I get it; she's imitating me, and how I told her to go get the watch. It's almost funny. But it's not.

"Cass, you're being unfair," I say, and she laughs. Hard.

"Oh really? I'm new at this, Ty. Explain to me, how does a girlfriend usually react when some hooker practically lap dances her boyfriend in front of her?" she asks.

"She's not a hooker," I say, rolling my eyes. I mean, please— I have standards. Cass is leaning on her hip, her lips pursed. Clearly, she doesn't think I have standards. "Before I met you, I dated. You know this."

"Yeah, *boy* do I know this," she says, throwing my past in my face. I don't like apologizing, and I won't apologize for things I can't change.

"Hey, you're throwing a lot of stones for a girl who could live in a glass house for all I know," I say back, my gut sinking again at the thought of my lost watch. I can't let go of it.

"What does that even mean?" she says, tossing her head to the side and yelling to the sky, her hands stretched out to her sides.

"It *means* that I've had a past. But for all I know, you've had one too. I mean, are you going to tell me that you've always been a sheltered little princess? That you're that good in bed just because? That you maybe haven't slept with a few guys who have taught you a thing or two so I can reap the rewards?" I'm getting nasty, pushing where I shouldn't push. I can tell I've pushed too far when her hand flies at my face—my head cracks to the side on impact from her slap. My cheek stings, and the cold air only makes it hurt more.

I like the hurt.

"You asshole," she seethes. "You can go fuck yourself! And go buy a new fucking watch, too! That one was ugly."

I hold my tongue as she walks away, but before she gets too far, I throw one more nail in our coffin. "Yeah, maybe we should take a break. I think we were getting too serious," I mutter, just loudly enough for her to hear. Like I even need to say this. I watch her walk away and hold two middle fingers over her head, like pistols shooting me through the heart.

I'm not sure when I started to cry, but it happens. Nothing over the top—there's no sobbing, no sniffles. I'm in the dark of night, and no one will ever know I've even done it. But I do. Three whole tears slide down my cheek, and I let them fall into the collar of my shirt before I swipe my sleeve across my eyes and chin.

"Goddamn it!" I say, loud enough that the girls who have just stumbled out of the bar look my way. "Yeah, yeah. Dude in wheelchair talking to himself. Mind your own goddamn business!"

It's just a watch. And I can *live* without it. I know I don't think I can. But I can. I'm not so sure I can live without Cass, though. Fuck, fuck, fuck, fuck, fuck! I've messed up. I know I've messed up. It was like a fire I lit over the desert, and every piece of brush in its wake went up in flames. All I'm left with is smoke. And it's suffocating me.

I pull my phone from my pocket and text my brother, because he's the only one who won't judge me too harshly. He'll judge, but it will come with sympathy. When he texts back, I tell him to meet me at the bar. I head inside and order a round of beer and shots, then don't bother waiting for him to show up before I down his drinks and mine.

I'll forget the watch tonight. I'll forget Cass too. And tomorrow, I'll suffer.

Chapter 18

Cass

The hand of Nick Owens is fast and swift. My father's law firm can handle most things just by flashing its name. He told me Paul Cotterman had turned in his resignation after his phone call. Just as he always does, my father makes my problems go away.

I thanked him. And of course, he told me I didn't need to thank him. What stung is that I don't think he actually believed me. I think he thinks that maybe, just *maybe,* I was acting inappropriately, and that I let things get out of hand. Just like last time. But he still made it disappear, because he loves me.

He loves me. He just doesn't believe me.

Rowe is still out of town. Paige is completely moved out, thanks to Nate's help. And I'm alone. For the first time ever, I'm completely alone. I used to wish for this. I think maybe all twins do. What I realize, though, is maybe I was confusing my craving for individuality with my desire to be alone. Individuality is liberating. Alone leads to one thing—loneliness.

I don't know what happened, other than the fact that my incident with Paul Cotterman left me crooked...feeling dirty. And I just couldn't shake playing the part.

Sabotage is a funny thing; self-sabotage even funnier. Ty and I—we were both at work—sabotaging left and right until there was nothing left but shreds and a shadow of our dignity.

For an hour, I've been staring at the picture he drew; the sad melancholy of The National is playing on random shuffle on my iPod. Even their "pop" songs are sad. The drawing is beautiful, done by his hands, days ago.

"That's how I see you," he said.

Not anymore.

I don't know how the ugliness showed itself—how he saw my history without me ever telling him. But when he put it out there, so bluntly? Promiscuity comes at a high price when you're a teenager, and it just keeps taking.

I got his watch. I had to. I don't hate him. I *far* from hate him. Now that I have it, I understand why it's so important. Or at least, I have a clue.

ALWAYS—that's all it says in simple engraving on the back. The letters are a little worn, but you can still read the words. Someone gave this to him, someone who meant that word to him.

Maybe they still do.

I run my finger along the small indents of the word, my mind imagining that I have the power to erase it. I could take a razor blade, scratch the lettering away from the metal right here, right now. But I would never be able to take away its power and everything it means. I know this without even asking.

My phone buzzes, and I jump, simply excited that someone from *out there* is contacting me. It's Rowe.

Hey, we're throwing a late-night party for Paige. Her idea, actually. She wants to thank Nate for his help with the move. Free drinks! I'll wait for you to finish your workout. We can go together. Miss you!

Rowe misses me. While the fact that she's enthusiastic about a party with my sister is, well, weird, I'm desperate for my friend to come home. I need someone, even if I can't tell her the entire story. That's another layer of Nick Owens's agreements—they are sealed. No talking about what happened if we want to keep things nice and tidy.

I'm in. I could use a drink.

Or five. Or six.

I tuck Ty's watch in my sock drawer and change for the gym, not really feeling the energy tonight. My body is tired from pushing so hard yesterday. And I should heed the warning and rest. But I have two hours until Rowe gets home. Idle time isn't doing me any favors.

Hoping that will ignite my fire, I run most of the way to the gym, searching for that inner competitor that takes over when I exercise and helps me forget everything else. But my inner soldier is tired, too. I end up walking the last four hundred yards. I head right to the locker room, swap out my clothes for my swimsuit, and spend the next hour in the pool.

I *really* wanted to be in the spa. But heat isn't great for MS, and hot baths always make my vision blurry. So even though this water is cold, I opt for it, and it still soothes my muscles. I don't even swim; I just float. I'm surrounded by a bunch of older students, maybe faculty members, who are swaying and swishing their way through water aerobics. Bizarrely, I feel right at home—the thump of the bass from the small boom box near the pool's edge pulsating in the water. It's all I hear—*boom, boom, boom, boom.*

Rowe is waiting for me when I get back to our room, and I actually run to her, hugging her so tightly that it makes her choke a little.

"Sorry. I think I missed you," I smile.

"I'm glad," she says, her smile reflecting mine. "Go ahead and shower. We'll walk over together."

I want to ask her if *he's* going to be there. I want to be prepared. But I don't ask, because at this very second, I'm happy and looking forward to something. Might as well not ruin it until I have to.

I speed through my shower. My stomach is twitching with the fast beats of my heart, my nerves tangling with my exhaustion. I slip on a pair of black leggings and a giant sweatshirt, just warm enough to keep me comfortable, and I blow my hair nearly dry.

"Okay, I'm set," I say, grabbing my wallet and keys and stuffing them inside the front pouch of my sweatshirt.

"You have to be the world-record holder for primping," Rowe says, reaching for the elevator button while we wait in the hall. "Paige would have needed an hour."

"Paige would have needed twenty-four hours notice," I laugh. There's some truth to that statement, though. "I'm lazy. I don't want to spend time on things I'm not good at."

I don't know why my words make me frown, but they do. Rowe reaches for my hand and gives it a squeeze. I lay my head

154

on her shoulder for the elevator ride. "Thanks for the invite. I think I need to get out tonight," I say, and I feel her tense under my touch. I know what that means, but I'm still not ready to pop my bubble of happiness.

"So, I'm thinking of joining the soccer team," I throw out there as we step off the elevator. I can't talk to my parents about this, and now that Ty's gone, I'm not so sure I have the guts to follow through with it any longer. As desperate as it seems, I think one little boost from Rowe might keep my dream afloat.

"You play soccer?" she asks, her feet stutter-stepping with her surprise. "I mean, I knew you were in great shape and all. I just didn't know you did anything like that? Are you...I don't know...good?"

I smile at her question, and I reach around her arm and link us together, giving her a squeeze as I pick up our step. "Yeah," I say, no longer doubting my dream. "I'm good."

Ty

Free rum and Coke. I've had to pay for all of my therapy drinking the last two days, so when Nate offered to take care of tonight's "medicine," I was all over it. Plus, the two hot chicks Paige brought to tag along were a pretty welcome distraction.

Paige hasn't hit me yet. I was, frankly, expecting to find her at my door bright and early this morning. My only guess is that Cass has kept our blowout a secret. Nate said that Rowe knew about it, because he told her. Of course, I'm the bad guy in this. At least, according to Rowe I am.

I probably *am* the bad guy in this. But I'll be damned if I was the *only* one being an irrational asshat in that fight.

I'm not even surprised when I see her walking up with Rowe. I think I knew this was an ambush all along. But now, I'm four drinks in, and I feel rowdy. I've been flirting with easy girls who don't want attachments, don't require work, and don't fuck with my heart and my head.

But the closer she gets, the more she comes into focus. She's beautiful.

"Oh fuck no!" I shout. Yeah, so maybe I'm a little drunk.

Rowe scolds me fast, putting me in my place. It makes me smirk. I like that girl. She's good for my brother. I wave her off and turn my attention back to Paige and her two girlfriends—mostly because they have the bottle of liquor.

"Fill 'er up," I say, holding my cup out for Paige. She holds her hand over the bottle and stares at me with a sharp look. I know I'm about to get the hammer I've been waiting for.

"You better fix whatever *that* is," she says, pointing to her sister with a swirling finger. "She hasn't said a word to me, but Rowe says you two had a fight. So help me god, if I find out you did anything that warrants me cutting your dick off, don't think I won't."

Here's the thing: when chicks make threats like that, it instantly incites a chemical reaction in the brain of a dude, and we imagine whatever it is they said, and then we feel it. However juvenile it might seem, however unlikely it is that Paige will *actually* cut my dick off—I just felt it happening. And that's enough of a threat for me.

Effective. That shit's highly effective.

"Your sister lost my watch," I say, somehow thinking in my state that Paige will have some clue what this means and cut me some slack. I'm sure my words must sound like gibberish though, because she just bunches her nose at me and shakes her head.

"So go get a new one," she says with her signature eye-roll. She was made to do that. It makes me chuckle, and I tip my cup back and feel the burn of straight rum, my chest and arms tingling with the warmth. Yeah, I should cut myself off now.

Cass stays close to Rowe, and Nate keeps giving me the look—*the* look. I told him everything, and he told me I was being an idiot. He's probably right. And I'm blowing this chance, too, blowing *right* through it with one more rum and Coke. Mmmmmmm.

There's giggling, and Paige's friends find me amusing. I focus on them, because they think I'm funny. Paige is a little drunk too. She must be—because *she* also finds me humorous. And she's no longer threatening to cut my junk. So that's good, right?

Cass isn't laughing. She's not having a good time. No, she's leaving. Wait...she's leaving? My cup is half full...or maybe it's half empty? How does that saying go...? I'm swishing the flat Coke around in circles in my cup—no more bubbles from carbonation, only the hot burn of rum. I could tip this back and forget everything, just stay here, see how the giggling plays out. Maybe wake up in the morning to Paige busting my door down and kicking me in the groin with one of her spikey heels.

But Cass is leaving. And she looks like she's going to cry. And...

I did that.

"I'm out of here, man. See ya later," I say to my brother, tossing the rest of my drink in the grass and pushing myself to the dirt where my wheels can move a little more easily.

She sees me coming, and she doesn't run. She's not running. My head is making everything look sideways, and I'm pretty sure my speech is going to sound like shit a green alien says, but she's not running. This is good.

"Hey," I say, moving up alongside her on the walkway. We're both traveling slowly, no rush—nowhere to go.

"Hey," she says, and she sounds broken. So damn broken.

"So," I start, but then my tongue suddenly feels fat. I'm fuzzy, my mind fuzzy. Everything, so...fuzzy. I'm aware enough to know that I won't be able to do this right, but I have to slide a rock in the door, keep it open, so I can fix this shit in the morning.

"Okay, so here's the deal," I say, doing my best to sound serious. Her arms are folded, her mouth is in a firm line, and her eyebrow is tilted up slightly in my direction. But she's still with me, and she's not giving me the finger. "I'm a little drunk."

"Statement of fact," she laughs. She laughed. Okay, at my expense, but also a good sign.

"Correct," I say, holding one finger up like I'm somehow accentuating her point. What am I, in a boardroom? "That is a fact. I am drunk. Another fact...I am sorry."

This stops her. Her face is still the same, and her arms are still guarding her body. But she's looking at me differently now. I hope I say the correct words, just enough to prop that door open until I can do this the right way.

"I'm sorry," I say it again, and this time, somehow by the grace of god, it comes out sober—sober and honest. "I am so unbelievably sorry. Sorry for what I said, how I reacted, for being a dick."

"Yes, you were a dick," she's quick to jump on that.

"I know, another statement of fact," I say with a smirk, once again holding up a finger. I look at my finger, and it makes me laugh, then I look back at her and she looks like I'm losing her. Pull it together, Tyson—slide the rock in the door. "I have a lot of groveling to do. And I'm in—I'm ready to do it. But if you could just give me the night, just...just wait for me to get my head on straight."

"Just let you go home, vomit, and then survive your hangover you mean?" she says, but there's a smirk. I see it. She's smirking.

"One," I say, holding the finger up again. I quickly put it down. "One, I don't vomit. I can hold my liquor, baby."

"Ohhhhh, definitely do not call me *baby*," she says.

"Right, okay, baby," I laugh, but she's not laughing, so I stop. "Right. No baby. I'm just saying wait with me, until the morning, so I can say everything that needs to be said in a way you deserve to hear it."

I'm not smiling anymore. No, I'm pretty sure I'm begging. Her arms are still crossed, but she nods to the dorm and I follow along, holding my breath until we get to her door and she opens it wide enough to let me inside.

She reaches under her bed and pulls a bin out with a big comforter and some extra sheets, tossing everything on the floor.

"Make yourself comfortable," she says. "And I don't have an extra pillow. And don't use Rowe's. I'd be pissed if she gave my pillow to Nate."

"Oh yeah...floor, so...I'll just be down here," I say, leaning forward and picking up the big comforter that suddenly looks very, very thin.

"Yep. You'll be down there. On the floor," she says, shutting the closet door behind her so she can change.

I've slept on the floor before. I've slept here lots of times. No big. And I'm pretty sure I'll be snoring in about two minutes, so I assemble my makeshift bed like a toddler camping out in his room for the night. Pulling myself from my chair to the floor, I tuck the excess pile of linens under my head. I'm awake enough that I hear the closet door creak open and see Cass's feet stop just short of her bed while she stares at me.

"Goodnight, baby," I say, unable to help myself.

"Don't call me *baby*," she says, and I smile and drift off to sleep, the door open and waiting for me in the morning.

Chapter 19

Cass

I've spent the last hour debating whether or not to wake him up. As drunk as he was last night, he was also incredibly sweet. I'm not sure what I'm going to get this morning.

I lay there and stared at the ceiling while he snored on my floor for hours. It was loud, but that's not what kept me from sleeping. It was the watch—and that word. *Always.*

This conversation is going to happen, and it's going to begin the second I wake him up. So, I might as well quit putting off the inevitable. I pick up the small circle pillow from my bed and toss it on his face.

"Morning sunshine," I say. His watch is tucked in my palm, behind my back, as I sit on the bed and stare down at him.

"Ohhhh wow, yeah," he grumbles, rubbing his hand harshly over his face and the stubble that is slowly morphing into an almost-beard. "So, I *might* actually be a little hung over," he says, stretching his mouth out and moving his tongue around like he's discovering new things about it. "Dry, so damn dry. Water?"

I leave his watch on my bed and roll my eyes as I stand. After I fill a cup with sink water, I hand it to him, and our fingers touch in the exchange. It still gets to me. He still gets to me. Our eyes lock, and I know no matter what he says this morning, I'm going to feel it.

"I got your watch," I say, reaching to the bed and tossing it on his chest. The thud it makes on impact is heavy, as it should be. "Told you I would get it."

He looks at it where it lies, his neck craned enough to view it, and his eyes don't blink for the longest time. The watch rises up and down with his slow, methodical breathing; his expression looks pained. Finally, he reaches for it with his hand and flips the band inside out, looking at the inscription, running his thumb over the word just like I did.

Then his eyes snap to mine. He's still holding the watch, his knuckles almost white, he's clutching it so hard, but his eyes are on me, a soft contrast from his straining fingers—as if he's trying to communicate a million things at once with that look. I see how sorry he is, but I also see so much more—something too overwhelming for him to translate.

"Kelly was my high school girlfriend," he starts, and I take a deep breath, sitting back down on the bed, my hands gripping the edge, but my eyes on his—I won't leave his eyes.

"Before we were boyfriend and girlfriend, we were best friends. I met her in kindergarten. I put glue in her hair in first grade, ate glue to impress her in third, beat up Michael Watson in fifth because he was her boyfriend, stepped on her toes in seventh at the junior high dance, and kissed her when we were freshmen."

Kelly was his girlfriend—his best friend. Kelly is the *Always*. I know it in my heart, and I'm broken immediately just knowing it.

"After my accident, I had to relearn how to do a lot of things in my life. I wasn't always the guy I am now—the guy who can figure out how to make the bench press work for him, and who can handcycle for ten miles. I didn't know how to lift myself up from the bed. I didn't know how I was going to get to the bathroom, or if I would ever be able to drive. I watched my mom pretend she wasn't crying when I wasn't looking. Watched my dad do the same. And Nate...he couldn't hide it, so I just watched him cry. That was the hardest part, because I didn't want to make it worse for anyone by crying for myself...for all I'd lost. I lost a lot of things, things like baseball, which, while I know that sounds so very unimportant and trivial, it's still a thing. It was *my* thing. And I had to let it go; I had to watch my brother take it over, love it, become it. I needed a new thing. And as much as my brother, my father, and even on some level my mom thought that I found other things to replace it quickly...I didn't. I found darkness. And Kelly's the only one I really told."

His story hits me with a weight of a thousand bricks. He's still lying on the ground in front of me, his watch slowly twisting between his fingers. He touches it with a fondness that I'm beginning to understand, with a fondness that scares me, because I don't know if I can compete with it.

"My physical rehab was brutal. I'm a lot like you, in that respect," he flashes his eyes from his watch to me, a small curve denting the corner of his lip. "I push myself too hard sometimes. I don't like hitting walls, don't like there to be things I can't find a way through or around. But I was finding those things everywhere I turned."

I slide from the bed to the floor, my back against my mattress, and my feet pushed in so I can fold my arms over my knees and lay my head to the side, truly listening to him.

"When Nate would visit, we'd play catch. If I missed a ball, he'd run and get it. Because it was faster that way, and I couldn't run and get it myself. He'd ask me to show him the weights in the therapy room, ask me to lift things, show him how strong I was getting. And I *was* getting stronger, but only on the outside. Inside...I was dying."

"Kelly would come every morning and night, on her way to and from school. She stayed longer into the evening than she should, and she failed biology our sophomore year because of it. But I couldn't get her to go; she wouldn't leave. She promised me she'd never leave, and I knew she meant it—she would stand by her promise. Then one night, I took advantage of her loyalty. I was so fucking depressed that I asked her to help me stop hurting."

The impact his words have on my chest is massive. They strike the air from my lungs with one pass and push the tears from my eyes the next. I let them fall in front of him. I let them slide down my cheeks, and chin, and neck, until they fall to the floor. I watch him struggle through this, swallowing hard, breathing deeply, closing his eyes until he opens them to rest on the watch again.

The watch. I get it. The watch.

"She refused, as I probably knew she would," he says, a painful smile coming and going. "And the next day, she didn't come. I thought that was it. I thought I had pushed her away because of how deep and dark and afraid and hurt I had become. And I was okay with that, because in a way, I liked the idea of not dragging her down with me—of her getting to go do all of those

162

things that we had planned, just with someone else. I was even okay with the someone else."

"And then the day after that, she showed up on her way to school, and she put a box on my lap while I was getting ready for my morning rehab. It was this old beat-up cardboard box that looked like it had been through a fire, but somehow the sides still remained intact and the lid still fit snuggly on top. I opened it and found this watch inside," he says, handing it back to me to take. I've seen it, memorized it in the twenty-four hours that I've had it in my possession, but out of respect, I take it from him anyway, turning the inscription over to say it aloud.

"Always," my voice is hoarse and beaten down.

"Kelly's mom bought this watch for Kel's dad after he was diagnosed with lung cancer. Her dad was a blue-collar man who worked hard, with his hands, his entire life. But the cancer left him weak, unable to breathe without a tank at his side and unable to provide for his family the only way he knew how. Kel's mom gave him this to remind him of the things that matter—to remind him that he doesn't have to carry everything on his own, and to remind him that he's loved—*always*. And that's why she gave it to me."

"You still love her. Why aren't you with her?" I ask, not in a jealous way, but in an earnest one. I am jealous, deeply so—full of envy for all of the things Kelly has from Ty that I don't. But his words have also opened my eyes to how deep his relationship is with this woman, this woman who I don't even know, who I envy, but cannot possibly hate because of what he's told me.

He laughs softly, a faint smile painted on his face as he pulls the watch over his hand and clasps it firmly to his wrist.

"Always," he says, looking at it. "Yes, Cass, I will love Kelly...always. But *this*," he turns his arm in front of me, flashing the silver band of the watch. "This was all so long ago. And my love for Kelly, it's different now. It's part of my past, and I honor it and am thankful for it. And for the last six years, I've had her friendship, and this watch. And I draw strength from that."

My head is down when he sits up fully. Soon, his hand is on my chin, tilting my face so I can look at him, into his eyes.

"It's just a watch. I know that now. I knew that then. And I'm sorry that I…I don't know what to call it, went *apeshit*? I'm sorry I went apeshit on you over a watch. And I'm sorry I was a grumpy asshole. And I'm sorry that you had to run into some girl from my past like that—and that I didn't go after you. I'm sorry I called you a tart for being a good lover—because damn, Cass, you are an amazingly passionate woman, and I am a spoiled man for having had the honor to have been with you in such an intimate way."

I blush from his attention, and as much as I'm still stuck on the watch and Kelly and everything it means to him, his words melt right through me, and I believe them as he says them. I lean into his hand, and I love the way he holds the weight of my worries.

"I had a great love, and then I had a great tragedy," he says. "That love, it put me right again, sent me on my way to where I am now. To you. And as far as I'm concerned, from now on, there is just you…and everything after."

There's nothing to say to this. His face, the way he's looking at me, his eyes moving back and forth between each of mine, his hands cradling my face, not letting go until he knows I am okay—it's not what I was expecting today. But it's what I wanted. What I needed.

"I'm really glad I waited for you to sober up," I smile. Ty shakes his head, laughing as he looks down, and then he brings my lips to his, kissing me softly and gently before pulling me to his chest to hold me close.

I touch the watch on his wrist, and he pulls it off and hands it to me to look at more closely. "Do you still talk to Kelly?" I ask.

"I do," he says, stopping short. I know there's more, and I wait, hoping he wants to share it. "I have a lot lately…and not because of anything with you. Kelly's having some trouble, it's been on my mind."

"You should help her," I say, handing the watch back.

"I will," he says, and again I fill the little sting of jealousy for how quickly he reacts for her. It's not a wanted emotion, but it's there nonetheless. I can't pretend it isn't.

"She'd like you," he says, and I don't know how I feel about that either, but I smile up at him, and wish for everything after.

Chapter 20

Ty

"Dude. How much did you drop on this tux?" My brother is taking his girlfriend to prom. Well, not *really* prom, but a fake prom date that he has all planned out—he got a limo and everything. Rowe was homeschooled, because she wasn't really keen on going back to her school after the shooting. Not sure I would be able to go back either.

"No comment," he says, fussing with his tie—untying, retying, untying.

"No comment? Uh, I'm pretty sure the lavender cummerbund is a comment. Or is that making a statement? I'm not sure—I think maybe both." I'm having fun with this. My brother looks like a Ken doll.

"Whatever, man. You wouldn't understand," he says, getting frustrated with the tie once again and moving to the mirror to obsess over it even more. I could help; I'm actually good at tying ties. But watching him struggle, for just a little bit longer? Yeah, I'm going to give myself this gift.

I've given Nate shit for days over this whole prom thing, but I actually think it's kind of cute. *Cute.* That's a word I've never used before when talking about Nate. Anyway, I've been giving him a ton of crap, but I'm borrowing his idea to use on Cass, of course, Tyson-ized.

My gym bag is stuffed with a bunch of lame CDs I got from the record exchange, some balloons, and a desktop disco ball from Target. The sentiment is there, and really—that's what my prom was, not that I stayed through much of it.

Nate's phone rings, and I watch him drop both ends of the tie with a defeatist attitude.

"Oh, good. You're downstairs then? No, that's fine. Just wait in the car. We'll be there soon," he says to someone on the other end. Curious, I head into the hall and the main study room to look at the parking lot below. Sure enough—fucker rented a limo. Damn, my brother might as well be a contestant on *The Bachelor* with this shit.

"Did you seriously get a limo?" I get ready for a new round of teasing as I come back into the room.

"I told you, I'm not messin' around. Prom is serious shit, and when you throw a prom, you do it right. Now come fix my damn tie," he says, holding both ends out for me. I take them because I don't want him to look like a sloppy loser, and while I'm tying, I can't help but snicker at the crappy dollar decorations and random things I've thrown together for my version of prom. Maybe it's just me, but I don't think you need a limo and suit to *do it right.* I'm pretty sure I can make tonight memorable all on my own—me and *Slow Dance Hits from the Eighties.*

"How are you my brother? I mean...seriously, I'm starting to think we need to give up on all the Barbie shit in our room, because you're making estrogen." I'm pissing him off, and I love it. It's like when we were kids and I used to make ghost shadows through his window with the flashlight to scare the crap out of him. I'm trying not to bust out laughing all together when I lift the leg of his pants—or dare I say, *trousers*—and check to see if he's shaved.

"Dude, don't touch my leg. What are you doing?" Nate yells kicking my hand away.

"Just checking to see if you've started shaving your legs. Your razors aren't pink, are they?" I can barely finish the sentence without laughing. It's that kind of laugh where I can't breathe now, and I'm turning red and coughing. When he gives me the finger, it only makes me laugh harder.

"No, jackass. And this is important, so cut the crap," he says, holding the loose ends of his tie again. He pulled it apart messing with it. Honestly, he should just wear a clip-on. That thought makes me chuckle.

"Important to whom? To Rowe? Because I was in that room an hour ago, and she was not a happy camper having Paige's hands all over her face and head," I tell him. Seeing Rowe get ready for tonight only made me like her more. She's not fussy. I like that.

I pick on him for a few more minutes, just long enough to finally get his tie to stay in place, and I send him off, blowing him a kiss and reminding him to be home by curfew.

"Shithead!" he yells as the door closes behind him.

I pull my duffel bag into my lap and look through my prom package again—and for a second, I feel bad that it's kind of pathetic. But Cass isn't Rowe, and I'm not really trying to create some full-blown experience. I'm just trying to be sweet and romantic, and I kind of suck at that, so I feel pretty good about this attempt. Maybe, though...maybe the workout clothes should change.

Most of my nice things go with jeans, and jeans take me a while, so I send Cass a quick text and tell her I'll be over in about twenty minutes. I wear the dark pullover shirt, gray and black stripes, because that's the one I wore the night of the party when I first talked to Cass—the night she slayed every dude in the room at that video game and drank me under the table. How the hell did she end up with me?

Finally satisfied that I look good, but not like I'm trying too hard, I lock up our room and make my way to Cass's. The door is open, so I knock lightly and move inside. Her back is to me, and she doesn't see me at first. Before I can warn her that I'm coming, she runs her arm along her face and eyes.

Shit! She's crying.

I freeze, then back pedal as quietly as I can, knocking at the door again, this time a little more loudly, and coughing on my entry just to be safe. She stands quickly, and she smiles. I know that move. I've fucking patented that move. And I can just tell her world isn't right. Her eyes are still puffy for Christ's sake. But she's pretending. Fronting—yeah, I've done fronting.

"Baby," I say, setting the bag down on her bed and moving closer so I can hug her waist and pull her close.

"Don't call me baby," she half giggles and half cries, pulling the end of her sleeve into her palm and wiping tears away before they have a chance to fall. She can't keep up the façade—it must be bad, whatever it is.

"Wanna tell me about it?" I want her to tell me about it, so when she says it's nothing at first, I'm actually sad. A girl is crying, and I want to help. I suck at this too, just like I suck at big romantic gestures—but I want to try.

"I'm good at listening," I say, stopping short of begging her to open up about whatever made her upset.

"My parents," she pauses, her lip slipping from its grip between her teeth and her breath heavy as she fights to stop her tears. "I'm sorry. I hate crying. It makes me mad. Makes me feel weak."

"You're not weak," I say, pulling her hand away from her face to kiss it. "I cry."

"You cry?" she asks.

"Well, no...not really...I mean, *hello*? Pathetic with a capital P!" She laughs, which was really my only goal.

"My parents...they don't think I should play. Don't think it's good for me," she says, and I can tell she's heartbroken.

"Did you tell them to fuck off?" I'm only half kidding, but I let her laugh and think I'm joking.

"No," she says. "I can't do that. My dad...he's *more* okay with it than my mom. And I can usually get my way if I win him over and get him on my side. But this time...my mom won."

"Does she have some dirt on your dad or something?" I tease, trying to lighten the mood because I can tell Cass is lost in these sad thoughts. She flashes a short smile at my joke, but it fades quickly.

"Something like that," she says, taking one more deep breath and slipping from my hold to stand in front of me. "Okay, enough of that. Enough of *them*. What's the plan for tonight? What's this *big idea* you said you had?"

"Well," I start, unzipping my duffel and pulling out the desktop disco lamp, which is met with a praising nod and laugh. I follow it with a few cheesy decorations and some pink balloons that honestly look like condoms when I blow them up. Cass helps me toss them around the room, kicking them and volleying them in the air for a few minutes. It's such a simple game—we're like children playing, but whatever had her heartsick is gone now, so we keep batting the condom balloons around until she collapses on the bed and sighs, her mouth still stretched in a smile as she watches a balloon float down to her face.

"We're having a party?" she finally asks, smacking the balloon into my face.

"Sort of," I say, pulling out the cheap CD player last. "I didn't think it was fair that Rowe got a prom tonight and you didn't. So...."

I finally get the CD player plugged in and start the first song, which is mostly incredibly cheesy saxophone music. When I turn back to Cass, she's shading her face like she's embarrassed.

"Oh. My. God. This is...like...the corniest thing ever," she says, and as if on cue, I tap the button on the light and the room illuminates with disco crystals. I move to the light switch, flip it off, and the effect is just as roller-rink-style as I thought it would be. I'm pretty pleased.

"No. No, wait. I lied. *Now* this is the corniest thing ever," she giggles. There's no trace of her frown left, no hint of a tear, and as ridiculous as this all is—she's looking at me like I just gave her a dozen roses. Yeah, I did good.

"Shut up, beautiful, and get over here and dance," I say, reaching for her hand while some song that I think was maybe from the movie *Footloose* starts.

Her fingertips graze against mine, and she's timid as she inches closer to me, her eyes moving from her feet to my shoulders, to both sides—she's unsure how this is done, of how to dance...*with me.*

"Relax," I nod, slowly. When she gets close enough, I put my hands on her waist, turn her to the side and sweep her up so she's in my lap, her legs kicked off to the side. "Put your arms around me. This is dancing, and we're allowed to be a ruler's length away from each other."

"Oh, really," she says, her smile sly as she looks off to either side of us. She gets close to my face, close enough to whisper, "I don't think the teachers are looking."

She pulls herself tight against me, her arms around my neck and shoulders, and rests her head just below my chin. Everything about right now is perfect. With my right hand, I reach for my wheel and turn us in a slow circle, my other hand flat against her back, making sure she doesn't go.

170

It isn't perfect. The CD skips a few times, and the battery-powered disco lamp makes a buzzing sound—like a vibrator. But if I had to venture to guess, I would say that this moment—this *prom experience*—kicks every other prom experience's ass.

"Thank you, Tyson," she says, nuzzling deeper into the crook of my neck as I spin us for another song.

"You got it, baby," I say, and she squeezes me a little tighter.

I like it when she calls me Tyson. And she just let me call her baby.

Cass

He's like magic. That's the only way to describe what Ty does when I'm feeling...*less.* He takes it all away. He doesn't think he's romantic, but my god. I don't like grand gestures. I'm not the girl who wants the proposal in front of thousands at the hockey game one day—not that I don't *love* watching that happen for someone else, because I do! I just don't want *my* face on that Jumbotron, not for anything other than scoring a goal.

I like simple. There's potency in simple. There's...*magic* in simple. And these simple moments are just for me and Ty, and nobody else.

He's held me close in his lap for three whole songs, and I marvel that his right arm isn't tired from spinning us in a slow circle. He's rocked me once or twice, too.

His left hand has slid around my shoulders, to my breast, finally coming to rest along the side of my face. It's the most tender of touches, and his thumb glides along my cheek in a way that honestly makes me feel beautiful. The CD starts to skip badly now, and even that somehow just seems right.

Ty reaches over and smacks the top of the player, and it makes the music skip ahead to some sort of reggae song that isn't remotely romantic, and it makes us both turn and look at the music player and laugh.

"Where did you even *get* this CD?" I ask.

"Record Exchange," he says, smacking it once more, causing it to start back at the beginning. I like the beginning. I like the thought of staying here, like this all night, starting over and over.

"I hope you didn't pay much for it," I say.

"No, got it for free. Well...sort of," he says, and I lean back, quirking an eyebrow up. "I traded in one of Nate's movies."

"He's going to be pissed," I say, laying my head down on his shoulder, my hand tucked under his shirt against his bare chest so I can feel the movement of his muscles, his heart, his skin.

"No, he won't. I watched it a shitload more than he did anyway. Nate's not really a porn kinda guy."

"Oh," I say, suddenly uncomfortable at the thought of Ty and porn and me. And Nate. And, *oh God!* He can feel the heat on my face, he must, because he's trying to look me in the eye, and I'm trying to bury myself under his arm.

"Cass, what kind of movie did you *think* I'd trade in for a shitty CD?" he says, amused by my embarrassment.

"I don't know. I just...*wow*. Do you, like...watch that stuff? I mean, with your brother?" I'm so uncomfortable. I don't know why. I've seen porn. The guys in high school used to play them at parties just to make the girls blush. It never bothered me. But something about talking about it with Ty is...weird.

"First off, you don't *watch* porn. You *use* it," he says, and I hold up my hand and slide from his lap to my bed. As much as I want to stay in his arms all night, in our dance, right now the urge to bury my face in my pillow is stronger.

"Nope, that's good. Don't need to hear any more," I say, and he pulls himself close to me, leaving his chair and lying flat alongside me. When I try to cover my face with my hands, he pulls them away.

"It's nothing to be embarrassed about. It's actually a really amazing business concept with high levels of demand and never-ending supply," he says, talking about it like a commodity. "We should watch one."

"Oooohhhhh kay. I think we're done talking about porn now," I say, red again, only to find him getting closer, teasing me.

"You know, that's what I'm getting my MBA for," he says, and my head snaps to him, I'm sure my eyes are wide and full of shock. "Oh yeah, I'm going to invest heavily in the industry. There's a ton of scratch to be made."

172

I hold his stare, trying to read his face, figure out if he's bluffing me. Ty is good. He could sell anything—even this story. Holding my breath, I wait, nodding lightly like I'm considering what he said, like I think there might be some truth to it, and he ups his game, shrugging. Holy fuck, I think he's serious!

"You cannot be serious? What does your mother think?" I'm holding my arms stiff against his chest now. He wraps his hands slowly around my forearms and slides them up, over my shoulders and into my hair, pulling me close again, bringing his lips close to mine. I'm still making an incredulous face, but he's ignoring it, his lips coming closer, closer, until I can feel the tickle of the static electricity working between us, pulling us together the rest of the way. And then there it is—the dimple. The smile.

"I'm totally fucking with you," he smirks. I bring my pillow up to his face and smack him across the head.

"I hate it when you do that!" I say, even though I don't. I love it.

"You liar. You love it," he says.

I do. I love it. I love you. I love you, Tyson Preeter. I love you. I love you. I love you. My lips almost feel like they're moving. But they're not. They're not, because I'm scared. Fucking chicken. God, Cass...just say it!

There's a pause in everything—Ty's hands stop their movement, his eyes don't blink, his breath holds, my pulse slows and then races. We've stopped time—I can feel it. It doesn't begin again until he sweeps his eyes upward as his fingers pull a stray wave of hair back in place over my head. His eyes stay on that hair for a few seconds before coming back to my gaze. His head tilts. His hands cradle my face. His focus on me, everything *me*, and all I see are his eyes, blue and honest and vulnerable. Every thought in his head is racing behind them, and I can read what's inside. I see it. He loves me too. I know he does.

His lips fall on me slowly, and I swear I feel them whisper the words—whisper *I love you.* I don't say anything, because the sound wasn't there. But I felt them. I feel them now.

He pulls himself above me, his elbows holding most of his weight and his forehead pressed to mine while our lips dance, grazing lightly. I let him take complete control. I surrender, and I wait—patiently wait for him to deepen our kiss, because I want more of him, more of his lips and his body and his everything.

When he begins kissing me harder, there's another shift—time no longer standing still, but racing. He lies to his side, next to me, his lips and teeth rough against my neck, but the feeling is so welcomed. He grips the bottom of my cotton T-shirt quickly, pulling it up and over my body and arms, my bra unsnapping in the front and falling to the sides. When I move to lower my arms, he traps them above my head with one hand, his body leaning into me as he kisses me again, moving his way down my chin, my neck, my chest, until his teeth find the hardness of my nipples, and he pulls them into his mouth, biting just enough to send shivers across my bare skin.

My back arches on instinct, and he's fast to move his right arm underneath me, pulling me closer into him while he devours my breasts.

Everything about our movements is hot, needy, wanting, greedy, hungry—a million selfish words. But there's also something else—more than passion, more than lust. It's like we both have so much to say, but the only way we're willing is through a physical connection.

My hands finally free, I let them glide down his chest until I find the edge of his shirt, and I pull it from his body. This is my favorite feeling in the world—the feel of his skin against mine. The heat from him takes away my chills as his hands glide around me, kissing his way up between my breasts and neck and back to my mouth again. This kiss is fast, his teeth holding onto my bottom lip as his forehead presses to mine and his eyes look down.

Down, down, down—his hands sliding down until he finds the band of my black cotton pants. A growl escapes him as he finally lets loose of his grip on my mouth, and his thumbs work my pants and panties quickly down my hips, then thighs, then knees until I simply kick them away.

Ty's eyes look drunk, they're so heavy as they follow the curve of my body—tracing the line he draws with one finger from my thigh to my inner thigh until he's where I'm craving him most.

174

There aren't any words. There are no jokes or role-playing or sweet-talking or flirting. We've moved past that, past the nerves. We're completely in sync, and as Ty runs the tips of his fingers over me intimately, I allow myself to gasp and whimper for him to hear exactly what his touch—what *he*—does to me.

His teasing is soft and sensuous, no rushing to get to the next part. We have hours, and the slowness of every move he makes is as if he plans to take every minute available to us to bring me pleasure. I'm not able to stop the pressure building inside of me, and when it becomes unbearable, I let myself go— wave after wave of tremors passing through me, against his touch. I let out a small cry again, and Ty groans, biting at my shoulder.

I want him to feel just as I do, want him to feel this with me. And the need inside me has only grown from his touch. My hands quickly find the button and zipper of his jeans, and he's not shy about helping me to work his clothes completely off of his body. My hand wraps around his length, and his eyes roll closed with my touch.

My touch is firm and continuous as I feel every bit of his hardness, and his breathing begins to grow more rapid with every movement. I stop only to reach into his jeans on the floor for a condom. I unwrap it and slip it over him, my hand feeling him one more time until his hand grips around mine to stop me. I'm expecting him to grab my hip, to direct me on top of him—to guide me just as he did the last time. But instead, he holds us here, paused, his eyes almost afraid.

"I want to hold you," he says, his voice barely a whisper, and his eyes trapped somewhere between need and despair. "While we do this...I want to hold you. I want to feel how you feel when I'm inside you. But..."

His breath catches, and his eyes close, almost as if he's searching deep within for the rest of what he needs to say, for the courage to say it.

"Anything, Tyson. What is it? You can tell me anything?" I say, letting my head fall forward until my lips can kiss his cheek.

"I want to hold you to me...but I don't know how," he says, looking down, but only for a moment. I don't understand at first, so I hold his gaze and my breath. And then I realize. When Ty's above me, his weight is held with the strength of his massive arms. They control his body, help him move, allowing him to do everything—everything but *this*.

I don't speak, because I don't think that's what he wants. Just getting the words out, just saying this to me was so difficult for him. It's not something that he wants discussion on. He just wants to feel me, for me to help him find a way.

With our bodies close, I bring both of my hands up to either side of his face, and I kiss him with the same reverence he's shown me—slow and deep and patient. I worship him with my kiss. When I pull away, I look at him and my eyes beg him to trust me. Slowly, I turn to my back, and then my other side. I lie against him on my bed, our bodies spooned together, my curves finding the hardness of his muscles and melding together.

I can tell he's unsure, afraid of not being able to do what I'm trying. He's afraid of failing to please me, but I'm just as afraid of failing him. My hands are slow, my first one reaching for his arm and hand until I find his fingers, weaving mine through his and gripping hard to reassure him that I've got this. With my other hand, I reach lower, between us, until I find his hardness ready for me, and I guide him into place.

As I slide against him, pushing him deeper inside, his erection completely filling me, I feel his grip tighten, and he brings both of our hands around my body, pulling me to him. His exhale is slow, and the tickle of his breath as his mouth finds the back of my neck only makes me want to move against him more.

My hips slowly rock, my body doing most of the work. His arms weave around both sides of my body as his hands splay across my breasts, my ribs, my stomach—he touches all of me, and my body reacts to every touch, my hips working harder, my body working harder.

His hands never rest, but his hold on me is always tight and firm, his forearms fully flexed to make sure the space between us is minimal. The more I move against him, the harder he breathes, and the more my own need grows again. As the intensity builds, my hips work harder and faster, and when Ty's hands both slide down my body to rest just above my pelvis, I lose all control. My body shakes, and the rocking of my hips becomes slower, but his hands pull me back to him tightly—over and over until he groans into my hair, his head pressed against the back of mine.

We lie still like this, holding each other just as we finished, for minutes—until I'm sure his arm is falling asleep, and my body begins to grow cold from being exposed. His grip on me loosens, and I slip away from him, pulling my shirt over my head so I can step into the closet to freshen up at my sink.

My reflection catches my attention, and I pause at the mirror, noticing the flushness of my face. My chest feels tight, and every nerve in me wants me to cry. I don't understand it, because I've never been happier. But something happened between Ty and me just now—something amazing, and beautiful, and special—but also something raw. And I want to hold onto it hard and fast.

When I slip back into the room in a fresh T-shirt and a loose pair of sleep shorts, Ty is already dressed in his boxers and is waiting for me, my quilt pulled back on the corner, a welcome for me to join him. I flip the light switch and crawl into his arms, this time my cheek finding the firmness of his chest. His lips touch the top of my head, resting there for several seconds before he turns his head, replacing his lips with his chin.

I love you, Tyson Preeter. I love you. I love you. I love you. I love you. I love you...

I mouth the words, shrouded in darkness. It's a rehearsal for the real thing, and I feel the quaking in my gut, because the thought of saying this aloud terrifies me. I've never said this, not to anyone, other than family. I rarely say it now to my parents and Paige; in fact, I think we were kids the last time I uttered those words to her. It's sad how hard it gets to love.

"Thank you," he whispers, interrupting my homemade panic attack. His whisper is soft, but perfectly clear. I don't say anything in return, because I know what he meant by *thank you.* I squeeze him tightly and kiss his chest once more before closing my eyes, my lullaby the chorus of *I love yous* that cease to end in my head.

Chapter 21

Cass

The debate over whether or not I would join the soccer team picked up right where it left off the night before. When Ty left for his workouts with clients, I turned the sound back on for my phone and endured the three messages waiting for me—one from my father, reiterating his reasoning; one from my mother pretending nothing was wrong at all; and one from Paige, telling me she heard about it all from Mom.

I don't feel like talking to any of them, but I call my dad back anyway because if I have to talk to one of them, at least he has a valid point. He isn't going to waggle a finger or feign like everything's fine and my spirit isn't destroyed.

"Hey, sweetheart. Just got in the car to head to the office, but I can talk for a few," my dad says. "How are you feeling about things this morning? Fresh perspective after a good night's sleep, I hope?"

I wait a few seconds before responding, half tempted to shock him by saying something like "...no sleep for me. Spent the night with my boyfriend. Thinking about getting pregnant. Oh, and then joining the team. And maybe I'll pose nude for Playboy, too."

I don't say any of those things. But I don't roll over either.

"Yeah, I thought. I'm still joining the team," I say, and his heavy sigh comes fast, just like I knew it would. He's disappointed. *What's new?*

"Cassidy, we talked about this. I know what your mother said, how she doesn't feel comfortable with you overexerting yourself. But it's more than that. If it were just the physical demands, Cass...if that were it...? I could hold your mom off. But this Paul Cotterman thing—Cass, we just don't know how it's going to go."

That's what had me in tears last night, more than anything. I called home to tell my parents I was going to play for McConnell, and in seconds, my father stripped my power away with news that Paul Cotterman was thinking about *not signing* the bargain—*not* following through with the carefully laid plans my father had constructed—the plans that would erase that awful experience from my life.

He was the one who was wrong. *He* was the one who should be punished. But *I* was the one who was going to suffer.

My mom found out. My dad tried to keep it between us, but the *Cotterman issue,* as it was now referred to, was just too big for him to keep hushed. She didn't really believe me either. I know she didn't. My dad said she knew, but my mother never brought it up when we spoke. Like so many things, she just liked to pretend that none of those *bad* things were real. Instead, after she told me *soccer would kill me*— exact words—she spent the next ten minutes filling me in on her bead workshop and the new things she got in the store.

"Cass, listen. I'm just pulling into the office. I've got a few calls out, and we'll see where things stand in a day or two. But for now, honey…" I hate it when he calls me *honey.* "For now, let's just sit on this. Sit and wait this out. Maybe next week…maybe the outlook will be different."

It won't be. I know it. But I am going to play anyway. And everyone trying to take this away from me can fuck off.

"Whatever," I say. Not even goodbye. My dad doesn't notice, telling me he'll talk to me Tuesday or Wednesday, like one of his clients. That's what I am.

Whatever.

It didn't take long for my mom to figure out that she could catch me. My dad must have told her we talked, because she called only a few minutes after. I let her go to voicemail. But she called again. She would keep doing this—I knew it.

Just before the second call fades to my voicemail, I catch it, taking a deep breath before I dive into a conversation where we pretend I'm not pissed, that she doesn't think less of me, and that the only things on the table to talk about are Thanksgiving plans and beads.

"Hi, Mom," I don't have the energy for the fake voice, so I don't put the effort into my greeting.

"Well, look who's finally awake?" She sounds like one of those workout videos, where the person counts down the reps with so much enthusiasm that you start to think they might be high on speed.

"Yes, I'm awake. What is it, Mom? I have things to do." I don't have anything to do—my homework was done Friday afternoon, and Rowe is probably spending most of her afternoon with Nate. And I'm sure, somehow, Paige is also caught up on the *Cotterman issue,* so I'm looking at an afternoon of reading and MTV until Ty gets back.

"I was just making your flight plans for Thanksgiving. Your sister said she was okay with an early-morning flight, and I wanted to make sure it would work for you," she says, knowing full well she already bought the tickets. I hate early-morning flights. You have to get to the airport before the sun is even up. But my mom uses Paige as our litmus test—if she's fine with it, then the other child must be as well. We're twins, after all.

"Early is fine," I say.

"Good. You'll be heading out at 7:50 a.m."

"Fuuuuuck," I moan. It just slipped out. It's my attitude. I'm usually able to keep it in check, but I think maybe I'm just done—done with it all.

"Cassidy!" Here comes the scolding.

"Sorry," I say, glad she can't see me shake my head and roll my eyes.

"This is that Tyson fellow's influence, isn't it?" she says, not even disguising the judgment. I'm sure I can thank Paige for this. I don't know why my mom acts like this. She's a textiles designer who owns a bead shop—she's borderline hippy. She's supposed to be open, accepting, and not...well, not a snob!

"Paige told you about Ty, I see," I say, sitting down on my floor with my back against my dresser. Might as well get comfortable.

"Well, it's not like *you* tell me about your boyfriends," she says, and I hear the little tone at the end of that statement too. Boyfriends—like I've ever had more than just this one.

"Mom, there's just Ty. He's it, and I like him. I like him a lot. You'd like him too if you'd bother to meet him in person—

180

instead of the version of him that lives in Paige's head," I admonish.

"Oh, she didn't say anything bad about him. She only told us that he's disabled, in a wheelchair? Is that right?" she asks, like she even has to.

"Yes, Mom. He's in a wheelchair. But I don't even notice. He's a physical trainer, and a grad student," I start to launch into my list of all of Ty's amazing qualities, but she's not listening.

"Right, that's what your sister said. He's *older*," she says, a special emphasis on that word.

"Yes, he's older than me, but not by a lot. And that shouldn't matter. Dad's older than you," by, like, ten years I continue in my head.

"Right, right. I know. It's just…" I don't like her pause. She's mulling, and hemming, and hawing. "—with this Paul Cotterman situation, Cass…are you sure you need to be having an affair with another older man?"

Another. She used the word *another*.

"What do you mean?" I'm back on my feet, pacing. Pissed. On fire.

"Honey, maybe you shouldn't be dating. Or, at least…maybe you should meet some of the boys in your class? You know, your age?"

I don't talk at first. I make it uncomfortable. I use this time to choose my words. I have one shot at this, and then she'll call my father, and then he'll lecture me. Of course, I'm not picking up my phone anymore today, so it doesn't matter.

"Mom, I'm only going to say this once. Paul Cotterman is a sick man who tried to touch me inappropriately, with physical force, in a classroom that I later found out was locked. I punched him—hard. And you should be proud that you raised a daughter who not only knew what to do, but has the physical strength to beat her way out of a nightmare," I say, stopping for a breath before launching into my disappointment in her. But she interrupts me, halts me, and then kills me dead.

"Cass, are you sure this wasn't like that thing with Kyle Loftman last spring?" Her question leaves me breathless. My father told her, told her *everything.* And I'm sure she told Paige. My secrets are not so secret.

I don't say anything else, and the sensation of my phone in my hand, against my ear, suddenly feels burning hot. I pull it to my lap and look at it; the text reads MOM to identify who I'm talking to.

"Cass? Are you there, honey?" I can hear her voice mutter from my lap. I stare at the phone though, don't pick it back up to continue our conversation. "Cass? Cassidy? Cass?"

She sounds like she's in a box—so I close it, and press my finger to the END CALL button. I put the ringer on vibrate, so I don't have to hear it loudly.

I wait for Ty. I need Ty. I love Ty.

Ty will make this all okay.

Ty

"Dude, so she bought you floor seats? For the Thunder game?" I'm looking at the tickets, holding them in my hand. They don't even have row numbers on them. They just say VIP and then a string of letters. I'm officially jealous of my brother.

"Third-row, but close," he grins at me. He should grin—turns out Rowe is even cooler than I thought.

My brother's birthday is this week, and Rowe surprised him with the tickets after their prom experience. I didn't bother to tell him about my prom, because I knew there was no way his could compare.

I haven't stopped thinking about Cass since she slept in my arms last night. I couldn't get back from workouts fast enough, and when I left the gym, I went right to her room. Rowe came home an hour later, and I got a feeling she wanted some time with Cass, so I came here. But I wanted to stay there. I would have stayed there all night, again—every night.

She didn't buy me floor seats to the Thunder game, but what she gave me...it was so much more. I'm not very eloquent at talking about feelings. I don't really know what to say. I'm good at honesty, and at calling people on bullshit. But I need to say something to Cass.

182

I need to say a lot of things to Cass.

"So, can I have them back?" Nate startles me. I'm still holding his tickets.

"Oh, yeah, sorry," I say, handing them back. He takes them slowly, one brow arched suspiciously.

"Just like that? No joke or maneuver to hork my tickets, or make fun of me, or say something about how if Rowe really had good taste, she'd take you to the game instead?" he asks.

"Well, while that last part is *very much* a true statement, no bro. I'm just glad you've finally met a girl worth all of your fine Preeter qualities," I say, turning my attention to the TV remote, switching the channel to ESPN. "And *hork* is a stupid word. Don't say it anymore. It's not even in the dictionary." I move toward my bed and pull myself up, my back leaning against the wall. It's Sunday Night Football, and Dallas is playing.

"That's...it?" Nate says, standing in the way of my view. I dodge his head, trying to catch the stats on the bottom of the screen, but miss something about someone who's injured for the Browns, probably my fantasy-team running back.

"Yes, that's it. Move your fucking head," I say.

Nate laughs, then sits on his bed and pulls the tab on a soda. The noise is irritating. His sipping is irritating. He's staring at me still, and that's irritating.

"Dude, are you trying to make me punch you?" I ask. He grins, then pulls the soda can from his mouth. "What?" I shrug.

"You're in love. With Cass," he says, and my stomach cinches tight. Instead of dignifying that with the guilty face I'm making on the inside, I turn my attention back to the TV.

"Toss me a Coke?" I'm avoiding. I'm completely avoiding this. Not going to touch it.

"Sure," he says, and I feel relief that he's bending down to pull a soda from the mini fridge. Moving on, yes...good. We're moving on. "Have you told her yet?" Not moving on.

This time, I don't look away from the TV. I can hear the way my breath sounds through my nose. It's that same sound my dad makes when Nate and I tease him and he gets fed up. But I'm not fed up. I just don't want to talk about this, because then I have to talk about it with Cass. And if I talk about it with Cass, I have to talk about it with Kelly—because Kelly's the only other one, and I always promised myself I would make it okay with her if there was ever another. And now her husband is a loser. And fuck, fuck, damn, damn. Nate is staring at me, but I keep my eyes on the ticker at the bottom of the screen. Great, it *is* my running back that's hurt. Well, there goes my fantasy week.

"You have to tell her," he says.

"Nothing to tell," I lie.

"Liar," he says. Yeah, he knows me too well.

"Whatever," I say.

"You talk to Mom about it?"

I blink, and keep my focus straight ahead. Fucking Nate, *no* I didn't talk to my mommy about it. He knows it's a sore spot for me, being the mama's boy. But he doesn't quite understand how much Mom was there for me when I was losing my way, when I was falling to depression. Mom pushed me into art, and *that*—and Kelly—saved me.

"Dude, it's a good thing…falling in love? Cass is awesome. You should let yourself have this, that's all I'm saying," he says.

"Got it. Good. Okay, are you done now? I'd like to hear some of the commentary," I say. I'm being a total asshole. It's what I do when I'm uncomfortable, and he knows it.

"Yeah, I'm done. Here's your Coke, dickhead," he tosses it on my lap so that I have to wait to open it. I'm tempted to spray it on his bed sheets. But I don't. Instead, I pull it into my hands and spend five minutes tapping on the top until it's safe to open.

Goddamned love. It's ruining football.

Chapter 22

Ty

This isn't quite how my night was supposed to go. When Nate and Rowe left for the game, Cass and I were settled in for some time alone. Pizza, a six-pack of Pabst, and Chunky Monkey ice cream. We were celebrating her official membership on the McConnell team—because her parents *weren't* celebrating.

I hate that for her. My parents wouldn't miss a single moment of something big in Nate's or my life. If I wanted to join a wheelchair knife-throwing league, my mom would ask if they had shirts for parents, and how she could get season tickets. Cass is doing her best to not act disappointed, but I can tell she is— she shows it in the quiet moments, when she's thinking—her eyes off in the distance.

Tonight was going to be all about forgetting the assholes. That was my plan. But then my brother became an asshole, and I had to deal with it.

An hour after he and Rowe left, I saw Nate's ex-girlfriend, Sadie, interviewed on television at the game. Sadie's playing college ball over at OSU. She's kind of big in the women's basketball world, and the Thunder invited the OSU women's team out for pre-game. Nate and Sadie's breakup was swift, but ugly. She cheated, he caught her, and that's the short of it. I knew things couldn't be good when he texted me in the first quarter, asking me to guess who he ran into. Seems the introduction of his new girlfriend to his *old* girlfriend didn't go well, especially for his *new* girlfriend. Needless to say, they came home early. Rowe needed Cass, and here I am, two beers in at Sally's—Nate a beer ahead of me.

"Dude, you called her your *friend*? Rowe is just a *friend*?" Honestly, I've said a lot of dumb shit in front of girls—things that have earned me a slap to the face more than once, and harder than the time Cass set me right. But I've never really minced words, had a slip of the tongue, just plain botched my ability to speak English. Nate? He's an idiot.

"I don't know, man. I don't think I can fix this." Nate is wallowing. I have two choices: push him into a drunken stupor, or give him hope. His girl lives with my girl. I'm man enough to admit that plays into my decision.

"Of course you can fix this." Here comes Captain Positive. I suck at this too, a symptom of my *tell-it-like-it-is* quality. But for Nate, I can spin hope. And I think it's there. Rowe's in love with my brother, and this won't be more than a blip.

"Dude, I'm supposed to meet her parents this weekend. They're coming to my tournament. She's going to introduce me as her asshole-neighbor down the hall, who sold her out in front of his ex...because he's too weenie to admit he's in love with her," he says, his own admission hitting him all at once.

And there you have it. The Preeter brothers—in love, and too big of pussies to do anything about it.

"While I agree that *yes,* she *should* introduce you that way, you know that's not going to happen. You were an idiot, a colossal idiot. Like, bonehead idiot champion of the universe," I say.

"Got it. Move on," he says.

"That girl loves your ass anyway," I say, and he sighs once, eyes staring into the half full glass of beer. "Just promise me one thing."

"What's that?" he asks.

"You won't let this relationship-shit fuck up baseball." He laughs, nods once, and tilts his glass back letting the rest of his draft slide down his throat. "I'm serious, man. You know I don't like shit fuckin' up baseball."

"Oh, I know," he says through a chuckle, standing up and tossing down twenty bucks before heading to the back for the men's room.

"Cass would never fuck up baseball," I think to myself, then I toast to no one and take a long chug to catch up with Nate. I drop my twenty on the table and wait for him at the door.

Things seem to have worked out for Nate. I knew they would. And he didn't play like shit in his tournament, despite all of the *drama-rama.* Rowe did have some dude come to the game

186

with her, pretty much hitting on her in front of my brother. That shit wasn't cool, but Cass said I didn't know the whole story, or whatever. All I know is if Cass brings some guy to tag along with us somewhere, I'm going to knock his teeth out—and I don't care *what* his story is.

Cass has had a full week of practice. Her body is holding up to the pressure. I know it's a concern for her, making sure she gets rest, stays cool. I made her take an Epsom salt bath in the physical therapy room on Friday. She hated it, but it's good for her muscles and nerves. Overheating isn't good for MS, and extreme cold isn't great either. Salt seems to be good for just about anything. I've been researching it as much as I can, because I want to help her, to be there to push back when MS tries to knock her down.

She's dodging calls from her parents. At first, it was really upsetting her, but now it's almost routine the way she just clicks END on the phone when she sees their names pop up. Thankfully, Paige doesn't seem to be bullying her about it. Cass says Paige is always on her mom's side, but I don't know. I think Paige might be in Cass's corner more than she realizes. Paige sure as hell let me know where she stood.

Cass has been out with the girls all day—Halloween shopping. I love this holiday. When I was a kid, I liked that I got free candy. When I was a teenage boy, I liked that teenaged girls dressed up in slutty costumes. And now that I'm twenty-two...? I like that college chicks dress up in slutty costumes.

"So, do I get to see?" I ask Cass, pulling the bag on her arm, trying to get a peek at her costume. I only get a glimpse before she jerks the bag away. I can see the skirt—red and white stripes. She's either a hot nurse or a cheerleader. I'm good with either.

"No, I want to surprise you," she says, her cheeks a little red when she smiles. It's cute when she's sexy like this. "What are you wearing?"

I laugh once at her question before I answer. "Like you don't know," I say. Yesterday, I got a ransom note in my mailbox. It was a picture of a teddy bear—more specifically *my* teddy bear. I've had Cookie since as long as I can remember. Honestly, I think he means more to Mom than me, but I like that he means that much to her. So, I keep him in my box of crap that I haul around with me—he's in there with a few trophies, yearbooks, homecoming pictures, and I think maybe my kindergarten report card.

Anyhow, the note with the picture said that if I ever wanted to see Cookie again, I better wear a tutu at the Halloween party. It's not so much about Cookie as it is about someone thinking they have something on me—so yeah, I'm going to wear the tutu. I'm going to fucking *own* that tutu—and the silver sparkly Speedo-style thong I'm wearing underneath.

"What does that mean?" Cass asks, and I try to size up the look on her face. Yeah, she's in on this. She's totally in on this.

"You know what that means," I say, and she rolls her eyes at me. Yeah. She's in on it. I can't wait for her to see the tutu.

Cass

Rowe filled me in on the Cookie thing after the boys left. I guess Ty's been picking on Nate, so to get back at him, Rowe kidnapped his teddy bear and is holding it ransom. My boyfriend has a teddy bear...named Cookie. Yep.

The best part is that she dared him to wear a tutu to the party tonight. I wish Rowe knew Ty as well as I do. If she did, maybe she wouldn't have taken the threat so far. I'm pretty sure everyone at the party has seen my boyfriend's penis. There's not a lot hiding it. There's a goodly amount of pink fluff that tufts up in the front as he's sitting, and then there's a very small silver thong...that doesn't fit well.

It's not attractive, like, in the least, but I kind of love that Ty couldn't give a shit. Most of the guys at this party tonight are dressed in stupid, scary masks, or with bad vampire makeup and their regular street clothes. The blend of the various colognes gave me a headache, so we've been hanging out outside.

"Okay, so again, explain this whole tutu thing to me? This is all because you tease Nate about making a *fussy fuss?*" I say, noticing a group of girls walking by, staring at Ty's lap, giggling, and moving on. That's right, ladies, get a good look. He's all mine. I laugh a little to myself.

I move to his lap, a strategic maneuver to cover the tutu, which he doesn't mind. His hand finds my knee quickly, and his fingers inch up my leg every few seconds, closer to the edge of my cheerleading skirt. I'm okay with this, too.

"When we were kids, I used to beat Nate up. You know, normal brother-wrestling kind of crap, not like bloody-nose stuff," Ty says. "Anyhow, he was easy to pin—all thin and gangly. I was four years older, and he never stood a chance. But he'd always start crying, running to Mom and telling her I was picking on him. Well, one day, she was busy...working on one of her sculptures. She was trying to get some welding equipment to work in the driveway, and here Nate was waving his arms, whining that I pinned him on the carpet and gave him a rug burn. She told him to stop making a *fussy fuss.*"

"So it's really your mom's fault?" I ask.

"Ha. I guess in a way, she started it. But no, I take full blame for giving him a complex over it," Ty says. "When she told him that the first time, it blew his mind. He couldn't believe that she would sell him out like that, not stick up for him. He turned around and looked at me—all I could do was grin. It was like a free pass. I could pin him over and over, and Mom wouldn't care. He was totally helpless. And the next time he started crying, I told him to stop making a fussy fuss, which only made him kick and scream more. Of course, I did it again. And then it sort of became my thing for him, whenever he would get whiny or act like a baby—fussy fuss. He hates it, and I *love* that he hates it."

I must be making a face, because Ty's hand stops its slow trip up my thigh and he leans back to look at me. "What?" he asks.

"I don't know. That just...that seems kind of mean," I say, almost feeling grateful for having a sister instead of this sick, demented, brother-relationship. *Almost.*

"It's not mean. It's a dude thing. Trust me, he hates it...but he also loves it," Ty says, his attention back on his hand now, which is where my focus goes immediately when I feel the hem of my skirt start to move up.

"Owens. Nice practice today," the voice pulls me out of my intimate bubble with Ty. It's Chandra, dressed as Wonder Woman. I'm not surprised. And her compliment is not a compliment at all. I was cramping at practice and had to leave before it was over. She's reveling in it. I hate her.

"Well, I thought I should give you a chance to work the ball," I say, my smile as fake as the bile in my mouth is real. She bites her lower lip, and when she slides her teeth over it, some of the cherry-red lipstick wears off, leaving a red mark on her front teeth. It makes me happy.

She's here with a few of the other girls, and some dude on the football team. I think he's friends with the guy Paige has been seeing. This guy seems clueless, so I give him a pass on his poor taste in women. He walks down the porch steps and the other girls follow, but Chandra stays behind. She doesn't like me having the last word, so I wait patiently for her to put an end to our conversation—happy to have Ty's hand on my leg, and his lips on my neck. He couldn't care less about her.

"I meant to ask you, Cass. How's Paul Cotterman?" The second she finishes talking she knows she has me. She smiles with her red lips pushed together tightly, bothering to give me a wink before turning and leaving me alone to bleed out from her attack.

My body is instantly covered in sweat, and the ability to breathe leaves. I feel sick, and not from drinking too much, because I've hardly had anything to drink at all. How does she know about Paul Cotterman? *What* does she know? And does she know about Kyle? Why would she do this...say this?

I quickly stand from Ty's lap, and he grabs my hand, turning me to look at him.

"What was that about?" He's not asking like he's angry. He's genuinely concerned, but I can't talk about it here. I'm not sure my brain has fully wrapped itself around what just happened. All I know is that I need to leave, and I'm probably going to vomit in the grass.

"I want to go. Now, Ty. Please? We need to go," I say, holding my hand over my mouth just long enough to make it to the lawn. I let out the little bit of alcohol I've had, shutting my eyes as shivers take control of my arms and legs and spine. Ty is next to me quickly, and he's holding my purse in his lap, over his tutu. The visual makes me smile through the tears that are already starting. This man loves me. I know he does. And I can trust him. Even with my ugliest parts.

"Not here. I'll tell you everything. But just get me home," I say, and he puts his hand on my lower back. We begin the long trip back to our dorm building.

We go to his room first, and I wait outside. Nate took Rowe home early; she was pretty blitzed. Ty whispers to me that she's passed out. He slips in and out quickly without waking them, his sweatpants and T-shirt in his lap when he exits. Once we get to my room, he changes, and I'm glad to have my non-tutu boyfriend back.

"Wow, I've never seen someone look so turned on by sweatpants," he teases.

"I was just getting worried that I'd never get *that* out of my head," I say, waving my hand over the pile of sparkling pink mesh on the floor.

"Yeah, you and about a hundred dudes whose day I ruined in that outfit," he laughs, picking the tutu up and straightening it out like he actually might save it to wear again. He finally tosses it back to the floor, and I'm relieved.

He's lying on my bed, his neck bent against my rolled pillow stuffed in the corner by the wall. He pats the space next to him, and I crawl up, folding my legs so I can sit and face him. I play with his fingers in my hand, pretending they're keys of a piano. I wish I knew how to play the piano. I wish for a lot of things.

"So...I think I should probably start with Kyle Loftman," I say, keeping my focus on his fingers, my pretend piano. I play *Mary Had a Little Lamb,* or at least, what I think is that song. He lets me play, tilting his head to one side and looking up at me, my glance shifts from his fingers to his eyes and back again.

"Is this story going to piss me off?" he asks.

That's a loaded question. I pause and cup his hand in both of mine, then lean forward to kiss it and press it on the side of my face while I look at him.

"Yes. No. Maybe," I say, through a truly pathetic smile.

"Okay, that sounds fair. Bases are covered," he says, wiggling his fingers again to let me play. I like that he does this, let's me have an outlet for my nerves. Or maybe he just likes it when I rub his hands. Either way.

"Kyle Loftman was a student teacher at my high school. He was about to graduate. Your age, really." I can feel his fingers grow stiff, but they loosen again quickly. I keep going, keep playing my song. "I was sort of...I don't know...one of those *easy* girls in high school."

His hand grabs mine, and he tugs for my attention. "Hey, don't do that. Don't ever apologize for things in your past. Not to me," he says. I nod, and my breath comes sharp and fast. I would cry if I weren't so nervous. I hate crying. "Go on. I won't judge you. Not ever."

I spread his fingers, weaving mine in and out while I talk. "Kyle was helping out our soccer team, and one night, he found his way to one of our parties. He was young, just a little older. Liking him was dangerous, but a safe kind of dangerous. So I slipped into one of the rooms with him at the house we were at, and we made out. That was it. Nothing heavy. No sex. Some...*touching*," I admit, my face feeling the burn of humiliation saying this to Ty—to anyone.

"Don't," he reminds me, and I swallow hard, trying to gain courage from him.

"The next day, there was a knock at my parent's door. My dad answered, and it was a young woman—short, brunette...pregnant. She asked for me, so my dad called me downstairs. He stood behind me when I cracked open the door the rest of the way. He stood there while she told me to stop sleeping with her husband. She spit on the screen door, cried, and told me I should be ashamed of myself. She called me a slut...and then she walked away."

Ty's hands wrap around mine, and I look at him. His face is exactly as I hoped—he's angry, but on my side. He's angry that I was accused, that I was spit at, that my father just stood by and watched it all happen.

"What did your dad do?" he asks.

"He told me I was being careless, that she could make this an issue with the school—which she did," I say, remembering the hell that was the end of my senior year. "He kept the details from my mom and from Paige. Or at least, I thought he did. My mom brought it up the other day, so somehow, the story got out. My dad's law firm worked with the district, kept things hushed. Kyle wasn't punished, because I never accused him of anything. He didn't do anything wrong, other than *not* let me know he was married. That...*that* was wrong," I say, letting out a huge breath, the weight of everything.

"That dick owes you an apology," Ty says, and I laugh.

"Which one?" I say, not sure who he was referring to—Kyle or my dad.

"Exactly," he says, and I kiss his hand and move to lie on his arm. "So, what does this have to do with Paul *whatshisname*? Whatever it was that Chandra chick said."

This part of the story...*this confession*? This one is going to make him angry. Not at me...but angry for sure.

"First of all, I need you to promise me you'll stay...calm," I say, mentally crossing my fingers.

"Can't do that," he says back fast, and I sink into him, my stomach churning and trying to convince me to backtrack, to *not* tell this part of the story. "I'm sorry Cass, but I won't make a promise I can't keep. I have a feeling I'm going to want to punch someone, and it might even be that Chandra chick by the time you're done."

"I'm okay with that," I laugh, cringing that I'm advocating for a man hitting a woman. I don't think it counts in this case.

"The day of tryouts...I had that physics makeup test, remember?"

Ty nods, his jaw flexing, his teeth grinding underneath.

"I knew something was off. The teacher, that's Paul Cotterman...he was...sort of flirty," I say, testing the waters. Ty's face hardens even more. Yeah, he's going to react badly.

"Go on," he says, his eyes focused on my lips, almost zoning out.

"He was that way with a few people in class, really. Not just me. But when I went in to take the makeup exam, the room was empty. It was just me," I say, closing my eyes and remembering how dirty his hand felt on my thigh, how hot his breath was on my neck, how demonic his voice was at my ear.

"I don't like this Cass. If that dude hurt you, I swear to god I will kill him. I. Will. Fucking. Kill. Him," Ty says, a menacing calmness to his tone.

"You don't have to. It's okay. He...he..." I can't say it, and Ty squeezes my hand to let me know it's okay. "He touched me, first on my leg, and then he tried to grab my breast. He was holding me to him, and things could have been really bad. But, I hit him, Ty. I hit him hard—first with my elbow, then with my fist. His nose bled, like a fucking faucet. Then I kicked him in the balls to make sure he couldn't follow me."

His mouth is slightly open, and he's still looking at me, just not at my eyes—like he's taking me in, but not completely. He's lost in his thoughts, no doubt reconstructing this scene in his own mind. I wait while he thinks, and then finally his eyes shift to me.

"I'll kill him," he says, his mouth open just enough to show the pressure of his teeth gnashing together. And I believe if Paul Cotterman were to stand in front of Tyson Preeter right now, he would die. And Ty would gladly take the punishment just to see the deed done. I lean forward and kiss his cheek, the tenseness in his muscles unrelenting.

"As much as I would love to see Paul Cotterman run into you in some dark alley, that wouldn't even come close to solving my problems," I say, and his mouth relaxes a small fraction with his breath, his eyes soft on mine.

"This is why your parents are upset, isn't it?"

Ty is so smart.

"They're referring to it as the *Paul Cotterman issue*," I say, a breathy laugh punctuating the end. "I'm pretty sure they think it's like what happened with Kyle. I don't think they believe things happened as I say they did. There aren't really any witnesses. My dad made sure he resigned."

"That's good," Ty says, not waiting for the rest.

"Yeah, that *was* good. But it seems Cotterman is thinking of fighting it. And like I said…there really isn't any proof. I could easily just be a student trying to get out of a bad grade."

"Faking an assault is a pretty steep move just to avoid getting a bad grade," Ty says.

"Yeah, but I hit him, Ty. *I'm* the assaulter!"

"No, you're not," he says, his hands quick to my face to force me to look at him. "No you're not. You're the victim. And you had every right to fuck that asshole's face up."

Without warning, my face grows weak, and the tears slide from my eyes. "Fuck," I swear, stuffing my face into Ty's chest, rubbing my puffy eyes against his shirt. "I hate crying."

"Yeah, well, I hate snot on my T-shirts, but what are you going to do," he says, and I laugh hard and long. He squeezes me and just lets me feel. He lets me feel bad, let's me laugh at his stupid joke, and then let's me just sit here and think about how angry I am at everyone and everything—everything, but him.

"That Chandra chick is a bitch," I say, finally.

"Yep," he says, his chin on my forehead.

I don't say the next part. That's what hurts me the most. That's what made me cry. Someone told Chandra about Paul Cotterman—and I'm pretty sure it was Paige.

Chapter 23

Ty

"Dude, you need to spend more nights with Cass. You're a pain in the ass to sleep in the same room with lately," Nate says. It was another night of tossing and turning, and my pain has been spiking more than normal lately. Fucking up a spinal cord does a number on the nerves, and they let me know when they're pissed off. Mine are *really* pissed off. But I don't like taking meds. Meds can sometimes lead to dependence and depression, and that shit ain't happening to me.

"Sorry man. Cass has had a busy couple of weeks, and finals are coming up. I've been putting in a lot of reading time," I say. I'm pretty sure I just fed Nate a bunch of excuses.

Cass has been busy working her ass off with soccer. She hasn't talked to her parents in weeks, and she's not really speaking to Paige either. I talked her into filing a police report on Paul Cotterman, and it took me days to convince her it was the right thing to do. She kept saying that it would ruin her dad's plans, but I told her that her dad's plans sound like bullshit. If this dude ends up fighting to get his job back, then there needs to be a paper trail that lays out what a douche he is.

All of the drama has gotten in the way of *easy* though. I miss easy. I miss that moment—her on my lap at the Halloween party, before Chandra set off a row of dominoes that tipped over every ray of sunshine in Cass's life, replacing it with a cloud. I don't know how to make her sun shine through again. The power doesn't rest with me, and the small places where it does, I just mess it up.

"Hey, thanks for inviting Rowe to Thanksgiving by the way. That didn't hurt Cass's feelings or anything," I say, throwing my rolled up dirty socks at my brother.

"First of all, fuck you very much. Second of all, you like Rowe. She needed a place to go, and I want her with me. If it's such a big deal, then suck it up and invite Cass," he says, throwing my dirty laundry back in my lap.

196

I'd love to invite Cass. I almost did. But Kelly's been calling me every night lately. Jared's been disappearing more often. He told her he's taking a class, something for his sales position. I promised Kelly I'd get to the bottom of it for her when I come home, and having Cass there…that complicates things.

I flop back on my bed and sigh, loudly enough for Nate to hear and chuckle at my helplessness. I'm helpless—utterly lost on the relationship roadmap; I'm off the grid.

"Is this why Tyson Preeter *doesn't do girlfriends*?" Nate jokes, absolutely loving every second of my stress. "What is it you always say? Relationships are full of…*fussy fuss?*"

"Oh, ha ha ha. You just love throwing that saying back in my face. Yes, I didn't do girlfriends. And now I do. And look—right smack dab in the middle of a pile of fussy fuss. *Fussy fuss* all over the goddamned place! It's making me nuts!" I say, my arms stretched above my head, holding the invisible weight of everything.

"Yeah…but you love it," Nate says, and I pause, not looking at him, not willing to answer aloud, but also unable to stop the smile that takes over my face because yeah, I love it. And I love her, too. I'm screwed.

Cass

It really hit me when I watched Rowe pack. She's going home with Nate for the holiday. I'm going home to a house full of people I don't want to talk to, and riding on the plane next to a sister I want to choke. I'll be in California for almost a full week, but I'd so much rather stay here, in my dorm room, alone.

"How about I just put you in my suitcase," Rowe jokes, zipping her small bag closed.

I pull my knees in close to my body, tucking my neck in, and trying to make myself small. "What do you think? Will I fit?" I ask, knowing I won't. I don't fit lots of places.

"Hmmmm, it might be a tight squeeze. I bet if I borrowed one of Paige's bags I could get you in," she says. I know it's only a joke, but it still makes my stomach roll thinking about the plane ride I'm going to have to endure.

"Ugh, Paige," I let out, surprising myself.

"Trouble in twinland lately, huh?" Rowe says, sitting next to me and pulling her knees in close. We both roll back like balls. I joked with her that this was my version of Pilates once, and ever since then, it's become our thing.

"I'm sort of mad at Paige," I admit, still holding my knees in to my chest, rolling to the side, knocking into Rowe. She nudges me upright with her leg, and we pull ourselves up to sitting, just to roll backward again.

"I noticed I haven't seen her around. I thought it was maybe just because she has a new boyfriend," Rowe says.

"That's part of it. When she's into a guy, everything else disappears. But honestly, I couldn't care less right now. I kind of welcome the excuse not to have to talk to her," I say, my eyes focusing on a small star sticker above my bed, left by the person who stayed in this room before me, or maybe it was left well before then. I plan on leaving it behind when I leave in the spring—someone else deserves to stare at it when they think too.

"I'm sorry," Rowe says, rolling into me lightly. I grab her arm once and squeeze, pulling myself back up to sitting, and I let my legs dangle off the end of the bed.

"Thanks. It'll work itself out. She just...she broke a promise. But it'll work out," I say, more to convince myself than Rowe.

I was alone for an hour after Rowe took off. Ty left his long-sleeved striped shirt with me, or rather, I took it from his closet, and he didn't make me give it back. I put it on, deciding to use it to give me strength on my plane ride.

Paige calls and tells me to meet her at the curb, so we can share our cab. By the time I meet her out front with my bag, she's already on the phone with someone else. She's talking about the winter formal her sorority is throwing, and she keeps saying how much stress planning this all is going to be.

Stress. This is *stressful* for my sister.

The longer her conversation goes, the more I feel the need to laugh, until finally I give in and let a few chuckles out. She continues to talk while we get into the cab, snapping her fingers and pointing to the driver so he can take her bag. We're only minutes away from the airport when she finally says goodbye, along with some stupid inside joke about rhinoceroses and hippos to whomever she's talking to. She's still laughing to herself, amused by the conversation, when I finally explode.

"You are so rude," I say.

"Uhm, excuse me? *That* was rude," she says, her compact already in her hand so she can check her lipstick.

"Your lips look fine. We're getting on a plane, not having our portraits done," I say. The seal is broken. The words from my mouth are only going to get worse.

"Wow. Someone woke up and put on her bitch costume today," she says. She tucks her compact back in her purse, so at least I get the satisfaction of that.

I manage to keep my mouth shut for the rest of the ride, and I bite my tongue in line, through security, and for the forty minutes we sit and wait for our gate to open. When we finally board, I pull my phone out and text Ty and Rowe, letting them know I'm about to take off. Paige pulls her phone out to check her texts too, and something makes me glance in her lap. I see the picture of her and Chandra, arms around each other, cups in their hands, at some frat party.

"Where was this taken?" I ask, pulling the phone from her fingers.

"First off, don't touch my phone. And second, at a party, duh," she says, taking the phone back and shutting it off completely.

I stare at her, my stomach so sick with hate that I fear I may actually need the bag tucked in the seat-back pocket in front of me. I had this feeling all along that Paige was the one to tell Chandra, but I held out hope. I knew they knew each other, but I convinced myself that they didn't know each other *well*. But my instincts...they are sharp. And as much as I wanted to ignore the arrows, they still pointed to Paige in the end.

"I can't believe you told her," I say, forcing myself to breathe in slowly, an effort to stave off the tears that want to ruin my face. I won't cry. I won't cry.

"Told who what?" Paige says, not looking at me. Her indifference infuriates me, so I grab her chin and pull her face to mine. Her first reaction is to pull back. But then she sees me. She *sees*.

"You told Chandra about Paul Cotterman."

She doesn't deny it. She doesn't blink. She stares right back at me, guilty as hell. The wheels of her mind are spinning, trying to find a version of history that doesn't match up to what I'm saying. But there isn't one. She told her. And Chandra probably told everybody on the team. And I am right back where I started—the girl in high school with the scarlet letter on her forehead.

"Cass," she says, her voice quivering as she pieces it all together.

"I can't trust you," I say, unbuckling my belt and standing quickly to grab my bag from the overhead bin.

"Cass, don't! What are you doing? Where are you going?" Her face honestly looks distressed. I can't deal with it.

"I'm not going anywhere, Paige. I just can't sit here, next to *you*, for four hours. I'm changing seats. That's all," I say, grabbing my bag and moving to the very last row. I can't lean my seat back, and there's less legroom here, but it's better than the alternative.

Paige did it again. I'm going home for a holiday where I'm supposed to be thankful for family—what irony.

Chapter 24

Cass

The festivities were in full swing at the Owens's house. Mom likes to make the house *smell* like the holidays. She says it's her way of combatting the California weather, which keeps things in the high seventies. It doesn't feel very much like fall outside, so my mom makes it seem like fall inside with batches of cinnamon, apples, and potpourri twigs in planters and bowls everywhere I look.

I used to love this when I was a kid. Today, the smell is making me nauseous.

Ty made it home okay. That was the highlight about my trip from the airport. Ty was already settled in, so I could text him for the entire hour ride from LAX to my parents' house, effectively ignoring Paige.

I could tell she was nervous when we got home. She took over the conversation quickly, making sure my mom and dad wouldn't notice how angry I was at her. She's probably more concerned over the fact that her spilling the beans on Paul Cotterman might mess up my dad's negotiations—break the nondisclosure clause. She doesn't like disappointing our parents.

I'll take care of the disappointment checkbox. Soon, my dad is sure to find out I filed a police report. I plan on telling him either way. I decided during the flight that I wasn't going to get walked on during my time at home. I was done playing the part of the mistress girl who *once* got involved with a teacher. I was going to be strong, talk back, stand up for myself, and maybe slam a door or two.

Right now, all I want to do is escape to my room. That's one thing my parents did right—even though they had twins, they never made us room together. My room is all my own, a space just for me. It's always been my retreat—my walls covered in posters of my favorite bands and David Beckham. I think about slamming the door, just to see how it feels, but I'm exhausted from being angry for the last several hours. I'm going to need something to fire me up again to be able to pull off a slam.

The soft knock on my door is unwelcome.

"Come in," I say, bracing myself. *Nobody* is welcomed from this house, it's just a matter of which unwelcomed guest it is. My mom has a fresh set of linens for me, and I know this is a setup, because she could easily have changed the sheets before we came home. I'm sure Paige's are done.

"I'll take them, thanks," I say, pulling the sheets from her hands. She holds on tightly to the pillowcase though, worming her way into the chore. She's not leaving.

"So," she starts. Great, we're going to feign small talk. In my head, I pretend she's going to say what she *really* wants to say.... "How's the Cotterman situation? How's your disabled boyfriend? Why couldn't you just join a sorority or something like your sister...?"

"How is practice going?" she asks.

Okay, I didn't plan for that one.

"Good," I say, with caution. There's a *but* coming somewhere. I wait for it, and wait for it. Mom keeps folding and tucking, and says nothing else.

"Okay, well, your sheets should be set. I'll wash the dusty ones and you can take them back to campus if you need an extra set," she says, smiling and moving to the door with my pile of dirty linens. She pauses right before she pulls the door closed behind her. "I'm glad practice is going well."

All I can do is blink. She was neither fake nor genuine—and nothing about the conversation felt like a mother and a daughter. All I'm hit with is an unbearable weight of sadness over this relationship I somehow don't have with her. Crawling under my freshly tucked blanket, I pull out my phone and slide through the few photos I have of Ty and me, and I think, for just a moment, about going to find my mom to show them to her.

But I don't. Instead, I just pull out my ear buds and play my favorite playlist while I scroll through Twitter looking for naughty photos and good jokes.

After an hour of noodling around on my phone, I give in and join my family in the living room. The sun is setting, and the sound of the local news makes me nostalgic. My dad is out on the grill, and he slides the patio door open and closed a few times before finally calling us all to the table.

"What did he make?" Paige whispers to me. I shrug, both because I don't know and because I still don't want to talk to her.

"Fish?" I say, looking at a long, thin, grilled...*something* on my plate. We never eat fish. And I don't think I really like fish.

"Salmon," my mom says, pulling out her chair to sit at the table. "We've been eating a lot of it lately. It's good for you."

Paige starts cutting hers right away, so I make a few cuts to mine to taste a small piece. It's fishy, but if I dip it in the salad dressing running from my lettuce, I can almost stand it.

"So," my mom starts. The same way she started her last question. This all suddenly feels rehearsed. "Tell us about this Ty fellow."

And here it is. I focus all of my energy on the fish meat on my fork. Heavy dipping in dressing. Long, drawn-out chewing. Hold my finger up to make my family wait for my response. And then, give them nothing of value. "What about him?"

My mom's shoulders slump at my response, and I feel a little bad. Maybe she is trying, and not just picking?

"He's nice," Paige answers for me, and I can't help but shoot her a glare. One, she doesn't like Ty. I can tell. And two, she is the *last* person I want talking for me right now.

"Ha!" I say. I dip a bigger slice of fish—dip, dip, dip, and chew.

"What does that mean?" she asks. My parents disappear from my reality, and I put my knife and fork down slowly, place my napkin on my lap, and prop my elbows on the table. I stop short of cracking my knuckles.

"You can't stand him. You *know* you can't! And that's why mom thinks what she thinks of him—whatever the hell that is. Because you just *had* to talk shit about him to someone, so you called up mom and gave her gossip before I got a chance to introduce him to her the right way," I say, and the feeling of freedom in my chest, of letting this go, is fucking fantastic.

Paige tosses her napkin on the table, whispers an apology to our mom, and then slides her chair out to leave.

"Ohhhhh, so now you're going to leave? We're just getting started, aren't we? Don't you want to stay and talk about the *Cotterman issue* next? Maybe you can bring up all of those boys who called me Easy Owens in high school. And while we're at it, let's talk about how I must have a thing for older men, how I'm a homewrecker, how I slept with Kyle Loftman, and broke up his marriage..."

"I never said you slept with Kyle Loftman!" she interrupts, her fist heavy as it pounds on the table so hard it vibrates the water from our glasses. "I didn't even know about him until mom told me!" This, of course, makes my mom squirm in her seat. My dad, though—he's still cutting his meat, watching us talk— oblivious to the part he played in any of this. "What do you think, that I'm really out to ruin my sister? That...that I have some secret agenda to spread rumors about you? Seriously?"

"Girls, that's enough," my mom tries to stop our flow, but we barely even acknowledge her. This has been building in me, and it needs to come out.

"I don't know, Paige! Somehow, when the rumors find their way to me, I always trace them back to you!" I practically shout.

"That's because I'm the one trying to tell the *real* story! God, Cass...I've been trying to fix this since I embarrassed you by yelling at those assholes who treated you like shit in high school. I never meant for it to start anything, I only wanted them to apologize—to not get away with using you," she says.

"Yeah, well, it started something anyway. You *ruined* my senior year, Paige. And now you're trying to ruin college for me, too," I seethe.

There's a long break in our words, and Paige keeps her eyes on me, her hands flat on the table between us. My mom is looking from her to me, then to my dad, begging him to step in. But there's nothing anyone can say. My last year has been a series of unfortunate incidents, miscommunications, poor judgments by my sister—and I'm just done having others speak on my behalf.

"I never meant to ruin anything for you," Paige says finally, her eyes bloated with water. I hate crying. And I hate that I'm making my sister cry. But I'm still angry. And none of this is okay.

"Why did you tell Chandra about Cotterman?" This is the wound that hurts the most.

"Paige! We can't talk about Cotterman," my dad says quickly, and I hold a hand up to stop him. This isn't a legal issue for me. This is a trust issue—a sister-bond, broken.

"Paige, why?" I ask, and she collapses into her chair, her fight completely gone.

"I thought Chandra was your friend," she says, her shoulders lifting faintly, a small signal to let me know she's being honest. "I thought...I don't know, that somehow...maybe she could help?"

"Paige," I sigh, sitting back in my seat, "Chandra hates me. I'm her biggest threat on the team. Why would she help me?"

"Because..." she says, her eyes slowly moving from the tabletop directly in front of her, along the distance between us, until her gaze meets mine. "—because she dated him last year."

Oh. My. Fucking. God.

My dad is already starting in with questioning. I know how his brain works. He wants to talk to Chandra, question her, see if she had a similar situation. Paige answers his barrage of questions with short one-word answers. They *dated.* He didn't assault her. It's different, though yes, inappropriate. But my dad wants to talk to her anyway...see if there's a pattern of abuse, of anger, anything he can have in his hip pocket. It's like I'm sitting in the middle of a pot of boiling water, bubbles bursting all around me, my skin on fire, everything poking and prodding to try to make me explode.

"I didn't do anything to deserve this," I say, standing up again and looking my dad in the eyes. I walk over to him and put my hand on his chest. "I love you, Daddy. I know you're just trying to fix this. But I'm tired. I didn't do anything wrong. Not once. And I'm just...I'm just done."

Nobody stops me from leaving the table. Nobody follows me into my room. And nobody checks on me for the next hour. The space beyond my door is quiet, which means dinner is over and everyone either retreated to their spaces or went outside to talk about me more. I don't care where they went or what they do, as long as I don't have to be a part of it.

When my phone rings, my heart dances. Knowing it's Ty makes my lips stretch into a smile for the first time in hours.

"Hey," I answer, doing my best to sound less like a girl who just had her hope stolen from her chest and wrung out in front of her.

"Guess who got his Cookie back?" he asks, the giddiness in his voice making my smile stretch even larger.

"Thank the lord. Seriously, I don't think I could endure another round of ransom embarrassment," I say. "How'd you get him?"

"Rowe caved," he says.

"Hmmmm, she...*caved?* That doesn't sound very much like Rowe," I say.

"What can I say, my charm won her over. She was no match," he says. I close my eyes when he speaks, picturing him here, his voice deep, thick with Southern drawl. I imagine his face—I want to see his face. "Oh, she also told me I was an asshole for not inviting you to come home with me. So..."

I sit up when he says this. Seconds pass, and I start to worry over what to say in response when he finally fills the void for me.

"I really wish I did," his voice no longer humorous. "I miss you like crazy."

"God, I miss you too," I say, pulling the sleeve of his shirt up to my face, breathing in deep and closing my eyes again. I can almost convince myself he's here—his smell and his voice with me.

"You should know, I'm going to visit Kelly tomorrow," he says, and just as fast he's gone—a thousand miles away...with *her*.

"Oh," I say. Small. Meek. Fragile.

"I don't want you to...I don't know...be jealous?" I'm embarrassed that he even says this. "I know it's not easy to hear about her. I wouldn't like you to have a Kelly."

"Yeah, well, lucky for you, all I have is a *Cotterman issue*," I say back, letting out a small, pathetic laugh.

"I don't like that you have that, either," he says, still serious.

"I know. Thank you," I say.

"I'm going to show her your pictures. She wants to see what you look like. I've been talking about you—kind of a lot," he says, and this time I blush in a good way.

"Saying good things, I hope?" I hold my breath.

"Well, I mean I did tell her that you don't like Leo. She's not too sure about that," he says.

"Hey! I never said I don't like Leo, I just haven't been exposed enough," I say, sitting up and gesturing like he's really here. Ty has this effect; he brings my energy back, puts the life back in my veins.

"Okay, well...maybe you get a pass then. Kelly *will* agree with me on one thing, though," he says.

"Yeah? What's that?" I ask.

"That you're beautiful," he says, and I lie down on my pillow, the phone pressed tightly to my cheek and ear.

"Thank you for saying that," I say.

"It's only the truth," he says, and somehow, my face turns even redder.

"Do you think, maybe...you can just stay on the phone? You know, while I fall asleep? It's been kind of a shitty day. And...I don't know. I just sort of need you tonight," I say. I feel vulnerable and helpless and foolish at first, but Ty annihilates those fears in an instant.

"I'll be right here," he says, and my breathing eases.

He reads some sports scores to me from his phone, then I listen to him watch *Sports Center* and *oooh* and *ahhh* over top plays. My eyelids grow heavy, and I only perk up to react when he speaks more than a few words as the half-hour show closes. The last words I remember his tender *goodnight* and the way he calls me *baby.*

Ty

Cass drifted off, and eventually so did I. But I never, not once, ended the call. She must have hit end before me, because she was gone from the other line when I woke up this morning.

I love Thanksgiving in our house. My mom hates turkey, and Dad doesn't care enough to make a fuss. So we always eat things we *really* want, and my mom makes enough for a week's worth of leftovers. This year is eggrolls and lasagna. The entire house stinks, but in a good way—*mostly*. It smells of onions and butter and maybe cabbage. I think that extra stench tacked on is from the cabbage for the eggrolls.

I treat myself to a handful of shredded mozzarella before my mom slides the lasagna tray back into the fridge, so she can time it with the eggrolls. She slaps my hand the first time, but when she starts washing her hands at the sink, I go in for one more pinch, smirking with pride that she can't stop me.

"I need the keys," I say, and Dad tosses them to me from his spot on the sofa. He'll be there for most of the day.

"You make sure you're home in an hour. You know your brother won't want to wait to eat," Mom says.

"I know. He's such a pig," I tease, and Nate reaches over the counter to the sink, flinging a handful of water at me, and then flipping me off.

"Can we have one finger-free holiday, for Pete's sake?" Mom says.

"I don't know who Pete is, but tell him I don't like him fingering you," I tease, my eyebrows high as I push backward out of my mom's reach. She tries to fling water at me next, but it's too late. So instead, she just flips me off. "Gosh, Mom. You're such a hypocrite," I joke.

"I'm serious. Be home in an hour," she says.

"Okay, got it." I cross my heart and leave the room, push through the front door and head down the ramp.

Driving the van is always easiest, because I can load my chair and lift myself to the driver's seat. The hand controls are better on this than my mom's Jeep, too.

Kelly's waiting for me. She lives only a few miles from my parents' house. Jared is home, and her parents are at the house. I had to promise her a thousand times that I wouldn't start something today, but I'm not sure I can help myself. Jared is being selfish, even if he isn't using. He's being selfish with his time—he needs to spend that on his wife and son.

I get to their house quickly, but as I'm rounding the corner, I see Jared bound down the driveway, his keys dangling from a finger as he gets in his car. He's probably running to the store to get something Kelly forgot. But maybe he's going somewhere else.

Paused at the corner, I wait for him to back out of the driveway and speed down the street in the other direction before I turn and stop short of Kelly's house. She won't want me to do this. But I *have* to. Kelly deserves answers, and I'm her friend. I realized recently that I'm her *best* friend. And as that, I need to do this.

Instead of pulling in, I keep driving. I follow the path Jared took down the street to the end of the block. I catch his car making a left turn, so I speed around the corner to catch him. I get another glimpse of him turning right as I round the last corner he took, and I speed forward again, saying a silent prayer for the cops to be on my side today, to be lenient, and not to be anywhere I am driving.

I'm able to catch up to him at a stoplight on the busier road, and I position myself a car or two behind him so he won't notice me. We drive for about ten minutes, several miles, to the next city over. We've passed a dozen grocery stores and convenience stores—all open for holiday hours. He's not running an errand. Or, at least, that's not his *real* reason for making this trip.

We drive three more blocks, and he pulls into a neighborhood diner. It's one of those pancake houses, a place for truckers to stop. I pull in to an end spot, one that gives me a good view of the entire parking lot and the bay of windows looking into the restaurant.

When Jared gets out of his car, he stops and pulls out his phone, probably to make sure Kelly hasn't called or texted...or maybe he's getting a message from his dealer. He looks around the lot, but thankfully his head never fully turns in my direction. I'm not very good at hiding. And I'm not sure I don't want him to see me.

After a few seconds, he walks to the diner entrance, steps inside, and moves toward the line of booths along the window.

And then it all becomes so painfully clear.

The girl is beautiful. Long, red hair, she looks to be about the same age as Kelly. She's wearing a blue sweater and jeans, and looks like she dressed up just enough to impress someone—impress a boyfriend or a date.

They kiss.

His hand moves to her face.

His other hand grips her hand.

They hold hands on the table.

He orders coffee. So does she.

They drink.

They laugh.

They talk.

They kiss more.

He puts some money on the table, and she follows him out to the parking lot.

He gets in his car.

She gets in his car.

He drives to the back of the lot, near the unkempt trees and bushes that block most of their view.

She climbs on his lap.

They kiss more.

I take a photo with my phone.

I leave.

He's not using. Goddamn how I wish that were it. I wish he were using. I could be angry at him, punish him, force him into rehab—make him do right by Kelly.

But this? I can't forgive this. For me, this is unforgiveable. This is unacceptable. You don't make promises of the heart just to break them. I never promised a girl something I couldn't give her. The only promises I've made are to Kelly and Cass. And I'm living by them both.

Jared is a coward.

Jared is a dead man.

And I have to tell Kelly, because he'll just keep doing this. And she deserves better.

I spend ten minutes in her driveway, trying to figure out what to say—how to pull her away from her parents, how to have this conversation. I sit there for so long, eventually she sees me out the window. She comes out of the house, down the driveway to where I'm parked.

"You know, you *are* allowed inside," she says when I unroll the window.

I can't even fake this, and she knows me too well to be able to ignore the expression on my face.

"What is it?" she asks. She looks so tired. But she's still Kelly, still the beautiful girl I've known for so much of my life.

"Can you...take a short drive?" I ask, hating that I'm pulling her away from her family on a holiday, but not knowing how to handle this any other way.

"Give me a minute," she says, walking back up her drive to the house. I notice her hand flexes as she walks. She does this when she's stressed, when she's angry. She knows something bad is coming.

She comes back out with keys and her phone in her hand. Picking up her step, she jogs to the van, rounding the front and getting inside. She smells like pie—she's been baking.

"My parents are watching Jackson. We have some time," she says, her gaze empty, her focus lost out the front window, her hands clutched to her phone and keys. She relaxes just long enough to put on her seatbelt. I back out and drive us a few blocks to the old elementary school. I pull in so we're facing the swings, the same ones she used to push me on—the ones where I used to look up her dress. The memory makes me laugh under my breath.

"I used to pretend to fall out of the swings, you know," I admit.

"I know," she says. "You were looking up my dress. That's why I wore shorts."

Her confession makes me smile, but now is not the time for smiling or happy memories, so I hold my hand over my mouth until I can regain my composure.

"I followed Jared," I say.

She doesn't respond, but her grip on her belongings gets tighter. I hear her swallow, see her throat move slowly, see her eyes twitch with both fury and tears. But she holds it all in, her breath heavy through her nose.

"Kel," I say, reaching my hand over to her arm, sliding it down to her hand, forcing her hand loose from its grip, until she holds mine back. Her eyes still stay forward. "He's not using, Kel."

She remains rigid, but her hand squeezes me tightly. A single tear falls from her eye, slides down her cheek, lands on her arm, and waits to dissolve completely.

"I know," she says. Somehow, her knowing makes this feel better. Everything is still awful, but her knowing, her not being surprised by what I'm saying—me not being the one to break it to her completely—somehow that makes this easier for me. And, selfish bastard that I am, I'm relieved by that.

"How long?" I ask. It's not my place. None of this is. But Kelly is family to me. And she's being disrespected. I need answers so I know what to do—how to avenge her.

"I think...I think maybe a few months," she says, her face falling to the side, her eyes moving to our hands. She lets go slowly, folding her arms up to stave off the chill. I push the heater up a level. "I found a text from her last night. Before he could delete it. He's been deleting everything. Or at least, I guess he has."

Jared is an idiot. Jared is an asshole. Jared is a poor excuse for a human being. Jared can eat shit. Jared is going to feel pain, really soon. It's a stream of rants running through my mind while I sit here in the van with Kelly, our view of simple times, of our innocence.

"I feel so stupid," she says, biting her lip, another tear following along the same path as the first. I reach over and catch it, holding my hand to her face, and she closes her eyes.

"You aren't stupid. You are amazing. And Jared..." I choke down bile from saying his name. "He doesn't deserve you."

Several minutes pass. I don't talk. Kelly doesn't talk. She lays her head on my hand, and I let her. Every now and then her face winces, like it's being attacked from the inside. She wants to cry, but she doesn't want to break.

"Do you want to meet Jackson?" she asks finally.

"I'd love to." I smile and move the gear into reverse to back out of the lot. We drive back to her home, her ruined and poisoned home with white siding and blue trim. I'm relieved that Jared's car still isn't in the driveway. I'm not ready to see him. I won't be able to help myself. And Kelly needs to call the shots on this.

She helps me from the van, just like she always did. I let her push me inside, over the lip of the door, and then I hug her parents. They look the same, only their hair a little grayer. Her dad looks stronger than when I saw him last, having survived another bout with cancer a year or two ago. Kelly brings Jackson over, a tiny human, bundled in an orange pumpkin onesie that covers his feet. He's perfect. He's beautiful. He's everything Kelly, and nothing Jared. Thank God.

Jared doesn't deserve him either.

I hold him for a few minutes, and he doesn't cry. His body feels warm, and his small movements are the coolest things I've ever felt—the way his legs jut forward, his hand reaches for nothing, his eyes open and close in slow motion. His yawn is adorable. And he smells like powder and strawberries.

We reminisce about high school, swap embarrassing stories about grade school, and I give them updates on college and life in Oklahoma. It's a pleasant, safe conversation, but there's always an undertone of regret when Kelly and I make eye contact. Regret that her world is crumbling, and I know about it, but there's nothing we can do to fix it. She's going to have to live through this pain, because even ignoring it would hurt.

Kelly pulls her phone from her back pocket, and her brow pinches as she reads a text. It's Jared. I know it is. I wait for her eyes to meet mine, and she motions for me to follow her to the door. She doesn't want me to see Jared. I understand. It's probably best I don't.

I say my goodbyes, making excuses for my quick departure. Mom wants me home in time for dinner. It's the truth in a way, though Mom would understand. I kiss Jackson's small, fuzzy head, and follow Kelly through the door back to the van. She helps me pack my chair, and I position myself in the driver's seat.

"He's on his way home. Said he'd be about twenty minutes. Apparently, they were out of pumpkin filling at five stores," she says with a harsh laugh.

"Kel, if you need me...if you need me here? If you want me to deal with him? Anything, just say the word," I say, and she leans in through the window and kisses my cheek, her hand trembling along my face. She's scared. And she's angry.

"I know. Not today. Today we get to have Thanksgiving. Jackson gets to have this. And my parents get to have this," she says, her hand dropping to her side with a heaviness. "But tomorrow...he's out of the house."

The blankness to her stare when she says that last part is serious. It's an expression she's never made for me, because of me, and I'm grateful I've never earned it.

I reach out and squeeze her arm one more time. She covers my hand with hers. Her gaze is soft and warm again when she looks at me, and she takes a deep breath. For a moment, staring at her, we're that same couple we were in high school—like I'm dropping her off after a dance, just having kissed her goodbye. She's so very much a part of me. And yet, what we are to one another is so different now. It's important all the same.

"You love her?" she asks, and at first, I'm nervous by her question. Not because of what she's asking, but because of everything that she's just been through. Because it doesn't feel fair for me to love someone when she's hurting like this. But the longer I look at her, the longer I think, the calmer I become. The more sure I am...sure of everything. The more I see in her eyes that she wants something for me—something *more* than I've been giving myself.

"Yeah, I love her," I say, allowing myself to be happy and smile cautiously in front of my heartbroken best friend. She wouldn't want me to be fake.

"Good," she says, and I know she means it. Her smile looks sad, but only for her own loss. "You should let her know that."

"I'm working on that. I'm not very good at...you know...sayin' mushy shit?" Her laugh is fast and raspy, and she looks to the side while she shakes her head and leans back from the van, her hands gripping the window frame.

"Ty," she sighs, coming back to me and placing both hands flat along the door panel, patting them down once for emphasis. "You are *especially* good at the mushy shit."

Her hands slip from the window, and she backs away, giving me one wink.

214

"Call me, Kel. For anything. I mean it," I say, and she holds up a hand to wave goodbye before pulling her arms in to hug her body. She doesn't break stride, doesn't pause at the door, doesn't let any of it show in front of her family. She walks back inside to pretend everything's fine for a few more hours, for today.

She's so strong.

She'll be okay.

I convince myself she'll be okay.

Chapter 25

Cass

The news was spreading all over the campus news sites when we got back to school.

ASSOCIATE FACULTY MEMBER FILES LAWSUIT AGAINST SCHOOL FOR WRONGFUL TERMINATION

I read the story a thousand times. No mention of my name. No mention of his assault either. A few quotes from school administrators, talking points that only circle the story, but never really saying anything. The closest anyone gets to the truth is when one faculty member uses the word *accusations*. Yes, someone made an accusation—based on an assault. Student reporters don't dig as deeply as they should. A little legwork would have turned up my police report. But they only worked off of the tip they received, probably from Cotterman's lawyer. A bigger city, a bigger state—the more the media attention would be. It's big enough for me as it is.

The plane ride here was just as quiet as the one going. And Paige didn't try to fix things when we got to campus. She has a big formal to attend, the fruits of her planning. She's distracting herself with that. And I'm glad.

In the meantime, I've come back to a lonely dorm room. Rowe left Nate and Ty's parents' house in the middle of the holiday. Her ex-boyfriend—the one who was barely living on life-support—died. Nate's not talking about it at all, and he's been completely closed off, spending most of his time at practice and alone with Ty. Ty told me it didn't go well, that Rowe is extremely upset. I guess Nate knew about it before she did; somehow her parents told Nate first, asking him to keep it a secret until she was done with finals.

They meant well. That's what everyone keeps saying.

They meant well.

Everyone means well—making decisions for you, taking things out of your control. But meaning well doesn't mean it's the right thing to do.

I text my friend again, hoping she'll say she's coming back, that she isn't leaving me here alone. I need her. But she doesn't write back. She's gone dark. And with two weeks left including finals, I worry that I may never see her again.

"You skipped!" Ty says, busting through my door with a pizza on his lap. I skipped my workout session with him this afternoon, not really feeling the energy.

"I know, I'm sorry. I'm feeling a little zapped today," I say, not really sure if it's my body, the stress, or my spirit. Maybe it's all three.

"Hmmmm, okay, you get one pass. But the next time you lose a whole letter grade," he says, flipping open the box and pulling a slice out on a napkin. The smell is glorious, and for the first time in days, I think I'm hungry.

"I didn't realize I was getting a grade for my workouts with you," I say, holding a slice to my mouth and blowing on it to cool.

"Baby, I'm always evaluating. Always," he says, winking. Cocky son-of-a-bitch. I love that about him.

"Oh yeah, me too," I say, handing him a napkin. He has a giant splotch of sauce on his chin. "That's going to put you at a C, maybe even a C minus."

"What, a little sauce? Damn, you grade hard," he says, wiping his chin. "That's fine though. I like extra credit."

"I bet you do," I tease.

Things quickly slid back to natural with Ty. He told me about his visit with Kelly, and I feel terrible about what she found out. I can't imagine being a young mother, newly married, and having a husband cheat. I think if Ty could find a way to take out both Paul Cotterman and Jared with one shot, and make it look like an accident, he would.

The threat of the lawsuit is wearing on me. It's there when I wake up in the morning, dangling above my head, threatening to ruin my reputation, yet again. I call my dad every afternoon for an update, and it's always the same. We're still talking with his lawyers, trying to find out what leverage he has.

Leverage.

I'll tell you what kind of leverage he has. He's a young faculty member, decent looking, and charming with his female students. And if he smells weakness in any form, he goes in after it, for his own pleasure. He uses leverage for evil. And I'd bust his nose again if given the chance.

The latest worry was that he was thinking of pressing charges against me. He has doctor's reports on his fractured nose. Suing me for breaking his nose. What an ass!

When my phone rings, I hold it and consider putting my dad off. I doubt he has anything new, and I don't like having these conversations with him in front of Ty. But there's also a part of me that's holding on to hope that one of these times, one phone call, my dad will say it's all over, that the case was dropped. That Paul is gone. That I get to play soccer without worry. That I get to be young, be in love, and just be me—just Cass. That was the plan all along.

I slide to answer, and hold my breath, ready to be debriefed on the *Cotterman issue.*

"Hey dad," I say, through a full mouth.

"Ah sorry, pumpkin. Did I call during dinner?" He's been calling me pet names lately, trying to soften our relationship. My blowup at dinner the night before Thanksgiving did a real number on my parents. My mom must have cried apologies to me a dozen times. My dad deals with things differently, just changing his behavior. What it's really going to take is time...and lots of it.

"No, it's fine. It's just pizza," I say, taking a big gulp from the soda bottle to clear my mouth. "So, where are we at today?"

"Things are looking good," he says. I almost spit out the sip I just took, shocked. Things haven't looked good in a while, since I gave Cotterman a bloody nose, to be honest. Good was not what I was expecting.

"Good. Wow. Really?" I say, turning to Ty and smiling. He gives me a thumbs up.

"We made an amendment to the original settlement, and Paul accepted," my dad says. His legalese is a little vague.

"An amendment...and he...*accepted?*" I ask, still not sure what this means.

"Yeah, we changed the terms of the settlement. Really, there was no way he could not accept, Cass. He would have been a fool not to," my dad says. Something about the way he says it, his phrasing, makes me itchy. So I push for more.

"Did we...*pay* him? Is that how we're making this all go away?" I ask, and the silence on the other end confirms it. "Dad...did you give him more money? The man who tried to...*ohhhh*...oh my god."

The thought of it all makes me sick, and I feel dirtier than I ever have before.

"You hit him, Cass," my dad says, like that's the only fact on the table.

"Yes, because he wanted to sexually assault me!" I bite back, tossing the rest of my uneaten pizza in the trash.

My dad's sigh comes through loud and clear, and it makes my head hurt. "Cass, the law isn't black and white like that," he says.

"Like what, like, you can't hit someone in the temple and kick them in the face so they don't violate you? Black and white like that?" I'm pacing in a circle, walking my pattern in front of Ty until he holds my waist to stop me. My eyes burn, my head hurts, my world is spinning. I don't understand any of this.

"Cass, the details, they're what you say and what Paul Cotterman says," my dad begins to explain, and I cut him off.

"You mean I could be lying, and maybe I came onto him and brought this trouble on myself. Just like I did with Kyle. That's what you mean, isn't it Dad?"

"Cass, I didn't say that. Don't put words in my mouth," he says, defending himself. He's fucking defending himself.

"No, Dad. If I put words in your mouth, they could never be as hurtful as the thoughts you have about me." I hang up before he can say another word, and I throw the phone on my bed.

I should be elated. This is what I wanted—the Cotterman issue put to bed. But somehow all I feel is worse. My phone buzzes from his call, and I silence it.

"I need to shower," I say, unable to look at Ty. I feel embarrassed, and I think I'm going to cry. If I can just make it to the shower, I can do it under the powerful spray of the water, and it will be like it never happened.

"Go ahead," Ty says. "I'll wait here. As long as you need."

I know he will. And even though I want to send him away, more of me *needs* him to stay, to wait...even though it could be hours.

Rowe left her small basket here, and I use it to carry my towel and pajamas, to have a place to set everything on the bench just outside of the shower stall. I see why Rowe likes to shower at night now; it's quiet in here. The sense of being alone is both comforting and frightening. But when you feel like I do right now—ugly, angry—the dark is welcoming, like a blanket.

The water does it's magic, washing away any sign of weakness to come from my eyes. The warmth pounds my back and my arms and my chest, working my muscles, the steam opening my lungs. After about thirty minutes, I almost feel right again. And then my vision

slides

to

the

right.

Everything. Doubles.

My world slants, and I trail my body down the wall to sit under the water.

The water can't erase this.

Blink.

Blink.

Blink.

I wait for it to stop. It's temporary. This has to be temporary.

Everything will fix itself. It has to.

You can't pay off MS.

Ty

I plan on answering her phone the next time it rings. I planned it the moment she said she was leaving to shower. It's impulsive. I'm good when I'm impulsive. It's never failed me.

I don't even let the ring finish when I press on the call to answer. And I know her father is shocked as hell when he hears a man's voice answer "Hello, Mr. Owens."

"Oh, I...I'm sorry. I...this is Cassidy's phone, right? Who...who is this?"

"It's Tyson, sir. I'm sorry this is how I'm meeting you. I really prefer to make an in-person first impression. This feels rude, so I do apologize," I say, letting my accent come out thick. The Southern thing—it's helpful when you're trying to work an angle, trying to make a point. For some reason, people let you talk just a little bit longer when you say things with a Louisiana accent.

"Tyson. While it's nice to finally speak with you, if you don't mind, I'd really like to talk to Cassidy," he says. He's a lawyer. My impulsivity might not work as well as I thought.

"I know, sir. She left. She was...upset. I'm waiting for her," I say, leaving it vague. I want to see if he worries.

"Is she all right? It's late there. Where did she go?"

This is the response I want.

"She's fine. She just went to the women's showers. She needed some time alone," I say, suddenly aware that it's late, and I'm with his daughter in her room. Ah well, fuck it. Let him think what he wants. "I was actually hoping...maybe you and I could talk? Cass, she's confided in me, about everything. And I was here...when you called the last time."

There's a long silence on the phone. Her father—he isn't as bad as she thinks he is. He's human. And I think he's trying to do the right thing. He's just stuck and doesn't know how. And Cass is so hurt that she can't unbury herself.

"I'm sorry, Tyson. I don't know if I'm comfortable talking about this private matter, with you. I hope you understand," he says.

"Of course," I say. "Just...if I may...I know we haven't met, and I'm not sure how much Cass has told you about me."

"Very little," he says, curtly. Ouch. That was...not nice. I shake it off, because, well, I'm used to being insulted.

"Okay, well, I'm sure she has her reasons," I say. I know Cass wants to introduce me, on her own terms. And I know her sister beat her to it. So I don't fault Cass for this at all. "I've been a paraplegic for a little more than six years."

221

He doesn't interrupt. I thought my words out while I was waiting for his call, and I knew I would share this and share it quickly. It's hard for people to stop you when you lead with this line. It's a perk of my circumstance. I've earned temporary patience. And I use it to my advantage.

"Stupid cliff-diving accident; dumbest thing I've ever done. Ruined my life. Or it could have. I thought it did for a while. But I had people in my life who saw me for everything *but* my disability, for everything beyond that stupid decision. They saw my potential. And they preached to me, pounded it into my head, day after day, hour after hour, until yeah...I saw my potential too. I'm getting my MBA. I'm sure Paige didn't mention that. I graduated magna cum laude for undergrad, on a scholarship. School...it's so easy for me, it isn't even funny. I don't have to study, because things just make sense to me. My brain is strong. My body is strong. I haven't run into something that I *can't* find a way to do. And you know why?"

I give him a second to answer, but he doesn't. It's okay—he hears me. I'm sure he hears me.

"Because when I needed people the most, my parents, my brother, my friends—they stood up. They were present. They didn't go for *easy*. My mom, she could have thrown medicine at me. I was a teenager, and she could have forced me to take drugs to help me cope with depression, to find courage, to sleep, to not feel the never-ending firing pain from my damaged nerves. I was afraid of what drugs would mean. I didn't want to take them. So she found another way. She led me through the hard way, and she didn't stop until I came out the other side."

"I train others with disabilities. I'm not sure if Paige mentioned this either. I train them because I like to see what happens when someone believes in themself. That's how I got to know your daughter. I trained her. I trained her right into believing in herself. And you know what happened? She started to want things again. She started to dream.

"My god, Mr. Owens. Your daughter—when she's running, pushing herself...when she's in her sport, competing—she's fearsome. I have never seen anything or anyone like her. And I love her. I haven't even told her yet, but I do. I love her for everything she is, and I love her for how much she makes me believe in the possible. She's defiance, in all of its glory. And I don't really care that it isn't my place to tell you this, but if you're too focused on taking the easy route to stop, just for a second, and watch her...and see her *as she is?* I'm not so sure you deserve to be the one she runs to in the first place."

I wasn't expecting applause. Though, the slow-clap does pass through my mind and briefly amuses me. I'm pretty impressed with my own speech, and even if Cass's father isn't, I feel pretty good about everything I said. I'd say it all to Cass and mean every word. The silence lasts for a few long seconds, and eventually, I hear him swallow—perhaps his pride.

"If you could tell her that I called," he says.

"I can do that, sir. You have a good night now," I say, one more little cherry on top.

I put the phone down and grab the remote from Cass's desk, flipping the television to *Sports Center,* and I wait for her to feel strong enough to come in and join me. By the end of the show, she's here.

"Your father called," I say. She rolls her eyes and crawls into her bed, patting the space next to her. I don't elaborate, because I don't want to freak her out. It's not a lie. It's omitting, a little. A lot. But I think this calls for an exception.

Chapter 26

Cass

Rowe's coming back.

Paige left early.

The *Cotterman issue* is now a *non-issue*.

I have to admit, the positives are starting to add up. I was even almost looking forward to the holidays. Mom has been calling me every day. It was annoying at first, because I knew it was all about making her feel better. But I find I'm starting to actually look forward to her calls. We still talk about nothing. She doesn't ask about Ty. I don't talk about Ty. She doesn't ask about practice. I don't talk about practice. And maybe that's okay—maybe I get to live my life separate from her knowing about it, and we get to meet in the middle, in the land of make-believe where I'm interested in the bead and textile expo.

She does try to ask me questions about Paige. She doesn't like it when we're fighting. And I don't like feeling this way about my sister. But I'm having a hard time getting over this one. It's always a matter of trust between her and me, and that bridge has just been burned so many times, I don't know if I can rebuild it any more.

I have one more final. Ty left for home with his brother yesterday, and Nate gave me a letter to give to Rowe. He told me not to read it—which was probably not wise. I don't think I would have if he hadn't made it so off limits. I steamed it open in the shower room, but you can totally tell I butchered the envelope. I think I'll just admit it to Rowe. She won't care.

The words in his letter...they were everything I want Ty to say to me in so many ways. Those boys are special. And I hope he and Rowe can figure things out.

I've been waiting at the window for an hour for the cab to drop Rowe off. I used to wait for my grandparents to show up on the holidays like this, my chair pulled right up to the windowsill and my face pressed on the glass. The thought makes me smile, so I breathe frost onto the window glass and draw a heart with

Ty's name in the middle. I feel silly and childish after, so I pull my sleeve over my wrist and erase it.

When the cab pulls up and Rowe steps out with her small bag, I slide my chair back from the window and step up on my bed and start jumping. I've missed her, more than I thought. And seeing her face when she walks into the room almost makes me cry.

"Yayyyyyyyy!" I actually scream when she comes in, like a child waiting for the fair to come to town.

"Uh...yeah. Yay," she says, looking at me like I'm a weirdo. Okay, maybe I'm a little overexcited. I've been alone for a full day, and the halls are empty, and it was getting to me. I've studied for my sign language final so much that I now feel qualified to teach the course.

Once Rowe gets settled in, we go to the dining hall, which is also empty, like a scene from *The Stand*. I fill my plate, I've been carb loading, probably from all of the running and workouts I've been doing. I tend to stress-eat, and finals, along with everything else, have been stressful.

"So, I'm officially on the team," I tell Rowe, and she smiles, happy for me, but still not quite herself. She's mourning her old boyfriend, and I think she's also mourning her relationship with Nate. I hope she gives him a chance.

"I guess that means you'll be pretty busy this spring?" she asks.

"Not any more than I have been. Instead of workouts, we'll have games. Soccer isn't like baseball and football. Women's sports, we sort of get the shaft," I say. I want to ask her if she'll be here next semester, but I'm afraid to open that door, so I just take her interest in my schedule as a sign that she will be.

She turns her attention to my overstuffed tray of food, picking on my lack of healthy choices, and when she jokes with me I can see glimpses of *my* Rowe. It almost feels like that first week of school again. The campus is empty, and Rowe and I nervously make our way back to our room, spending the rest of the night watching TV.

It's nice not sleeping alone. Last night—without Ty, without *anyone*—was hard. I don't think I ever fully fell asleep. The dorm hallways are full of strange noises at night, the creaking of the heating pipes, the echo in the hallway when someone shuts a door from far away. Even the sounds from the outside creep into the inside when nobody is around. I started to focus on the chirping crickets and the occasional car driving by.

We're watching one of those reality shows on MTV; I'm not even sure which one. There's a lot of yelling and relationship drama. It's funny how that's not how it looks like in real life, yet this is supposed to be *reality.* I turn my head to Rowe and imagine her standing on a table, drunk, and telling Nate off like the girl on the TV is right now, and it makes me laugh to myself.

No. Not reality at all.

"Have you talked to him yet?" I ask her, and she just shakes her head *no.* What I want to do is pull out Nate's letter, show it to her, fawn over it, and watch her heart melt just like I know it's going to. But I can't, not until tomorrow. I promised Nate I wouldn't give it to her until her finals were done.

Nate poured his heart out in his words to her. I cheated and read some of it to Ty over the phone. He made fun of Nate, called him a lovesick puppy, but I think it's only because he was uncomfortable hearing his brother's honesty. I get it. Guys don't do chick flicks, and Nate's letter—it's one big-ass chick flick. I wish I made a copy of it I love it so much.

"I don't know what to say. Everything is all...I don't know...messy?" Rowe says.

I understand messy. I've been in what Ty would call one *messy fussy fuss* for weeks. But my mess...it's kind of over. And I'm starting to appreciate the fact that my dad put an end to it, even if I don't like the *way* he put an end to it.

"You know, Nate was sort of really put in a crappy position," I say, rolling on my side to look at my friend. Her parents asked him to keep a secret, and he didn't want to. She has to forgive him. She will, once she reads his letter. "He's been a wreck."

As much as Rowe wants to stay in this somber place, her lips can't help but twitch into the faintest smile when I let her know how Nate has been feeling—*feeling*...about her. And I

226

know the second she reacts to what I say that they're going to be fine.

We're all going to be fine.

The hours of solitude spent studying earned me a perfect score on my sign language exam. I don't even need to see the grade to know. I had to hold a conversation with my instructor for five minutes, and I anticipated every question she would ask when I studied. My hands were perfect today, my signs perfect. She smiled at me when our time was up. She never smiles, so I know I did well.

I gave Rowe the letter just as Nate instructed, as soon as she was done with her finals. I was risking being late to the airport for my own flight home, but my task was too important. I wouldn't mess this up.

When I got off the plane, I turned my phone on and saw I had two messages, one from Ty, and one from Rowe. I knew the letter worked. I called Rowe quickly and promised her I would help pull off whatever she needed to do to reciprocate his letter. I also apologized again for reading her business. But I'm not really sorry. It was beautiful. Rowe was planning on finding Nate when he traveled to Arizona for the first seasonal baseball tournament. She said something about singing to him, which sounds scary as hell to me, but Rowe...she can actually kind of sing. I want to be there with her for it, to support my friend through whatever crazy stunt she has planned. I'm also a sucker for big romantic gestures, just not when they put the spotlight on me.

My smile flips when I see Paige parked at the curb to pick me up. My mom had said she would do it, and I honestly expected my dad to be the one waiting for me. Paige was the last person I wanted to see, even though I admit to myself that I miss her. At least she's not in my Charger.

She pulls the lever to pop her trunk, and I put my things in the back. Paige drives a Mazda. It's pink. I swear it's the only pink car Mazda ever made.

"Thanks for picking me up," I say, slamming the door closed a little harder than I mean to. I really want to be nice, or at least pleasant. But being near her, it just brings everything back to the surface. I'm fighting so hard not to be mad, to remain rational.

"Sure," she says, signaling and pulling out into traffic. Some guy honks at her, and she looks rattled from it, nervous. That's not like her. Paige doesn't get pushed around. "I asked Mom if I could get you instead. I wanted to. I hope that's okay."

"Yeah, it's okay," I say, still not really sure if it is, but I feel like that's what needs to be said right now. I think I've kicked her enough, and she's still down. And today I don't feel good about it.

She turns the radio up when we hit the highway, and we listen to the hits station for the next hour, not talking, only soaking in the familiar sounds of home. This is normal for us, riding together in silence. But it used to not feel so uncomfortable. We usually sing along with the chorus, for the few songs that we both actually agree on. There's so many things unspoken floating between us now—I can feel them.

When we get to the house and pull in the driveway, I leave the car and move to the back to grab my things. Paige stays in the driver's seat, her hands low on the steering wheel while she watches me through the rearview mirror.

I close the trunk and shrug at her to come inside, to get out of the car, to move, or say something. But she just sits there, staring at me. My bags are heavy, but I hold them to my sides, my duffel slung over my shoulder, while I drag everything to the car door next to her, her window now rolled down. She's turned the ignition off, but she's still staying in the car. It's weird. And it's irritating me.

"Paige, just come inside. Seriously...I'm tired. It's late. I'm hungry. I'm not in the mood for your drama right now," I say. She shuts her eyes and shakes her head, her lips curling like they want to laugh, but no sound comes out.

"I am so jealous of you. I actually used to fantasize about what it would be like to hate you," Paige says. She won't look at me, keeping her focus on the place where her skirt skims the tops of her knees. She runs her hands down the material, straightening it, pulling the fabric lower. Demure—she's being demure...now.

"Wow," I say, not really sure what else to add. I let my bags fall to the ground next to me, my muscles almost seizing from the build up of lactic acid. I have a feeling Paige and I might be out here in this driveway for a while.

"It used to be the attention, the way everyone worried about you. They don't worry about me. I know, I know...it's stupid and petty. And I don't feel like that now, but I used to," she continues. I'm still stuck on that word *hate*, wondering if I've ever wished that about her. I think I might have, as recent as yesterday. And it makes me a little ashamed, because my sister is at least big enough to admit it. To my face.

"You said am...*am* jealous. What in the world could you possibly have to be jealous about now?" I ask.

She breathes in deeply, and closes her eyes, shaking her head slowly, before looking up at me with so much honesty that it drives her words right into my chest, making my heart hurt for her. "You know exactly who you are," she says.

"Paige, that's ridiculous. So do you. You're the most confident person I know," I say.

"I'm a faker," she says. "I fake to fit in, for everybody. I play up the pretty because that seems easy, so I go with it. I joined a sorority, because that's what I thought a girl like me should do. I'm dating a guy who only halfway pays attention to me, who makes me feel small and insignificant—a guy who my sister would probably punch in the face if he tried to be her boyfriend. But he fits a checkbox. You know who you are. I have no idea."

There's a long silence while my sister sits in the car, keys in her lap, and a dress on her body that's fit for a night out at the club. I've gotten so used to seeing my sister wear this part, and she's good at it. I never thought in a million years that she didn't want it.

"I don't know, Paige. I just don't rule anything out as an option. That's all. You...you sort of rule things out, without even trying," I say.

She laughs lightly at my suggestion, turning her attention to our parents' house straight ahead. "You have no idea how true that is, Cass. *No idea,*" she says, biting at her lip and squinting her focus to the nothing in front of her before pulling her purse from the center console and finally stepping out of the car near me. She looks down at her feet, then at the heavy bags surrounding mine before she meets my eyes.

"I'm really sorry about Chandra," she says, pausing short, her breath held, her tongue held, her mind deciding if she has more to say. "I never thought she would use what I told her to hurt you, but..."

"But..." I almost finish it for her, my heart absolutely ripping in half because I know what she's going to say.

"But there was a small part of me...that sort of wanted her to," she says, her lips open, more words needed. But there's nothing more to say. I can see the regret in her eyes, but she respects me enough not to lie, not to throw fake apologies on top of her confession.

I let her walk away. I wait for the door to close completely behind her. My sister is gone. Somewhere on our path together, our roads split, and I lost her.

Ty

"You come up with your big move yet?" Nate asks, flopping down on the sofa next to me. He's making that annoying sipping noise, puckering his lips to try to suck up the spillover around the top of his Orange Crush can.

"No, someone had to go and write their girlfriend the Nicholas Sparks of all love letters, so now the expectations are out there at, like...well, let's just say they're unrealistic expectations now! And dude, can you stop licking the top of your soda can? You look like a junior higher learning how to French kiss!" I might be a little irritable.

Nate chuckles while he takes a full drink from his soda, and I secretly wish for him to inhale some of it, make it come out his nose. But no, he goes back to the sipping.

"Why don't you just write her a letter then, since it works so well," he says, his legs crossed, all relaxed and shit on the coffee table.

"Don't get too comfortable there, Casanova. You still haven't heard from Rowe yet. You don't know that your letter worked." He deflates a little when I say this, and I'm hitting below the belt. I know his letter worked. And I know when we head to Arizona for his tournament tomorrow she's going to be there to surprise him. Of course his letter worked. Hell, he even picked up *my* girlfriend with his apparently poetic, Shakespearean prose. Nate's letter is all Cass has talked about.

"Your brother's letter, oh my god, Ty. Beautiful...Nate's letter was so amazing...OMG, I can't quit thinking about Nate's letter...."

Yes. There have been OMGs. I hate OMGs. Cass is not an OMG girl, and OMG, Nate's letter has turned her into one!

As much as I want to give him crap for it, I can't. It was a damn good letter. So good that I've gone to jewelry stores—actual jewelry stores, where women in suits have to pull things out of cases for me to look at—just to find the right...*something*! I keep putting the jewelry back, though, because no matter what's inside, when you give a chick a small velvet box like that, it gets weird. Even if it's not a ring—*and it's totally not going to be a ring*—there's the small moment, that brief second where she thinks "what if" and you think, "oh shit, she thinks it's a ring."

I'm done looking in jewelry stores.

I've been trying to tell Cass I love her now for days. It was easier to say it to her dad. When I get with her, when we talk on the phone, there's just this block, like my brain falls apart.

"Dude, I know you want to make this special, or whatever, but I gotta tell ya, you're *way* overthinking it," Nate says.

"Easy for you to say. You're practically a damned Disney fairytale," I say, moving back to my chair to head to my room.

"Don't call me Disney until I get the girl," he yells as I move farther down the hall. "If that letter doesn't get a response soon, I'll be more like one of those depressing gangster movies you like where everybody dies."

"No, you'll be like Leo in *Titanic*," I yell back over my shoulder. "Martyr. You'll be a total martyr."

"Your obsession with DiCaprio is not healthy!" he yells, sending one of Mom's throw pillows down the hall behind me with a fling. It falls short, which makes me smirk. He missed.

"Don't dis Leo. And pick that up, Mom doesn't like it when you throw her things around," I say, waiting for three, two...

"Nathan! I don't throw your things on the floor," my mom says, stepping out of the laundry room to pick the small pillow up and put it back in its place. The child in me still loves getting my brother in trouble, even when it's meaningless.

I move to my bed and work my jeans off so I can pull on my sweatpants. It's barely eight at night in California, but Cass likes it when I call her before bed. I haven't been sleeping well lately, sharp nerve pains in my back and neck. I've spent the last two days helping Kelly box up things to put in the garage. She and Jared officially separated, but he came over for Christmas. Kelly wants to work things out, but I'm not sure Jared's capable of that. I don't trust him. I don't like him. But I've been keeping my opinion to myself, because right now is not the time Kel needs to hear it.

Once I hit CALL on my phone, I let my eyes close for a few seconds. Tonight, I just can't seem to keep them open.

"Hey, you're early," she answers. I flip my lamp off and tug the heavy comforter up to my chest.

"Yeah, I know. I'm so sorry, but I don't think I can sit up much longer," I say through a yawn.

"Uhhh, that's what I get for dating an old man," she jokes.

"Hey, don't tell me you don't appreciate the blue-plate specials," I say. "You love a good buffet."

"Yeah, the senior discounts are pretty swag," she says. "And you can still get it up, so...I'll stick around for a while longer."

"You know I'm not rich, so there's no money in this for you when I die," I say.

"Damn. Forget it. I'm out," she says, waiting a few seconds before she lets her laugh breakthrough. I love her. I love her. I love her.

"How are things...with Paige?" Some nights we talk about Paige a lot. Others, I can tell talking about her sister is off the table. Cass can't seem to decide if she's sad about her sister or angry with her.

"We actually went to the mall today. We had gift cards, from Christmas," she says.

"Well that's progress, right? Shopping—that's the girl equivalent for football, breaks down all barriers, the ultimate common denominator, right?" I ask.

"Hmmmm, I think I'd rather have football, but I get your logic," she says. "Yeah, I guess things were a little better. We talked in the car. A little."

"It's just going to take time," I say.

"Says the man who has never gone a day without talking to his brother," she says back quickly.

"I know. I'm lucky. They don't make all siblings like Nate. But don't you dare tell that little turd I said that," I say, tilting my neck up to see if the hallway is still quiet. It is.

Cass giggles. "Turd is a funny word," she says. There's a long silence after this. Palpable. It's not uncomfortable, but just the opposite. There's nothing grand about this moment, nothing remarkable at all. It's one of hundreds of phone conversations Cass and I are going to have, have had.

But something. Just. Feels. Right.

"You know I'm in love with you, right?" I put it out there. I haven't said it. But I know she knows. And I know she loves me back. The words—they're just like a period on the end of our very long, run-on sentence.

"I know," she says, almost a whisper. I can't see her, but I know she's smiling. And blushing. And beautiful.

"Good," I smile. I'm not as sleepy as I was a few minutes ago. Instead, now I feel warm and happy and ready to stay awake all night.

"I sorta kinda love you too," she says, her voice meek and embarrassed. It's sweet.

"Well don't go crazy there and get too committed with those words. Best to hedge your bets," I tease. I know she's just nervous. Her laugh is muffled, probably by her pillow. "So, since I love you more, and I clearly said it first, I think that means I'm the winner, right?"

"You are sooooo not the winner," she says, stronger now. My little ninja princess.

"I don't know. I'm pretty sure if we called up to the booth they would rule in my favor," I say.

"Nooooo," she protests—always so competitive. "They would see through your sneak attack. The playing field was *definitely* not even. I think you'd get disqualified."

"Only one way to know," I say, covering the phone with my hand. "Nate! Nathan, Nathan, Nathan, Nathan—" He hates it when I use his full name, so he makes his way down the hall to my room fast, pushes open the door completely, and flips on the light.

"What?" He's so pissed off. This will be funny.

"Cass and I need you to settle something for us," I say, and his eyebrows rise, barely interested, so very annoyed. "I *clearly* said *I love you* first. But Cass thinks because I didn't give her a fair warning that mine doesn't count and she wins *the I love you* game."

Nate is staring at me, doing that blinking thing he does when he's not sure what to say; then he takes a deep breath. "This is stupid," he finally lets out, and turns his back to walk away. "Cass is right; she wins."

"I think the judge is biased!" I yell.

"Yeah, well...the judge thinks you're an asshole for making him get up with fifteen seconds left in the game," he hollers.

"I win! I win, I win, I win!" Cass squeals on the phone.

"I'm filing an appeal," I say, smiling and loving her. Loving that I said it. Loving how easy it was. Loving that everything about this was so very us—that there is an *us,* and it's simple to define.

Chapter 27

Cass

"I can't believe you actually sang in front of, how many people?" I ask Rowe, who has been talking a million miles per second for the last ten minutes, still feeling the adrenaline from her surprise visit to Nate at his tournament game.

I knew the second she read Nate's letter she would have to chase him. Ty hooked her up with one of the public-relations reps for the tournament venue, and got her in to sing the national anthem. He said she was coming in from McConnell, and had sung a few times at the school, "Always a crowd favorite," he told them. I'm pretty sure the only people who have ever heard Rowe sing before are Ty, Nate and me. She's not bad, but I'm guessing the crowd probably wasn't blown away either. My boyfriend can sell anything.

"A few thousand. Oh my god, Cass. It was so crazy! My hands were shaking, and I swear I thought I was going to drop the microphone when I got to the part about the bombs bursting in air," she's still talking fast. It's cute. And she sounds so happy.

"I wish I could have been there," I say, squeezing my eyes shut, and wishing when I open them again that everything looks right, straight—not blurred. It's my right eye. It's been like this for more than twenty-four hours now. It's been like this for two days. And I probably shouldn't ignore it. But I'm going to. It's going to go away. This is going to go away.

"I know, me too," Rowe says. "Hey, it's getting hard to hear with the crowd, so I'll call you later. Ty wanted me to let you know that he's leaving right after the game, and he'll call you from the airport."

"Thanks, and sounds good," I say. "Call you later." I end the call and hold my phone to my chest, lying flat on my back, eyes closed again. They just need rest. I'll just rest until six, until I need to go to the airport.

Ty is coming to visit, flying here from Arizona since it's such a short flight. My parents are letting him stay in our guest room. I asked, expecting a battle, but my dad surprised me, saying it wouldn't be a problem at all. My mom didn't protest. I might be in the *Twilight Zone*. I don't care. I'll stay here in fantasyland if it stays like this.

I put the cold compress back over my face, pushing down on my eyes. I don't know if this works, or even helps, but I read it on one of the MS blogs. I'll try anything. Rest...yes. I just need rest.

"Cass, your phone alarm has been going off, for like, forty minutes!"

Why is Paige in my room? I must have slept harder than I thought, longer—deeper. Everything hurts. The cold compress on my head feels lukewarm, not at all relaxing. I slide the gel pack from my face, my arms tired, tingling from being folded over my head for so long.

"I need to pick Ty up. He's coming in at seven. I need to get ready," I say, rubbing the tiredness from my eyes.

"It's six-thirty. You're going to be late," Paige says, turning my phone alarm off and tossing it on my bed next to me.

"Shit!" I stand quickly, the blood rushing from my head. Woozy. I'm woozy. I sit at the edge of my mattress and focus on my flip-flops—where they sit on the floor. They're...cloudy. Everything's cloudy.

"No, no, no, no, no!" I squeeze them shut. Deep breath. When I open, everything will look fine. Everything's fine. I'm fine.

Fuzzy. Everything I look at through my right eye is fuzzy. That's okay. It's better. I think it's getting better. Clearing up.

"Cass," Paige says, her voice cautious. She knows. My sister knows. "Cass, are you having a flare-up?"

"I'm fine," I say, standing quickly and moving to my closet. I miss my target, my steps suddenly off-balance, and my right rib crashes into the corner of my dresser. "Damn it!"

"Cass, you're not fine. And you're not driving. I'm getting Mom," she says, moving to my door.

"No, I'm fine. Paige, look at me," I beg. She stops short of the door and turns to face me. I close my right eye and she looks normal. I close my left eye and she looks like she's standing in the rain.

I'm not fine. My lip quivers. I'm not fine, and now I'm starting to cry.

"Goddamn it! I hate my body!" I scream, stroking my arm along the top of my dresser, knocking over some pictures and knickknacks.

"I'm getting Mom," Paige says, her hand around my arm. "I. Have. To."

I look at her, in her eyes. She doesn't want to do this to betray me. She has to. I know she does. I have to see my doctor. This isn't normal. I've been through this before. I nod, a slight movement, but enough that Paige gets the answer she needs.

"I'll tell Mom, and then I'll go pick up Ty," she says, and I move to the floor. Being lower, it helps. I have my bearings, and I crawl back to bed and lie down. And I cry. I hate crying. I hate my body.

None of this is fair.

Ty

I know the second I see Paige that something isn't right.

"She's having a flare-up," Paige explains as we wait for the elevator to come to take us to our level in the garage. "She's probably been having it for a while. Did she tell you?"

Her tone is accusatory, and my gut instinct is to say something back to her in the exact same tone. But I don't. Because no—Cass hasn't said anything to me. If she's been feeling things, she's been keeping it to herself. And it hurts a little that she didn't tell me. I shake my head *no* and move into the elevator as it opens.

"Mom is getting her in with her neurologist. Hopefully tomorrow."

I nod again.

"She's been pushing herself," Paige says.

That one was directed to me. She's making this my fault. That's not happening.

"She's also been stressed," I say back, keeping my eyes forward. That one was for her.

"I brought Cass's car. She has more room," Paige says, pulling the passenger door open for me, and then stepping back. She's not sure what to do, and that's okay. I understand. I pull myself into the passenger side and then reach over to collapse the chair for her.

"You'll need to get it in the trunk. It's not as heavy as it looks," I say, and she nods. She struggles with it a little, but she doesn't say anything. I watch her in the rearview mirror as she pushes and grunts until my chair is in the trunk, and then she closes the heavy top.

Cass's car is hot. It's something I would drive. And I bet she wanted to be the one to show it to me. I only let myself look at the interior, and not awe over it for long, so that way she can take me out in it again when she's ready. I bet she drives it fast.

Paige drives it like a grandmother. It takes her four attempts to back out of her spot, and she rides the break all the way down the turn-ramp for the garage. I keep my mouth shut, though. I could easily make her more nervous, pick on her—like I would if Nate were driving. But I don't feel like joking around with Paige. Our last conversation consisted of her telling me I didn't deserve her sister. Now I felt like saying the same thing to her.

"They can't make her quit," I say after a few long minutes of silence. Turns out I'm not very good at keeping quiet.

"Hmmmm?" Paige says, looking over her shoulder to switch lanes on the highway. She drives this car like a boat. It's a little funny. And scary.

"Soccer. Your parents can't make her quit," I say, keeping my eyes on her, putting a little pressure on her so she gets my point.

"That's not up to me," she says finally, still not glancing in my direction.

"It's not up to them either," I say back, turning my attention to the passenger window for the rest of the drive. My first trip to California, and it's too dark to see the beach. Just one more thing I'll save for Cass.

The driveway is dark when we pull in, and no one comes out to help. "Cass is probably inside. She's a little wobbly on her legs. Or at least, she was this afternoon," Paige says, popping the trunk and moving to the back of the car. I hate that I have to depend on her right now.

She manages to work my chair out and unfold it so she can push it next to me. "I've got it from here," I say, pulling myself in and grabbing my bag from the floor of the passenger side.

I push the door closed and follow Paige up the driveway through the garage to a back door. There's a little bit of a lip, but I manage to make it over and into the house.

"We're here!" Paige yells, dropping her purse on top of the washing machine in the laundry room.

I follow her through the kitchen to a large living room with a gigantic television and fireplace. Cass sits up quickly and looks at me over the back of the sofa. As painful as the ride here was with her sister, seeing her eyes light up like that made it all worthwhile.

"Hey," she says, her voice raw, like she's been sleeping. Good, I hope she's been sleeping.

"Not cool," I say, pushing closer until I'm next to her at the sofa arm. "Faking a flare-up for attention."

I'm kidding, and Cass knows I'm only joking. Her Mom, however, does not.

"Tyson, Cass is not well," she says in the most serious voice I am pretty sure I've ever heard.

"Mom, he knows. He's joking," Cass says over her shoulder, turning back to me to roll her eyes and shake her head. She leans forward and places a hand on either side of my face. "God I'm glad you're here," she says, kissing me and holding her lips to mine like she needs them to breathe. I think she just might.

"Well, that's not a very funny joke," Cass's mom says, standing up from her chair, looking for an excuse to leave the room. She doesn't like me, but I don't want that to be my fault, so I move to meet her before she can leave the room.

"I'm sorry, ma'am," I say, Southern drawl doing it's thing. "I didn't mean to be disrespectful. Humor—sometimes it takes the edge off, that's all. Thank you for having me as a guest in your home."

I hold my hand out, hoping she'll take it. She finally does, though her grip is weak and timid. Nothing at all like her daughters'—either of them. "Let me show you to your room," she says, leading me down a hall to the back of the house. I look over my shoulder to Cass, and she's laughing quietly at me, but she gives me a wink.

"I hope you don't mind, the only other guests we have are usually my parents, so the room is a little...Victorian," she says, reaching for a pillow on the bed and straightening the ruffled case that's covering it. This room puts the pink Barbie room to shame.

"It's fine. And again, thank you," I say, her mom turning to look at me with a pause. She breathes in, ready to say something—before pushing her lips into a tight smile, and nodding as she turns to leave. Cass comes in a few seconds later.

"Your mom is not a big fan," I smile. I don't think her dad is a very big fan either, based on our phone conversation, but I don't tell her that.

"She's just not used to a boy being here. It's weird for her. I was sort of surprised she said *yes*, but my dad made this face at her. I think he's sort of on your side," she says, her smile bigger. There's a part of me that thinks her dad may have lured me here to murder me. But I keep that to myself too.

"So, how long?" I ask, unzipping my bag and pulling out my few toiletries. I don't look at her while I do this, because I don't want her to see the hurt on my face. She senses it anyway.

"A few weeks...nothing big until a few days ago, though. I'm sorry..." she says, and I look up with a soft smile.

"Sorry for what?" I shrug. I don't want her apologizing. I'll get over being hurt. This isn't about me. It isn't about Paige or her parents. It's about her, and people need to let it just be about her.

"That I didn't tell you," she says.

I shrug again and go back to putting my things on the night table. I pull my watch off and hold it in my hand, running my thumb over the *always*, soaking in it's meaning. "I get it. You

240

were scared. And talking about things like weaknesses makes them real," I say, handing my watch to her.

She takes it and looks at it closely. "Something like that...yeah," she says, her fatigue showing through. I don't know how I didn't see it before.

She hands the watch back, but I shake my head *no*. Her brow furrows.

"You keep it," I say. She looks back down, rolling the metal band through her fingers until she gets to the *always*. "This...isn't meant for me."

"It's meant for whoever needs it," I say quickly, holding my hand around hers, clasping the watch in her fingers tightly. She looks up at me, unsure. "It's mine to give. And you need it."

Her hands stay in mine for a few more seconds, and I relax my hold slowly, until I'm sure she's going to keep the watch. She puts it around her wrist, clipping the clasp. It's about five rungs too big for her thin arm, and it makes her laugh.

"You can push it up to your bicep, wear it like an iPod," I joke, and she chuckles back.

"Yeah, that won't look weird," she says, twisting the silver around her arm a few times, her breath held, until she looks back at me. "Thanks, Ty."

"It's nothin'," I shrug back. That was a lie—it's everything. I never thought I would be able to live without that watch. Now, I don't think I can live without Cass's smile. I'll do whatever it takes to get that back, make it permanent.

"You hungry?" she asks.

"Does a bear shit in the woods?"

She stops me at the doorway as I follow her out. "Yeah, uhm, maybe turn the Ty down, just a notch, until my mom warms up to you?"

"What? Your mom hates bears? Damn, what kind of household is against Leo *and* grizzlies? I don't know, Cass, I'm starting to think y'all have some prejudices that I just can't look past," I say, wincing like I'm serious. I drop the act fast though when I can tell she's not in the mood. "Got it, tone down the bear shit. Done," I salute her.

I watch her carefully for the rest of the night. Her mom hovers, bringing her a plate to eat on the sofa. I join her there, deciding to stay near her instead of at the table with her mom and Paige. Even if laser beams of disdain didn't come from their eyes, I'd still sit with Cass. I can't be close enough to her. I missed her. And she's faltering. She needs me now.

We watch television, a full couch cushion apart while her mom and Paige are in the room with us. It's weird how nobody is talking. In my house, everyone is *always* talking—we talk over each other. Hell, I'm not sure any of us actually listen we love talking so much. Here, it's pin-drop kind of quiet.

"Where's your dad," I whisper to her, after her sister finally leaves the room.

"He works late. His office is downtown," she says, the corner of her lip curling in apology. "You'll see him tomorrow though. He has the day off. We make the doctor-visit thing a *family affair.*"

I don't have an answer for that. I know how she feels. It's smothering. But I also know that her parents—though they show it in freakishly overbearing ways perhaps—are probably just worried.

"Well, I'm totally coming too. I mean, this will probably become the topic of conversation at dinner tomorrow, right?" I ask, and she smiles, amused. "I don't want to feel left out. It would be like not watching one of those big cable shows and then trying to decipher everyone's *OMGs* on Twitter."

I OMG-ed. It felt dirty. But she laughed, so it was worth it. Maybe.

"You may have noticed, HIPAA laws don't apply to Cass Owens," she says, a wry laugh coming through.

"Welcome to the club. I was a medical-student case. Had twelve doctors. Oh, and...my legs are in *Newsweek.*"

"Shut up!" she says, shoving me on the shoulder.

"Google it. Look up my name, Louisiana Samaritan Hospital, and Dr. Bunshee," I say, and she studies me for a few seconds, waiting for me to break. I cross my heart and her eyes widen.

"Okay, I'm Googling that. Tonight," she says.

"Go right ahead," I say.

"Oh I am," she says back.

"Whatever. That's fine, go do it," I tease back.

"I'm totally doing it," she smiles.

"Go on then. Go ahead," I hold my arm out, and she stands, challenging me.

"Okay. Here I go. This is me...going to Google you and your famous legs," she says, folding her arms over her chest while she walks by stomping. Her body is perfectly straight, and her steps come easily. No weaving or stumbling. I notice. Her mom notices. Neither of us says a word.

"Whatever. You'll find it online," I say back, keeping our silly banter going.

"Oh, I'm sure I will," she says over her shoulder.

I watch until her door closes to her room and then I turn my attention back to the television. It's some nature show, and it sucks balls. "Mrs. Owens?" I ask, trying to be as polite as possible, and not insult her absolutely horrid taste in television. "Would you mind too terribly if I maybe changed the channel, for just a few minutes?" *And then lost the remote and somehow stabbed this channel so you could never get it back?*

Cass's mom closes the magazine she's been reading, pulls her glasses from her face, and then clicks off the small reading lamp next to her chair. She stops in front of me and hands me the remote. "You can call me Diana, Tyson," she says during our exchange. And then she smiles. Not a fake one, but a real one.

"I'll do my best, Mrs. Owens," I say, and her eyes soften.

As soon as she leaves the room, I switch the channel for *Sports Center*, and I watch just long enough until I feel like it's safe to follow Cass's steps down the hall to her room. I knock with the tips of my fingers, just loud enough for her to notice, and she opens her door. Standing. Not swaying. Her eyes focus on me. Her laptop is closed on her bed where she was sitting.

She pokes her head out and scans the hall, then she opens her door wide and waves me inside.

And somehow I end up holding her until the morning.

Chapter 28

Cass

It was literally a caravan to my doctor's office. There were five of us in the waiting room, and everyone wanted to join me when they called me back. The scene was a bit mortifying. My neurologist sees mostly older people, seniors. My visits already garner a lot of attention because I sort of *stand out*. But when I walked in with a posse?

I really only wanted Ty, but that would have opened up a whole new shit storm. So I let my mom come. It seems like doctors are places moms are supposed to be at with their daughters. We should do some things that are...normal.

Nothing was a surprise. I was relapsing. I haven't relapsed in a while, since I quit playing soccer. My mom hasn't said it, but she's thought it. I can see it behind her eyes. My body was fatigued—under unnatural stress—and even though the doctor threw in that flare-ups can happen at any time, for any reason, I knew on some level that those things probably played a part. It was my mom's conclusion. It was *my* conclusion, even if I didn't like it.

Dr. Peeples ordered intravenous steroids at the medical center for a few days, plus an MRI to see if there was any active cell damage happening in my brain that would be causing the blurry vision, or maybe one of my old lesions is getting bigger. Either way, the steroids should calm everything down. Then, I'd be good to go. "Good to go," Dr. Peeples said.

I had a feeling my parents and I were bound to have different definitions of "good to go."

"He said you could start today, if you want. I really think that's best," my mother says as we all stroll through the parking lot. I nod in agreement. Steroids make me sick to my stomach and turn my face red and puffy, like an Oompa Loompa. So Ty should get to see that during the week he's here. Awesome.

The medical center is the next parking lot over, and I really wasn't up for having the posse follow me to my next stop. "Mom, why don't you and Paige head home? Dad can take Ty and me," I suggest, hoping she gives me this. Please, just give me this.

"Oh, there's a really cute store that just opened up at the strip mall down the road. Great jewelry. Let's go; we can meet them after for lunch," Paige says, tugging on my mom's sleeve. Her eyes meet mine for a brief second. I may be imagining it, but I think she's doing me a favor.

"Well..." my mom says, swinging her keys back and forth between my sister and me. I think she's actually saying "eeny, meeny, miny, moe" in her head. "I guess you know what you're doing, Cass. You've done these before. And we can all meet up after?"

"Sounds good," I say, tugging on my dad's arm, dragging him to his car. I'm not giving her a chance to flop on this decision.

"Subtle, Cassidy," my dad says as he pushes the UNLOCK button and waits for Ty at the side of the vehicle to take his chair for him. I notice my father's gaze fall to Ty as he lifts himself to the edge of the seat, his arms fully flexed as he swings his body inside. It's a move that Ty somehow makes look effortless even though there are about a hundred moving parts in his body doing the work. My dad doesn't stare, but he notices. And I notice that.

My dad pulls up front and drops me off with Ty so we don't have to travel far while he parks. I sign in and say hello to the nurse working at the station. Her name is Heather, and I remember her without having to check her tag.

"Come on back, Cass. Dr. Peeples sent your files over. It's a slow time, so might as well get this over with, huh?" I always liked Heather. She was newly engaged the last time I went through this therapy. I see now that she has a band next to the engagement ring, and her belly looks about seven months pregnant.

"This is new," I say, looking down, and she laughs lightly, rubbing her hand over her large belly.

"Yeah, and I'm about ready to be done with this part," she says, turning her focus back to my file. "I'll have this ready to go in about ten minutes," she says, giving my shoulder a squeeze before she leaves the room to get my dosage. It's amazing how much of this I remember. It's like riding a bike, though *nothing at all* like riding a bike, I muse to myself.

"Wow, you're like famous here. I bet they have a picture of you. No! A shrine," Ty says, moving to face me and bumping me with his knees. He can't feel our touch, but I can.

"You must have missed the sign. We're sitting in the Cassidy Owens wing," I say.

"No shit!" Ty says, reaching for my hands. His watch slides forward out of my sweatshirt when I reach to grip him, and he flips his eyes to mine when he notices. No words, just a tender smile, his eyes saying everything that needs to be said.

"Okay, let's get you hooked up," Heather says as she comes back into the room with my drip bag ready to hang and a needle ready to pierce my vein.

"Do you mind waiting for my dad in the hall, just so he knows what room I'm in?" I ask Ty while Heather connects the various tubes and begins prepping the IV for my arm.

"You got it, babe," he says, and I scowl at him for the *babe* part. "Too late, you've already given me babe permission. No going back."

"Uhm, I'm pretty sure I only okayed *baby*," I say.

"You missed the fine print, babe. I get Baby, and ALL derivatives. It's locked in," he says, his voice fading as the door closes behind him.

"He's new," Heather says, a little gleam in her eye. She knows better than to tease me. She and I talked a lot when I went through this in high school. Teasing was always off the table, because well...boys were always off the table.

"He is," I say back, unable to help the grin that spreads the width of my face—teeth show and everything.

"I like that boy. You did good, missy. *Real* good," she says, nodding for me to turn and face the window. I'm a fainter. "Now this will only hurt for a second."

Usually, Heather is a liar, because I normally feel the pinch and the burn for much longer than a second. But today, I don't feel a thing. Too much love in the way to let the pain through.

246

Ty

I don't really like hospitals. They remind me of physical therapy, of waking up in a hazy fog to a beeping sound in the ICU. They remind me of my mom's face when I finally opened my eyes long enough to recognize her. My mom's tears. Nate's crying. My...crying.

I'm happier here in the hall. But I'll go back in when I need to. When Cass's father enters through the sliding doors, I hold a hand up to get his attention before he veers off to the nurse's station. He came home late last night, and I snuck back to my own room early this morning before anyone was awake. He and I haven't been alone once yet, and I haven't really been looking forward to it. I was braver over the phone with him. Too brave, I fear. But I wouldn't take any of it back.

"She's just getting set up," I say.

"Good, good," he nods, looking through the small window-slot in the door, and then running his hand through his graying hair. He's worried.

"She kept this to herself. Otherwise...I would have made her talk to someone. I promise you," I say, because I still feel like maybe Cass's parents hold me responsible for this. Maybe I am.

"You can't make her do anything, Tyson," he says, looking at his daughter through the door window and pushing his hands into the pockets of his jeans.

"Yeah," I laugh once. "You're probably right."

"You...you want a coffee or anything from the nurse's station?" he asks me. "This usually takes about an hour."

"No thanks. I'm good. But go ahead," I respond.

He just shakes his head, letting his gaze drift off. "I'm good too," he says. I move toward the door, but before I get too close, he halts me. "It's nice to finally meet you...in person, by the way," he says, extending his hand. His grip is firm, and maybe a little threatening—as a father's should be.

"Thank you for letting me stay with you all. It was really nice to be able to come here from my brother's tournament. I know it was sort of a last-minute thing, so...anyhow," I say, suddenly aware that I'm sweating. And rambling. Yeah, I'm definitely braver over the phone. I haven't had to talk to many fathers. Just Kelly's. And he was my Little League coach, so...

"I wanted to tell you," he says, his eyes on me at first, but then at his feet. He sucks in his lips to think, and his posture grows stronger. He's a prosecutor, and from what Cass says, he's damn good. I have the distinct feeling he's about to deliver a closing argument meant just for me.

"I appreciate what you said the other day...that you stood by Cass like that. It was...maybe a little surprising," he says, his head cocked to the side as he looks at me with a knowing smile, one eyebrow raised.

"Thank you...sir?" I'm a dead man. I feel like a dead man.

"But I just wanted you to understand something, and please...don't take this in a bad way, like I'm attacking. I...I just get the feeling that you and my daughter might be a whole hell of a lot more serious than her mother and I thought you were, so I thought this was important for me to say," he says, and I can feel the sweat run down my back.

"The choices I made for my daughter, with this Paul Cotterman guy...they aren't the easy route. You insinuated I was taking the easy route, but let me be clear—nothing about what I've done concerning that man, my daughter, and this case has been easy. Every fiber in my being wants to drag that asshole through court—to spread his story through every front page I can get to print it, to have him become viral on social media and the punch line for late night television shows. I want to spend months digging through his list of old girlfriends, hiring private investigators to uncover dirt, to make a case so strong that there's no doubt in anyone's mind that my daughter is right. I know she is. God, Tyson—I've known it all along. But what would that do to her life? Dragging this story out, making it bigger, and bigger, and bigger, until it followed her forever? She'd have to live *this*. So as much as it kills me to let that asshole off the hook, as much as it killed me last year to appease the talking heads at her high school district, I struck a deal, and paid them all to keep their mouths shut. Forever. Because my daughter doesn't deserve a media circus, and I have the means to make her nightmares go away."

248

He's looking down the hallway again, his jaw flexing, his teeth gritting.

"I think you should share that with her. I think she could really use hearing it," I say.

"No, she needs to be angry at someone, until she's done feeling angry," he says. "And I'll take the hard way, Ty. I'll be that person she's angry with. As much as it breaks my heart, I'll be it for as long as she needs."

His head hung low, he grips the handle to the door and takes a deep breath, trying to replenish his energy, his spirit—so that way when he walks into that room with his daughter, she has no clue how broken he is on the inside. I let him go in first, and I listen to his now-booming voice, confident and strong, and I move forward to watch him lean forward and kiss his daughter's head. She shuts her eyes, wincing when he does. And I know that breaks him even more. But he sits down in the chair next to her and waits, all the while his jaw muscle clenching, biting his tongue, being *that* person.

For as long as it takes.

Chapter 29

Cass

The nausea was better this round, maybe because I was expecting it and didn't eat anything that would make things worse. After five days, my flare-up seemed to be under control. My vision was back to normal, and steroids always leave me feeling strong and full of energy, so my wobbly legs were once again dying to run.

Ty's heading back to Louisiana today; I don't want him to go. I've said all along that he's magic. Since he's been here, my family has never felt more like...well, *mine.* Ty was *really* interested in my car, so my dad and I took him for a spin out along highway 101 at sunset a couple of nights ago. The farther north you get, the less crowded the roadway is, and my dad gave me the nod—the one he saves for when my mom isn't looking. I hit about one-ten before my dad put his hand on my arm, warning me to slow down.

I was back to that innocent sixteen-year-old again, the one who learned how to change her own oil from her dad the day she got the keys to Uncle Lou's Charger. Paige got a new Mazda, and she apologized to me over and over, feeling bad that I was slighted with the *used* car. My dad and I never laughed about it in front of her, but on our own, in the garage, we'd cut loose. I'd been eyeing this car since I was five.

Ty being around somehow brought those feelings back. And I'm afraid as soon as he goes life at my house is going to go back to lectures about my health, orders to quit playing soccer, and...*the Cotterman issue.*

"You know, I still haven't seen the beach. I mean, up close," Ty says, holding his coffee mug up to his lips, blowing the steam away. Even my mother is in his pocket now, as she runs over with two ice cubes to cool it for him. "Thank you, Mrs. Owens."

"Diana," she practically sings.

I shake my head at him, amazed at his skills.

"What?" he shrugs.

"You can charm the pants off anything, can't you?" I say, regretting it immediately as I watch his smirk curl above the steam from his coffee. "Don't even think about saying it."

"What, me? Cassidy! Always the pervert, you are," he says, sipping and slurping loudly just to annoy me.

"You wanna see the beach or not?" I ask, mostly to get out of his razzing.

"Let's do it," he says, sliding his mug on the counter and pulling his McConnell baseball hat low on his head. I love that hat on him, the way it barely shades his eyes. He's downright sinister looking, but in the sexiest way.

"Oh, careful there, Cassidy...it looks like I might be charming the pants off—" I slap my hand over his mouth quickly, and I can feel him smile under my touch.

"We're going to the beach! Back in time to get Ty's things and get him to the airport," I say.

Beaches are meant to be visited in the middle of the day on a workday. No tourists, no picnics—just the diehards. I envy the surfers, the way they seem to be able to get up early, stay up late, and live and die by the tide. There are a few still riding this morning, and I watch Ty look at them as I pull in to the parking lot.

"I always wanted to try that," he says, his eyes squinting a little as he focuses his attention on a single surfer. It's like he's memorizing his movements for later, studying him as a pupil would.

"You should. It's mostly upper body strength. I bet you'd be good," I say, popping the trunk, and moving to the back to pull out his chair. Ty's still watching the surfer when I pull his chair next to him, so I don't interrupt. I lean on the side of my car and watch along with him as the stranger in the ocean zips through the water, back and forth, until a larger wave eventually pulls the board away from him.

Ty nods when he's done, then pulls himself into his chair.

"There's a path for most of the way," I say, zipping my hoodie over my chest and pushing my hands deep into the pockets. The breeze is light, but there's still a little chill in the air.

We take the path down to the guardhouse, but stop at the sand.

"You have beaches in Louisiana, right?" I ask.

He looks out over the water, almost memorizing the patterns of the waves. "Yeah, but...not like this," he says, his mouth settling into the most content smile. "Not like this."

We stay here, under the shade of the guardhouse for a while, people-watching and listening to the sound of the waves. I used to love taking naps here, falling asleep to the sound. I've paid for it with sunburns many times.

"Hey, you think I can get you in the sand?" I ask, looking at the wheels of his chair, contrasting them with the softness of the sand ahead.

"I don't know. Maybe?" he says, looking at his wheels, and rocking them back and forth with his hands. "It'll be tough. Are you...strong enough for that?"

"Psssshaw," I say, hand on my hip. "Have you met my trainer? He's a hard-ass." This makes him laugh.

Ty pushes himself to the very edge, but before he rolls from the concrete into the sand, I stop him, holding up a finger. "I have an idea," I say.

I reach into my bag and pull out the two large beach towels I brought and unfurl them, stepping hard on the material to compact the sand underneath. "That should get us sixteen feet at a time," I say. Ty's lips tug at the corner as he looks at the brightly colored path ahead.

When I grip the handles behind him, I pause. Ty doesn't let others push him often, and it isn't lost on me how special this is, how much trust he's giving me. I lean forward and kiss his neck lightly, and he brings a hand up to caress my face.

"Careful, babe. We might not make it very far if you keep doing that," he says, and I smile against his skin.

The first push comes easy, and momentum carries us a good ten feet before I feel the sand building around the tires and working against me. Ty holds up a hand and tilts the chair back slightly, nodding for me to push again; we make it the full sixteen feet. I grab the towels each time we make it to the next one—

building our distance until we're a good forty or fifty feet away from the guardhouse, almost to the smooth, wet sand.

"This is good," he says. "You won't have the energy to get me back if we go any farther."

"What? I've got energy coming out of my ears. Haven't you heard? This girl's on steroids," I say, and he smiles in response, but holds his hand over mine and pulls me to his lap to stop me anyway.

"Yeah, about that," he starts, and I suddenly feel trapped.

"Ty, don't. I don't want to talk about it, not now," I say, and he takes a deep breath.

"I know. Just hear me out, and then I promise we'll move on to making out on that pile of sand right there." His words make me blush. "You don't have to do this. You've proven a lot, to yourself, to everyone. Just, your parents, they may have a point."

"Don't, Ty. Don't you dare give up on me," I say, my stomach fluttering with anxiety. He can't back out on me now. I need him. I want this, and I'm only strong enough with him.

He purses his lips and breathes in long through his nose, his eyes washing over my face, my neck, down my arm...to the place where his hand grabs mine. He pulls it to his mouth and kisses my knuckles, then pushes the sleeve up on my hoodie until his watch shows. He twists it around so the face is on the inside of my wrist, and taps it twice, then lets the tip of his finger graze over the thin skin underneath.

"*Always*. I'm always on your side. I just didn't want you to think you had to prove anything to me," he says, and I hug him tightly and kiss him hard. When I pull back and look at his face, my champion is back. The only thing I'll ever need in my corner. "Think you can hold my weight just long enough to get me...down there?"

I bite my lip and slide from his lap until I'm next to him, pulling his arm over my shoulder. "On the count of three," I say, letting Ty count down when he's ready.

His body is heavier than I expected, and I can't support him for long. But we make it to the flat sand right in front of us, and I lay back and let him hover above me, his strong arms caging me in while the waves cascade in and out a hundred feet away. The way he looks at me, the slowness at which he bends down, bringing his lips to mine, it's all so perfect. The boys in high school, the mistakes I've made, my doubts and self-loathing—it all washes away with every kiss, every pass of his nose against my cheek, the sensation of his teeth along my neck, the whispers in my ear.

"You know I love you, right?" It's the first time he's said that in person, and it's just as perfect as it was in my dreams.

"I know," I say, my smile undeniable against his lips. "You know I love you back, right?"

He pulls himself back, looking over me, his eyes moving down my body and back up again, the potency of his gaze making me sweat. "What?" I ask, unable to handle the heat of his stare.

"How'd I get so lucky?" he asks, teeth pinching the corner of his lip as he considers me, my worth—my worth of him.

I don't have a response, and the longer he looks at me, the more I blush, and then out of nowhere, a tear slides from my eye, over my cheek and onto the sand. And I don't even mind. I let it fall. This cry...it feels okay.

Ty

The Pacific Ocean is better than the Gulf. It just is. I'm probably biased because I spent an hour making out with a hot blonde on the sand. That'll sway just about any location into my favor. But this morning definitely falls into my top ten favorite-moments category.

Cass's strength is unreal. I'm not even sure Nate could have pushed through the sand like that. She took the towel to my wheels back at the car, careful to keep sand out of the grooves, and then she stowed it back in the trunk. She was still blushing when she turned the engine over, sneaking glances at me, catching me staring at her.

"So, I saw your legs...in *Newsweek*," she says as we pull back out onto the main road.

"Yeah? What'd you think? Pretty hot and famous, huh?" I say.

"They were all right. I mean, I've seen better. The nerve graphic, the one they overlapped? You know, the one that made you look bionic?" she says, and I narrow my eyes, giving her my best suave Bond expression. "Yeah, that was pretty cool. But, still not quite *Sports Illustrated* swimsuit."

"That's only because they didn't keep the Speedo pics in the mix," I say, and she laughs so fast she snorts. She gets embarrassed by it; it's cute. She keeps her focus on the road while we wait through four or five stoplights, but she seems pensive the entire time. Finally she breaks.

"I saw the pictures of you playing ball, too. In high school?" She's being cautious. Truthfully, I forgot about those photos in the article.

"Oh yeah. I made that uniform look good, huh?" I turn the other direction quickly, watching the cars in the lane next to us, staring at drivers—anything to avoid the look I know she's going to give me. I don't turn when she speaks again, but I know the look is there.

"You...you were pretty good, huh? Good, like Nate?" It's not quite pity, but it's close. I know she doesn't mean it that way.

"I was good," I sigh.

The silence gets thicker before it starts to fade away the longer we drive. I keep my eyes on anything other than her...until I feel like that topic—the concept of me missing baseball—fades almost completely. It always leaves a little mark behind, and I'll probably feel the punch of this conversation during my flight.

We get back to the house with just enough time to grab my bag and freshen up, shaking the sand from our clothes. My farewells from Cass's parents are most definitely warmer than their greetings, but there's still an element of trust—or resistance to fully trust—lurking. And maybe that's just based on experience. I'm willing to put in the work, earn it over time.

Paige is another story. She treats me with the same huffiness and indifference as she always has. And that feels better. Nothing's changed between her and me, but over the last few days, I've seen moments between her and her sister. I caught Paige looking at Cass differently, regretfully, perhaps. I haven't mentioned this to Cass, and we try not to talk about Paige much. I can tell it makes her sad, so I don't go there.

We get to the airport with little time to spare, and Cass doesn't have time to park. Our goodbye is rushed, and I hate that. But even with my guaranteed spot on the plane, I get to the gate barely on time. I charm my way on in the middle of the final boarding group, and the male flight attendant takes quite the liking to me. I laugh to myself, and pull my phone out quickly to send Cass a text that she may have competition; then I shut the phone off and spend the next three hours learning about my flight attendant Shawn, and how I remind him of his ex. By the end of the flight, I'm honestly flattered, and I get Shawn's number, with the promise of having drinks sometime—with his new boyfriend and my girlfriend.

Before I get through the gate to where Nate should be waiting for me, I pause and turn my phone back on and chuckle at Cass's response.

CASS: Yeah, well, I finally watched The Departed. And Leo, yeah, uhm...I'm a fan. Does that sway things in my favor?

ME: I think you may have taken this Leo thing too far, it sounds like you like him not in the 'bad-ass' way but in the 'hot for his bod' way.

CASS: Your fault. You made me look.

ME: I think that's enough Leo.

CASS: Too late, already started Gangs of New York. I'm marathoning. Gotta go.

ME: :-| I don't like this.

"Dude, move your ass," Nate yells the second he sees me.

"Are you seriously pretending you have any power over me?" I say, eyes back to my phone, waiting for Cass. I think she was serious, and I may have created a monster.

"I'm parked weird. That's all, and what's up your ass?" he says, grabbing my bag and swinging it over his shoulder.

I look up with my lips pushed into a half frown. "I think I may have pushed Cass into Leo's arms," I say, and Nate pinches his brow.

"Good, you and Cass can share your man crush then. Come on," he says, leaving me behind. I push hard to catch up.

"I don't have a *man crush*," I say in defense.

"Yeah, *sure* you don't. Saying every one of his lines along with him is totally normal. Totally," he says, laughing over his shoulder.

Damn. I do have a man crush.

"Yeah, well...shut up," I say back, and his cackle echoes into the elevator.

Chapter 30

Cass

My bags are packed. Paige's bags are packed. My cleats, my old knee braces, my shin guards, my ball—I packed it all. I know I have new things, but sometimes I like the way my old equipment feels. My parents and I haven't talked about it. There's nothing to talk about. I'm playing.

I'm about to zip the bag closed when my dad walks in, a large envelope in his hand. His focus goes right to the bright green ball I've managed to wedge into my suitcase, and he smiles tightly when he sees it, then nods.

"I have to play. I need it. I just...I need this," I say to him, and inside I say *please, please, please* over and over again, praying we don't make this a thing—that they don't try to take this away.

"I know you do," he says, tossing the envelope on top of my things and helping me to zip my suitcase the rest of the way. "You're going to need those. They're medical forms, judge endorsed, explaining your treatment, any steroid injections. There are three copies, and there are two doctors' signatures— Peeples and one of his colleagues."

"Dad—" I start, but my breath leaves me quickly. His warm arm wraps me from the side, and he pulls me to him tightly, kissing the top of my head. "We still worry. Just promise me one thing, if you feel something...if you feel *off*...at all? You'll talk to someone and listen to your body. It doesn't mean you have to quit, it just means...we modify. Can you do that?"

"I can do that," I say, pulling both of my arms around my father's chest and holding him tight, my cheek resting against the wool of his suit jacket. "You're off to work?"

"Time to make the donuts," he says. He's been saying that to me since I was a kid, when I used to get up early just to see him before he left for the office. He kisses my head one more time, then turns to leave through the door, his hand knocking once on the frame as he passes.

My phone buzzes, and I sit at the edge of my bed to answer. It's Rowe. I've texted her a few times, but we haven't talked. I'm afraid to talk to her, afraid she's mad that I kept this from her.

"Hey," I answer, my heart beating fast with my nerves.

"Hey, when do you get in? I just got here. Our room...Cass," she's talking a million miles a minute, and I fade out for a second as she goes on, awed that our friendship is somehow just the same as it's always been. No MS. No questions, no mention—I'm just still Cass.

"What about our room?" I ask, smiling nervously, for a different reason now.

"It's...brown. Like...I'm sorry, but it's caca brown. Maybe a little orange? No, it's brown. Definitely brown. And not a cool brown, like taupe or chocolate. It's awful, like that burnt sienna color you get in your box of crayons that you never wear down because you don't use it, because it's seriously the ugliest color ever made," she says, breathless by the end of her panicked speech. "Cass...we can't live with this. I'm so sorry, I didn't think they had it in them."

The laughter creeps in quickly, and soon I can't control it, and it infects Rowe; she's laughing on the other line just as hard. "I'm serious, Cass," she says, practically through tears, she's laughing so hard. "It's hideous. I'll go to the hardware store and start repainting so maybe when you get here, I'll be almost done."

"Don't you dare," I warn her. "We don't give in, just like they don't give in. I've got this."

"Okay, but I'm not kidding when I say it's ugly," she says, and I smile, because I know the trump card, and it's going to be awesome to throw it.

I needed Paige's help, and I was nervous to ask at first. Our relationship was healing, but slowly. She seemed more excited at the prospect of beating Ty—so I used that in my favor, and she called a few friends to help pull things off.

We needed to time it just right, everything like clockwork from the moment our plane touched the ground. I called Rowe, and she made plans with the boys for dinner at Sally's. We'd meet them there, so that way they could save us a table before it got too crowded. The only risk left was whether or not they left their room unlocked—their keys inside. Something they do...often.

Rowe is jumping up and down at the elevator when Paige and I get upstairs, and her smile means we're in luck. I leave my things in the hallway, by our room, and we hand Paige all the keys she needs, and she promises that her assistants are on their way.

In exchange, I promise Paige a free bailout, no questions asked, the next time she's a little in over her head at a party—something that hasn't happened in a while, now that I think of it. Her lips curl at the edges, a faint smile at my promise—a baby step. And maybe just saying this to her was enough.

"I can handle this," she says, reaching into her bag for a band to tie her hair. She pulls her jacket from her shoulders, and rests it on my suitcase, kicking her gigantic pumps off so she can work barefoot. The scene makes both Rowe and me laugh.

"What? I'm not lifting things in those," she says, blowing her bangs up and out of her eyes. It's funny mostly, because Paige isn't likely lifting anything. Our suspicion is even more confirmed when we swap places with three extremely large guys on the elevator, and as the doors shut, I think I catch a glimpse of one of them lifting her in his arms.

"Do you know that guy?" Rowe asks. I'm glad she saw that too.

"No idea who he is," I say, my eyes wishing they could see through the elevator doors as we start our decent. "Someone's been keeping a secret."

Whoever he is, he isn't a jock or frat guy...or anyone I've seen around any of Paige's parties. He's way off the radar, and nothing like anyone I'd ever pair with my sister based on her tastes. I hope like hell I see him again.

Rowe and I somehow manage to keep our smiles in check throughout dinner—even pretending to be pissed about the brown room, about how they one-upped us...finally. And when my phone buzzes in my lap with a message from Paige that "the deed is done," I tug my ear to signal Rowe, and her smile grows wicked.

"I almost want to sprint home," she whispers in my ear as we wait at the front of Sally's while Nate and Ty linger by the bar to check the score of a game.

"Play it cool," I say, and she folds her arms and smirks at me.

"Look at you. When did you get all ballsy and good at this?" she asks. "The student has become the teacher."

"Okay, you and Ty seriously need to stop with the *Kung Fu* thing," I say, and Ty catches the end of it.

"You can never talk too much *Kung Fu*," Ty says, and Rowe nods in agreement, jutting her fist forward for a pound.

"Damn straight," she says.

"So what has my young grasshopper mastered?" His question makes me panic, but only for a second, because Rowe is *way* better at this than I am.

"Oh, you'll find out," she says, waggling her eyebrows, and instantly Ty assumes we're talking sex. It's easy to take his mind there, and Rowe is a genius for thinking of it. She didn't really lie, because he will find out soon. He's just going to be even more disappointed now.

We take our time getting back, as if there's nothing to be excited about. I stop at our mailbox downstairs, and pull the sets of keys out, dropping them in my pocket before anyone can notice, and we continue to the elevator.

"Mail's empty," I say, winking at Rowe behind their backs.

"Well duh, we just got here. Nobody has any mail yet," Nate says, totally going along with our plan. Ty, however, makes a face, and the second I see his eyebrow tick up, I look away; I know I won't be able to bluff him if he looks right at me.

I have to nudge Rowe in the ribs once to get her giggles under control, and when the doors open, we step from the elevator and move toward the boys' room.

At least, what *used* to be the boys' room.

"I'm kind of tired. You know, I think I'm going to go to bed early. Long flight. Hope you don't mind," I smirk, and Ty knows instantly.

"Son of a bitch," he says, his head shaking as he looks to his lap and bites his lip, then lets out a reluctant laugh and folds his hands together, his thumbs tapping one another because he knows. He knows!

"Oh, that's fine," Nate says, trying to be polite, still not caught up with the rest of us.

"Good, well...you're going to need your keys," I say, tossing them to him. He catches them at his chest, and then realization settles in slowly. Rowe and I push in through our *new* door, all of our things inside, as if we'd always been here.

"Good night boys," she says, and we both blow them kisses as we close the door behind us, locking it too, just in case.

My phone buzzes about two minutes later with a text from Ty.

TY: *Well played, Ninja.*
ME: *Enjoy your shit-brown room ;-)*
TY: *Oh I will.*
ME: *I don't doubt it.*

I think I may be more proud of this than I am of making the women's soccer team. I fluff out the Barbie comforter and layer it with my quilt, then crawl into bed, kicking my shoes off and letting them fall to the floor. Rowe does the same.

"You know, I kinda like their room better," she says, scooting into the deep corner of what used to be Nate's bed with her blankets and pillows piled around her.

I smile at her, then say, "You mean *our* room." I let myself relax, and when my phone buzzes under the blanket, I dip my head underneath to read Ty's message privately.

TY: *You know I love you, right?*
ME: *Yeah. I know.*
TY: *Good. Now watch your back...babe ;-)*

My face buried deep in my sheets, I shake my head and grin from ear-to-ear, stopping short of kicking my feet and squealing because of how he makes me feel. I'll let him get over this, and stew for a little while. Then I'll give in and make my way to the brown room to spend the night—trading places with Nate, because that's where I really want to be. I'll watch my back, and he'll probably get me with something way better than this prank eventually. But I won't care.

I won't care, because I love him. I'm *in* love with him. I love his funny side and his serious side. I love that he's protective, and I love the part of him that sometimes misses baseball and won't admit it out loud. I love the way he can talk to me with his eyes, yet never say a word with his mouth. And I love the part of him that thinks he can do anything—especially the impossible.

Tyson Preeter is my boyfriend—a real boyfriend, the kind that takes me on dates and leaves me love notes. The kind I wished for—the kind I promised myself I would have. The kind who loves me.

The kind who made me love me, too.

And I love him for that most of all.

Epilogue

Four months later

Ty

"Okay, so this series...it's important," I say, leaning over Rowe, ignoring Cass's glare.

"She knows that, Ty," Cass says, and I wave my hand at her, hushing her.

"I'm just making sure. This series, if we win, moves us to number one. Number. One." I hold up one finger. Just to make my point totally clear.

Rowe leans forward, effectively ignoring me, talking to Cass. "Does he think I'm stupid?" she asks, pointing at me. "He thinks I'm stupid."

"Yeah, I kinda think he thinks you're stupid," Cass jumps on the bandwagon. I pull my hat from my head and rub my face.

"Oh ha ha ha, yes, very funny ladies. Let's cut the cutesy," I say, and Cass punches my arm. "Oww!"

"You're kind of crossing the line," she says, giving me the face. The one she uses when I'm being *too Tyson,* as she likes to say.

"What was too much? Cutesy? Fine, I take back cutesy. Now focus," I say, and now they're both laughing at me. And I'm frustrated. "Forget it. This is no use. I'm just going to hope you don't fuck up baseball, since you're not taking me seriously."

"Aw, Cass, look at that. Tysie Wysie's making a fussy fuss," Rowe says, and I can't take it anymore.

"You know, I'm going to try sitting over there," I say, pushing back from the aisle. Cass stops me though, sitting on my lap and weaving her arms around my neck, pulling my hat from my head, and putting it on hers. It looks better on her anyway. Damn, I'm easy.

"We're just teasing you," she says in my ear, kissing my neck, almost making me forget I'm at a baseball game. Almost.

"Yeah, well...it's just important," I say, this time seriously. She takes a deep breath and locks onto my eyes with hers.

"She knows. *We* know. And he's going to be great," she says. And with one kiss, I'm calm again.

There are scouts here for this series. We're playing OSU. And usually it's OSU that brings in the big teams, the serious scouts, the ones who are looking to pad rosters and fill triple-A ball clubs with talent that can be moved up sooner rather than later. But the Cardinals and the Cubs are here for someone else. They're here for Nate Preeter. And my brother is a nervous fucking wreck.

"Sorry I'm late," Paige says, and Cass stands up from my lap to go hug her sister. They've gotten closer. It's taken months, but the effort on both of their parts has been genuine. I want this for Cass. I want her to have a sibling like I do, one that you count on and trust with everything.

"She brought him," Cass whispers in my ear when she moves back to my lap. I look past her to see who she means. Houston is with Paige again. He's been with her a lot. I like him. He's a good guy, as far as I can tell from the few times we've hung out. Paige always says they're *just friends*. But I don't think that's how Houston sees it.

"Hey man, you want to save me from all this girl talk over here? They're determined to ruin baseball," I say, and Cass rolls her eyes.

"He's just being a baby," she says.

Houston looks at Paige, whose attention is on her phone, and then looks at me with a slight shake of his head. He's going to stay right where he is. Wait...for her to notice. I hope like hell for that poor bastard that she does.

"Excuse me, are you Cass Owens?" A skinny kid with a wrinkled notebook slides into the seat next to me, the one Rowe just left to go talk to Nate. She better not be messing up baseball.

"Yeah, I'm Cass," she says, looking at me, like I know who he is.

"Hi, uhm...okay, well, I'm the beat reporter for the McConnell Times," he's nervous, and he's dropped his pen twice in the span of a single sentence. Heaven help this kid if he ever tries to become a reporter anywhere bigger than a school with an enrollment of twenty thousand.

"Okay," Cass says, waiting for him to get to the point. I'm waiting too. There's a game about to start. Why is this not important to everyone else?

"I was wondering...would you let me ask you a few questions, maybe for a short profile, for the women's soccer team? Since you've overcome so much, playing with MS and everything," he's getting his ground now. Unfortunately, he's hit on that taboo topic. I feel for the kid, really.

"You know what? Yeah, sure. But we have to sit back here—they're really into the game," she says, shocking the hell out of me.

"You sure?" I whisper to her as she steps in front of me to follow the reporter to the last row.

"I'm absolutely sure. I've been thinking about it a lot, about talking about my MS. There aren't a lot of teenagers out there who are like me, but there are some. And they need to hear what I have to say," she says, nodding with a smile as she steps to the back, a few rows behind me.

I can still hear their interview, and even though my heart is focused on my brother and on the field, a part of it is also stuck behind me, so unbelievably proud of my little Ninja Princess.

"So, what are your thoughts on the whole Chandra scandal? Did you have any idea about her drug problem?" he asks. I listen close to this question, waiting for Cass's response, and when I turn my head to the side, I notice that Paige is listening too. She's looking at her phone, but nothing's open. She's eavesdropping.

"I had no idea. I was shocked, and it's a big blow to our team for sure, losing her. But you know what? We'll get through it," Cass says, not dwelling on Chandra for long at all. While she talks, I watch Paige's reaction, and her mouth curls up slightly to the side. And it's more than just being proud of her sister and her ability to dance around a tough question.

"Crazy how that whole Chandra thing blew up, huh? The way those pictures found their way online?" I say, looking at Paige, calling her bluff.

"Yeah," she says, everything about her expression disinterested, as if she couldn't care less. But her eyes—they're just narrowed enough, and I read her loud and clear. "Definitely...*crazy*," she says, her lips careful with that word.

She stands up and tells Houston that she's thirsty. She steps around him, and looks back at me one last time as she walks up the ramp. Her nod was just slight enough, not enough for anyone else to notice. But I know what she did for her sister. And I'll keep this secret for her—because damn, I'm impressed.

We get through the National Anthem, the play-ball kid and the first pitch, and by the time Nate's up to bat, Cass is back sitting next to me, Rowe on my other side. And they're both crossing their fingers, holding their breath. They get it. No fussy fuss.

After he hits for a double with one RBI, I lean over to Cass and kiss her cheek. She sweeps her hair behind her ear when I do, then turns to me, her cheeks a little pink from the warm spring sun.

"What was that for?" she asks.

"Nothin'," I shrug. "Just proud of you, I guess."

I turn my attention back to the field, cheering loudly as my brother steals third, but Cass keeps her eyes on me. I can feel the heat of her stare, and I grab my hat from her head and tilt it to the side to block her view, because *wow*, I'm getting a little inspired by her attention.

She grabs my hat back and puts it on her head, where it really belongs, then puts her hands on my face, pulling me to her lips, stopping just short of a kiss.

"You know I love you, right?" she says, and I smile and pull her the rest of the way in until her mouth crashes into mine. I kiss her longer than I should at a baseball game, and I totally miss my brother sliding into home. I miss the next two batters too, and I don't stop until I'm sure every single guy at the stadium has seen me kiss this girl.

This girl.
My sexy Ninja Princess.
The only girl I need to know...anywhere.

THE END

Don't miss book 3 in the Falling Series!
The Girl I Was Before – Paige and Houston's story
Coming 2015

Preview:

Paige

I'm only half listening to Chandra bark orders at me over the phone.

"We're going to need more food. The homecoming parties are always crowded. Sigma is coming, and they'll easily push us over five hundred. And get more shrimp. You didn't get enough shrimp."

Somewhere along the way, she hung up. I must have said goodbye. I'm sure I said goodbye.

I hate her.

I hate her for what she did to my sister, when she confronted her about her assaulter in front of people. I hate her for this invisible power she has over me because she's the president of our sorority. I hate her because her boyfriend is friends with my boyfriend.

I hate her because part of me wants to be like her, and I hate her because the weaker part of me doesn't.

And I hate the person I am when I'm around her.

"Seventeen!" My number is called. Great...it's the same guy working the deli counter today. He was the one who took my order for the party last week. Carson was with me. He was drunk...and an asshole. This guy, he knew—and he judged me for it. Or at least, it felt like he did.

"I'm seventeen," I say, stepping up to the glass case and handing over my number.

"I don't really need the number," he smirks. Maybe he doesn't remember me. "Adding to your order?"

Shit. He remembers me.

269

"Yeah. Party just got a little bigger," I say, smiling. I can't help but smile at him—he has one of those faces. It's like a forced reflection, and I want to mimic whatever he does.

"Okay, hang on. I'll get the file from the back," he says, patting the counter once and winking.

Houston.

I noticed his nametag the last time, too. I like the name. That's why I noticed. Not because he's tall, broad shouldered with dark hair that flops over the top of his visor and green eyes that practically glow under the shadow.

I like the name. That's it.

"Okay, let's see...Paige. Right...I've got you right here," he says, pulling the pen from behind his ear and clicking it to take more notes. "What are you adding?"

"You better not have ordered yet!" Carson's voice bellows from behind me. "Did she order yet? Get mine in on this ticket. I don't have a lot of time."

"I haven't ordered for lunch yet. This was just the party order, relax," I say, turning to face him, dreading turning back around to face Houston, the guy with the cute name. I turn anyway because I have no choice, and that same look is on his face again—the judgmental one.

"Order that crap second. I've got practice, so I only have a few minutes. Hey, yeah...so, get me one of those burrito things," Carson says, leaning over the counter and pointing down as if Houston wouldn't know what he was talking about. When he leans back on his heels, he lays his heavy arm over my shoulder and pulls me into him tightly.

"I guess I'll have one of those too," I say, my eyes on Houston's nametag instead of his eyes. I don't want to see the look in his eyes.

"We only have one left," he says. Of course they do.

"Oh," I say, sucking in my top lip and looking into the case of food for an alternative. I'm not hungry anymore. "I'll just take a sandwich then. Tuna."

"Right...okay," he says, reaching to the side for a bag. He pauses, though, before picking out one of the pre-made sandwiches for me. "Or...maybe *this guy* could pick something else and let *you* have the burrito."

"Fuck that, bro! I ordered first. Give me the burrito. She's fine with a sandwich," Carson bellows. His phone rings, so he steps to the side and answers the call. "Yo, what up, man?"

I can still hear his entire conversation even though he's twenty feet away. Everyone can hear him.

Houston is standing still, his arms propped on top of the counter and his brow bunched while he stares at my boyfriend. Carson is pacing and talking so loudly that he's starting to interrupt others eating lunch at the small tables in the corner of the market.

I used to like his big personality. His confidence and swagger was what turned me on when we first met at the Sigma-Delta mixer. He's a starter on the McConnell team, a fullback. He's a year older than I am, and I liked that too.

Houston is moving again, wrapping the burrito and dropping it in a plastic bag. He lets the burrito hit the counter with a thud, and he watches Carson pace the entire time. When he sees his burrito is ready, he reaches across my body and grabs the bag, holding his phone to his chest and kissing me with nothing but forceful indifference. "I gotta run. You got this?" he asks...sort of.

I nod, only because he's already gone before I could answer.

"That guy's your boyfriend?" Houston asks, finally packing up my sandwich. Normally, I'd respond with something snarky, something strong that would put him and that damned disapproving look on his face in its place. I can't seem to find that fire today, though.

"I still need to make the party orders," I say, instead opting to ignore his question completely.

"Right," he says, his lips pushed into a tight, flat line.

I add two more trays of shrimp and up the order of meat and cheese, and Houston notes it all on the order sheet. I wait at the register while he walks to the back office and tucks my order file away again. When he comes back, he slides a bottle of tea toward me—the same sweet tea I ordered and drank the last time I came.

He remembered. It makes me smile.

Propping my purse up on the counter, I pull out my wallet and start to unsnap the clasp so I can pay for my lunch, but Houston stops me. The warmth of his hand is surprising against mine. I don't jerk or flinch; I only freeze. It takes me a second or two to look up at him, to register that he's stopping me from paying for my lunch. I don't like that. I don't like being beholden to someone. Favors—they're like making a trade sometimes.

"It's on me," he says, and I refuse quickly, shaking my head no. His hand squeezes mine tighter. "I won't take your money. Not for your lunch...or *his*. It's on me."

"I can buy my own lunch, thank you," I say, starting to resent being ordered around. I shake his grip from my hand and hold out my card. He takes it and swipes it hard along the register, shaking his head and mumbling under his breath.

"Damn, you mean that asshole can tell you to do something and you just obey, but me—an actual *nice* guy—I can't buy you lunch without getting your foot up my ass?"

"I'd like my receipt," I say, ignoring him again. He rips it off and crumples it in his hand along with my card and throws it on the counter. "Thank you," I say, stuffing it in my purse and clutching my sandwich bag in my other hand.

I can feel the force of his eyes on my back as I turn to leave, and my heart is kicking the insides of my chest in anticipation of his voice. The closer I get to the door, the stronger the sensation is, and I almost make it outside when I feel his hand on my shoulder. I spin around, ready to lay into him now—my fire flickering.

"You can do better," he says before I can open my lips to speak. His gaze is direct, and it halts me, if only for this moment. "That's all I want to say. I just thought you should know. You. Can do. Better."

His face is serious. There's a part of me that wonders if this is flirting, if he's flirting. But it doesn't feel like a pick-up line. Houston—his being here today, his words—*this* feels more like a rescue.

I smile, perhaps a little indignantly, and spin back around through the exit. When I round the building, I tuck my purse higher on my arm, and I clutch my sandwich and tea to my chest, running my hand along the cool spot on my skin where Houston touched me seconds ago.

Save your rescuing for someone else. I have a plan. I'm sticking to it. And I don't need rescuing, I think to myself.

No, I don't need rescuing...

Acknowledgements

You And Everything After is my sixth book. Six. This number blows my mind. Finishing my first book was a dream for so long. And not a day goes by that I don't stop, for at least a moment, and wonder at where I've arrived. When *This Is Falling* went live, I held my breath—as I always do—and crossed my fingers that someone…anyone…would love it. Just a little. Or almost as much as I did.

And then someone did.

This book—book two in the series—is for you. It is for the readers and book bloggers out there who have graciously given their time to my words. It is for those of you who have left reviews, posted about my book, tweeted me, sent me emails, messaged me, told a friend to give me a try or cheered me along the way. And it is for those of you who found me, stumbled upon *This Is Falling,* and decided to take a chance. I am blessed to have connected with each and every one of you, and you have no idea what your support has meant to me.

Writing a book is such an incredibly personal journey; sharing it with the world is borderline terrifying. I took a leap, and you caught me. For that, I will be eternally grateful.

There are so many people I owe thanks to for helping me tell Cass and Ty's story accurately and with heart. First and foremost, I must thank Ashlea Miller for schooling me on multiple sclerosis. An awesome beta reader, your medical knowledge and personal experience kept me honest, and your time on this story was truly a gift. I must also thank Kathy from Love Words and Books as well as a good friend (you know who you are) for answering my questions on spinal cord injuries and nerve damage.

My amazing beta readers: Shelley, Bianca, Jen, Debbie and Brigitte—thank you for always opening your inbox to me, for meeting me with piles of paper and Post-It notes, and for reading and telling me exactly how my words make you feel. May you never close your inbox to me!

Thank you, Tina Scott and Billi Joy Carson, for being more than editors. You are the safety net into which I fall easily. I am so glad to have you!

A special shout out to my boys, my husband and son, who make me smile morning, noon and night. You are the reason I live. You *are* the good in my life, and you are *real* men who deserve stories that prove you exist. Thank you for making me believe in love, hope, romance and joy on a daily basis.

And last, but not least, thank you, baseball. I love you, and I'll see you again in the spring.

About the Author

Ginger Scott is a journalist and writer from Peoria, Arizona. A proud Sun Devil, she is a graduate and associate faculty member of Arizona State University's Cronkite School of Journalism. When she's not typing feverishly on her MacBook during the wee hours or reading in the dark on her iPad, she's probably at a baseball diamond somewhere watching her son or her favorite team, the Arizona Diamondbacks, take the field.

Books by Ginger Scott

Waiting on the Sidelines
Going Long
Blindness
How We Deal With Gravity
This Is Falling
You and Everything After

Coming in 2015

The Girl I Was Before – Book 3 in the Falling Series
...and...
A raw, dark, heartbreaking, yet hopeful and (I think) beautiful, high school romance – title to be released soon. This one might be my favorite thing I've written.

Ginger Scott Online

www.littlemisswrite.com
www.facebook.com/GingerScottAuthor
Twitter @TheGingerScott

Made in the USA
Columbia, SC
11 March 2020